THE TRAIN TO [illegible] DGE

By Julian Smart

The Hawksbridge Angels
The Train To Hawksbridge
The Ramsburgh Variations
Emma Vernon's Northminster Ghost Stories (with Harriet Smart)

THE TRAIN TO HAWKSBRIDGE

A THOMAS RUFFORD MYSTERY: 2

by

Julian Smart

Published by Anthemion

First Edition

ISBN 978-1-907873-74-4

Made with Jutoh

PREFACE

YOU may be sure that after the adventures documented in the first volume of my memoirs – which I titled 'The Hawksbridge Angels' – I was in no mood to repeat such excitement and once more do the work of the police. I would have been content simply to enjoy the company of my new friends, engage more fully with the management of the Pottery, and improve my estate. I had, after all, come within a whisker of meeting my maker on several occasions. But, as is so often the case, Fate was not content to honour my plans. I was soon to be embroiled in lethal intrigues springing from passion and greed, disturbing the equanimity of our town like lava bursting through a tranquil landscape and branding it with a blackened trail.

It has been suggested that, seeking to consolidate my nascent, and I might add, extremely modest reputation as an amateur detective, I solicited such work. Some have gone so far as to say that I somehow exaggerated my role for the greater glory of Thomas Rufford, but how that might possibly be, I must leave to those with a greater imagination than mine. If these libelling pests are envious of my position, then let me be quite clear: I am not one who enjoys putting myself in peril, and neither do I value fame. I would rather sit down with a Dickens or a Tavistock than follow a trail of clues; but if I am called, I will answer.

I do not wish to give the impression that my experiences during this period were entirely harmful. Humanity had displayed itself again in fascinating extremes, and some of my own weaknesses were made wretchedly plain. It is no bad thing to be tested occasionally, even if, as you will see, some of these tests I regrettably failed.

Without further ado, I present my exploits in 'The Train to Hawksbridge', for – I fervently hope! – your pleasurable diversion.

— Thomas Rufford, November 1862

If in his study he hath so much care to hang all old strange things, let his wife beware.

— John Donne, from *The Antiquary*

CHAPTER ONE

November, 1848

"IT was kind of Mrs Ambrose to invite me," I said, encouraging Jenny up a steep incline in the road. "I think I will like her, but you said very little about Mr Ambrose, except to mention his temper. Is he an ogre?"

"Not exactly," Flora said, "but I feel more comfortable when he is out of the house. He is obsessed with his antiques – in fact, I suspect he loves them more than his family – and he has an unpleasant habit of using sarcasm against people he disagrees with."

"Oh dear," I said. "Poor Mrs and Miss Ambrose."

"Quite," said Flora. "That is why the kindness may be as much on your part as Isobel's. You will dilute him."

"I see," I said. "Well, I'm happy to make myself useful, and to make new friends."

"Just be careful with Felicity," she said. "She's at an impressionable age, and she has asked a lot about you in our drawing classes. You are probably some kind of Hawksbridge hero to her, after your recent triumph."

"A 'Hawksbridge hero'! I like that," I said. "But I shall try to downplay my genius."

Flora indicated a right turn, and Jenny pulled us up a drive and to the door of the Ambrose residence. Houndswood was a modern house, faced with gleaming sandstone and with a rather functional, unornamented appearance that brought to mind an exhausted architect with many client briefs to get through. "That will do, for a man of his type," he might have said.

And yet, as we were ushered into the hall by the butler, the exterior plainness belied a quite different interior: it was stuffed with treasures. Well-executed paintings, from ancient portraits to large landscapes, and a huge tapestry, left little wall on show. A beautiful painted cabinet under the hall window looked as if it dated from the seventeenth century, if not earlier, and an ornate carved high-back bench looked similarly ancient. Above the bench, several species of fowl looked beadily out from within their glass case.

I was peering at a miniature of a young woman holding a cat when Mrs Ambrose came into the hall. She was a slender, short woman of fine features, around forty years of age, and with bright blue eyes that, by a trick of nature, seemed tinged with sadness.

"I see you have found my favourite picture!" she said. "Isobel Ambrose – I am so glad you could come."

"How do you do, Mrs Ambrose?" I said, putting out my hand. "Thomas Rufford. Thank you for inviting me."

She smiled and shook my hand warmly. "Flora, how lovely to see you," she said. "I must say, Felicity's drawing has been improving amazingly – how lucky we are to know you, both as a friend and a tutor! Especially when you have your important work at the Town Hall to occupy you."

"The luck is all mine," said Flora. "Felicity is an ideal pupil – she has talent and patience in abundance. Thomas! You are getting distracted."

It was true; it was hard not to be entranced by the fine workmanship on show.

"You're welcome to look," said Mrs Ambrose, "but my husband will be able to describe them better than I. Shall we go into the drawing room? Would you like a little Madeira to warm yourselves after your drive?"

The drawing room resembled an auction house, such was the clutter of furniture – all of it valuable, no doubt. My eye was drawn to a mahogany secretaire, much like the one in

Francesca's bedroom. Above it hung an astonishing painting from the seventeenth century, depicting in vivid colour and great detail an aristocratic family picnicking in a glade with their mansion in the distant background. The small children were playing with their dogs, while the young parents looked lovingly at each other.

"Thomas?" said Flora. "A glass of Madeira?"

"Oh," I said. "Thank you – yes, please."

"My husband will be gratified," said Mrs Ambrose, although I thought I saw her wince when she glanced up at the picture. "Mr Rufford, you seem to be quite an art aficionado."

I turned, and joined Mrs Ambrose and Flora. "I'm mostly an ignoramus about art and antiques, I'm afraid," I said, "but I greatly appreciate them. There is something about old things that calms the soul."

"That should be the case," said Mrs Ambrose, "but it is not always. If Yorick finds competition when he has the scent of a piece, he becomes anything but calm. Ah, Felicity! Come and meet Mr Rufford."

Felicity had nervously entered the drawing room, and was standing a little way off, smiling at me and fiddling with a button on her dress. She had blue ribbons in her wavy, auburn hair, and she looked just as appealing as the portrait in the hall, despite, or perhaps due to, inheriting her mother's sad eyes.

"I'm glad to know you, Miss Ambrose," I said, walking towards her and shaking her hand. "Miss Davison – and your mother – have been telling me how well your drawing is coming on."

"Oh – thank you," Felicity said, looking away modestly. "Flora – I mean, Miss Davison – is such a good teacher. My favourite thing is botanical drawing. Would you like to see some of my work?"

"Perhaps after dinner, Felicity?" said Mrs Ambrose.

"Yes, of course, Mother," she said, and went to sit down. "May I have some of that too?" she added as she saw the butler bring a tray in.

Mrs Ambrose laughed. "That's only for cold travellers. You may have a small glass of wine at dinner. One, mind!"

A middle-aged man with a greying beard and an intense expression strode into the room and held out his hand. "Mr Rufford! How delightful to have such a distinguished guest. Yorick Ambrose."

"How do you do, sir? I've been admiring your beautiful house." I gestured towards the picture over the secretaire.

"Aha!" beamed Mr Ambrose. "You are a man of taste. The Huysmans is one of my best acquisitions, and hard won, eh, Isobel?"

His wife forced a brief smile.

"I have a good dealer," Mr Ambrose continued. "Known him for many years. He manages to get the best pieces, and he knows what I like – no, what *we* like, is that not so, my dear? But he's not the only game in town now, so he'll have to watch his back."

There was the sound of voices in the hall. "Excuse me," said Mr Ambrose, and left to greet the new guest. He appeared a moment later with a stout man, slightly older than Mr Ambrose, sporting a well-groomed moustache and spectacles.

"Mr Rufford," he said, "let me introduce my friend Mr Leonardo Fountain. Leonardo, this is Mr Thomas Rufford, of whom you have no doubt heard."

Mr Fountain nodded politely at Mrs Ambrose and her daughter, and then turned to me and offered his hand. "But of course! The scourge of Hawksbridge criminals! Pleased to meet you, Mr Rufford."

"Leonardo is a founder member of the Hawksbridge Antiquarian Society," said Mr Ambrose. "He is a veritable fountain – forgive the pun – of information about local history. So he's your man if you have questions about Hawksbridge. He might even be able to tell you a thing or two about your own house that you didn't know!"

"The less said about the recent history of my house, the better," I said with a smile, feeling that frankness was the best way to head off any overtones of unpleasantness on that score.

"Surely it's a castle, not a house," said Felicity.

Mr Fountain turned and looked over his spectacles at Felicity. "Not really, Miss Ambrose. Strictly speaking, Ramsburgh is a fortified fifteenth-century tower with later additions."

"Well, it looks like a castle to me, and I shall call it a castle," said Felicity, her lips showing the hint of a pout.

"You may call it a turnip, my dear; it's no skin off my nose," said Mr Fountain, rather haughtily.

I laughed. "Whatever the case," I said, "I'm just grateful to live amongst such interesting people, and to have a turnip I can call home." I was pleased to see that Felicity's frown at being contradicted had been replaced with a smile.

After we had been ushered into the dining room and had settled ourselves gingerly into our inevitably precious old chairs, Mrs Ambrose said, "What adventures you have had since coming to Hawksbridge, Mr Rufford! I hear the police treated you abominably. And yet Flora told me you have hardly said a bad word about them."

I reached for my wine glass. "Our police leave something to be desired, certainly. But we still need them to protect us – so I don't wish to erode confidence in them. Besides, Inspector Simmons did apologise to me, in his gruff way. They're only human, and they should be forgiven some mistakes."

"What admirable sentiments, Mr Rufford!" Mrs Ambrose said, and smiled sweetly at me in a way that I found extremely pleasant. "I hope the police have learned their lessons, so that our faith in them is entirely restored."

"Speaking of restoration," Flora said, "Mr Fountain, I gather there is some talk of refurbishing Hawksbridge Castle. What news of that?"

"Ah yes," said Mr Fountain, clearly in his element. "Obviously it cannot be reconstructed fully – it is much too far gone for that – but some of the standing walls should be strengthened before they collapse, and some walls can be rebuilt from masonry – what hasn't been stolen, anyway. I am proud to say I have founded a committee to look into it and raise funds."

"What a noble goal," said Mrs Ambrose, laying down her spoon. "I love to walk in the castle grounds, and it makes me sad to see all the fallen stones – recent, some of them."

"Indeed," said Mr Fountain. "The traces of our history have a habit of disappearing if you don't cherish them. And given how the castle has looked after our ancestors, the least we can do is look after it."

"Hear, hear," said Mr Ambrose. "May I propose a toast to the Hawksbridge Castle Preservation Committee – and may the castle still be standing in a thousand years!"

We raised our glasses, Miss Ambrose's being conspicuously almost empty, the redness having been transferred to her face in a becoming fashion.

"If I may ask," I said, "who owns the castle, and its land? Is it the property of the town?"

"Good question," said Mr Ambrose. "Not the town. A Mr Dunton owns it – he has farmland nearby – but the public has rights of access and he has given permission for improvements. Though the old miser won't donate a penny, or lift a finger to help. He says the castle is more trouble than it's worth."

"Ah – that thought crossed my mind after several large bills from my builder," I said.

"Two troublesome turnips," said Felicity, hiccuping.

"Now, Felicity, I do believe you are tipsy," said Mrs Ambrose. "I should never have let you have that wine. Why don't you have a walk in the garden and clear your head?"

"Oh, very well," said Felicity, and she left the room

humming a tune. Then she popped her head around the door, and added, "But I shall bring my drawings for Mr Rufford to see later. And I might bring Pantoufle!"

"Don't you dare bring that rodent downstairs, Felicity," Mr Ambrose shouted after her.

"Pantoufle?" I enquired.

Mrs Ambrose sighed. "Felicity found an injured baby squirrel in the garden, under a tree. She's been keeping it in a cage in an attic room, with a slipper to sleep in. Hence Pantoufle."

"Good Lord!" I said. "How wonderful."

"Not at all," said Mr Ambrose. "The scrawny thing will probably give us a disease. And if I find one squirrel-claw scratch on my furniture, or a chewed chair leg, I will take pleasure in wringing its neck."

"Mr Rufford is also a friend to animals," said Flora, ignoring Mr Ambrose. "He got extremely ill after rescuing my cat in a storm. And Fox – his dog – was a stray."

"Indeed!" said Mr Ambrose. "Not only animals. How is the poor widow Shannon?"

"Oh, Yorick!" murmured Mrs Ambrose.

Flora was unaware of my intimate friendship with Bess, and I hardly knew what to say when she looked questioningly at me.

"I am glad to say that Mrs Shannon is very well," I said, carefully keeping my temper. "She is a talented woman –"

"So I've heard, Mr Rufford, so I've heard," said Mr Ambrose. Mrs Ambrose looked daggers at him, and I was touched by her sensitivity.

"She is a gifted harpist, and –" I persisted.

Mr Ambrose leaned over to Mr Fountain and whispered something to him about plucking, no doubt of an obscene nature.

Mr Fountain was not receptive to this style of humour and retained a studiedly neutral expression on his face, sipping his wine.

"Oh, I'm sorry, Mr Rufford," Mr Ambrose said. "I'm only joking with you. I have every respect for the widow Shannon, and visited her husband's shop often. Have some more wine."

I stole a look at Flora. She was clearly mortified on my behalf, as was Mrs Ambrose. There was an awkward silence in which Mr Fountain's pursed lips could be heard sipping his wine.

Mrs Ambrose rose from the table. "Shall we adjourn, Flora?" she said.

The ladies left. "Excuse me," I said. "Nature calls."

"Down the passage, second on the right," said Mr Ambrose. "You may admire the Allan Ramsay on the way! Or on the way back if you're in a hurry."

I was too annoyed to obey Ambrose's instructions, even though I was partial to a good Ramsay portrait – the porcelain-skinned duchess kind, not the bewigged old philosopher kind. My host really was an unbearable oaf when drunk. Or perhaps when sober, too.

On the way back, I found Felicity waiting in the hall with a portfolio. Her burning cheeks had calmed down.

"Mr Rufford! Would you like to look at my drawings now? If you're not busy, that is..."

"I would like nothing better," I said. "If you can take them into the drawing room, I will be there in a moment."

She smiled, and scampered off with her drawings.

I went back to the dining room, where Mr Fountain was pontificating on the origins of Hawksbridge Castle. "If you don't mind, I'm going to have a look through Miss Ambrose's drawings," I said. "Otherwise I will be tempted to drink too much wine."

"Very well, Mr Rufford," said Mr Ambrose. "I will rescue you from the ladies later, and then I will show you some of my more interesting acquisitions."

In the drawing room, Felicity had drawn a table closer to the sofa and laid open the portfolio, while Mrs Ambrose brought out some embroidery for Flora to examine. I came and sat down next to her and admired the first picture: a group of autumnal trees. They were drawn with admirable sensitivity and skill.

"This is remarkable, Miss Ambrose," I said, turning to the next page.

Next was a dahlia, with some clever shading of the petals.

"Superb," I said, and went through the others, which were equally good. "You could be a book illustrator."

"Thank you, Mr Rufford," Felicity said with obvious pleasure. "But I don't know if they allow women to do that."

"I think they will, and if not, you can be a pioneer. After all, women can make a living out of novels under a male pen-name. And my friend Miss Phyllis Drummond – that is, Iona Tavistock – dispenses with a change of sex."

"Oh! Your friend! Do you know her well?" Felicity said, her eyes lighting up.

"Yes, I have that honour – and she has come to my rescue on several occasions, like a heroine in one of her own books. She is delightful, and we must arrange for you to meet her."

"Oh, Mama!" Felicity said, leaping up and going to her mother. "Did you hear that? Mr Rufford says he might be able to introduce me to Iona Tavistock!"

"No! Mr Rufford, how marvellous! Felicity has all of her books. You are a quite a follower of hers, aren't you, my darling?"

"I think she's the best author living!" Felicity said.

"Then we both have impeccable taste," I said. "I admire Miss Drummond hugely."

~

"Pantoufle! It's Felicity and some friends to see you."

Felicity had led Flora and me up to an attic room where there was a cage containing some tree branches, a lot of sawdust, a bowl of water, and an old slipper.

Felicity poked a walnut kernel through the bars, and a young red squirrel emerged from the slipper. It stood up and looked at us suspiciously, and then came over and grabbed the nut, turning its back on us while nibbling.

"What a handsome chap," I said. "Is that a splint on its leg?"

"Yes, our groom did that. He's quite knowledgeable about animals, but he's never mended a squirrel leg before!"

"Will you turn him loose, when his leg is fixed?" I asked.

Felicity sighed. "I expect so. I don't really want to, but it would be better for him."

"You should try drawing him," I said.

"I have tried," Felicity said, "but just when I get started, he skitters off, even with a sore leg. Oh – that reminds me. Would you like one of my botanical drawings? You can choose one."

"If you're sure you can spare one?" I said. I looked up at Flora for guidance, who was looking slightly amused, but did not seem inclined to discourage this gift.

"Of course I can!" Felicity said. "Let's go back to the drawing room, and you can look through them. You two go on ahead, and I will give Pantoufle the rest of his supper."

In the drawing room, I sat down in front of Felicity's portfolio again.

"Mrs Ambrose," I said, "your daughter has offered to give me one of her excellent drawings. Would this be all right?"

"Oh, what a sweet child she is!" said Mrs Ambrose. "Yes, I don't see why not."

I chose the autumnal trees. When Felicity came back into the room, she said, "I thought you might choose that one! I was very pleased with it. Let me find something to put it in."

She went away with the drawing, and when she came back, she had placed it in between the cardboard covers of an old sketch book, tied up with a ribbon.

"Thank you, Miss Ambrose," I said. "I will enjoy it immensely, especially for cheering myself up when I am miserable."

"Oh, no!" said Felicity. "Do you ever get miserable? Surely someone like you..."

"We all have our bad days," said Flora. "Everyone does, I'm afraid – even kings and queens."

"I suppose so," said Felicity.

"Especially kings and queens," I said. "All that responsibility, and not knowing who your true friends are – you couldn't pay me enough to do it."

Flora coughed. "Speaking of bad days," she said, "I'm very sorry, but I seem to have a cold coming on. Would you mind terribly if we headed for home? I hate to leave, though."

"Yes, you must go home at once, you poor thing," said Mrs Ambrose. "But you will come again soon? Please?" There was a hint of desperation in her tone, not just politeness.

"Very soon, Isobel, I promise," Flora said, putting her hand on Mrs Ambrose's shoulder reassuringly. Mrs Ambrose smiled and pressed Flora's hand.

"And Mr Rufford, Mr Ambrose will be cross not to have embroiled you in a discussion about his antiques," she said.

"Please send my apologies, and my thanks," I said. "It's been good to meet you all. Including the handsome Pantoufle!"

~

When the front door closed and Flora and I were settled in the pony trap, I first had to disentangle a knot in the reins. During this short delay, we heard raised voices through an open window.

"How could you speak to him like that!" Mrs Ambrose was saying. "I could have killed you!"

"About Mrs Shannon? It was only a joke. You are being over-sensitive, as usual, Isobel. And anyway, remember what you are!"

"What am I, then, Yorick? I am your wife! God forbid that you might ever treat me as one."

I heard a bitter laugh, but his reply was muffled by a gust of wind in the trees.

Then: "You may strike me all you want, Isobel, but it won't make me share your bed."

A window was slammed shut, and we heard no more. I realised we had been eavesdropping, sitting rigid with horror in the trap, and I spurred Jenny down the drive as quickly as I dared.

Flora turned to me. "What did he mean about Mrs Shannon? What is Mrs Shannon to you?"

"Bess is a good friend," I said. "I'm very fond of her." I wondered how Mr Ambrose had found out about our association, and whether it had scandalised Mrs Ambrose. But she had been more shocked by her husband's behaviour than by mine.

Flora was silent for a moment. "Of course, it's none of my business. I'm just – surprised, that's all. I thought you might have mentioned her to me."

"I'm sorry," I said. "Perhaps I should have."

"Well, that was an... interesting evening," Flora said, yawning and then coughing. "Isobel and Felicity obviously liked you. But I didn't realise things between Isobel and Yorick were quite so fraught."

"Yes, that was disturbing," I said. "Still, I expect some people's marriages are full of unpleasant scenes like that, after which they come to terms."

"I hope so," said Flora, "especially for Felicity's sake. But their arguing like that makes me wonder whether... oh, no, I'm being silly."

"Whether what?"

"It's just that several years ago, Mr Ambrose was the subject of a horrible rumour about their maid. Susan, I think she was called. Susan Lipton. She left suddenly, and then the poor girl killed herself."

"How very sad," I said. "So what was the rumour about?"

"You can guess, can't you?"

"That Mr Ambrose dishonoured the maid, so she killed herself in shame?"

"Something like that."

"Unfortunately, these things happen more frequently than one cares to think," I said, "and I can quite believe it of Mr Ambrose."

"So can I." She blew her nose. "Oh – I'm feeling dreadful. I hope this is no more than a cold."

I put a hand on her forehead – it was worryingly hot.

CHAPTER TWO

FLORA accepted some assistance up the stairs to her rooms, and I saw that she was comfortably settled in bed, with her housekeeper Meg Northcutt fussing around her and opening the window.

"My work at the Town Hall!" she said, feverishly. "I can't let Johnny down."

"The mural can wait," I said. "Besides, this thing may have passed by Monday. And you will give Mr Falkirk time to catch up."

She nodded. "Good night, Thomas. Can you look in on me in the morning?"

"Of course I will," I said. "Good night!"

I went to bed, somewhat worried by Flora's illness. Perhaps long hours painting in the Town Hall had worn her out – it was more exertion than she was accustomed to – and travelling on a cold November evening might have compounded it.

It also troubled me to think that Bess Shannon was the subject of gossip, but I hoped that it was confined to a small number of people and would not change the way townsfolk saw either of us. Besides, I doubted anyone would find evidence of anything really scandalous.

The next day was Sunday. After checking on Flora, who was still rather too hot, but sleeping soundly, I went to church, largely in order to see Phyllis. After the service, which was conducted in a bland fashion by a rector from a nearby parish, she and I met in the churchyard.

I greeted Phyllis and said, "I must say, Mr Benton almost makes me miss Mr Neville. Is your father not here today?"

"It's his arthritis," she said. "It's a little worse, and bending to kneel is painful."

"I'm sorry to hear that," I said. "The autumn chill can't be helping. Would you care for a walk?"

"Certainly. Have you been to Hawksbridge Castle yet?"

"Not yet," I said. "I was at a dinner last night and someone was talking about its restoration. How much of a wreck is it?"

"Enough to make you grateful for the state of your own house – you will see. The most picturesque way is via the walls."

The castle had fallen into disuse several centuries ago, and it lay outside the town's own, more recent defensive walls. Phyllis and I climbed up to Knight's Mount, savouring the view beyond Hawksbridge as we had in September. The River Gill gouged a valley that provided a southern boundary for the town, and its northern cliff added to the sense of reassurance that the walls provided.

We walked for a few minutes before climbing down stone steps and following a path that led to the castle. I had seen the tops of the remaining walls above the trees, but I had not realised how majestic they would be. Traces of the curtain wall around the castle and its associated towers and other structures, mostly reduced to waist height or less, enclosed a field around which several goats were wandering.

"This is the best-preserved part – the Great Hall," Phyllis said. We went over, and stood in the roofless space, peering up at the birds roosting in the windows and ledges. At around fifty feet wide, and a hundred feet long, it was an impressive accomplishment, and the walls still projected some thirty or forty feet into the air. But even such monumental walls had no lasting defence against time and the northern weather.

"It's enormous. Imagine all the banquets they would have had here," I said.

"And servants would sleep on the floor," said Phyllis.

"Which would not be pleasant after a banquet, I imagine."

"Quite," I said. "So the decline of the castle is to be halted by Mr Fountain's Preservation Committee. I'm glad. I'm not a subscriber to the belief that the present may disregard the past."

"I have had many good plot ideas, pottering around here amongst the goats," Phyllis said.

"Then on that basis alone, the castle should be preserved, with a plaque recording your inspiration."

Phyllis laughed. "I'm sure no one will ever be interested in where a novelist dreamed up a story. Only, I hope, in the story itself."

"Speaking of which," I said, "how is your soldier-girl, fighting her own relatives?"

"I have put that one aside, for now," Phyllis said. "I am bored with her, and I have made her far too heroic to be sympathetic."

"I'm sorry to hear that," I said. "It sounded promising."

She grunted and kicked a fallen tree branch with evident annoyance at herself.

"On another topic," she said, brightening, "I have had an interesting letter."

"Yes?"

"From a young woman called Victoria Clitheroe, who professes to be an admirer of my work."

"So far, so natural. You must get quite a number of such letters."

"Yes," Phyllis said, "but she is different. She speaks with particular warmth, and decorates her letter with charming animal drawings! And she is coming to Hawksbridge soon, and wishes to meet me."

"Good Lord," I said. "And will you? I know how protective of your privacy you can be."

"That's what's odd. I feel no inclination to refuse her. She sounds great fun."

"Then I heartily approve," I said. "Is she coming to Hawksbridge solely to meet you?"

"No, she says she wants to set her first novel in a place like Hawksbridge. I should be wary of the rivalry, shouldn't I?"

"You have quite a head start," I said, "so she's unlikely to be any kind of threat. From your description, she would be a good dinner party guest. I should like to meet Miss Clitheroe."

Phyllis looked at me dubiously. "I'm not sure that would be good for you, or for her, Thomas. I have a feeling you will flirt most dreadfully with her, if she is remotely presentable."

"And what, may I ask, is wrong with that?" I said, amused.

"Oh, nothing, I suppose," she said, walking towards the gaping end of the Great Hall. "If you enjoy toying with a woman."

I stood for a moment and observed her elegant form and the gracefulness of her movements as she picked her way over the weeds and fallen stones. Far from being needled by her words, I admired her straightforwardness. And perhaps there was a grain of truth in what she said.

Snapping out of my reverie, I quickly caught up with Phyllis as she emerged into the open field, and mildly alarmed a goat in the process. I stood in her way and said, "No woman can possibly compare with you! You have the finest mind of any person I know."

She frowned. "That's hardly what I meant, but... I'm not sure I like your characterisation of me as a dry old scholar."

"That's because I'm not as good at words as you," I said, "and also because I know you don't like sentimentality."

"What *are* you prattling about?" she said, and dodged around me.

"Just that I am very glad to know such a magnificent creature as you," I said.

She tried to suppress a smile, but it was clearly not working.

"Thank you, Thomas," she said. "I'm sorry I was crotchety."

"Don't mention it," I said. "It's part of your charm."

"You're very silly," Phyllis said, brushing off an autumn leaf that had landed on my shoulder. "Now, let's go home, and you can help cheer my father up."

~

"It's good to see you, Mr Rufford," Dr Drummond said as the chicken soup was laid in front of us. "How's your head? Recovered, after all your recent adventuring?"

"Thankfully, yes," I said. "I'm hoping for a quiet life now. Phyllis was showing me the old castle this morning – it's more impressive than I imagined."

"Ah yes," Dr Drummond chuckled. "Phyllis' mother and I used to court in the Great Hall. No one to see us kissing but a couple of goats."

"Father!" said Phyllis, colouring. "I'm sure Thomas doesn't want to hear about that."

"Perhaps not," Dr Drummond replied, "but let me enjoy my memories of your dear mother. And Mr Rufford," he added, putting his hand on my arm, "don't imagine you have all the time in the world. It goes more quickly than you think."

Phyllis shot me an embarrassed look. "Anyway," she said quickly, to avoid me having to reply, "would you like to see Victoria's letter?"

"I would," I said. "It sounds delightful."

Phyllis left the room, and came back with the letter a minute later, and put it next to my bowl.

Miss Clitheroe's hand was neat but it had extravagant, energetic flourishes. Up the margins of the letter climbed a variety of small, well-drawn creatures, including mice, some beetles, and a fox, and it reminded me of an illuminated manuscript, albeit lacking colour. It was an unusual way to write to a stranger, but it had a charming quality that seemed to override considerations of convention. I read the missive aloud.

> Leeds, November, 1848
>
> Dear Miss Drummond,
>
> I hope you can forgive the impertinence of this letter! but as a devotee of the inimitable Iona Tavistock, I could not resist writing to you, as I am travelling to your beautiful town for a few weeks in the hopes of inspiration for my first attempt at a novel. Leeds fills my head with smoke and noise, and I must find some peace so I can hear the faint voices of the characters that are beginning to form.
>
> You have, as I am sure you have for countless others, enthralled me and stirred my imagination, made me weep, and saved me from my own melancholy. In short, you have improved me, and I am moved to try to possess this witchcraft for myself.
>
> Nothing would give me more pleasure than to talk to you, however briefly, and perhaps some of your sorcery will rub off on me – and at least I can show my gratitude in person.
>
> If you have time to reply, I will be at my Leeds address for the next week, and from then, at The Black Bull in Hawksbridge. If you do not have time, then thank you for reading my letter, and I wish you fair winds with your next book, which I await eagerly!
>
> Yours faithfully,
>
> Victoria Clitheroe (Miss)
>
> P.S. I got carried away with my doodles as I wrote this letter – I cannot help myself. I hope to combine illustration and writing some day!

"Good Lord," I said. "She has been bitten badly by the Tavistock bug. But I know exactly what she means."

"I confess it doesn't hurt to be told these things, once in a while," said Phyllis. "My newspaper reviews are much more guarded."

"What's it like to have such a gifted daughter?" I asked Dr Drummond.

He thought for a moment, and then said, "Aye, well, worrying."

"Worrying?" I repeated.

"Aye," he said, taking his time, evidently enjoying our puzzled expressions. "That she might not find an equally gifted man to appreciate her."

"Ah! yes," I said. "I can understand that."

Phyllis ignored this exchange, and said, "I will write back. She is obviously a thoughtful person, and I should be kind to my readers."

"Talking of readers," I said, "last night I met another devotee of yours – a fifteen-year-old by the name of Miss Felicity Ambrose. She is Flora's drawing pupil. I'm afraid I suggested that I might introduce her to you: she was entirely thrilled at the idea! And now you are being swamped with eager followers."

"That's quite all right," said Phyllis. "It's not as if my mind is working properly at present anyway. I haven't hit on the right theme for my next book. Perhaps the well has run dry."

"Nonsense," I said. "You probably just need a rest. Or perhaps a holiday? You could both go to Italy, and fill your heads with beautiful art and opera."

Dr Drummond laughed. "Not me, lad," he said, pointing to his legs. "My arthritis. I hate travel. Besides, I have patients who need me. But my dear, you could find someone to go with, could you not?"

"It's tempting," said Phyllis. "Perhaps in the spring. I don't know who I'd go with, though."

"Francesca?" I said. "You would be guaranteed an

exciting time."

"Too exciting, I suspect," she said. "I'll see. But perhaps I do need to take the time to fill that well up again."

I could see Dr Drummond looking at me pointedly, and I knew what he was thinking, but even he could not find a subtle way to imply how Phyllis might legitimately travel to Italy with me in the spring.

CHAPTER THREE

WHEN I returned home from my lunch with the Drummonds, I found Fox full of energy and demanding a walk. Having accomplished this, I withdrew to my little study with a jug of coffee and watched the light drain from the grey November skies. I thought about Phyllis. I had not allowed my feelings for her free rein; I felt unworthy of her, and my dalliance with Bess cut off certain avenues of thought and action. It would be hard to wrench myself from Bess' welcoming arms, but Dr Drummond's remarks had hit their mark.

As had often been my habit when faced with an uncomfortable conundrum, I diverted myself with another task, namely sifting through the late Mr Kington's correspondence that still lay in his – now my – bureau. Under the invoices and business communications, I found a packet of letters tied in a blue ribbon, that I had not noticed in my previous cursory inspection. Looking at the first one, I saw it was from a Mr Jeremy Davison: Flora's father. It was dated April, 1823, and most of the letter's contents were pedestrian and involved news about relatives and tiring journeys to London.

However, one passage stood out.

> I must ask you about a delicate matter that has been on my mind. Perhaps I am being over-anxious, but did it not strike you on our visit last month that your friend Dr Rufford appeared rather familiar with my wife? I felt that Rufford was complimenting her in an inappropriate manner. I hope I am wrong about the man! Alice did not seem disturbed by it, so I may simply be finding fault where there is none. After all, Alice is – like her sister – a handsome woman.

Perhaps I should be flattered that she receives such attention.

This was a double shock to me: firstly, that my father apparently had eyes for Flora's mother, as well as Mrs Kington, and secondly, that he was visiting Ramsburgh so much earlier than I (and my father's solicitor) had realised – when I was around four years of age. The letter also implied that he was a friend to both of the Kingtons, not just Margaret, in which case the coming betrayal must have been all the greater.

The next letter made no mention of Mr Davison's concerns, but in the one after that, in October of 1823, the topic had resurfaced.

It was wonderful to be back at Ramsburgh last week, and the shooting was glorious. However, I was tempted to aim my gun at Charles, as he was talking to my wife again in that impertinent manner I have mentioned before. Perhaps it is just his way, but my wife seems to enjoy his asinine flattery. I am sorry – after all, he is your friend, and in other respects, he is fine company – but his air with my wife grates.

I wondered how Mr Kington had fielded Mr Davison's concerns. I thought he had probably dismissed them out of hand, else he might not have entertained my father in his house over such a long period.

I decided to postpone the reading of the remaining letters – I dreaded further revelations about my father, having, as I had thought, made my peace with the irregular way in which I had inherited Ramsburgh. Instead, I turned to Miss Ambrose's drawing – delightful, innocent Felicity with her recuperating squirrel. I opened up the cardboard sarcophagus that protected my drawing, and as I took it out, a small note fell out.

Dear Mr Rufford,

It was very nice meeting you today. Please come again soon. Pantoufle liked you too!

I hope my drawing helps when you are melancholy. Trees are my favourite subject to draw at present. Perhaps you can hang it in your office – so you can see it when composing all those dull letters about business things that grown-ups have to write!

Yours faithfully,

Felicity Ambrose

I smiled. She was quite right, I thought – everyone should have aesthetic objects to help them through the humdrum matters of life. I thought of Felicity dashing to her bedroom and scribbling this note, concealing it with the drawing. I doubted her parents would have approved.

~

The following day, I had an appointment with Francesca Campbell to which I had been looking forward: to ride together, and no doubt to foolishly gossip.

The sun reluctantly emerged as I approached Francesca's Elizabethan domain, Halfpenny House. Its warm, red brick façade seemed a match for Francesca's personality: bold, welcoming, hiding a wealth of surprises, but ultimately embodying the best English qualities and traditions. The tradition I had come to participate in suited Francesca aesthetically: sitting high up in her feathered riding hat and green habit, confidently wielding her riding crop, she was a picture of feminine sensuality and vigour.

She was walking her horse from the stables as I approached. "Good morning, Thomas!" she said. "How are you and Celeste?"

"Good morning, Francesca," I said. "I am well, and Celeste is in good form and as patient with me as ever. And you?"

"Now I have you to chase away my *ennuie*, I have nothing

to complain about," said Francesca. "Our usual route?"

I nodded, and we followed the dirt track that wound around the edge of a forest, and then exercised our mounts by chasing one another around sheep-filled fields.

We stopped to rest and watch a dirty, rain-filled cloud move across the valley.

After a few minutes, Francesca turned to me and said, "I have met an interesting gentleman. I must introduce him to you. He has some amusing business ideas, and is good company."

"Oh?" I said. "I hope he is reliable. What is his name?"

"Mr Reginald Wakeley," she said. "And I believe he is. But he has had some bad luck lately, and a business partner absconded with much of his wealth. But he is undeterred. I like a man who does not easily give up."

"I see," I said. "And he's looking to replace his lost wealth with some of yours?"

"Don't be so silly," said Francesca. "He is not that kind of person. And I have not agreed to anything."

"He must be very handsome," I said, feeling a pang of jealousy that was entirely unreasonable.

Francesca laughed and said, "You may rest assured – not as handsome of you! Of course not. But he possesses a certain charm."

"Like Mr Walker?" I said, and then regretted saying it.

"Not at all like Mr Walker," she said, unfazed. "Much more dependable, in my view – and more sober."

"May I ask the nature of these business proposals?"

"I'm afraid he wishes them to remain confidential for now, so I can't say, but perhaps he will tell you about them himself."

I was not entirely happy with what I was hearing, but put my reaction down to innate male rivalry.

"Have you a need for business schemes, Francesca? Forgive me, but I thought you were well provided for. And your splendid house...”

“I am bored with living off money I haven’t earned,” she said. “And besides, I have inherited some investments I’m not proud of. It would amuse me – and be good for me – to have new sources of income.”

“Ah,” I said.

She looked at me and I stared at the horizon, feeling irritable and unwilling to return her gaze.

“Anyway,” she said as brightly as she could, “I can see I have put you in a bad mood, for some reason. I’m sorry. Let me console you with tea and cake! And I have some acquisitions I want to show you.”

We returned without further exchange, but the distraction of tea helped my mood a little.

“I’m sorry, Francesca,” I said. “I suppose I feel slightly protective of you, that’s all.”

“That’s quite all right,” Francesca said, taking a forkful of cake. “But I’m a grown woman – I can take care of myself. There is no need for your shining armour at the moment.”

“I know,” I said. “So – what are these mysterious treasures of yours?”

“Oh, yes! Let me show you,” she said, putting down her fork, and she led me into the sitting room in which, not long ago, I had participated in a tableau vivant. “I haven’t worked out where to put everything just yet.”

The room was filled with a jumble of furniture, a wrapped picture and a couple of tea-chests.

“Good Lord,” I said. “Someone else with an antiquarian obsession.”

“Someone else?”

“I’ll tell you about it another time. This is magnificent,” I said, looking at a clearly ancient, highly carved cupboard, over six feet in height. Three semi-naked caryatids adorned the two sides and the centre, and the panelled doors were also intricately carved with shields and scrolls. The centuries had aged the wood to a satisfying texture and shade.

"You approve?" Francesca said. "It's sixteenth-century, and according to Mr Blackwood, from Burgundy. He has recently returned from the Continent with a haul of pieces; he was almost reluctant to part with this one. I thought it was appropriate for the age of this house."

"It's incredible," I said, running my hand over the carvings. "Such workmanship."

"Of course," Francesca said, "it's not very fashionable now: people prefer plainness. Which means that things of this period are undervalued, in my opinion."

"So these are some of your investments?" I said.

"Well, that might be overstating it. I just liked it. Mr Blackwood said that one of his regular customers would be cross, as he has been eyeing it up."

"Ah," I said. "That I can understand. I wonder if it might be –"

My speculation got no further, as Francesca was opening up a tea-chest and laying out some miniature paintings on a table. "Come and look at these!" she said. "I can't believe how little he was asking. Well, it was still substantial, but look at the detail!"

I went to examine the paintings, which were indeed of a high quality. Faces from the Elizabethan era, judging from the extravagant ruffs, and maybe a century later, looked at me as fresh and vivid as the day they were painted. Their demeanours were variously impassive, proud, self-satisfied, serious, coquettish, and in one case – a royal-looking gentleman in a huge wig – a little disgusted, as well he might be after being retrieved from a bed of sawdust and paper to be confronted with two commoners impertinently peering at him.

It was a substantial collection – I counted twenty-four. "They must have been someone's life work," I observed. "They are extraordinary!"

"I know," Francesca beamed. "I was lucky to get them."

"What else?" I said, turning round. "Ah – nice chair." I had spotted a fruitwood country chair with unusual grooves in the back slats, and polished from a good few decades of use.

"It's quirky, isn't it?" Francesca said. "I thought you'd appreciate that one – good and simple this time! Not very old, but such a pleasing, plain design, I couldn't resist it."

"Now the best item!" said Francesca, and she pulled the brown paper from an oval picture, and turned it around. "Voilà! A self-portrait, from around 1690."

A curly-haired beauty met my gaze, with an expression of confidence. 'As you can see, I can do this as well as any man,' she seemed to say. She wore a blue shawl over a gold dress, the folds of which were cleverly depicted, and she held a drawing to indicate her profession.

"She's gorgeous," I said.

"A French artist called Élisabeth Laurent," said Francesca. "I will put her in my bedroom to inspire me when I get up."

After we had examined the remaining items – a couple more chairs, a Pembroke table, and a glazed cupboard – I said, "You have done well. It's quite an Aladdin's cave. I see why you need to replenish your coffers!"

Francesca laughed. "Yes, that is a consideration – to feed my terrible habit. But that wretched Blackwood has such a good eye. I fear I will run out of space soon."

"You will just need to buy another house for them," I said. "You could rent it out on the condition that you can regularly visit your precious artefacts."

"And have people damage them?" said Francesca, carefully putting the miniatures back to bed. "I will be in a perpetual state of worry!"

"Then extending your home is the only solution," I said. "Or rotating your possessions."

"Oh, I'm a greedy fool, creating problems for myself," Francesca said. "But how am I supposed to resist such beautiful things?"

~

On Tuesday morning I put in an appearance at the Pottery for a briefing on the company's operations and sales. Mr McPhee was usually in good spirits, but I was learning to detect when his expression betrayed a more than usual amount of satisfaction, and this was one of those occasions.

"A very good morning to you, Mr Rufford!" he said, ushering me to a chair in his office. "Coffee? Walton – two, if you don't mind."

Mr Walton went off to fetch the coffee, while McPhee pushed a pile of papers across his desk in my direction.

"These are advance orders for Marbleware from a dozen or so shops to whom we have offered the new range. Judging by the response, we will have to increase production to keep up with the demand. The greatest enthusiasm is shown for the Hawksbridge Angels! And the Earl of Monmouth – a very old customer of ours – has ordered one for each of his houses. What do you think of that?"

"Very impressive," I said, "although not surprising, considering the quality of our products – and our staff."

"Not forgetting Miss Davison's invaluable help. Of course, it's early days, but I believe we'll steal a march on our rivals. And we have already turned around our previous unfortunate balance sheet thanks to the popularity of Hawksbridge Dragon."

"All very good news, Mr McPhee," I said. "Please pass on my congratulations to the staff! Perhaps a bonus for all might be due, especially since Christmas is coming?"

"Capital idea," said Mr McPhee. "I will insist upon it at the next board meeting."

It weighed upon me that I breezed in and out of the Pottery like a powerless monarch, but since for many years the company had grown used to working with largely absentee owners – first Mrs Kington after her husband's death, and then my father, whom I doubted would have concerned himself with any company business – I was careful not to overstep the bounds of my role. Besides, I was content with my influence via McPhee, and did not trust myself to make more substantial decisions. The Marbleware project showed that they were capable of adapting to new markets, and it looked as though I would finally be seeing dividends as the company's finances improved. I would then have the dilemma of how to invest or spend it – Francesca's recent acquisitions set a tempting example.

After my meeting with McPhee, I went to Hunter's bookshop. Mr Hunter had a picture-framing business as a sideline, and I left Felicity's sketch with him and headed off to see Bess Shannon. Buoyed by news of the Pottery's success, I entertained thoughts of an afternoon of indulgence and pleasure, as I had been fortunate enough to experience before.

As I approached her house, I could hear the sweet sounds of Bess' harp, and I lingered for a moment by her sitting room window to listen. I hesitated to interrupt and bring to an end this innocent pastime; and then I thought of Phyllis, and so, accompanied by the fading, melancholy beauty of plucked chords, I turned Celeste around and made my reluctant way home.

CHAPTER FOUR

ON my return, I found a brief note from Phyllis. It read:

> Dear Thomas,
>
> I have met Victoria! and she is quite as delightful as her letter. We get along strangely well, and I feel moved to assist her with her writing. To show that I can share my friends, please come and take tea with us tomorrow afternoon around 3 o'clock – that should allow you enough time to get home safely afterwards.
>
> Yours,
>
> Phyllis

And so on Wednesday, Celeste and I duly braved a rainstorm and sharp wind to visit the Drummonds and their guest.

Phyllis appeared in the hall as I dried my face with a towel that the maid had provided. "Oh, Thomas!" she said. "This is Miss Victoria Clitheroe!"

Victoria was slightly younger than me; her features had an understated beauty and she wore a stylish turquoise hat over her flaxen hair.

"I'm very pleased to meet you, Mr Rufford," she said with a disarming smile, holding out her hand. "I have been hearing about your adventures. You must be a good person to know, if one is in peril!"

I shook her hand. "Pleased to meet you too, Miss Clitheroe," I said. "I fear you wouldn't think that, if Phyllis had been candid about my recklessness."

"Recklessness, courage – let's not split hairs!" said

Victoria. "I would like to hear your story some time, without the distortions of the press."

She turned and smiled at Phyllis. "On the subject of stories, Miss Drummond has been so helpful in telling me how I might approach my novel. I can't wait to put it into practice, when I get back to my room!"

We were ushered into the drawing room, where Dr Drummond was already installed in his favourite armchair. We greeted each other, and after we had all sat down, I asked, "How is your room, Miss Clitheroe? I gather you are staying in The Black Bull. I had heard the place was a trifle... basic. Is it satisfactory?"

Victoria grimaced. "Well – to be frank..." She glanced around as if the proprietor of The Black Bull might be lurking in a corner, and whispered, "It's shockingly awful!"

"Oh no!" said Phyllis. "Really? Are there cockroaches?"

"Not quite," said Victoria, "at least not that I've seen. But I saw a mouse near the kitchen – or it might have been a rat – and the whole place is filthy. And as for the privy..." She shrugged and raised her hands to indicate that she was lost for words.

Phyllis looked distressed, and said, "You can't possibly stay there another night!"

"My dear, Miss Clitheroe must stay here," Dr Drummond said earnestly to his daughter. "The inn sounds most unhygienic."

"Certainly!" said Phyllis. "Oh – but the spare room! It's being redecorated, and is quite topsy turvy. We put the bed in the stable to get it out of the way! Bother. We could share my bed – but that's a shabby offer!"

"It's quite all right," said Victoria. "I dare say I'll survive another night, and then I'll try to find another inn."

"Which may be just as bad," said Phyllis.

As the tea tray arrived, I cleared my throat. "Miss Clitheroe, this may be an impertinent suggestion," I said, "but you're very welcome to stay at my house, where Phyllis stayed not long ago."

Phyllis added, "Yes, why not? You will have a kind of chaperone in the form of Miss Flora Davison, the niece of the former owner, who lives in a part of the house."

"You can stay as long as you need while you make further arrangements," I said.

"I can't possibly –" began Victoria, but Phyllis interrupted with "Of course you can! It's the ideal solution. And I can vouch for the impeccable behaviour of my friend Mr Rufford. The house is lovely, and the bed comfortable."

"I agree with my daughter," said Dr Drummond. "I would strongly advise against staying another night at The Black Bull, for the sake of your health."

Victoria's expression showed that her resistance was crumbling. "Would I not be a frightful inconvenience?"

"Not in the least bit," I said. "And my dog Fox will enjoy having fresh company."

"Oh! I look forward to meeting Fox," Victoria said. "I must draw him. But mostly I shall hide myself away and work on my book: you won't know I'm there. But this is so kind – thank you, Mr Rufford! It is an enormous relief. I was absolutely dreading going back to that place. Though I will have to fetch my things and settle up."

"I will take you in the trap after tea," said Phyllis, "and see that you're settled in Ramsburgh. A problem easily solved."

Victoria smiled at Phyllis and me in turn. "You are all being so kind to me, a perfect stranger..."

"Nonsense," said Phyllis. "You are a stranger no longer. Now, try Mrs Jackson's almond cake. I could make myself positively rotund on it."

~

As we talked, I was amused to see how Phyllis had let her guard down with Victoria. It was touching to see her new friendship blossom. As far as I knew, Phyllis had not found a female friend with whom she could be truly comfortable since she became estranged from Flora. It was easy to see why Victoria appealed to her: she was intelligent, charming and funny, combined with a shrewdness that may have been attributable to her city upbringing. She was going to be an asset to our circle.

Still, I had a disagreeable, half-formed notion that if Phyllis had feelings for me, she might not be so keen for her attractive friend to stay at my home. But I imagined that Phyllis' trusting nature and generosity of spirit had overcome any such consideration.

After tea, I returned to Ramsburgh and waited for Phyllis and Victoria. Victoria was delighted with her new lodgings, and as I had predicted, Fox was excited to have someone new to make a fuss of him.

Phyllis decided to stay for dinner. My housekeeper, Mrs Felton, was still acting as cook, as we had not yet found a suitable candidate, but she had made an excellent fish pie.

"This is excellent," Victoria said as she tucked into the pie. "Where is this chaperone you spoke of, if I may ask? Will she be joining us?"

"Unfortunately she's not well at the moment," I said.

Phyllis sighed. "But even if she were, she might choose to avoid me. I regret to say we fell out a long time ago. But she is quite close at hand, in the tower you saw to the right of the front door. Her rooms are accessible via the first floor landing. I'm sure you will get on."

"Oh!" said Victoria. "I'm sorry to hear you are not friends. I'm sure you will be again, in time. How could anyone resist you?"

Phyllis smiled sadly and nodded. "Thank you. Perhaps. Thomas – how is she?"

"She is still not right," I said. "I have suggested summoning your father, but she says she is not ill enough to trouble him with all those stairs. It's probably influenza."

"Oh dear," said Phyllis. "I wish I could see her."

Victoria took a sip of wine. "The proprietor of The Black Bull, Mr Harkness, told me of another relative newcomer to Hawksbridge – but not, I think, staying at The Black Bull – who is apparently a very canny man with money, and is about to make him a considerable profit. I have some money I need to invest – I don't suppose you have come across him? His name is – let me try to remember – Wakeley, that was it. Reginald Wakeley. Might you know him?"

"How strange," I said. "I have recently heard the name. My friend Mrs Francesca Campbell spoke of him in relation to some investment she was thinking of making. So we can arrange a meeting, if you wish."

"What a coincidence! That would be kind – thank you!" said Victoria.

Phyllis looked dubious. "I'm not sure I like the sound of Mr Wakeley. Only recently arrived – I would be very careful, Victoria."

"Oh, of course," said Victoria. "I would get several opinions before I invested. But I find my own bank very unhelpful when I discuss what to do with my money, and I get the impression they would rather not be talking to a woman at all. Anyway, I can't lose anything by just talking to him, can I?"

"Probably not," said Phyllis. "But if you would like me to accompany you –"

"Certainly!" said Victoria. "I would be glad of your company."

I flicked my empty wine glass with some annoyance at Wakeley's name cropping up again. "Mrs Campbell wouldn't reveal the nature of the investment," I said. "I felt a little suspicious, to tell you the truth. But I haven't met him, so perhaps I'm being unfair."

"I will of course be on my guard," said Victoria. "Thank you for your concern! Now, to change the subject, how beautiful your house is – no, your castle! It is so grand, but comfortable."

"I have been told it is not a castle," I said, "but merely a fortified tower, with additions."

"What nonsense," said Phyllis. "Which curmudgeon said this?"

"A Mr Leonardo Fountain," I said, "a rather ossified member of the Hawksbridge Antiquarian Society, whom I met on Saturday at a dinner party. He may be right. No doubt he was comparing it unfavourably with Hawksbridge Castle, for the care of which he has set up a committee."

"It would have been an impressive castle in its day," said Phyllis. "I must take you to see it," she added to Victoria. "It might inspire you, as it does me!"

I refilled my wine glass and sat back, imagining the two of them staring up at the Great Hall, their charming, absorbed faces illuminated by the sun, their dresses making blue and green splashes against the tan of the sandstone walls. I put an imaginary frame around them, taking care to show, on one side, some of the river that wound below, and on the other side, a grazing goat. Such a picture would be a fine replacement for the indifferent hunting scene that currently hung over the fireplace.

"Do you think you might, Thomas? Thomas?"

I felt a prod on my arm: Phyllis was trying to get my attention.

"Oh – I'm sorry," I said. "I was in a dream. Do I think I might what?"

"Go along to the next meeting of the Antiquarian Society," said Phyllis. "I gather from my father that there will be talks about the castle – and of course we women are forbidden to go. So I thought you might invite yourself as a guest. I'm anxious to know what they will do to the castle."

I nodded, since Phyllis was giving me the kind of look that made it impossible to refuse anything she asked.

"And besides," she continued, "if you're looking for something to occupy yourself with, you might find some part to play."

"Very well: I shall make enquiries and see if they will allow me to observe. They may not welcome guests, especially one so new to Hawksbridge. But I will look into it."

~

When Phyllis left, Victoria spent a few minutes admiring and fussing over Fox, before wishing me good night and disappearing up to her room. It felt strange to be hosting a woman I had only met that day, but I had got somewhat used to turning my house into a hotel for distressed gentlefolk.

I went and sat in the drawing room, with Fox curled up at my feet and the fire dwindling in the grate, contemplating the invitation I had received that morning: lunch with Francesca and her new friend, Reginald Wakeley. I had decided not to mention this fact to Victoria and Phyllis out of an instinct that I should size Wakeley up before any further meetings could be proposed.

"Would you like some more logs on that, my dear?" said Mrs Felton, coming in to check all was tidy.

"Ah – no need, Mrs Felton," I said. "I'm just about to go to bed. Thank you for an excellent dinner."

"My pleasure, my dear," she said. "You have so many pretty young things coming to the house! Such a choice, if you were in a courting mood!"

"Yes, you may have a point," I said. After several glasses of wine, I was disinclined to be either offended or embarrassed at her frankness. "Dr Drummond is always dropping hints."

"As well he might," said Mrs Felton. "Miss Drummond is a fine young woman, and such a clever one! You would make a handsome couple."

I nodded. "Perhaps. But I need to make sure I'm worthy of her, first."

Mrs Felton was adjusting a crooked rug, but she immediately stood up and stared at me. "Mr Thomas Rufford! My sainted aunt. I can't believe you would say that, when you have proved yourself to be such a courageous and honourable man over the last few months. To Miss Flora, to Miss Drummond, to everyone in Hawksbridge!"

She came and perched on a chair adjacent to mine. "And to me!" she said. "Not that it was at all my place to approve or disapprove, of course – but it must have been hard for you to come to Ramsburgh, in such strange circumstances, and you have a humility that – forgive me – your father never had. So what can you be speaking of, my dear?"

I grunted and drained the wine glass that I had brought with me from the dining room. "That's very kind of you, Mrs Felton. But sometimes I have... indulged myself. I don't know if I can be forgiven by any woman I would care enough about to marry."

Mrs Felton looked at me with wide eyes. "Is *that* all you are worried about? Men do indulge themselves, for sure, that's how they are made. But you are not married yet, so I don't think you have to be too hard on yourself."

I smiled. "Perhaps... but it seems too easy an excuse. And it's so hard to stop indulging myself. I am so weak."

"The very fact you are saying this is an excellent sign," Mrs Felton said. "It means you have a conscience, and in my opinion, too much of one for your own good! What if the right woman decided to marry someone else, just because you had scruples? That wouldn't be in your interest, or hers."

"No," I admitted. "Damn it, I need more wine. Or perhaps some port. Would you like to join me in a glass? You deserve some for counselling me."

"Well, if you don't mind," Mrs Felton said, "that would be very welcome. I'll go and fetch it."

As Mrs Felton went to retrieve the port, I sank lower in my armchair and felt a wave of gratitude to her, heightened by a pleasant haze of alcohol. I had no male friend to discuss such things with. I could talk about some personal matters with Bess, but of course – not this. Mrs Felton was a very sensible, practical woman, and remarkably unjudgemental.

"There we are, my dear," she said as she came in with a tray and took her seat.

"Now then," Mrs Felton said after taking a sip of port, "what was I about to say? Oh yes – me and my Charles. I loved him, but he wasn't perfect. Who is? So, his brother got ill, and Charles took to spending time with him and his wife, Abigail."

"Ah," I said. "I fear I can see where this is going. Like my father...?"

"Exactly, my dear," Mrs Felton said. "Eventually his brother died, and Charles continued to visit and... comfort his widow." She said the word 'comfort' with ironic emphasis.

"Oh dear," I said. "When did you suspect something?"

"I gave him the benefit of the doubt for a few weeks, and then one day, I went to call on her when Charles had made one of his usual excuses in the evening. I knocked, but there was no reply, so I went into the house, and finding no one downstairs, and hearing a racket upstairs, I went to investigate."

I grimaced, anticipating what she was about to say. Mrs Felton took a strengthening draught of port, and refilled her glass and mine.

"I went into the bedroom, and there he was comforting Abigail with all his might! And – forgive me – she was squealing like a vixen on heat." She laughed. "I can find it funny now, but of course it wasn't at the time."

"I should think not," I said.

"They were making such a noise they didn't hear me. In fact... can I say this? I've never told this story. You will be shocked."

"I assure you I won't," I said, thoroughly intrigued by what Mrs Felton was about to confess, her tongue loosened by the port.

"Very well. Her bed was opposite the door, and they were both facing the bed head, if you know what I mean."

"I see," I said, forming a picture in my mind.

"They couldn't see me, and his backside was a convenient target. So I tip-toed up and gave it a tremendous whack. They absolutely screamed, and he fell off the bed. Poor Abigail – she was so mortified for me to see her like that. She just kept saying sorry, and crying."

"And what about Charles?" I said.

"He was struck dumb with shame for several days. Then he said he was truly sorry, and I said you will be, if you ever do something like that again!"

"How wretched that must have been for you," I said.

"Yes, but I got over it, and Charles realised he wasn't in love with Abigail, and after that we got along more than well enough until he died. And what was the point of me rambling on about all this? Ah, yes – that trespasses can be forgiven, for the sake of everyone's happiness! There is no point in cutting off your nose to spite your face. And whatever you think you've done, my dear, I'm sure it's nothing compared with Charles' little escapade."

"Thank you, Mrs Felton," I said. "I will try to be more sanguine about my defects." I rubbed my head. "Damn – the port has given me a headache."

Having expressed sympathy, Mrs Felton made me some coffee, which I took up to my bedroom. Rather unsteadily, I changed and got into bed, and fell asleep dreaming of Mrs Felton's story. I played the part of Mr Felton, Bess the role of

Abigail, and Mrs Felton – I am embarrassed to say – played herself, and dealt me a bracing slap.

CHAPTER FIVE

IN the morning I breakfasted late, suffering the effects of the wine and port, and Mrs Felton told me that Victoria had already eaten hers. I did not allude to our well-oiled conversation the night before. Mrs Felton looked a little sheepish to have confided so much in me.

After breakfast, I found Victoria in the library, a notebook in one hand, her other hand touching her cheek, staring dreamily out of one of the large windows. I stood in the doorway and watched her for a moment, as the morning light illuminated loose wisps of her fair hair.

Then I coughed, and said, "Good morning, Miss Clitheroe!"

She turned around at the sound of my voice. "Oh! Mr Rufford. You startled me. Good morning!"

"Please call me Thomas," I said. "May I call you Victoria?"

"Of course," she said, smiling.

"Good," I said. "Did you sleep adequately?"

"Oh, far more than adequately," she said. "It was bliss after that wretched inn. How lucky you are to live here. It'll be hard to go back to an inn after this luxury. But you have been so kind to let me stay last night."

"It was easily done," I said. "In fact, why don't you stay on here? I don't like to think of you having to lodge cheek-by-jowl with any Tom, Dick or Harry. Not to mention the possibility of rats."

"I wouldn't mind if all the Toms were like you," she said, "but yes, the rats..."

"Then stay here. I know it may look somewhat irregular,

but I'm used to having guests in my house."

She stared at me. "Really?"

"Yes, as long as you like," I said. "Being a bachelor, I enjoy having people about in the house: otherwise it's rather too quiet."

"That would be wonderful," said Victoria, and she came and kissed me on the cheek, which I thought made up for any slight inconvenience her continued presence might be about to cause. "Thank you, Thomas. Oh – but Phyllis is due to pick me up shortly, to hunt for lodgings."

"Well, instead you can go for a ride in the country, or you can take tea and wander around the gardens here. I'm afraid I have to leave shortly, to have lunch with a friend. But Mrs Felton will look after you. And Phyllis. You can discuss your writing – which I would like to hear about some time."

"I'd be delighted to tell you my novel plans, but they are flimsy at present." She indicated her notebook. "I had meant to make some notes, but your view distracted me."

I winced and pressed my hand to my head, and she said, "Are you all right? You look rather –"

"It's nothing," I said. "I had too much to drink last night, while Mrs Felton imparted some of her considerable wisdom about..." I searched for a summary of our curious conversation. "About original sin. Or rather, recently accomplished sin."

"And what did you housekeeper advise on this subject?"

I wondered how to answer this without giving anything away. "If the port hasn't completely confounded my memory, the general gist was of forgiveness – for others, and for oneself."

"What can you have to forgive? I'm sure very little."

"Perhaps, perhaps not," I said, regretting straying down this path.

"Some sins are forgivable," Victoria said. "And other sins" – she twisted her shawl in her hands, as if wringing a chicken's neck – "must be punished."

She looked at me intensely for a moment, and then broke into laughter. "I'm sorry. My friends tell me I have a strange sense of humour. You must go to lunch, and I must go and meet Phyllis – I think I can hear her pony trap!"

~

As Celeste carried me to Francesca's house, I did not feel in the mood for conversation, let alone meeting Mr Wakeley. All I wanted to do was to crawl back into bed and sleep. My head still ached, and the rhythm of Celeste's gait was making me nauseous. I tried to apply my sluggish mind to my encounter with Victoria. With her graceful movements, wit and striking looks, she was highly marriageable, and yet I sensed depths of seriousness that any suitor would be advised to explore. She was going to be an interesting person to get to know, at any rate.

"Ah – well met, Mr Rufford!" Mr Reginald Wakeley said when Francesca had made the introductions in the drawing room. "I have been hearing all about your exploits. Congratulations are in order. We had all better watch ourselves, if you are a better policeman than the police themselves!"

"Good to meet you too, Mr Wakeley," I said, shaking his hand and taking an instant dislike to the forced charm of the man. "However, it was mainly luck and I will not be making a habit of it."

Wakeley was of middling height, with a prominent jawline and an unfortunately formed mouth that implied a sneer even when serious. It gave him an untrustworthy aspect, even though I knew that his features were hardly his fault. I judged him to be in his late thirties, and he had a full head of dark brown hair that he was inordinately proud of, judging by its impeccable appearance.

"How modest you are," said Mr Wakeley. "Now, let's get the man a drink."

I did not like his proprietorial air: he seemed to have made himself far too much at home here. But I took the drink, reminding myself to consume it slowly given my already delicate state, and we were ushered into the dining room.

As we waited for the first course to be brought in, Francesca said, "Now, Thomas, what news do you have for me? How is Phyllis? And Flora?"

"Phyllis is well; but Flora has a cold, or perhaps influenza, and is sleeping it off," I said. I added with some satisfaction, "And I have a young lady staying at Ramsburgh."

"Really?" said Francesca, her eyes widening. "How delightfully scandalous! Tell me all about it."

"A new friend of Phyllis' – she had appalling lodgings in town, so she is staying at Ramsburgh for a short while."

"Is she pretty?" asked Francesca.

"Very," I said. "She is an author, and Phyllis is helping her."

"A wealthy dilettante, perhaps?" said Francesca. "She sounds as though she must have independent means."

I shrugged. "She has investments she is looking to place."

Mr Wakeley, who had been looking distinctly bored by the discussion, perked up at this. "Interesting," he said. "Fruitful investment is something I like to think is within my ambit – perhaps I can help."

"Well, I would like to meet this young woman," said Francesca. "Miss –?"

"Clitheroe," I said. "Miss Victoria Clitheroe."

"Miss Clitheroe. She shall be our guest, and you and she can discuss financial matters," she said to Mr Wakeley.

I was starting to regret encouraging such an association, especially after the pheasant dish arrived and I had to listen to the sound of Mr Wakeley eating.

Francesca said, "I must say, Reginald has the most ingenious ideas. You will be amazed. Reginald, are you at liberty to...?"

"Not yet, my dear, not yet," said Mr Wakeley, with his mouth full. "I hope you understand the need for confidentiality," he said to me, removing a small bone from his mouth. "If word got out, it could compromise some delicate negotiations."

"How very intriguing," I said, in truth more alarmed than intrigued at the familiarity this implied. "I look forward to hearing about it in due course."

"Of course! When we are ready, we will happily spill the beans."

"We?" I said, looking at Francesca. "You are definitely investing?"

"Oh yes," she said. "You don't need to look so grave. It is perfectly sensible. Indeed, beyond sensible!"

Mr Wakeley laughed. "I like that. I might have business cards printed. 'Reginald Wakeley, Investment Advice: Beyond Sensible.'"

"There is no charge for the idea," said Francesca.

I was itching to give my opinion on what lay beyond the realms of 'sensible', but I knew it would offend. So instead I started on an innocent topic.

"I hope you are enjoying Hawksbridge," I said. "Have you walked along the old walls, Mr Wakeley? There are some fine views. And Hawksbridge Castle is interesting. Perhaps a good antidote to thoughts of finance."

Mr Wakeley stopped chewing, and he and Francesca exchanged odd looks. "Ah yes, I have indeed been to see the castle. Most interesting, yes, Mr Rufford – most interesting." He again exchanged a smile with Francesca. They were behaving rather oddly.

I carried on regardless. "I'm going to attend the next

Antiquarian Society meeting to see what they are planning. There are moves to improve the site and strengthen the remaining ruins."

"Are there, by Jove!" said Mr Wakeley. "Well, I'm not sure they should put too much effort into it. After all, there was a reason why the place was abandoned. We should surely concentrate on the useful buildings, that still have some life in 'em."

"I take your point," I said, my temperature rising, "but surely we owe something to history, and to the aesthetics of the place? It's part of the town's heritage. If we're not careful, it'll just be a field with a pile of stones in it."

"Would anyone really notice?" Mr Wakeley said. "And in any case, an empty field could be put to some use. As could the stones."

Francesca must have noticed that my cheeks were starting to burn, and intervened to calm the conversation. "Now then, gentlemen, we must agree to disagree," she said. "How are you finding the pheasant?"

I had just taken my final mouthful, so I nodded enthusiastically, while Mr Wakeley said in a bombastic tone, "It was wholly adequate!" before laughing.

Francesca rolled her eyes. "Since you're nearly finished, I will show you my latest treasure from Mr Blackwood's! Wait a minute, please!"

There was an awkward minute during which I had to suffer Mr Wakeley's company on my own. We both drank our wine and avoided each other's gaze. He had started to hum, when Francesca returned with a birdcage, and placed it on the dining table before winding a key at the side.

"Whatever have you bought this time, Francesca?" said Mr Wakeley, who had evidently been shown her other recent purchases.

Inside the cage, a small, rainbow-coloured bird began to wag its tail, open and close its beak, and sing in an engaging series of chirps and whistles.

"Ha!" said Wakeley. "That is delightful."

"Very ingenious," I said. Although I should have been entertained, my overwhelming feeling was discomfort at Francesca's self-indulgence. My attack of puritanism puzzled me, because, individually, I could appreciate the objects that Francesca had gathered like a superior magpie. In a way, her excitement was quite endearing. And yet... perhaps it was getting out of hand. Her concentration on material things tarnished my perception of her as a free spirit, somehow above the trifles that concerned most others. That feeling, I realised, spoke as much about my preconceptions and prejudices as it did about her. But I still had a visceral sense of disappointment.

I did not stay long after lunch, and I made my way back to Ramsburgh with my headache worsened by the wine and my irritation with the pair of them.

~

In my little room at the top of the house, I fell asleep on the couch with Fox on my legs. When I awoke, I found I was quite refreshed. My eye was caught by the bundle of Mr Davison's letters on the bureau, and felt strong enough to read another. In a letter dated June, 1823, Mr Davison was growing frustrated with my father.

> My dear John,
>
> How are you, friend? I hope your old trouble is being kept in check. Physically I am in good health, but my mind is awash with unpleasant thoughts. You will scarcely believe it, but Charles Rufford had the audacity to call on us at home last week – or more particularly, my wife, since I had little to say to him. In contrast, my wife conversed far too freely with the

damned fellow, and was all smiles, while my own remarks were met with a look of contempt from her. After he left, I told Alice that Charles was not welcome in the house again, and we had a fearful row, which is still not made up.

I do not even trust her not to entertain him when I am away. I have instructed our staff to be on their guard. Beware, John! Beware of this man. He is not to be trusted with women. And he a doctor!

I put down the letter, mortified that my father could be described in such terms. Granted, his behaviour with Mrs Kington was common knowledge, but the insidious effects of his womanising were painfully laid out here. To pursue both sisters in such a blatant way was more than even I had thought possible of him.

And yet, preoccupied as I was with my family shame, I did not at that moment see the larger implications of Alice's association with my father. Instead, reminded of Flora's indisposition, I went to her tower and gently knocked on the door. Meg answered, wearing a frown, but her usual animosity towards me was in abeyance.

"She's still not right, Mr Rufford – hot as coals, and making no sense." She led me into the bedroom, where Flora was sleeping fitfully. "Surely we should get a doctor, whatever she says? But she couldn't bear Dr Drummond to trouble himself, and I know what she means – these stairs are the devil on my knees."

"Quite – but I would feel better if she were to see a doctor."

"Well, how about the new one, Mr Rufford? Dr Weldon, I think his name is. Set up a new practice a few weeks ago. Young fellow."

"Interesting," I said. "Yes – it's a good thought. I will ask Mr Shipley to fetch him. I will be interested to observe his manner. Perhaps he will be full of new ideas."

"I don't like the sound of that," said Meg. "But needs

must."

CHAPTER SIX

TO Meg's evident relief, Dr Weldon did not have any outlandish new prescriptions for Flora. He merely suggested plenty of water, an open window, and complete rest for what he confirmed was influenza – a serious bout, but nothing more sinister. His reassuring manner and his looks were such that I imagined Flora would have enjoyed his attention, had she been well enough.

On Sunday afternoon, I took tea with the Ambroses. The previous day, an invitation had arrived for Flora and myself. Flora was still not strong enough to come, but I felt bad for Mrs Ambrose after the conversation Flora and I had overheard. Besides, I needed to ask Mr Ambrose about attending the Antiquarian Society. So I suppressed my usual instinct to avoid people I did not care for, and hoped that Mr Ambrose would be in an affable mood.

Mrs Ambrose was glad to see me, and in her drawing room, I was soon ensconced in an armchair near the fire, enjoying a pleasantly unchallenging exchange.

"Yorick will be here shortly," said Mrs Ambrose, "and Felicity has gone for a walk, but while I have you to myself, tell me: what do you like to read? Perhaps you have some recommendations for me?"

"I'm a great admirer of Swift," I said, "so a copy of 'Gulliver's Travels' is never far away; but of late I have found it rather too thought-provoking, so I am working my way through the Iona Tavistock canon. Still intelligent, but also providing me with hope for humanity!"

Mrs Ambrose laughed. "Ah, the talented Miss Drummond. You are so lucky to have her as a friend. I am tremendously fond of her work – and I'm glad to find that a man may enjoy it too! Have you a favourite?"

I considered the question. "I think 'The Author of Kingshorne Priory' is my favourite so far," I said. "Georgina is so brave, and the ups and downs of her adventures are described so well. I was reluctant to break away from it, even with my dog jumping on me."

"Oh yes!" Mrs Ambrose said, her eyes shining. "We have that in common. Sadly, Yorick has only contempt for this kind of novel. He says they're full of cheap sentiment. Isn't it curious what men may see as a weakness, when women find it a strength? And vice versa. And yet – I'm happy to be proved wrong by you."

The tea arrived, along with some shortbread. "Well, I can't speak for all men," I said. "We are all different, thankfully."

"Yes – thankfully!" she repeated, with some emphasis.

We got no further in our discussion, as Mr Ambrose stormed in with a red face. "Would you believe it, Isobel!" he said, tearing off his gloves. "Some bloody scoundrel is competing with me for the castle. Dunton said I would need to offer more. Is he making it up to swindle me? But he seemed pretty he sure he could sell without me. Damn the man! And who could this new buyer be? Is it the same blaggard who's been swooping in and taking the pieces at Blackwood's that I've had my eye on?"

"My dear, please be calm!" said Mrs Ambrose, obviously distressed and embarrassed. "We have a guest."

Mr Ambrose paused for breath, and finally noticed me. "Ah, Rufford. Sorry, you have come at a bad time. I'll make no bones about it, I'm absolutely boiling mad to have been taken by a ride by Dunton. He as good as guaranteed the castle to me, and not for a small price either."

"Hawksbridge Castle?" I asked.

"The same," he said. "I intend to preserve it, with help

from others, and allow it to be kept as a site of historical reflection, whereas another owner might simply level it for farmland. It will be the pinnacle of my antiquarian pursuits – if the idiot Dunton hasn't sold it already!"

I realised with dismay just who the competing buyer was. Or rather, were – it must be Francesca and Mr Wakeley. Their expressions when I mentioned the castle made complete sense now. But what on earth did they want it for? Was it just another bauble for Francesca? But then, what interest could Mr Wakeley have in it? In what way could it be a clever investment?

I was also grappling with the notion that such a beloved ruin could be bought and sold so easily. "Should the town not have a chance to bid?"

"No," said Mr Wakeley. "The council doesn't have the funds. Besides, Dunton is under the impression that the council could simply seize the land if they heard it was about to be sold, though that's nonsense. So he has been secretive, and doesn't want the council to know about the change of ownership."

"Perhaps some kind of trust would be appropriate, and a public subscription...?" I suggested.

Mr Ambrose made an exasperated tutting sound. "No! It was in everyone's best interests that the castle should be under my protection, and now some Philistine will probably get hold of it."

"Are you going to increase your offer, Yorick?" said Mrs Ambrose.

"You can be damned sure I will," said Mr Ambrose.

There was a small lull, and I took my chance. "Mr Ambrose – I would be interested in attending the Antiquarian Society's next event, which I understand involves discussion of the castle. Would this be possible, do you think?"

"Yes, yes," he said, waving his hand expansively. "I will be there, and you can give my name if anyone asks. This

Tuesday at five o'clock, at The White Hart."

"Thank you," I said. "I look forward to it."

"Just keep quiet, please, and especially don't mention the sale of the castle. I'm sorry, I'm too agitated to stay," Mr Ambrose said. "I'm off to my study to smoke. Good afternoon, Mr Rufford."

When Mr Ambrose had gone, Mrs Ambrose sighed. "Oh dear. He was so looking forward to being the king of Hawksbridge Castle, and impressing all the other members of the Society. What a coup that would have been! He could have had them eating out of his hand."

"He might still manage it," I said, "if he has deeper pockets than the competition."

"We shall see," she said. "Would you care for more tea?"

At that moment, Felicity arrived. "Hello, Mr Rufford!" she said. "Have you got my picture framed yet?"

"Felicity!" said her mother. "What a thing to ask. Where are your manners?"

"Sorry, Mama. Sorry, Mr Rufford. Oh, shortbread! Lovely."

She sat down and took a piece, which kept her quiet for a couple of minutes.

"As a matter of fact, Miss Ambrose," I said, "I took it to Hunter's on Tuesday. It should be ready soon, and I will hang it in my study to cheer me up as I work, as you proposed."

Felicity beamed at me with a full mouth.

"How is Pantoufle?" I asked.

When she had finished her mouthful, she said, "Oh, very well, Mr Rufford. Growing tremendously. Would you like to come up and see him?"

"Perhaps later, Miss Ambrose, thank you – I would like to talk further with your mother first."

Felicity looked slightly put out, and wandered off, though not before grabbing another piece of shortbread.

"I apologise for my daughter," Mrs Ambrose said.

"Sometimes she lacks refinement." She smiled and added, "I think she admires you! But who can blame her? A handsome young man comes to Hawksbridge, and saves one man from the gallows, and ensures justice is done to another! And still a bachelor, which is unfathomable."

I shrugged and smiled back at her, aware that any protestations from me would seem like false humility.

She took a sip of tea, and as a maid came into the room, Mrs Ambrose leaned towards me and to my surprise, put her hand on my arm, and said, "I have half a mind to poison my husband, and make sheep's eyes at you, before you are taken."

She removed her hand quickly when she realised that the maid was present. The maid left hastily, nearly dropping the tray in the process.

"I'm flattered, Mrs Ambrose," I said, "but you are far too good for a rogue like me. And Felicity might have something to say about her mother straying."

She laughed. "What a good sport you are, Mr Rufford! Indulging my silliness. You are so kind to come here and listen to this old fool spouting nonsense."

Something about her demeanour made me think that there might be a grain of sincerity in her play-acting. I felt deep pity for her: longing hopelessly for what her marriage had failed to provide.

"It's a pleasure," I said.

"Would you like to take a walk in the garden?" she said. "It's dry, at least."

Outside, we walked down a path between beds that had been carefully maintained.

"I can't wait for the summer," she said, "when these roses will be flowering. I wish they came out in the winter – when we really need them."

"True!" I said. "But it's something to look forward to." I turned to look at the house, and noticed Felicity staring out of the drawing room window looking a trifle sulky. I waved at her, and she waved back, before disappearing into the house.

"Don't worry about annoying Yorick," Mrs Ambrose said. "Everybody and everything annoys him these days. Especially me."

"I'm sorry," I said. "That must be wearying."

"Yes, rather," she said. "However, he is away a lot, which helps."

"Oh?" I said. "On business?"

"That's what he says, but not always what I believe."

"Ah," I said.

"Yes," Mrs Ambrose said, "but what can I do? It's not as though I deserve..."

She trailed off, and I looked at her expectantly. "Deserve what?" I prompted.

She smiled and said, "Oh, nothing. Ignore me."

"Of course you deserve happiness," I said. "Mr Ambrose is a fool not to see what he's got."

"The trouble is that he does see what he's got, and he doesn't like it."

"I find that hard to believe."

"Thank you," she said, and sighed. "Anyway, I made my choices, and he made his, and that's that. I have Felicity, so I am blessed in that regard."

After our perambulation in the garden, it had started to get dark, so I had left without seeing Pantoufle: this I would need to make up for on another occasion. I felt I had not been as good a counsellor to Mrs Ambrose as Mrs Felton had been to me. But what could I offer, except sympathy? It was not for me to advise her to stay or leave, nor pass judgement on the marriage, about which I knew very little. Still, it had been distressing to see Mrs Ambrose's pain; and perhaps my visits were helping in a small way, for as long as Mr Ambrose tolerated me.

~

In the dining room of The White Hart, I sat aloof from the members of the Hawksbridge Antiquarian Society but exchanged brief pleasantries with Mr Ambrose and Mr Fountain. Everyone, myself included, had availed themselves of a drink or two.

Mr Fountain presented a summary of the first meeting of the Hawksbridge Castle Preservation Committee, which involved ideas for funding and the solicitation of plans and quotations from local craftsmen. This appeared to be received well, and I felt Phyllis would be pleased when I reported back. But then someone put his hand up for an opportunity to speak.

"Ah, Mr Redpath," said Mr Fountain. "What is your question?"

Mr Redpath stood up. I judged him to be in his late fifties; he looked well heeled, and his expression was a mixture of disapproval and smugness. The way he looked around at the assembled antiquarians made me think he had something shocking to reveal, and he was obviously enjoying it.

"Gentlemen," he said after a moment. "May I just express my thanks to Mr Fountain, and other members of the committee, for the plans that have been explained to us. They all sound eminently sensible, and necessary steps to preserve what the town might refer to as its castle – one intimately associated with Hawksbridge's history."

He pursed his lips and stroked his beard. "But is it ours? Are all our efforts futile? I fear they might be, because I have heard that the land and the castle are being sold."

There was a murmur amongst the audience.

"Sold?" said Mr Fountain. "Surely not, Mr Redpath. Perhaps you are mistaken."

"Alas, I don't think so," said Mr Redpath, and he looked

towards Mr Ambrose. "I have heard that Mr Dunton is quietly selling it, either to Mr Ambrose here, or to a mysterious bidder. Is that not so, Mr Ambrose?"

Mr Ambrose looked furious, but said nothing, staring stonily at his accuser.

"Mr Ambrose," said Mr Fountain, "is this true? I can hardly believe you would have kept this from me – from all of us!"

The antiquarians were now all staring at Mr Ambrose in disbelief. I thought Mr Redpath was looking much too pleased with himself, as the bearer of scandalous news.

"It's a kick in the teeth to us all," Mr Redpath said. "Had we known, we would surely have formed a plan to purchase the property together, and put it into a trust. Or am I speaking out of turn, Mr Fountain?"

"You're quite right, Mr Redpath," said Mr Fountain. "What is the meaning of this, Yorick? We have been planning the future of the castle for some time – and yet you omitted to inform us you would be taking charge of it."

Mr Ambrose cleared his throat. "I assure you, the secrecy was purely Mr Dunton's requirement. He did not want the council getting wind of the sale, in case they made a compulsory purchase and left him out of pocket. He wanted to keep knowledge of the business to as few people as possible – two bidders. I had to respect his wishes. My motivation in this has been to safeguard the property for the benefit of the town, nothing more."

"Mr Ambrose," Mr Redpath said. "Much as I respect your contributions to this society in the past, I find your actions constitute nothing less than a betrayal of the society, and indeed of all the individuals present." There was a cry of "Hear! Hear!" and he continued: "We might have wasted large amounts of time and money, only to have the castle sold to the highest bidder and then disposed of in Lord knows what manner."

Mr Fountain shook his head. "Yorick, I confess I'm disappointed. Well, I'm sure you had your reasons, and perhaps we will come to understand them. Please let us know the outcome of this sale, won't you? Gentlemen, that will be all for tonight. Thank you, everyone." He gathered his papers and left the room, nodding coldly to Mr Ambrose as he left. The others followed, casting hostile looks at him.

As Mr Redpath was about to leave, Mr Ambrose put out his arm and stopped him.

"How dare you betray a business confidence like that, Mr Redpath?" he said, red-faced and evidently struggling to control his temper. I thought he was about to hit his tormentor. "How dare you embarrass me like that in front of everyone? Could you not have talked to me in private like a gentleman?"

Mr Redpath smiled. "I'm sorry, Mr Ambrose," he said. "But I thought it best that everyone know. You saw their faces – it was a bitter blow. You should have told Mr Dunton that secrecy was not possible, or at least invited us all to bid, not just yourself. What were you after, anyway? The glory of owning Hawksbridge Castle? Another jewel for your collection? Well, it would be a tarnished jewel, after going behind our backs."

Mr Ambrose shook with fury. "You are completely wrong!" he fumed. "I would have saved the castle! That's all I wanted to do. And this is the gratitude I get for my efforts! Damn it, I shouldn't have bothered."

"You're right," said Mr Redpath. "You shouldn't have."

As he walked out of the room, Mr Ambrose shouted after him, "Watch your back, you snivelling blabbermouth! I won't forget this!"

This was a step too far, for Mr Redpath stopped and came back, standing in front of Mr Ambrose with his left arm across his chest, and his right hand on his chin, as if he were casually admiring a picture in a gallery.

"A threat? Oh, come now, Mr Ambrose. Do you really want to provoke me? That would be even more foolish than your dealings with Mr Dunton. By the way, have you heard what happened to poor Mr Harper the other day? What a terrible accident. But I'm glad to hear he is recovering well. We must all remember to look after ourselves. Good evening, Mr Ambrose."

I was left alone with a quivering Mr Ambrose.

At this point, I felt sorry for him, and temporarily overlooked the way he had spoken to his wife. He appeared completely desolate. "Let me get you a drink, Mr Ambrose," I said. "You obviously thought you were doing the right thing. I'm sorry for how it turned out."

After a few moments of breathing heavily, his anger began to subside, and Mr Ambrose turned to me and said, "Thank you, Mr Rufford. I'm glad you understand. Confound it all. Yes, a drink is what I need."

When we were seated in the tap room with beer in front of us, I said, "Have you any idea who Mr Harper is, and what happened to him? Is Mr Redpath some kind of gangster? He certainly spoke like one."

Mr Ambrose took a draught, closing his eyes to enjoy it. "Mr Oswald Redpath is a builder, with a reputation for ruthlessness in his business. I expect he's been asked to bid for the castle renovation: a detail that Mr Fountain chose to omit from his summary. Mr Harper is another builder who used to work for Mr Redpath, and is now his competitor. Sounds as though their feud is turning nasty. It's what I would expect from Redpath."

He sighed. "This evening has turned out to be a fiasco. I should not have picked a fight with Redpath. Damnation."

"I'm sure he wouldn't dare to try anything with you," I said. "After all, I heard what he said."

Mr Ambrose laughed. "Redpath wouldn't be too worried about that. He was quite blatant about Mr Harper, after all.

But thank you, Mr Rufford. I feel better for having you as a witness."

I swirled the beer around my glass and said, "Why would someone like Mr Redpath bother with the Antiquarian Society? He doesn't strike me as the cultured type."

Mr Ambrose shrugged. "He likes to have his ear to the ground. And even rogues must have their pastimes. I expect it helps him to feel respectable."

"Yes, that makes sense," I said. "Do you think you might still get the land?"

"I doubt it," he said glumly. "And now I'm not sure I even want it. Redpath was right about one thing: it will be tarnished. My fellow members will now be against my involvement with the castle, when I might have persuaded them of the benefits had Redpath not been so dramatic about it. Well, to hell with all of them. Another drink?"

~

I did have another drink; in fact, several, and when I emerged from the inn and took my leave of Mr Ambrose, I was distinctly unsteady on my feet, and it was dark. I did not want to risk the journey back to Ramsburgh, and neither was I in the mood to stay at the inn, so I walked – or rather stumbled – to Bess' house, having left Celeste at the inn.

When she opened the door, Bess looked at me in surprise. It was a curious time to call, and she soon noticed my inebriated state.

"Hello, Bess!" I said. "Do you have room in your bed for a sick traveller, with nowhere to go?"

"What a state you're in," she said. "What happened? Come in, then."

"Oh, nothing happened, really. Just been drinking with a

man who... who I don't really like."

"How odd. Come and sit down," she said, gently guiding me to the sofa in the sitting room, "and I'll get you some tea. Then you can tell me all about it. But really, Thomas! I don't see you for weeks, and then you come to me in a drunken stupor!"

There was no sign of the maid, but Bess' black cat – now bigger than when I first handed her over to Bess – stared at me with ears cocked with suspicion.

"There's no need to look at me like that," I said. "You know me. What did your mistress name you?" I patted the seat next to me, and she jumped up, sniffing at my fingers that still smelled of beer. I picked her up and put her on my lap, which she accepted, and she settled down, purring.

Bess came in with a tray. "Lizzie is in her room. She was tired and I didn't want to disturb her. Now, I made the tea nice and strong. It should help."

"Thank you," I said. "May I stay?"

"Well..." she said. "Oh, all right. I'll make up the spare bed."

"There's no need for –"

"You might snore, for all I know."

"I don't think I do," I said. "And anyway, it's November. Don't you want some of my heat?"

"The cheek of the man!" Bess said. "We'll see."

The cat had relaxed, resting the side of her head on my knee.

"Look at that!" I said. "She appreciates me, at least. What did you call her?"

"Cadenza," she said. "Silly, I know."

"Cadenza," I repeated. "I like it. Cats are free spirits, after all. She's quite attached to me," I added, carefully moving a paw whose claws was digging into my flesh.

"Perhaps because the beer has made you warm," said Bess. "Why were you drinking with someone you didn't like?"

"I went to an antiquarian meeting to hear what they were doing to Hawksbridge Castle. But Mr Ambrose got into a row with one of them, and I felt sorry for him, so we had some beers."

"And who is this Mr Ambrose?"

"An irascible man with a lovely wife, and a sweet daughter," I said, drinking my tea.

"I see," said Bess. "Well, I don't really. Mrs Ambrose is a friend, then?"

"Yes," I said. "I suspect she has a thing for me." I laughed. "A handsome woman. Mr Ambrose is vile to her, though. She deserves better."

Bess looked at me, her lips pursed. "And will you make her your mistress? This sounds like a dangerous game, Thomas."

"Of course not, Bess!" I said. "Not at all. Flora introduced me to her, as she teaches her daughter, and I find her good company – but nothing like that. She lacks your delightful rear, for one thing."

Bess slapped my arm, which fortunately was not holding a teacup, and I started, causing Cadenza to run away.

"Is that all that matters to you?" she said.

"No," I said. "Your lips are also irresistible." I kissed her, which she permitted, despite her annoyance with me.

Nevertheless, the next morning I awoke, shivering, in her spare bed.

CHAPTER SEVEN

IN the morning, I arrived back at Ramsburgh in time to change and enjoy breakfast with Victoria. I had a mild headache from the previous night's indulgence which I dosed with several cups of coffee.

"I don't feel like writing this morning," declared Victoria. "Have you any suggestions for me?"

"Let me think," I said, impaling a rasher of bacon. "Read a book? We have plenty here."

She wrinkled her nose and shook her head.

"I see," I said. "No reading or writing. Then a walk, perhaps?"

She sighed. "What are you doing today?"

"I was thinking of visiting Blackwood's – the antique dealer. Everyone else seems to be buying old stuff – and the Pottery is doing quite well. I want to have a nose around."

Victoria clapped her hands. "That's it! I will accompany you – if you don't mind?"

"Of course not. I'd be glad of the company. You may be able to save me from my own fecklessness."

"What fun," Victoria said. "I could hardly visit on my own account. It will be like going to a museum."

"How's the writing going?" I asked.

"Oh – you know," she said, waving a hand dismissively.

"As well as that!"

"You wretch!" she said. "You're supposed to be encouraging me."

"That's Phyllis' job," I replied. "My job is simply to provide a roof over your head. But if you wish to involve me," I added, lest my levity be taken seriously, "I will try to help, lacking in qualifications though I am."

"Thank you, Thomas," she said. "If I need advice on my heroine's wardrobe and millinery, I will be sure to ask you."

"Touché," I said. "If you've finished, shall we meet in twenty minutes? I'll have the pony trap brought around."

~

Mr Blackwood's shop was on Cheswick Street, off the High Street, and sprawled over two eighteenth-century, three-storey terraced houses. We left the trap with Howard, the groom, and entered Mr Blackwood's treasure store. I felt strangely nervous and exposed: I was no knowledgeable collector like Mr Ambrose, and neither was I possessed of Francesca's fearless extravagance.

There was no sign of the owner, and we stepped slowly through the first room, almost piously as if in a cathedral. All around were the results of extraordinary craftsmanship over several centuries, but there were also objects of military interest: uniforms, guns, medals, and a club adorned with terrifying spikes.

Victoria stopped at a walnut escritoire – which even I in my relative ignorance could see was from two centuries ago – with its many drawers and pigeon holes, and pleasingly intricate cornice. Perhaps more attractive than this piece was Victoria's expression: fascination, wonder and desire entwined. I stood and watched as she took it in, stroking its precise lines and gently opening and closing the drawers. She reminded me of Bess' cat, kneading her mistress' legs in a similar slow, deliberate and sensuous way.

"Isn't it beautiful?" she said. "Close to perfection. Surely a god made this, not a man!"

"Yes, astonishing," I said. "I could easily imagine you or

Phyllis writing your novels on it."

"It's almost too good for that," said Victoria. "One should be signing a historic peace treaty, at least."

"You are discerning," a voice at the end of the room said. We had been so absorbed, we had not noticed Mr Blackwood come in. "She's exquisite, isn't she? Sixteen-eighties, original condition, yours for only two hundred guineas. Good morning, ma'am, sir."

"Good morning – Mr Blackwood?" I said.

"That's correct, sir," he said. "And I believe you are Mr Rufford – I recognise you from your – how shall I put it? – intervention in church. Most gratifying, sir."

"Thank you, Mr Blackwood. This is a friend of mine – Miss Victoria Clitheroe."

"Very pleased to meet you, Miss Clitheroe," he said with a small bow. "Are you looking for something in particular?"

"Only for inspiration," I said. "I don't have a specific need, but I'm open to being charmed by the right piece. Unfortunately this beauty" – I indicated the escritoire – "is beyond my means at present."

"Don't worry – not everything is as dear," said Mr Blackwood. "I will let you look at your leisure – please call me if you need some information."

He disappeared into another room, and we continued our exploration.

"Perhaps I should simply buy some antiques instead of investing my money in boring old stocks and shares," said Victoria. "Then I could enjoy them, and sell them when I needed the money. And perhaps they would have increased in value. Speaking of investments, have you by any chance arranged anything with Mr Wakeley?"

"Ah – sorry, not yet, but I did meet him, and when I mentioned that a friend wanted investment advice, he was keen to speak with you."

"And what did you make of him?"

"I'm afraid I didn't like him much," I said.

"Well, I don't have to like him to hear what he has to say."

"I will arrange something," I said. "Now – what do you think of this?" I pointed to a dumpy Davenport desk, with drawers at one side.

Victoria turned to examine it and winced. "It's absolutely hideous!" she whispered. "It looks cobbled together – a veritable chimera!"

"Good," I said. "I'm glad I'm not the only one to think that."

In the other half of the shop, the second street door opened.

"Good morning, Yorick," I heard Mr Blackwood say. "You've not come to see the cassone...?"

"Indeed I have," came the reply. "I have nearly made up my mind, but I wanted to take another look."

"Then I have bad news for you, I'm afraid. It has been sold. I'm sorry."

"What?" Mr Ambrose exclaimed. "The devil it has! God damn it, Peter, you knew how interested I was. You could have let me know! This is intolerable."

"What can I say?" said Mr Blackwood. "They offered cash. Prompt payment is not something I can often rely on. And I have acquisitions to make."

"After all the business I have had with you! This is how you repay me!"

"It's more of a question of you repaying me, Yorick. I'm still waiting for settlement for a couple of pieces."

"Nonsense. We have had this out – you have been compensated."

"You know that not to be true," said Mr Blackwood. "Now please don't make a scene – I have other customers."

"And who bought it?"

"She is... I can't say," said Mr Blackwood.

Mr Ambrose snorted. "She? You sold it to some confounded woman? What woman would buy something like that?"

"A wealthy woman of taste. Now, please, Yorick..."

"Don't worry, I'm going. I may not return. There are other dealers. Good day."

The door slammed.

I exchanged glances with Victoria.

"Oh dear," she said.

Mr Blackwood emerged from the other room. "I am so sorry, sir, ma'am," he said. "That was most unfortunate. Beautiful objects can inspire deep passions."

"That's quite all right, Mr Blackwood. But it must be some piece!"

"Oh, it is, sir, it is. An exquisite fifteenth century marriage coffer, from Italy. With superb paintings – the best I've seen. My customer is a very lucky woman. I might have kept it for myself, but falling in love with the merchandise is bad for business!"

"Has your customer taken delivery of it yet?" I asked.

"No, sir, not yet."

"Might we have a look?"

Mr Blackwood looked uneasily at Victoria, and then back at me. "Ah – it's not really... I mean, you wouldn't want to, sir. It's not exactly..."

"Yes?" I said.

"It's not for a lady to see, sir, if you know what I mean."

"Well, not really, Mr Blackwood," I said, "since a lady has purchased it."

Mr Blackwood shrugged, but made no reply.

Victoria smiled, and intervened. "We will put aside our curiosity, Mr Blackwood. Perhaps we will get to know this lady, and then we may see it for ourselves."

"We might well," I said, having an idea who the mysterious collector might be.

~

I may have returned empty-handed, but the intrigue had been stimulating, and Victoria finally settled to some novel planning, like a well-exercised spaniel curling up to dream. Shipton handed me a letter from the Harrises, inviting me to dinner on Friday. I was sorry that this time I would not be accompanied by Flora, who was still recuperating.

Mrs Harris was in an ebullient mood, helped by a glass or two of champagne. "I'm so glad to see you, Thomas! We haven't spoken since your ordeal! You must tell us how you are and what you are doing now the excitement is over. But first, meet Mrs Florence Tambard! Florence, this is Thomas Rufford."

I shook hands with a woman who was a few years older than Francesca; her hair was greying unevenly, but the brightness of her clothes, her strength of grip and air of energetic curiosity showed that age was of little consequence to her.

"How splendid to meet you, Mr Rufford," she said, squeezing my hand. "Olivia has told me all about you, and of course, I read the newspapers. I expected a handsome knight, and I am not disappointed!" She spoke with a resonant contralto that had a pleasant husk.

"Thank you, Mrs Tambard," I said, a little taken aback. "Mrs Harris will have exaggerated my capabilities, no doubt, being extremely kind."

"I doubt it," said Mrs Tambard. "She is kind *and* truthful!"

"Of course," I said, deciding not to take the bait of her playful implication.

"Now, Florence," said Mr Harris. "You had better give Thomas his hand back before you stop his circulation."

"Oh!" said Mrs Tambard. "Excuse me, Mr Rufford! I am

old and forgetful." She released me with a mischievous smile.

"So," she continued, as I took a glass of champagne from the butler, "how do you occupy your days, now you have retired from bringing villains to justice?"

"Let me see," I said. "Pottery business; walking my dog; reading; and a few days ago I went to look at antiques. A pleasant pastime, but I fear if I start collecting, I'll never stop."

"That is certainly true," said Mrs Tambard. "At least it was for my late husband. I came second to his treasures. And not even a close second!" She laughed. "Did you buy anything?"

"No, but I enjoyed looking nonetheless. And I had the additional spectacle of an irate customer who had just missed buying a very precious item. He was beside himself!"

"I sympathise," said Mrs Harris. "Years ago, when we lived in the city, I went past an antique shop window every day, and I would covet a delightful painting that was far more than I could afford. I eventually persuaded David that we should buy it, but the very day I went in with my mind made up, it had been sold! I still feel the burning regret of it."

Mr Harris fondly rubbed her shoulder. "Never mind, my dear. We have all manner of lovely things now, don't we? We are very lucky."

"Yes, of course, David," she said, "I really have nothing to complain about! But it's funny how these things rankle, all the same."

"And what was the contentious item, Mr Rufford?" said Mrs Tambard.

"An old Italian coffer – a cassone, Mr Blackwood said."

"Ah – Mr Blackwood," said Mrs Tambard. "Then I believe you're speaking of the Wicked Cassone."

"Goodness," said Mrs Harris.

"It has a name?" said Mr Harris. "Then it must be a truly extraordinary piece. However do you know of it, Mrs Tambard?"

She smiled. "My husband's interest rubbed off on me. Sharing his interest was a way of getting his attention. I still keep my eyes and ears open."

"But why 'Wicked Cassone'?" said Mrs Harris. "You can't keep us in such suspense, Florence!"

"Alas, I shall have to," said Mrs Tambard. "I have not had nearly enough champagne to go into details. You must not press me, Olivia."

"Then you might have avoided mentioning its name – how tantalising!" said Mrs Harris, half in jest, but clearly also a little put out.

"I'm sorry, my dear," said Mrs Tambard. "May we change the subject?"

"In that case," said Mr Harris, "I have a topic that may be of some interest. Hawksbridge Castle! Just as its future seemed assured, thanks to the Preservation Committee, it seems that it's being sold! To whom, I have no idea. Does anyone else have any news about this?"

"That is worrying," said Mrs Tambard. "I often walk there and think about my husband, who was always sure he was about to see a ghost in the ruins. Sadly, he never did."

"I confess I know something of it," I said. The company turned towards me. "Just that Mr Ambrose was hoping to purchase it, but –"

"Mr Ambrose!" said Mrs Tambard. "But he never said... Sorry – carry on, Mr Rufford. I interrupted you."

"He seems to have been pipped at the post by someone else," I said. "He was quite furious about that, and then the Antiquarian Society got wind of it all, and Mr Ambrose had a stand-up row with another member over his secrecy. I witnessed it, and tried to calm him down with a few drinks."

"That was kind," said Mrs Tambard. "He will have appreciated that."

"But why should Mr Ambrose want to buy the castle?" said Mrs Harris.

"The prestige?" I said. "He's an avid collector of old things. A ruined castle probably seems the ultimate prize. But there is another bidder, and I suspect I know who it is. I probably shouldn't say, though."

"Oh, for heaven's sake!" said Mrs Harris, who was flushed with champagne. "Another secret! I can't bear it. Can't anyone just speak plainly tonight?"

"Very well," I said. "Francesca Campbell and her new acquaintance, Mr Reginald Wakeley, have been cooking up an investment scheme, and I believe it's the castle."

"Investment?" said Mr Harris. "What are they going to do, charge an entrance fee?"

I shrugged.

"Francesca! Good Lord," said Mrs Harris. "What is she playing at? I invited her, but she declined – politely enough, of course – due to a previous engagement. I wonder now if she's deliberately lying low. This castle business might be embarrassing."

"Well, my dear, you must ask her about it," said Mr Harris. "No – Mr Rufford, you should, since you know some of the details already."

"I will try," I said. "I hesitate to pry – but I agree, it's a puzzle."

CHAPTER EIGHT

THIS puzzle was irking me so much that the next morning, a Saturday, I rode over to Halfpenny House. I wanted to see if I could mend the coolness between Francesca and myself, as well as satisfy my curiosity. However, I suspected that these two goals were irreconcilable.

Francesca was in her drawing room, absorbed in some embroidery, when I was shown in.

"Thomas! What a nice surprise," she said, getting up. "I hope you are in a better mood today! And why not? – see, the sun is shining. Let's have a walk in the garden."

The earlier frost was melting, and the sun warmed us despite the fresh breeze. I tried to keep away from controversial topics for a while.

"Have you arranged all your new pieces yet?" I asked.

"Nearly all," she said. "But I need to find a home for something even more precious. I will be taking delivery of it in a few days."

"A cassone, perhaps?"

She turned sharply to face me. "How did you know about that? No one knows about the cassone!"

"Sorry," I said. "I was in Mr Blackwood's shop a few days ago, and I overheard Mr Ambrose getting irate because he had missed out on a piece. I'm sorry to steal your thunder!"

"Never mind," she said. "I will enjoy showing it to you. You will be scandalised. It has a name –"

"The Wicked Cassone," I said.

"Goodness, Thomas," Francesca said. "Do you know all my business?"

"Not quite all, it seems," I said.

"Ah," she said. "You are referring to my investment with Mr Wakeley. Is that what you came to ask me about? Well, you had better do your worst. What would you like to know?"

"Why you are buying Hawksbridge Castle. I understand it's a private transaction, but a lot of people in Hawksbridge are agitated about it. They love their ruined castle, and all they hear are rumours. Can you not put their minds at ease, Francesca?"

"I didn't know those old ruins were held in such high esteem," said Francesca, kicking some loose gravel off the path. "After all, the town walls are far more interesting and more complete."

"Are you telling people what they must lose, and what they may keep?" I said. "I don't think they will see it in those terms. And you make it sound as though the castle will truly be lost. What is to become of it?"

Francesca sighed. "I love the remnants of the past, you know I do. Why else would I have bought this house, or all those old things? But at the same time, I recognise that human progress is inevitable. I'm sure you do too. You have your conveniences in your house – your plumbing, your clever bells, cloth that was woven in big factories, and so on. Your own factory is, no doubt, a modern marvel."

"What are you getting at, Francesca? Please spit it out!"

She stopped on the path and looked at me. "The railway, Thomas," she said. "The railway is the future, and it's changing everything. The railway is coming to Hawksbridge, and it will need land."

I detected shame on Francesca's face. Defiance, but also shame.

"And it will consume the castle?"

She nodded, and turned away from me so that I could not read her expression.

"I'm sorry, Thomas," she said quietly, after a moment. "I know it will pain you – and others. But it's not my doing. It will happen with or without me."

I stared at the fields beyond the garden, trying to find calmness and words that would not betray my anger.

"Everything is becoming clearer," I said. "Mr Wakeley and you are simply middle-men, about to get rich off the back of the railway."

"And what is wrong with that?" Tears were visible on her cheek.

"Look in the mirror," I said, "and you will see the face of a woman who knows exactly what is wrong with it."

"You will have to argue better than that, Thomas," she said. "Let me try to justify myself. Mr Wakeley and I have taken a calculated business risk that the railway will have to pass through the castle. If it doesn't, then Mr Dunton is the winner, for selling the land at an inflated price. Then nothing need change: the castle can remain. If the railway does pass through it, then perhaps I can help persuade the company to preserve at least a token of it: some of the curtain walls may not need to be removed. Mr Dunton would not have cared about that. So am I really so bad? You know me – you cannot think me such a wicked person."

She looked at me with her head cocked, an appealing expression on her tear-streaked face.

"Surely, Thomas?" She reached out and touched my arm.

"Do I know you?" I asked. "The last time I was here, I began to doubt it. You were so wrapped up with Mr Wakeley, whom I cannot like or trust. He has an unhealthy grip over you."

Francesca let go of my arm. "That is not for you to judge. He is my friend and business partner, whether you like it or not. But I can assure you, Thomas, you don't need to worry about him."

"Very well," I said. "But how did he settle on Hawksbridge Castle as being valuable to a railway company?"

"He is cleverer than you give him credit for," Francesca

said. "He has been studying the local geology and landscape. The land around Hawksbridge Castle is – he says – the only economic site for the railway to cross the river, without demolishing buildings that are in use. And it's convenient for town."

"I see," I said. "And this deal with Mr Dunton – has it been signed?"

"Not quite," she said. "The paperwork is being drawn up. But it should be ready soon."

"One final question, Francesca, and then I will hold my tongue about it. Why does Mr Wakeley even need to involve you?"

"Because he can't afford it on his own, of course!"

"And you're paying the lion's share, I would imagine?"

"It's none of your business, but yes! Ninety percent."

I whistled. "Well, you must know what you're doing. You are more shrewd than I."

"Naturally, Thomas," Francesca said. "With great age, comes great wisdom. Now – let us have a strong cup of tea and speak no more about it. Tell me about life at Ramsburgh!"

~

I went to church the following day in order to see Phyllis, and tell her what I had found out about the castle. At Halfpenny House, I had pushed Francesca's news to the back of my mind in order to remain civil, but since then I had been brooding and cursing. But who or what was I to curse? Francesca? Mr Wakeley? The railway company? Progress itself? She had been quite right that the forces of modernisation could not be stopped by anything so trivial as a crumbling, useless arrangement of stones.

After the service, I found her waiting for me on the path.

"Do I detect a frown, despite the sunshine?" she said.

"You may well do. I have news... shall we walk on the walls?"

She nodded, and we made our way up to Knight's Mount.

Turning to me, she said, "So – did you attend the Antiquarian Society meeting?"

"I did," I said. "It was... eventful."

"Oh?"

"One of the members revealed the fact that Mr Ambrose wanted to buy the castle, and it became a little ugly."

Phyllis stopped in her tracks. "*Buy* the castle?"

"Unfortunately, yes," I said.

"But whatever for?"

"I suspect Mr Ambrose's intention was to be able to lord it over the other members. And the town in general. Imagine how insufferable he could be!"

"I see," said Phyllis, taking this information in. "But that would spare the ruins, surely?"

"Ah," I said. "This is where it gets more complicated. There is another, higher bidder for the land. So Mr Ambrose will not be the owner after all."

"For goodness' sake! Who will, then?"

I shuffled uncomfortably.

"You won't believe it, but..."

"Out with it, Thomas! Who?"

"Francesca."

"No! Francesca Campbell? But that's..."

"Ridiculous, yes," I said, starting to walk again. "But she and a man called Reginald Wakeley are buying it, and hope to sell it to a railway company. Apparently there's a good chance this is the only economic spot for a railway bridge to land on the north bank. I'm sorry."

We stared at the innocent river beneath the walls, ignorant of what might soon be thrown across its back. Phyllis thought for a while before saying, "So that will be the end of the castle. After all these centuries."

"I fear so," I said. "I suppose it's some consolation that it's been enjoyed by so many people over so much time. It will remain in the history books. Perhaps we need to worry more about what other changes a railway would bring to Hawksbridge. It won't be the same."

"Yes; yes, you're right. I'm sure there will be many benefits too," she said. But I could see that it was a bitter blow to learn of the potential disfiguring of her beloved town.

"Francesca and I had a small falling out over it," I said. "I thought she looked unhappy with her decision – although she defended it – but this damned Wakeley fellow has seduced her."

"Not literally, I trust?" said Phyllis.

"Good God, I hope not," I said. "A more slippery-looking fellow I have rarely met. I don't know why Francesca can't see it. She has been in a strange mood lately."

Phyllis put her hand on my arm. "I'm sorry you fell out over this. Can you repair it?"

"We left on cordial terms. When the dust has settled, I expect we will speak more easily to each other. Would you like to walk to the castle?"

"I don't think I could bear to just now, Thomas. Let's just stay on the walls, shall we?"

"Of course," I said, and decided to change the subject. "Is Victoria proving a good pupil?"

"Yes, and a fine companion. We have had some good discussions. In fact, she has helped me see aspects of my own writing more clearly."

We had reached Lover's Bastion, and took the broad path that wound around the bottom of it, though this was still high above the town. I was emboldened by our shared distress over the castle. "Perhaps you had better take my arm," I said. "It's a long way down."

"If you wish," said Phyllis, and she put her arm in mine.

"I'm a trifle jealous of Victoria," I said.

"Oh?"

"She gets to spend so much time with you. And I want to be able to talk about writing with you."

Phyllis looked at me and smiled. "Then you should write a novel, Thomas."

"I wouldn't know where to start," I said. "Is that a necessary condition for your time?"

"No, of course not," she said. "Anyway, you might discover that I'm very annoying."

"I think I would know that already," I said. "We have, after all, collaborated in a dangerous adventure. And that simply accentuated your virtues. You rescued me, twice!"

She laughed. "As if I could forget." She tightened her grip on my arm. "I'm glad I did."

"I almost wish you needed rescuing, Phyllis," I said. "But you are very self-reliant."

"Really?" she said. "I suppose I might give that impression."

At that moment, I saw her not as a revered author and eminent member of Hawksbridge society, but as a desirable woman with vulnerabilities and unfulfilled potential; a woman who, with an insight borne of writing about the agonies and ecstasies of human life, might love with a powerful fierceness and loyalty. That she was my friend, I found an incomprehensible blessing. That she might one day be my lover – this was an idea that I hardly dared to entertain. But with her arm pressed against my body, it became a notion within the realms of possibility.

I moved in front of her to block her path, and placed my free hand on her other arm. She looked up at me, slightly afraid, and yet her eyes told me that she was prepared to countenance this manoeuvre. She did not wrest free of me. I bent my head and kissed her, lingering as long as I dared, and she closed her eyes and pressed her lips back against mine.

CHAPTER NINE

HOW long we had stood there, oblivious of the wintry breeze and everything around us, I cannot say; but when I opened my eyes and finally allowed both of us to breathe freely, the world had been renewed. Whereas a moment ago, we had spoken of change as destructive, now we both were aware of a glorious transformation: a progression from friendship to a deeper bond. But we were not prepared to enunciate where this might be leading, and we treated what had passed between us with the reverence accorded to a priceless and fragile vase, taken from a high shelf for examination, and placed carefully back to be considered. It was therefore in silence that we walked back to her house, the only acknowledgement of our altered state being her arm locked in mine, for all to see.

And so through the days of that week, until Friday, that scene had occupied my waking moments, and some sleeping ones. Victoria had told me of a change in Phyllis' demeanour, and I tried to devise a meeting with Phyllis that could come close to the bliss of holding her, and would not be in danger of setting our relations back with prosaic formality.

While I contemplated this, another invitation from Mrs Ambrose demanded my attention. Had I foreseen the merest shadow of the events that transpired over the next twenty-four hours, I would have stayed at Ramsburgh in the company of Fox, or gone to seek out Phyllis and begun to tread the path that had opened up. In short, I would have minded my own business. But I confess I was flattered by Mrs Ambrose's interest in me and my apparent ability to soothe her, and Felicity was a delight, so I took Celeste and went to tea.

When I was shown into the drawing room, I was surprised to see that Pantoufle was out of his cage, and Felicity had him on a lead. He was scrambling on and off Felicity, and darting around the back of the sofa. He stared at me for a moment before resuming his mad caper.

Felicity beamed at me with pleasure and pride, and Mrs Ambrose said, by way of explanation, "Yorick is away! He would be furious if he saw this. But isn't Pantoufle adorable? I'm sorry – good afternoon, Mr Rufford! How lovely that you could come and see us. Do come and sit by me on the sofa."

I obeyed, and tea arrived. "What an extraordinary animal!" I said, admiring Pantoufle's antics. "You have quite a bond with him, Felicity. How are you, Mrs Ambrose? Have you read any good books since I last saw you?"

"I am well, Mr Rufford. And yes, I am trying to read 'The Count of Monte Cristo'" – she held up a volume – "but I confess I am daunted by the length. It promises to be an exciting tale, though. I just hope I can keep all the characters in my head. There appear to be hundreds of them!"

"I have heard good things about it," I said. "But certainly Monsieur Dumas is not the most concise of writers. I suspect he was paid by the page."

"And he didn't think all of it up himself," put in Felicity. "That's cheating, isn't it?"

"An interesting point," I said. "I shall have to ask Miss Drummond about the ethics of it. It does seem disingenuous not to credit your collaborator, but no doubt it's easier to sell a 'Dumas' novel than a 'Dumas and Maquet' novel."

"Mr Rufford," said Felicity, earnestly, "do you think one should take revenge on people like that? If they've been really bad?"

"As I understand the plot from a review," I said, "not having actually read it, Dantès was sorely provoked. Years unjustly spent in a prison would twist your mind and make you want to do dreadful things. I sympathise with him, although strictly speaking, a Christian should not take justice into his own hands."

"I suppose so. Oh, Pantoufle is tired. Let me take him up to his slipper." Felicity left with the exhausted squirrel resting on her shoulder, half-buried in her hair.

"Or *her* hands," said Mrs Ambrose, in answer to my last remark. "Let me tell you, I have been sorely tempted to administer justice to Felicity's father! I wish I were joking, Thomas."

I glanced nervously at the maid who was bringing a fresh pot of tea. It was unfortunate for her to have to hear about the divisions in the household.

Mrs Ambrose was warming to the topic. "What would you say, Thomas, as an amateur detective? Poison? A quick stab with a paper knife? A pillow over his head?"

"None of these, Mrs Ambrose," I said. "Rather – distance, and a new lover!"

She laughed. "You make it sound easy. But to just walk out of here in disgrace with nothing, not even my daughter – no, I could not do that."

The maid left, and Mrs Ambrose said, "Oh, of course this is all fantasy. I could never do such a thing. It makes me feel better to be defiant. But a part of me still loves Yorick, despite... everything."

"That is to your credit," I said. "Where is he, by the way? Is he joining us?"

"Who knows! I don't enquire too closely. All I know is, he often comes back home in a better mood than he left it, which I suppose is a small mercy."

A door slammed, and I heard a raised voice. Mrs Ambrose flinched and said, "It seems this is not one of those times. Speak of the devil..."

The sitting room door was flung open, and Mr Ambrose strode in.

"God damn that conniving bitch," he said. "Oh, hello, Mr

Rufford. Sorry, but you find me once again in a hot temper."

"Do try to calm down, Yorick," said Mrs Ambrose. "It's not good for you. Which conniving so-and-so are you talking about?"

"Mrs Francesca Campbell, that's who!" he said, pacing in front of the fire. "Not only did she steal that cassone from under my nose, but I find that she's the one buying the castle. Or rather," he said, rubbing his hands, "formerly buying the castle."

"What? What are you saying, Yorick?" said Mrs Ambrose.

"Merely that I am raising some more funds from shares, and a couple of pictures, and I have a verbal agreement from Mr Dunton that my raised bid is acceptable."

"Oh, Yorick! Are you sure we can afford –"

"Oh, Isobel," he mocked, "yes, we can. And I'm going to the Antiquarian Society meeting this afternoon, and I'm going to tell the buggers that I'm buying the land, and I'm going to raze the castle to the ground and sell the stones to a builder! Mr Redpath can have his precious monument – as a heap of rubble!"

"What?" said Mrs Ambrose. "Are you serious?"

"Absolutely serious. It will give me the greatest satisfaction."

"But what's the point of doing that, Ambrose? Then you'll just have an empty field."

"Well, it's obvious, isn't it?" said Mr Ambrose. "Mrs Campbell may be a conniving bitch but she's not stupid. She obviously thinks it's worth something – and the only way I can see it being worth that much is if it's on the route of a new railway. So I'll get my money back, and more, but better than that, I'll have the pleasure of seeing their faces when the castle is reduced to dust."

Mrs Ambrose had turned pale. "But we shall be in disgrace! We shall have to leave Hawksbridge, Yorick! Please don't do this."

"I welcome a move," Mr Ambrose replied. "We could get a fine town house in Newcastle, and it will be easier for me to do business there."

"You mean, easier to find a... oh!" Mrs Ambrose burst into tears and fled the room.

Mr Ambrose looked briefly bemused, and then chuckled and sat down, taking a glass of wine that the butler had brought in.

"I had the misfortune to marry a temperamental woman. Well, here's to the clever, smug, Antiquarian Society, who have guaranteed the destruction of their precious castle."

He raised his glass, and I considered how to respond.

"Unfortunately, sir," I said, "not only the Society will be upset. Many of the town's inhabitants are fond of the castle. Might you not reconsider, in that light?"

"Why, Mr Rufford! I thought you were made of sterner stuff," he said. "If that land is valuable, then there can be only one outcome."

Felicity bounded into the room, and then said with disgust, "Oh, it's you," and ran out again.

"Felicity!" shouted her father. "Do not speak to me like that! Come back here and apologise!"

Felicity did not obey. Mr Ambrose drained his glass, and shrugged. "Don't know why I bothered having a child. It's not as if the getting of her was a particularly pleasant duty. And I had hoped for a son."

He stood up and checked the time on his pocket watch. "Well, Mr Rufford, I wish I could stay to talk, but I have to be getting along to my last meeting of the Society. I have to say I am relishing it. It will be like pricking a balloon!"

I nodded, and was relieved when he left. After I heard his horse disappear down the gravel path, Mrs Ambrose came in again. She had composed herself: no doubt she had had much practice at that.

"I'm sorry about Yorick, Mr Rufford," she said. "He must

have been brooding about that land for days, and his treatment by the Society, leading to this horrible decision. It is a pattern with him. Things fester, and drive him almost to the point of insanity."

"Perhaps fate will intervene and somehow the castle will be saved," I said.

"Oh, what a mess," Mrs Ambrose sighed. "No matter. He is gone for now, and we can have some intelligent conversation!"

I smiled and said, "I will do my level best!"

Mrs Ambrose asked for some sherry to be brought, and we talked pleasantly about literature and art.

After a while, Felicity reappeared. "It's snowing!" she said. "Look!"

"So it is," said Mrs Ambrose, looking out of the French window. "Goodness, such large flakes. Do you think you will be all right getting home, Mr Rufford?"

I was feeling drowsy from the sherry and the heat of the fire, and was not much inclined to hurry home. "I will be fine, thank you! But – sorry, am I outstaying my welcome?"

"Poppycock, Mr Rufford! What an idea. You could never do that. Do just sit tight – you look so comfortable. You can always stay the night if you wish."

"Oh yes!" said Felicity. "Do stay. Pantoufle will wake up in the morning, and you can play with him before you go."

"You silly thing," said Mrs Ambrose, looking adoringly at her daughter. The poignancy of this unhappy mother taking solace from her innocent daughter, combined with the intensifying effects of the drink, touched me greatly, and my eyes filled with tears. I sniffed into a handkerchief and wiped my eyes, discreetly as I thought, but sharp-eyed Felicity said, "Mr Rufford! You're crying! Are you all right?"

Embarrassed, I said, "Oh – am I? Perhaps it's a cold. Or this charming domestic scene. Sorry. I'm perfectly all right."

"I didn't think men cried," said Felicity.

"Oh, they do," I said. "Just not normally in public. I blame the sherry. And I am far too much at home here!"

"I'm glad," said Mrs Ambrose, smiling at me. "That's a fine compliment to us. Especially when things can be rather..." She waved her hand to complete the sentence.

"Horrid," said Felicity. "That's what you meant, Mama. I hate Papa's moods."

"I know, my dear, I know. It's very trying."

~

Even when the light was gone, and the snow on the ground had grown ever thicker, I made no effort to leave, and neither did Mrs Ambrose show any inclination to speed my departure. I was vaguely aware that I was encouraging an unhealthy familiarity, and yet I was in such a pleasant miasma of human company, sherry, and warmth, that the thought of venturing out into the cold and dark was unappealing – and by now, quite unsafe.

I suggested a tune, and after some modest protests, Mrs Ambrose sat down at the piano and played a chord.

"That sounds so much better than it did!" she said. "I insisted on having the piano renovated, despite Yorick's meanness when it comes to musical pleasures. Now it makes even me sound tolerable!"

She performed an increasingly confident rendition of 'The Waves and the Wind', which all three of us joined in with enthusiasm. To the others' amusement, I sang the final chorus in falsetto to portray the song's unfortunate protagonist:

So pity me, pity me, maiden am I
No lover to kiss me, nor with me to lie
A maiden I'll stay, unkissed will I be
Till the waves and the wind bring my true love to me.

We laughed when Mrs Ambrose energetically repeated the final chord in the style of the music hall. Felicity had particularly relished singing the slightly racy lyrics, glancing at me to see whether I was shocked. I was sorely tempted to reveal the real author of this piece, which would no doubt have elicited highly satisfying gasps of surprise, but I managed to keep Phyllis' secret.

By midnight, Felicity had gone to bed, and Mrs Ambrose and I had lapsed into a companionable silence, watching the flames in the fireplace shrink.

A maid came in. "Shall I put some more logs on, ma'am, or...?"

"Oh, no, May, that's all right. We should be getting to bed. But can you check the spare bed is made up? The one in the attic. And please put a bottle in it for Mr Rufford, and make up the fire!"

She turned to me. "Well, I don't know when I had such fun! Thank you, Thomas. May I call you Thomas? I would like you to call me Isobel."

"Please do," I said, "and I will. I enjoyed this evening. I'm sorry to be an inconvenience –"

"Nonsense," she said. "I'm glad you could stay. I expect Yorick has found himself a warm berth in town."

She stood up and stretched. Looking at her mature but pleasingly formed body, I could not imagine how Mr Ambrose had found making love to his wife to be a chore.

"The attic room is quite cosy, and the most private one," she said. "The main spare room is large and less friendly, to my mind. Anyway, you should be comfortable."

"I'm sure I will be, Isobel!" I said, standing up. "Thank you."

"Oh – I should have asked May to prepare the room earlier. Sit down and I'll just go and check everything is in order."

When she returned, she said, "That's better. You should have everything you need now."

She went over to the French window and stared out at the falling snow, illuminated by the lights of the house and the moon. I joined her.

"Isn't it beautiful!" she said. "Snow is so mesmerising. It is so pure, it makes you forget everything else. I could pretend that all the bad things in my life were gone, leaving just my daughter, a few nice things, and the occasional handsome visitor!" She smiled at me, and then sighed.

I had no ready response to this, so I just smiled sympathetically in return.

After a few moments, she said, "Come – May should be finished. Let me take you to your room."

The attic room had obviously been intended for servants, but a fire had been lit in the small fireplace and I saw that this was a better option than a grand but chilly room. A pot of white cyclamen had even been thoughtfully placed on the chest of drawers, next to a jug of water and a pile of towels.

"Well, good night, Thomas!" Mrs Ambrose said. "Thank you for such a cheerful evening!"

"Good night," I said. "I have enjoyed it immensely."

I stripped to my shirt and gratefully slipped beneath the covers. The stoneware water bottle had heated my bed beautifully, and as I was exhausted by socialising and sherry, it did not take me long to fall asleep.

~

Cadenza was climbing all over me; she turned into a squirrel, who was holding a large nut. It stood on my shoulders, and started to break the nut on my skull. Crack, crack, crack!

"Stop it!" I muttered, and tried to shoo it from my shoulders. But then I realised I had awoken, and the cracking noises were knocks on my door. The door opened; a figure in white stood there with a candle. My eyes were bleary, and I could not recognise the intruder.

"Yes?" I said. "Who is it?"

"It's just me," the person whispered. "Isobel!"

"Oh," I said, confused. "Are you all right? Is something wrong?"

"No, it's just that... it was so cold in my bed! And I couldn't sleep. I kept thinking about... how nice you have been to me."

There was a sniff, and the sound of teeth chattering. I sat up in bed, my eyes beginning to focus. Isobel was shivering, and had evidently been crying.

"I'm so cold," she said again. "May I come in...?"

For a moment, I was torn. On the one hand, clearly this would be a huge breach of society's rules. On the other, why should I not take pity on this poor creature, suffering with cold and misery? The rules would have to be suspended, I decided: this was a special case. Even my female friends would surely not condemn me.

"Of course," I said, and moved aside, pulling back the bedclothes.

"Oh, thank you," she said, her voice cracking with gratitude, and she put the candle on the chest of drawers. She climbed into bed, drawing the bedclothes about herself and shivering.

"Hold me, please, Thomas," she said. "I need you to hold

me. Just this once. I need your warmth."

Having crossed a Rubicon, I was beyond evaluating my decisions and motivations, and did as she asked. She faced away from me, and I pressed up against her, gently putting my arm around her. She sighed and I felt the stiffness in her body melt away. I, on the other hand, had the reverse experience, and was consumed by mortification.

After a moment, I felt her shift her lower body a small amount, back and then forth, and she made a contented noise. Our night clothes had ridden up, and the cause of my embarrassment had lodged in a most intimate place, flesh against delicate flesh; and the more she moved, the more my animal desires were roused. So, it appeared, were hers. I became quite giddy with physical desire, all the more so for the transgressive circumstances. There was no denying her deliberate movements against me, and I felt emboldened to clasp her breast. She did not object, neither when I traced my finger around her nipple, nor when I moved my hand to stroke her enticingly smooth, soft rear. Indeed, her delight at this was audible.

"Be a husband to me, Thomas," she whispered, "just for tonight. Please?"

I needed little persuasion, electrified as I was by lust. I gently manoeuvred myself, and we were soon joined together, each of us bearing against the other with a surprising and almost desperate energy. I had not had the pleasure of this sin even with Bess, and so, part of me long-starved, I was driven by an ancient and unquestionable imperative that overwhelmed all of my judgement. Across the canvas of my mind passed the reasons to desist, and the knowledge of the guilt that would result – but they did not impress my animal self. I perceived the workings of my conscience with the merest prick of regret for the self-disgust would undoubtedly afflict me when I was in a different state of mind, the demons of passion once again chained in their lair.

The head-board clanked purposefully against the wall, and Mrs Ambrose was charmingly and encouragingly vocal, her wordless song of desire reaching an impassioned crescendo as my own crisis overcame me. Even as I endured the almost painfully intense waves of pleasure, it occurred to me that this remote, private attic room had been chosen with care and forethought.

We lay for some time, catching our breath, still locked together.

"Thank you," Mrs Ambrose murmured. "I'm warm now."

"It's a fine activity for that," I said.

We unlocked ourselves and she rolled onto her back, a smile playing on her lips as echoes of pleasure reverberated within her.

"I am catastrophically wicked," she murmured, "but I don't care. Kiss me."

I obliged, but it gave me no satisfaction. I was thinking of Phyllis.

CHAPTER TEN

I WAS rudely awoken by a banging on my door, much less refined than Mrs Ambrose's knocking. I started, and for a panicked moment, checked for another person in my bed, but there was none. Perhaps that had merely been an interesting dream.

"Come in!" I said, and May entered, in a flustered state and out of breath.

"Begging your pardon, sir, but I was to ask you to get dressed. Something awful has happened!"

I flew out of bed, my shirt still rucked up around my waist, and May looked away.

"What, May? What's happened? Is Mrs Ambrose all right?"

"Yes, sir, she is – well, she is very upset. It's Mr Ambrose, sir. He's been found in the driveway."

"Is he harmed?"

May looked at me with wide eyes. "He's dead, sir! Dead!" And she rushed out and down the stairs.

I got dressed as quickly as I could, in the process falling over my trousers and nearly braining myself on the foot of the bed.

When I got to the hall, I saw Rayner, the butler, with a tray. He nodded at the tray and said, "Hot toddy for the mistress, sir. She's in a state of shock."

I was about to enter the drawing room, where I could hear both Mrs Ambrose and Felicity crying, when Rayner said, "A word before you go in, sir. I need to tell you what's what."

He drew me into a corridor and lowered his voice. "Mr Ambrose is lying dead at the end of the driveway, sir. He's in a shocking state. Great gash on his throat. The horse was found wandering not far away, on the road to Hawksbridge. I've had a lad go and fetch the police – shouldn't be long." He shook his head. "Never known anything like it," he said, and proceeded to take the tray into the drawing room, while I paused and tried to think of what I might say to the two of them.

Failing to come up with a suitable form of words, I went in anyway, and found Mrs Ambrose and her daughter huddled miserably on the sofa. There were red stains on Mrs Ambrose's dress.

"Oh, Thomas," Mrs Ambrose said in a weak voice. "Thank goodness you're here. Yorick..."

"Rayner told me," I cut in, to save her having to spell it out. "I'm so sorry. This is shocking. The police will be here soon, and they will make some sense of it."

"But who would want to do this, Thomas? I went for a walk early this morning, as I my mind was all muddled and I couldn't sleep." She looked at me, and then quickly away, as if in guilt. "It was so beautiful in the snow... and then I found..." Mrs Ambrose burst into tears, and Felicity squeezed her arm and tried to comfort her, although her cheeks were streaked with tears too.

"It was done so cruelly!" she said. "A wire..." She had to compose herself once more. "A wire strung across the driveway, so when he returned on horseback – oh!"

Felicity could bear to hear no more, and ran out.

I was stunned by her words. "Horrible," I said. "Obviously a very premeditated act. I will go and examine the scene."

"Would you?" she said, looking up. "It will be hard to look at, but I would be so very grateful."

"Of course," I said, and knelt down and touched her arm. "I will do all I can. You are not alone in this."

"Thank you, Thomas," she said. "Thank you!"

The snow was now a couple of inches deep, and my approach to the scene risked destroying any suspicious footprints and other evidence. I tried to step lightly and in a straight line so that my route could easily be tracked, although this was probably futile since there had already been much coming and going.

I stopped a few feet from the body that lay sprawled in a bed of crimson-stained snow. It was clear that his throat had been severely lacerated by the wire, which Rayner had already cut down to avoid further tragedy. By the looks of it, the victim had bled to death after being knocked from his horse. Not even a man as unpleasant as Mr Ambrose deserved this fate.

Snow was starting to fall again, so any footprints were likely to be obscured soon. I cast around for footprints, and found some that led into the wood, in a southerly direction towards Hawksbridge. I attempted to memorize the size and shape of the prints, comparing them to my own footprint. They were slightly longer and wider, and they led into thick undergrowth, so I could not track them further, but at least it was something.

There was nothing unusual I could discern about Mr Ambrose's body, so I made my way back to the house. As I reached the door, I heard a carriage turn into the drive and stop, followed by expletives. I recognised Inspector Simmons' voice.

I went inside and into the drawing room, where Mrs Ambrose was still in a miserable heap on the sofa, alone.

"I found some footprints, which may be of use to the police," I said. "Nothing else of note, though. But I'm sure whoever did this will be caught. Someone of such monstrous temperament cannot hide for long."

"It's my stupid fault for wishing him gone," Mrs Ambrose said tearfully.

"You did nothing, Isobel," I said. "The two events are

entirely unconnected."

"I don't know. I can't think straight. What happens now?"

"We wait for the police to interview us. They will be here in a moment. And after that, I will help you make arrangements. I imagine they will want to keep your husband's body for a post-mortem."

"I'm sorry about last night," she said in a small voice. "I was weak. I didn't give you much choice, did I?"

"I am capable of making my own decisions," I said. "At least, I should be." I could hear approaching footsteps. "But I suggest we keep it to ourselves."

Mrs Ambrose nodded.

The door swung open, and Mr Simmons appeared, with Constable Taylor. He nodded to me, and turned to Mrs Ambrose, his hat in his hand.

"Allow me to offer you my sincere condolences, Mrs Ambrose," he said. "I give you my solemn pledge to hunt down whoever did this terrible thing. I will, of course, need to speak to everyone in the house. I take it no one has left since Mr Ambrose was discovered?"

"Thank you, Mr Simmons. No, no one has left the house. I'm sure everyone will be as cooperative as they can be. Please do ask the staff for sustenance for yourself and your officers."

"You are most kind, Mrs Ambrose," he said. "Now, if you feel up to it, I'll ask you my questions, and then I can leave you to rest."

Mrs Ambrose nodded, and Mr Simmons said, "If you don't mind, sir?"

I took the hint and left. Trying to find somewhere to collect my thoughts, I wandered into the library, and there I found Felicity sitting at a desk, her head buried in her arms.

She looked up, her face a picture of misery. "Who would want to do that to Papa?" she said, sniffing into a handkerchief. "I can't understand it."

"No one of sane mind," I said. "I suspect we won't know for some time; the not knowing will be difficult to bear. But the police will get to the bottom of it, eventually. And it will get easier to bear as time goes on."

"Will they want to talk to me?"

"Yes – everyone in the house, I'm afraid."

"I was vile to Papa yesterday. But he can – that is, could – be so horrible to us. I didn't want him dead, though. Just different. I don't understand why he couldn't just be nice. But I feel such a terrible person for having bad thoughts about him, now he's... gone."

"That's natural," I said. "You will have all sorts of conflicting feelings: but the fact that he's gone doesn't excuse what he did. You have every right to be sad about that, but now it might help if you and your mother remember the good times – the better side of your father."

"I don't know if I can any more," said Felicity. "He used to be fun when I was smaller, but all I remember of the last few years is him upsetting Mama."

"Perhaps your mother will be able to jog your memory," I said.

"Perhaps," she said. "It's going to be so... different here. And at school. Everyone will stare at me and whisper."

"Surely not," I said. "I hope they have better manners than that."

She snorted. "Girls can be as horrid as boys. Worse."

"Then you must train Pantoufle to bite them!"

Felicity laughed and said, "Mr Rufford! That's horrible. But so tempting. Especially Alice. She's an evil, ugly troll. She will just love to taunt me about Papa."

"You must pity her, then – only a miserable, empty-hearted girl would do such a thing. Take comfort from the knowledge that you are a wholly superior being!"

"Thank you, Mr Rufford," she said. "I wish you had... I mean, that Mama had..."

"Yes?"

"Oh, nothing." She went to the window. "It's still snowing. Poor Papa will be quite covered up."

"I expect they will have taken him away by now," I said.

There was a knock on the door, and Constable Taylor looked in. "Excuse me, sir, but Inspector Simmons would like to talk to you now, in the dining room."

"Very well," I said. "Will you be all right, Felicity?"

She nodded. "I'll go and talk to Pantoufle. He always cheers me up."

When I entered the dining room, Mr Simmons was reading through the notes from his interview with Mrs Ambrose, and muttering to himself. He looked up and said, "Mr Rufford! What an unfortunate business for you to be mixed up in. I thought we might have a longer rest from one another, but it seems it was not to be."

"Indeed, Mr Simmons. I wouldn't exactly say 'mixed up in', which implies involvement in the crime! But I'm sure you didn't mean that."

"Of course not, sir, of course not," he said, in the dry tone that in my previous experience indicated that he was humouring me. "But kindly explain how you came to be here."

"Certainly. I was invited to tea by Mrs Ambrose, and so I arrived yesterday at around three in the afternoon."

"You have been here before?"

"Yes," I said. "Twice – I consider Mrs Ambrose a friend. My neighbour Miss Davison teaches Miss Ambrose."

"But you don't consider Mr Ambrose to be a friend?"

"Unfortunately not, no. I find – I mean, I found – Mr Ambrose brusque, with a tendency towards cruelty."

"Interesting, interesting," said Mr Simmons, scribbling in his notebook. "So you had tea yesterday – and you spoke to Mr Ambrose, as well as his wife?"

"Yes, he was in briefly. He came from a business meeting, and left to attend a meeting of the Hawksbridge Antiquarian

Society. We spoke for a few minutes before he left."

"Mrs Ambrose has appraised me of what these meetings consisted of. It seems Hawksbridge Castle has been causing some very bad blood, if you'll pardon the expression."

"Yes, Inspector. It's ironic, considering what a serene place it is."

"Would you care to speculate whether this castle business might be related to Mr Ambrose's death?"

"I couldn't imagine anyone would want to kill over it," I said. "However, I acknowledge that there may a significant sum of money involved. Mr Ambrose didn't divulge how much."

"Do you know if Mr Ambrose had any enemies?"

"He had a slight quarrel with one of the Antiquarian Society members – a Mr Oswald Redpath. It was he who revealed Mr Ambrose's ambition to buy the castle land, and Mr Ambrose was enraged."

"Ah yes, Mr Redpath. His name does come up now and again. Not a person one would cross lightly."

"Quite. Mr Redpath threatened Mr Ambrose, though not with any specific action. Redpath isn't in competition with Ambrose, as far as I'm aware, so I don't see a motivation to actually kill him."

"You may be right, Mr Rufford, you may well be right. But I believe there is someone who was in competition with him, and who might now be a beneficiary of Mr Ambrose's death. Do you know of such a person?"

I hoped that I would not have to mention Francesca, but I was cornered.

"Mrs Francesca Campbell expressed an interest, and will presumably now be free to purchase the land. But, Inspector – I know Mrs Campbell very well and she is not even remotely capable of murder."

"But we don't know much about her business partner, eh, Mr Rufford? I gather a Mr" – he looked at his notes –

"Reginald Wakeley is in business with her. Have you met him?"

"Yes, I have, and while I didn't much care for him, I would not think him likely to kill anyone. All they had to do was offer more than Mr Ambrose was offering, and Mrs Campbell has deep pockets."

"I see," said Mr Simmons, scrutinizing me as though he could extract more information from my countenance. "So – you had a short conversation with Mr Ambrose, and then he left – at what time, would you say?"

"About five o'clock," I said, "although I was not aware of the exact time."

"And you continued to talk to Mrs Ambrose and her daughter. And then she kindly put you up for the night."

"Yes, I had left it too late to go home, and the snow was quite deep by then."

"What time did you go to bed?"

"It must have been around midnight."

"And there was no sign of Mr Ambrose? Or anything unusual?"

"No, Inspector. No sign of him, or anything out of the ordinary."

"And after you went to bed, what were you aware of next?"

I knew at this point I had to lie, at least by omission, and I hoped to God it was not written on my face.

"I was awoken by the maid, May, and I got dressed quickly and rushed downstairs. I spoke briefly to Mrs Ambrose, and then I went outside to take a look at the scene."

"Ah, yes – this is where you play detective. I thought this was coming. And did you see anything of note?"

"No, just a trail of footprints leading into the forest, in a southerly direction. The prints were slightly bigger than my feet. I expect they will have disappeared under fresh snow by now."

"I see. There were no such footprints when I examined the scene, so I will need to take your word for it."

"Then I came back into the house, spoke again to Mrs Ambrose, and then you arrived."

"Very well, Mr Rufford," said Mr Simmons, making further notes. "If you could please remain in the house for now, I will continue my interviews. Thank you, sir."

I went back to the library, and pulled out a few books, but I could not concentrate, so I fell to staring out of the window. The snowfall had now stopped, and sunshine was beginning to prick holes in the blanket of white. I wondered when I would be allowed home; Celeste would be getting restless.

Half an hour became an hour, and my mind settled on the events of last night. Mrs Ambrose must have been starved of physical affection for many years, and my attentions had kindled passions whose eruption easily pierced the thin membrane of accepted social protocol.

In turn, her desires had lit the touch-paper on my own. I was not yet thirty years of age, and my instincts to propagate were at a peak. Could I be blamed? It had been a sore temptation, but perhaps a stronger man than I could have drawn the line and taken Mrs Ambrose at her word, and let her warm herself before sending her to her own bed. Or perhaps I could have removed myself from my bed to allow her to use it, or even asked her to leave when she first stood at my door. And yet such cool treatment would have been cruel in the face of her own generous hospitality towards me.

As I was grappling with my faults, the library door opened and Constable Taylor appeared again. "Sorry, sir – Inspector Simmons would like another word."

Once more I took my seat opposite the Inspector in the dining room. He was wearing a frown that I did not like the look of.

"I have been talking to the staff, and again to Mrs Ambrose," he said.

"Yes?"

"It has been thought-provoking," he said. "Yes, thoughts have indeed been provoked. And provocation is a notion that I have been considering in this case."

"You've lost me, Inspector."

"Mr Ambrose was a very difficult man, wouldn't you say, Mr Rufford?"

"Yes, he was – he spoke his mind, often without regard to the feelings of those around him."

"Did Mrs Ambrose convey an animosity towards him, in your conversations with her?"

"I suppose a little – that they had both been disappointments to each other."

"Perhaps more than disappointments. Do you recognise these words, Mr Rufford? 'Poison, or stabbing with a paper knife, or a pillow'?"

I had a churning sensation in my stomach, which had still not settled from the wine last night. I began to feel slightly nauseous, and struggled to respond.

"I – they might have been spoken in jest, last night," I said.

"By Mrs Ambrose?"

"Yes. But it was entirely –"

"The maid, May, is clear on this point. She has been alarmed by the hostility displayed by Mrs Ambrose to Mr Ambrose."

"Oh, Inspector – you cannot possibly think –"

"And did not Mrs Ambrose also say, a few days ago, words to the effect: 'I wish I could poison my husband, and have you, before you are taken'?"

"Good God, man! No, I don't think she said that. That is, you are twisting what she said. She was again joking, as long-married women are apt to do about their husbands. You cannot draw any conclusions from mere banter."

"And yet the butler, John Rayner, tells me of terrible

arguments between Mr and Mrs Ambrose, where Mr Ambrose would strike his wife, and his wife would express a desire to kill him."

I sighed in exasperation. "Couples have arguments and say things they later regret."

"Many couples do indeed," Mr Simmons said, "and occasionally it leads to awful consequences. And now a husband is dead."

He picked up his pencil and tapped his cheek with it, gazing at me intently. "What is the nature of your relationship with Mrs Ambrose, Mr Rufford? Have you given me the full picture? Is she infatuated with you?"

"Of course not, Inspector," I said. "We are merely friends."

"And yet May tells me that she has seen Mrs Ambrose touch your arm when confiding in you. And she speaks warmly to you, in a way she does not with her husband."

"Isobel – Mrs Ambrose – is simply a demonstrative woman. This is hardly unusual."

"Isobel," he said, writing in his notebook. "Interesting."

"Damn it, Inspector!" I said, twisting in my chair with frustration. "You are on utterly the wrong track, believe me. Can you really be suggesting that Mrs Ambrose crept out of the house last night without anyone noticing and strung up some piano wire in order to slaughter her own husband? Apart from the sheer lunacy of this scenario, she would hardly deprive Felicity of her father, however bitter she was about him. She loves her daughter more than her own life."

"Perhaps enough to release her daughter from an overbearing and cruel father, and present her with a better substitute – a wealthy landowner and proprietor of a thriving pottery business."

"Preposterous nonsense," I said. "She has no designs on me. And Mrs Ambrose is very clear about the sacred bond between a father and his daughter. And she is not the sort to sit in judgement, not even of her own husband."

"Who knows what a person is capable of, when pushed past the farthest reach of their patience? And another interesting thing, Mr Rufford. I gather her piano was repaired a couple of weeks ago, at her instigation. It's perfectly possible for her to have gathered some piano wire on that occasion."

"I cannot believe you are even contemplating this!" I said. "What are you intending to do?"

"Thank you for your time, Mr Rufford," Inspector Simmons said, closing his notebook and standing up. "This interview has not altered my suspicions, and I will shortly arrest Mrs Ambrose for the heinous murder of her husband."

CHAPTER ELEVEN

I TRIED to follow Mr Simmons into the drawing room and speak to Mrs Ambrose, but Constable Taylor stopped me at the door. I had to listen to the detective say the dreaded words, "Mrs Ambrose, I am arresting you..." and then hear Mrs Ambrose's shriek of shock and misery.

"I'm sorry," I heard Mr Simmons say. Constable Gawley came out holding Mrs Ambrose's arm; she was sobbing, and she looked as though she might collapse at any moment.

"Isobel, don't worry," I said. "It's all a terrible mistake, and I will come and see you. Inspector, can we visit Mrs Ambrose today?"

"Perhaps tomorrow, Mr Rufford," he said.

As she was taken out of the house, she looked back and said, "Thomas – please look after Felicity!"

"I will," I said, and followed the police into the driveway as they bundled her into the police carriage. Glancing down the drive, I saw that Mr Ambrose's body had been removed and the red-stained snow cleared. At least Mrs Ambrose would not have to see that again on the way out.

I turned back into the house to see Felicity in the doorway.

"What's happened?" she said. "Where's Mama?"

"Let's go back inside," I said.

In the drawing room, I sat next to Felicity on the sofa.

"I'm afraid the police have arrested your mother," I said. "They have taken her to the police station."

"No!" Felicity wailed. "That's impossible! Why would they do that? They can't think she killed Papa!"

"Unfortunately they do, at the moment," I said. "But it

cannot stand. I know she is innocent, and I'll do everything I can to make sure they release her and find the real culprit."

Felicity broke down, and buried her face in my shoulder, howling uncontrollably. For several long minutes, I comforted her while her fit of misery ran its course.

"Please don't worry," I said. "She will come home: you must just be patient. We'll go and see her tomorrow."

"But you will go home," she said, the tears beginning to flow again, "and I will be alone in this house, where Papa died! I can't bear it."

"Then we must find someone for you to stay with. Have you any relatives nearby?"

She shook her head. "Only in Newcastle," she said.

I considered this. "Then you shall come home with me, if you wish, and we shall find some friendly people for you to stay with."

She dried her eyes. "What about Pantoufle?"

"You can bring Pantoufle, of course."

"Oh, thank you," she said. "Shall I go and pack some things?"

"Yes, good idea. I will tell Rayner what's happening."

She hurried off, and I sought out the butler.

"Terrible business, sir," he said.

"Yes, one that wasn't helped by staff repeating confidences," I said. "What happened to staff loyalty?"

"There's no need to take that tone with me, sir," he snapped. "We may be humble, but we were all of us brought up by our Christian parents to tell the truth."

"Well, the result of all this so-called truthfulness is your mistress being falsely accused of murder. But be that as it may, I am just here to inform you that Miss Ambrose is coming with me to Ramsburgh, and then we will find suitable guardians until her mother returns. She does not want to stay here."

Rayner frowned. "I'm not sure about that, sir, not sure

about that at all. I don't think you can just take her away without permission."

"Her father is dead, her mother is in jail, and her relatives are far away, so unfortunately there are no satisfactory alternatives. However, I will make the arrangements and get Mrs Ambrose's approval."

The butler had to accept this. "Very well, sir. Would you like the trap brought around? I can arrange for someone to ride your horse back."

"Yes, please, Rayner. I would appreciate it."

~

Mr Shipley and Mrs Felton came out to greet us.

"Goodness! Thank the Lord you are all right, sir," said Mrs Felton. "I was convinced you were dead in a ditch covered in snow."

"I'm sorry to worry you, Mrs Felton," I said, helping Felicity down from the trap. "I left it too late to return last night, but I have brought back a guest – Miss Felicity Ambrose."

"Very pleased to meet you, miss," said Mrs Felton, looking puzzled. Felicity nodded, her face wet with tears shed on the journey.

"Her family are indisposed," I said. "I shall be finding somewhere suitable for her to stay today. Let's get the cage down, shall we?" I added to Felicity.

"Oh, Lord – miss!" cried Mrs Felton. "There's something moving in your coat!"

Pantoufle poked his head out from behind Felicity's coat, and Mrs Felton screamed. The animal's head quickly disappeared again.

"It's all right, Mrs Felton," I said. "It's only a squirrel.

Miss Ambrose has been looking after it."

"Merciful heavens!" said Mrs Felton, putting a hand over her palpitating heart.

Mr Shipley helped me release the cage, which had been tied to the back of the trap with string. "The boot room?" Mr Shipley asked, and I nodded and said, "That should do for now."

The Ambroses' groom handed Celeste over to Howard, and set off in the trap.

"Let's get you inside, miss – you look frozen," said Mrs Felton. "The kitchen's the warmest place. How does a hot chocolate sound? And I can find some nuts for your friend."

"Yes, please," Felicity said, and followed her into the house.

In the drawing room, I found Victoria and Phyllis in earnest discussion. When they noticed me, they both turned and smiled in a gratifying way.

"Oh, Thomas!" said Phyllis. "There you are. Were you caught out by the snow?"

"In a manner of speaking," I said. "I'm sorry, but I have to be rude and skip pleasant conversation: I need to ask your urgent advice."

Their smiles turned to concerned expressions. I came and sat down next to them.

"Phyllis, I spoke of the Ambroses before. Mr Ambrose is dead, and Mrs Ambrose has been arrested for his murder."

"No!" Phyllis said. "How terrible! What on earth happened?"

"He was killed by what looks like a piano wire stretched across the driveway, and I'm sure Mrs Ambrose was not responsible."

Victoria grimaced and Phyllis looked as though she was about to be sick.

"I will of course try to find out what happened. But the pressing thing is how to look after their daughter Felicity. She is fifteen years old, and does not want to remain in her house, as you can understand. So I have brought her here, but I don't think it's a suitable place for her to stay – somewhere in town would be better, preferably with a couple. Do you have any thoughts?"

"The Harrises?" said Phyllis immediately. "They have raised two daughters, and they seem to be kind people – I believe you and Flora are quite well acquainted with them. I only know them slightly, but they strike me as the sort who would welcome the chance to help."

"That's a good idea," I said. "They will also need to be agreeable to looking after a squirrel."

"I beg your pardon?" said Phyllis. "Did you say squirrel?"

"Yes, you shall see. He is called Pantoufle – Felicity rescued him."

"How adorable," said Victoria. "A new model for my sketches!"

"I shall make sure Felicity is comfortable here," I said, "and then we should visit the Harrises this afternoon and see if they are amenable to a guest. Well, two guests."

"That will be an excellent solution," said Phyllis. "But Thomas, why would the police suspect Mrs Ambrose of killing her own husband? Did you have any inkling of such a thing?"

"No, it's preposterous," I said. "Mr Simmons has interpreted a few sharp remarks – the kind any dissatisfied spouse might make in a jest, merely as a release of tension – as confirmation of her murderous plans. The staff have reported back a few phrases, which Simmons has leapt upon because he has little else. There is no concrete evidence to support such a charge."

I got up and went to the window, agitated at the injustice. "The poor woman has lost her husband and the father of her daughter, and then the police compound her misery with this cruelty. I don't quite know where to start, but I will damn well get to the bottom of it."

"I'm sure you will," said Phyllis.

"*We* will!" said Victoria. "If there's anything we can do, we'll do it, won't we, Phyllis? There's obviously a monster at large. He must be hunted down and exterminated."

Phyllis nodded, though visibly surprised at the strength of Victoria's language. "We are at your disposal, of course. But as you say, where to start?"

Victoria stood up and started to walk around the room. "If you say that the detective could find no real evidence at the scene, apart from the wire, then I imagine the first thing to do is to look at who Mr Ambrose's enemies might be."

"Indeed," I said. "I know of several who were at odds with him – though not enough to want him dead. Strangely, Francesca Campbell is on that list, along with her business partner."

"Then you – or we – must talk to them, without arousing their suspicions," Victoria said.

"I assume the police will be speaking to them, also?" said Phyllis.

"I would hope so," I said, "but they are distracted by Mrs Ambrose, so they may not be as thorough as they should be. Unfortunately, they have a record of that type of neglect."

Just then, Felicity appeared shyly at the door.

"Oh – Miss Ambrose? Do come in and sit down!" said Phyllis.

"Felicity," I said, "I had hoped this would be under different circumstances, but I have the pleasure to introduce Miss Phyllis Drummond – better known to her readers as Miss Iona Tavistock!"

Felicity's eyes widened. "Truly? Oh, Miss Drummond! Your books are so..." The poor girl was overcome with emotion again, and burst into tears, but Phyllis handled it beautifully, jumping up and guiding her to the sofa, where she held Felicity close while she sobbed into Phyllis' chest.

I was glad that Felicity now had the comfort of a fellow

female – I had done my best, but she needed a temporary mother substitute. Mrs Harris would, I thought, also enjoy coddling her.

"You poor thing," said Phyllis softly. "I heard about your parents – I'm so sorry. We will all do what we can. Your mother will soon be back at home."

When Felicity had dried her eyes and sat up, I said, "And this is Miss Victoria Clitheroe – a student of Miss Drummond's. She is staying here for a few weeks."

"I'm delighted to meet you," said Victoria. "Do you really have a squirrel called Pantoufle?"

"Yes," said Felicity. "He's resting now, but I can show him to you later, if you like."

"I would very much like that," said Victoria. "I should also like to try sketching him, if I can."

"I have tried," said Felicity, "but he doesn't stand still long enough!"

"Miss Clitheroe is quite an artist," I said. "Her animal sketches are amazing."

"Oh!" said Felicity. "Might you be able to teach me? My usual teacher, Miss Davison, is too unwell at the moment."

"I would be honoured," said Victoria. "I have been wanting to make myself useful – all my friends here are being so generous to me, they are making me feel selfish!"

~

"Flora! It's Thomas," I said gently. Flora had been muttering something to herself, but she turned her head towards me.

"Oh! Hello, Thomas," she said. "I have been so tired... I feel as though my arms and legs have been tied down."

"The influenza has hit you hard," I said. "Are you feeling less feverish?"

"Yes, a little," she said. "What's been happening? I feel such an idiot, not being able to work."

"You shouldn't worry about that. Just concentrate on getting strong again. The mural has waited decades already, and it can wait a few extra weeks. But I'm afraid I have some disturbing news. I debated whether to tell you –"

"That's all right," Flora said. "I'm not as pathetic as all that. Tell me."

"Mr Ambrose is dead."

I let that sink in before elaborating.

Flora gave me an uncomprehending look. "Dead? Surely not! He was fit and healthy when I saw him the other day – when was that?"

"About three weeks ago now."

"That much? Oh! I have been malingering longer than I thought. What happened?"

"Unfortunately he was murdered," I said. "He was found early this morning."

Flora closed her eyes and sighed, almost too tired to react. "Oh, God," she said. "That's too awful."

"And the worst of it is – Isobel has been arrested for his murder."

Flora opened her eyes again, and tried to sit up. "No!" she said. "That's impossible! She would never do such a thing!"

"I know," I said, and Flora sank back on her pillows in a state of misery. I began to wish I had not told her, but Mrs Ambrose was her friend, and she had a right to know. "I will of course try to find out the true culprit. And in any case, Mr Simmons might not charge her. He will have to decide soon."

"But – Felicity!" Flora said.

"Don't worry – we will ask the Harrises to take her for the time being."

"Good – good," said Flora. "Oh, how strange. I am too tired to even understand."

"I will leave you to rest," I said. "I just thought you

should be informed. I'm very sorry."

"Of course," she said. "Thank you."

After a moment, the rhythm of her breathing indicated that she had fallen asleep, and I tip-toed out of the room.

~

After lunch, Phyllis and I set off in her trap to see the Harrises. It was the first time I had been alone with her since our amorous encounter on the town walls, and we were slightly nervous with each other.

"I haven't asked how you are," I said.

"Oh, I'm all right," she said. "Work is very slow, which is frustrating, but I have been enjoying my discussions with Victoria."

"You and your father must come to dinner soon," I said. "I haven't seen enough of you lately."

"Well, you have been busy running headlong into adventures again."

"This is not an adventure I relish," I said. "I would prefer a different kind of adventure, with you."

"Oh? What do you have in mind?"

"Perhaps the holiday in Italy we talked of. Culture, sunshine, interesting people, time to properly talk..."

"I see," said Phyllis. "Without a chaperone? My reputation would not survive that."

"Unless..." I began.

"Don't be silly," Phyllis said. "You must not make light of such things."

I leant over and planted a kiss on her lips. She allowed it for a moment before turning her head away in a pretence of admiring the view.

"Was that silly?" I said. She was trying to suppress a

smile.

"I don't know," she said. "I don't know if I'm the kind of person..."

"The kind of person to what?" I asked. She shrugged, and I continued, "I have a theory about you."

"Do you really?" she said. "This I must hear."

"You are a writer. You are in control of every aspect of your story, and every aspect of your characters' lives. You tell them where to go, what to say, what to eat, what to think, what to feel."

"Of course," she said. "So?"

"But there is one character who doesn't have these instructions, this carefully planned path laid out for her. She doesn't always know what to think or what to feel. Her destiny is not written anywhere. When faced with choices of the heart, mere storytelling fails her: because real life is not a story. There is more nuance – yes, even more than in the best Iona Tavistock – and more compromise. There is cold, hard reality, unalloyed with a novelist's romantic haze, that does not fit a tidy script. And that is frightening for this character, who therefore retreats back inside her fairytale house, where strangers cannot complicate her life with the unknown."

Phyllis opened her mouth to react, and then shut it. After a minute, she said, "Thank you," and stared out at the passing landscape, lost in thought.

"Phyllis, I'm sorry, I didn't –"

"No, I mean it," she said, and pulled a notebook and pencil out of a pocket in her coat. She found a blank page and began scribbling in it. "It's perfect for my book. May I use it?"

"Yes, of course, but –"

"Good," she said, and muttered, "'Her destiny is not written anywhere.' I might change that around; but maybe you should write after all, Thomas."

"It's possible that I may have got carried away with my theory," I said. "Is your current book about a writer?"

"Yes, another one, I'm afraid – a topic I can't resist. It's self-absorbed of me, I know."

"You are anything but that," I said.

She shut her notebook. "Let's suppose there is a tiny grain of truth in your diagnosis," she said. "Is there a remedy for this affliction?"

"I believe there is a good chance of it," I said. "We shall have to wrack our brains."

She smiled and leant towards me, but before any remedy could be applied, we arrived at the Harrises' house.

~

"Of course you must bring Miss Ambrose here!" said Mrs Harris, her face a picture of horror after I had described the circumstances of Felicity's misfortunes. "What an appalling tragedy."

"I agree," said Mr Harris. "She must come here. It's been a long time since we had a girl of her age in the house – it will be most stimulating."

"Yes, the house can be so quiet," said Mrs Harris. "Perhaps that's why we have so many parties!"

"That would be so good of you," said Phyllis. "It's an enormous weight off our minds. And Felicity is lovely – I only met her today, but I know you will enjoy having her to stay."

"There is something we haven't mentioned," I said. "What is your opinion of... squirrels?"

"Squirrels?" said Mr Harris. "I have nothing against them, except when they get into the attic and chew the rafters."

"Ah," I said. "Felicity is looking after a recuperating squirrel – it stays most of the time in a cage, and when she brings it out, she puts it on a lead. So there should be no danger to your rafters, or anything else in the house."

Mrs Harris laughed. "Well! How unexpected. Yes, of course we can accommodate her squirrel, if she's careful."

"Good," I said. "We will bring her here later today, and then I will take her to see her mother tomorrow. I will make occasional visits here to see Felicity, if you don't mind."

"I never mind seeing you, Thomas, you know that," said Mrs Harris.

"Feel free to come and go as you please," said Mr Harris. "I'm glad we can help! Oh – I nearly forgot. I found out something that might be of interest to you."

"Yes?" I said.

"It concerns this business with the castle. Well, I was playing golf last week – lucky I got some in before this damn snow – and got talking to a fellow there, up from Newcastle. Name of Edward Thornton."

"Should I know him?"

"I suspect you will soon. He's a director of the North British Railway Company. I was beginning to suspect that the land purchase might relate to a new road or railway, so I immediately had my antennae up. I had a conversation right out of a novel. He said he was from the railway company, and I said, 'Reconnaissance?' He said 'Maybe', in an evasive way, and I looked at him squint, as if I knew something. I decided to take a gamble. I said –"

"Oh, Charles," laughed Mrs Harris. "You are being so melodramatic!"

"That is my prerogative, my dear. We live a quiet life, and the occasional melodrama is not to be sniffed at. As I was saying: I took a gamble, and I said, 'Aha! The castle route' and nodded. And his reply? 'The devil, sir! How do you know about that?' And I tapped the side of my nose, and took my shot, as cool as a cucumber!"

He guffawed at the recollection. "How do you like that? I glanced round, and the fellow looked like I'd hit him with my five iron!"

"Fascinating," I said. "So we now know who the land will be sold to, assuming there are no other competing railway companies."

"The North British have deep pockets," said Mr Harris. "And they've got the East Coast sewn up. I'd bet good money they're the ones who'll be bridging the river."

CHAPTER TWELVE

I WAS grateful that the snow had turned to slush on the hill up to Ramsburgh, and not ice.

"So Francesca will get the castle land after all, and sell it to the North British Railway Company," I said.

"After all?"

"Mr Ambrose had bid higher, and thought he would shortly be the new owner of the castle. Which he said he was then going to completely destroy, to spite the Antiquarian Society."

"He was going to do what?" said Phyllis, staring at me. "The man must have been insane! How horrible. Surely this must be related to his murder?"

"You would think so. Obviously the police don't."

Phyllis shook her head and pulled her coat tighter around herself. "So if it is," she said, "do you think this Mr Wakeley could have done it?"

"I didn't want to believe it, but in comparison with pointing the finger of suspicion at Mrs Ambrose, it's starting to strike me as more plausible. I must talk to him. And to Francesca. She must be feeling uncomfortable about Mr Ambrose's death, at the very least."

"Thomas," Phyllis said after a pause, "how well do you know Mrs Ambrose? We at least need to consider the possibility that her husband drove her to extreme behaviour, before we dismiss it."

I considered how to characterise Mrs Ambrose. "She is dignified, while somehow having a deep shame about herself. Does that make any sense? She seems to think that she almost deserves her misery. When Flora and I came away from

Houndswood, the first time I met them, we heard a conversation we were not meant to hear. Mr Ambrose said 'Remember what you are!' I don't know if that's relevant. Perhaps not. But I have no doubt she is a frustrated woman – Mr Ambrose treated her with contempt. And yet I saw much kindness in her, and she certainly loves her daughter very much."

"Too much to kill Felicity's father?"

"Precisely," I said. "That's what I told Inspector Simmons. But my opinion doesn't count for much."

"Might she think of you as her knight in shining armour, perhaps?" Phyllis said.

"I hope not," I said. "But it's possible. She was... attentive to me. I don't think I actively encouraged it, but nevertheless..."

Phyllis sighed. "It's not surprising."

"That damned policeman thought that my presence provided a motive for her to kill her husband. He even suggested that I was going to be an alternative father for Felicity! The cheek of the man."

"Interesting," said Phyllis. "Well, you would make a good father."

"Would I?" I said, meeting Phyllis' gaze. "I have no idea."

"You are kind, generous, and fierce in the defence of your friends. That's just the sort of father I would like my child to have."

Despite this compliment, I fervently hoped that Mrs Ambrose had not made a father of me last night. Might not the same resolve with which she had invaded my bedroom have also compelled her to act against her husband? I could not be sure that her appearance in an emotional state was not part or wholly contrived. I naturally tended to a less cynical view, but if she had been exaggerating her misery in order to possess me, both last night, and – heaven forfend – later, by means of parenthood, then who was to say she was incapable of more?

"That's very generous of you," I said. "My instinct is to take Mrs Ambrose at face value, but I confess to an iota of doubt. I will try to keep an open mind, while making the working assumption that she is innocent. Otherwise, my efforts for her might be impaired. And I need to do everything I can to find the truth, so Felicity may have her mother back."

"Quite," said Phyllis. "It's unthinkable that she should lose both parents."

But once the seed of doubt had been planted in my mind, it quickly began to germinate. As we neared Ramsburgh, I wondered whether Mrs Ambrose might have been planning to use our encounter to her advantage in other ways. If I had raised my own suspicions, she could have threatened to expose my injudicious behaviour.

And she had been out in the snow early in the morning. Perhaps, if the cold had not interfered too much with the processes of decay, the post-mortem would reveal that he had died too early for Mrs Ambrose to have laid the trap in the morning.

A shocking thought occurred to me. Was Mrs Ambrose so cold last night because she had been outside? There was no one to verify where she had been in the night, before and after she had been with me.

~

When we returned, we found that Victoria and Felicity were busy drawing squirrels, while Pantoufle jumped all over Felicity and the sofa, attached to his lead.

Felicity looked up as we came into the room. "I'm getting better, Mr Rufford!" she said triumphantly, pushing her sketchbook towards me.

I was impressed by her lively drawings, and also that Victoria had contrived to make Felicity temporarily forget her woes – although there was a pile of handkerchiefs on the sofa, and a thickening in Felicity's voice, that suggested that many tears had been shed.

"That's very accomplished," I said. "Flora will be amazed!"

"Miss Ambrose is a talented young woman," said Victoria. "I believe a career in illustration beckons."

Phyllis bent over the sketchbook. "These are very good," she said. "It makes me wish I wrote books for children. What fun it would be to have someone bring one's stories to life with pictures!"

"May I suggest Pantoufle as the hero of such a book?" I said. "'The Adventures of Pantoufle', by Miss Iona Tavistock and Miss Felicity Ambrose."

"Oh, that would be a dream!" said Felicity. "But you are far too famous an author for such a thing."

"It's a lovely idea," said Phyllis. "It would make a pleasant change for me. I will ponder on it!"

Felicity looked awestruck, and retrieved Pantoufle, bringing him up to her eye level. "Do you hear that, Pantoufle? You might become a hero in a story!"

"Now, about the Harrises," I said. "They would be delighted to have you – and Pantoufle – for as long as you want to stay. I'm sure they will dote on you, and you should find them easy to get on with. They have grown-up daughters, so they'll know what to expect! And it's near your school, so you can walk there – but only when you're ready to go back."

"Thank you, Mr Rufford," Felicity said. "But will you all come to see me? I have made such good friends today!"

"I'll visit frequently," I said, "and I'm sure Miss Drummond and Miss Clitheroe will come and see you too."

"You may dependent upon it," said Victoria. "We can continue our art lessons."

Phyllis nodded. "I will also call!" she said. "It's fortunate that the Harrises enjoy company."

~

Having introduced Felicity and her whiskered friend to the Harrises, and dropped off her meagre luggage, I took her to the police station to see her mother. Mr Simmons was not there, but the duty constable allowed us to see Mrs Ambrose in the interview room, one at a time. I awaited my turn with anxiety, knowing Felicity would be in emotional turmoil after speaking to her mother. I was not wrong, and after comforting her for a few minutes, I suggested she return to the Harrises, which was a short walk away.

Mrs Ambrose's tears were drying on her face. I could not imagine how difficult it must have been to see her daughter under these circumstances.

"Are they treating you well here?" I asked.

"Oh, I have nothing too much to complain about," she said. "Other than being wrongly accused, that is."

"Quite. As you probably know," I said, "I have spent a night here myself, so I am well acquainted with the comforts of the accommodation. It must be much worse in winter. Please ask the constable for extra blankets if you need to."

"Thank you, I will. What I fear most is having to leave my cell – to go to Newcastle Prison, away from Felicity, if they charge me." She leant forward earnestly. "I know I have not helped myself by my remarks about Yorick – but please believe me when I say I had no part in this... this awful thing. I did not want him murdered, however unkind he may have been to me."

"Of course, Isobel!" I said. "Of course." At that moment, seeing her distress and sincerity, I chose to trust her word, even while knowing that later I would need to be more objective. "Has your solicitor been informed?"

She shook her head.

"Then I will notify him tomorrow morning."

"Thank you," Mrs Ambrose said. "It's Mr Barrowman."

"This might be painful, but I wanted to go through the evidence the police think they have, to get it straight in my mind."

"Very well, if you wish."

"You went out quite early in the morning – can you remember when?"

"I suppose around seven o'clock: I woke and couldn't sleep. I wanted to feel the cold air against my skin, and to think, so I went outside with a lantern. Perhaps I was punishing myself."

I did not need to ask what for.

"And you found Yorick dead?"

"Yes, there were no signs of life, and there was a lot of blood."

"So he must have come back quite early in the morning."

"Yes," Mrs Ambrose said. "He's an insomniac, so that must be why."

"Do you know where he might have been staying?"

"No," she said, with a firmness and an expression of distaste that suggested that an unpleasant possibility might have formed in her mind.

"The police thought you might have had access to piano wire. I assume this is a fiction?"

"Of course," she said. "The fellow I engaged for the repairs was very tidy, and did not leave anything behind after he renovated the piano. I certainly did not attend him while he worked."

"And Mr Simmons also suggested – as very slight circumstantial evidence – that on several occasions, you expressed a desire for Mr Ambrose's death. What did you tell

Mr Simmons about that?"

"What I just told you, Thomas – that in truth I had no such desire, whatever the servants might have said about him striking me. It was simply my stupid chitter-chatter, borne out of frustration. I had grown used to my husband's tempers, and bore them for the sake of my daughter."

"I understand," I said. "Well, this is thin gruel indeed for any prosecutor. I regret to say that my next task is to learn as much as I can about your husband. Then there's the chance of finding some piece of information pointing to the person responsible. I hope the police are doing the same."

"I don't know what I can tell you, Thomas," Mrs Ambrose said. "But I will try to think. There's the Hawksbridge Castle land, and the unpleasantness surrounding that. I cannot imagine who might have hated him this much."

"What was the source of Mr Ambrose's income, if I may ask?"

"Oh, he had some investments from his father. He dabbled in stocks and shares, but he didn't have any significant success with it. It meant he had far too much time on his hands for buying antiques and..."

"And?"

"Oh, nothing," she said, looking away. "Just for buying antiques, and hanging around the house being disagreeable."

"Is that all you were going to say?"

"Yes!" she said, defiantly. "What do you want me to say?"

"As much as you know, Isobel. It may be important."

She shrugged.

I recalled what Flora had told me after my first visit to the Ambroses. "I'm sorry to bring this up, but I heard that a maid killed herself several years ago after leaving your employment. Can you tell me about that?"

She winced, and sighed. "That was extremely tragic, and I'm sure her death has absolutely nothing to do with Yorick. Susan was always highly strung, and she was... impertinent, so we had to let her go."

"Impertinent, how?"

"Oh, I don't remember."

I gave her space to say more, but she had lapsed into silence, so I said, "I see. Well, with your permission, I would like to go through your husband's papers."

She frowned. "I don't think that will be necessary," she said.

"But I don't have very much to go on," I said. "It may be vital to find something amongst his things – perhaps a letter from someone with a grudge against him. Anything I can find to divert the police investigation towards more fruitful enquiry."

"I'm sorry, Thomas," she said. "I don't like the idea of needlessly exposing Yorick's private business. You won't find anything interesting," she continued, in a manner that led me to think the opposite. "And as far as my supposed guilt is concerned, the police have so little incriminating information that there may be no reason for you to exert yourself."

"But Isobel," I said, "what have you got to lose by it? And it's not needless – on the contrary, it may be crucial for saving your life. We must not be complacent. A jury may be swayed by an appeal to the emotions, regardless of the lack of direct evidence. If it gets that far, of course."

She hesitated, and I added, "Think of Felicity! She needs her mother back."

"Very well, Thomas," she said. "If you must. But please guard anything you find very carefully. It is essential that only you see it."

"Thank you."

She sighed and said, "No, thank you, Thomas – I'm sorry, I'm rather tired. It was kind of you to come and see me. And thank you for finding Felicity somewhere nice to stay: that is a relief."

I felt I was being dismissed, and was reluctant to go after

such an unproductive meeting, but I squeezed her hand and assured her I would be back soon. She gave me a sad smile as I left.

I went home via the Harrises, to make sure Felicity was settling in. Mrs Harris showed me up to her room, which was airy and cheerfully decorated in a floral print.

"This is splendid!" I said.

"Isn't it?" said Felicity. "Mr and Mrs Harris are very kind. It feels like a holiday, only not. At least I'm close to Mama."

"True," I said, not wanting to think when or if Mrs Ambrose might be removed from the police station to a more distant and less amenable incarceration. "Felicity, I was saying to your mother that I need to find out more about your father, so I can see who might have been involved. I wondered if you might help me."

"Of course, Mr Rufford. But how?"

"I don't like prying, but I will need to go through his papers, assuming the police haven't already removed them. And I thought you might be able to come with me to look in your father's study. It would make me feel better about rummaging through it, and otherwise the staff would probably think I didn't have permission."

"Yes, Mr Rufford – I'll do whatever might help Mama."

CHAPTER THIRTEEN

IN the morning, I went into town to tell Mrs Ambrose's solicitor to attend to her, and then I took Felicity to Houndswood to conduct a search: she was keen to help her mother. I was able to satisfy Rayner, the butler, that Felicity was being well looked after, and he let us into Mr Ambrose's study when I explained our purpose.

Felicity's father had crammed as many antiques as he could into his study, and the pictures were equally tightly packed. He evidently had not been able to choose between desks, as there were two of them: a secretaire and a bureau. This was despite there being a distinct lack of business to do, save receive his dividends, at least according to Mrs Ambrose.

Felicity sat in a captain's chair reading, while I went through the drawers of the secretaire. Here I found many receipts for Mr Ambrose's purchases, most of them from Mr Blackwood. It appeared that Mr Ambrose had been a mainstay of Blackwood's business. I dug deeper into the pile of receipts, and noticed that some of the older ones had substantial deductions marked with 'Special Discount'. Mr Ambrose was getting some bargains, no doubt through long association with Blackwood. Perhaps, I thought, if I made enough purchases, I too might earn the discount; but I doubted I could compete with Mr Ambrose's spending. Francesca, on the other hand, might even surpass Mr Ambrose's extravagance at the rate she was buying.

Spread across the drawers of both desks, there were other letters and documents of a mundane, administrative nature, and nothing to arouse my suspicions. All in all, it was a great disappointment.

I decided to take away a single envelope containing receipts, which I had briefly sampled. There was an element of deliberate self-delusion, in the same way I would delay looking at a pile of letters until after breakfast, so I might entertain the pleasant fantasy that there might be an interesting letter amongst them. Thus I could still carry away a small flame of hope from this failure. And it was a trivial enough quantity so that a police search would not be compromised. I put the envelope in my coat pocket.

Felicity noticed my expression of defeat. "Nothing?" she said. I shook my head.

"Oh dear. I suppose there is one more place you could look," she said.

"Yes?"

"Papa has a safe," she said.

"Ah. Where is it?" I said.

Felicity got up and carefully took a seventeenth-century portrait from its hanging, revealing the door of a safe.

"Ta-da!" said Felicity triumphantly, gingerly placing the portrait on the ground against a bookshelf.

"Good Lord!" I said. "Your father went to some trouble with this. How did you know about it?"

"Once I saw through the window when he was putting something in it. He didn't see me."

"Well spotted," I said. "I don't suppose you noticed where he put the key?"

Felicity pulled a face. "No," she said. "No such luck."

"Never mind," I said. "We can ask your mother. Perhaps she knows."

I helped Felicity to put the picture back, and after she had collected a few things from her room, I returned her to the Harrises.

~

I was out of sorts after my fruitless search, and in need of a small success, so instead of going home directly, I took the pony trap to Halfpenny House. I considered Mr Wakeley to be my prime suspect, and I wanted to see if Francesca was nervous.

However, she greeted me with an innocent smile. "Hello! I'm glad I didn't frighten you away for good last time. Still, you have a serious expression – how alarming! But you must give me a kiss before we become solemn." She closed her eyes and pointed at her cheek.

I obeyed, and she ushered me into a seat in the drawing room and summoned coffee.

"Well, Thomas?" she said, clasping her hands. "I am all ears."

"Have you heard about Mr Ambrose?" I said.

"No, I have been ensconced here for the last few days, happily pottering around my house arranging things. So I have not been disturbed by the outside world. What news of my business rival?"

"I'm sorry to say he's dead."

Francesca's expression quickly turned from amused anticipation to horror.

"No!" she said. "How awful. How did it happen? And when?"

"On Saturday morning. Or Friday night. It was murder."

She covered her mouth. "God in heaven. Murder? Are you sure?"

"Yes – I'll have to leave it to the police to release any details they see fit. But it wasn't pretty."

"How terrible," she said. "How are his wife and daughter? What an awful shock for them."

"Yes, but it's worse than that," I said. "Mrs Ambrose has been arrested on suspicion of her husband's murder."

"Oh goodness!" Francesca said. "You don't suppose...?"

"No," I said. "It seems highly unlikely."

"Lord... what about her daughter?"

"I have found her somewhere to stay for now – the Harrises. She is in reasonable spirits, all things considered."

"A good thought," she said. "Olivia and David will be perfect guardians."

The coffee arrived, not a minute too soon for me.

"Thank goodness for coffee!" I said, taking a sip. "I have been looking through Mr Ambrose's things, but there was nothing of interest."

"You *are* thick with the Ambroses!" Francesca said. "And Mr Ambrose such a great competitor of mine."

"Now conveniently removed," I said, immediately regretting my bluntness.

"Oh, my dear boy!" Francesca said. "What an appalling thing to say! Kindly explain yourself."

"Sorry, that was uncalled for," I said. "I just meant that now the way is clear for you and Mr Wakeley to buy the castle land. I take it you heard that Mr Ambrose made a last-minute offer that was accepted by Dunton?"

"Yes, it was a great blow. Mr Dunton informed us by letter. I assume that we will now be able to purchase it, but I assure you, it is not my intention to profit from tragedy."

"No, of course not," I said. "I'm sure of you, but I'm less sure of Mr Wakeley. Are you certain you know him well enough to say he was not involved? After all, he was enthusiastic to the point of obsession about this project, and put a great deal of effort into identifying the route of any prospective railway. He wouldn't easily let this opportunity slip out of his hands."

Francesca looked shocked. "Are you seriously suggesting I have gone into business with a murderous thug? Oh, Thomas – surely you respect my judgement more than that?"

"The cleverest and most well-meaning people can be deceived by equally clever rogues," I said. "History is littered with such cases. Even I might be susceptible, in the right circumstances. So it's no shame to be taken in – the shame is all on the perpetrator."

"Well, your diagnosis in this case is entirely wrong, Thomas. And I can prove it."

"Yes?"

"Yes. Mr Wakeley was my guest here on Friday night."

It took a few moments for this to sink in.

"Now are you satisfied?" Francesca said. She seemed inordinately pleased with the effect her words had had on me.

"May I ask the nature of his visit?" I said.

"No, you may not. But you may have some more coffee if you wish – assuming our conversation will be moving in a more civilised direction."

I nodded, and sighed. "I have a strange feeling of foreboding. And I don't want it to make me fall out with you."

"Then don't let it!" said Francesca. "We shall ride together again soon, and talk of pleasant things, as we did before. Shall we not, Thomas?"

~

When I returned to Ramsburgh, I only had Fox for company, and it was quiet after the events of the previous few days. Without people to fill this house and give it purpose, its size and grandeur mocked me. I missed the sight of Felicity absorbed in her sketching, and even Victoria scribbling in her notebook: no doubt she was out discussing plots with Phyllis. I found myself unjustly cursing Victoria for occupying so much of Phyllis' time. I resolved to be bolder, and claim more of her attention, now that kisses – however brief and few in number – had been exchanged.

In the meantime, poor Mrs Ambrose was unfairly incarcerated, and time was not on her side. I would have to marshal my thoughts. I went up to my little study with the envelope I had taken from Mr Ambrose's house, and first considered whether I could extract anything useful from my visit to Halfpenny House.

Francesca had apparently been genuinely shocked at the news of Ambrose's death. I had carefully observed her, and I did not think that her modest theatrical talents would have allowed her to concoct such a reaction. She had been unaware of his death. But I knew I would have to talk to Mr Wakeley; I did not trust the alibi she had given for him. He might well have been able to slip out without arousing Francesca's suspicions. However, it was still something of a blow to my supposition of his guilt.

And what of my interview with Mrs Ambrose? It was strange that she had been so reluctant for me to search for evidence. It spoke of circumstances in the Ambrose household that she did not want to be revealed. And yet, surely, it was exactly this kind of secret that might eventually lead to Mrs Ambrose's own freedom. I would need to quiz her again, however resistant she might be.

Sitting at my desk, I pulled out the contents of Mr Ambrose's envelope.

The receipts catalogued an impressive if motley collection: a secretaire here, a Huysmans portrait there; a large collection of coins; a Roman bust; ancient books; a medieval tapestry, and more – and this was only a selection of Mr Ambrose's records. Several of the larger items were marked with 'Special Discount', which had enabled the purchase of items that might otherwise have drained even Mr Ambrose's ample resources. None of this brought me closer to understanding why Mr Ambrose might have had a mortal enemy.

As I was leafing through the last of the papers, I discovered a letter that had been left with the receipts, seemingly by accident.

Ambrosial Yorick,

Thank you for my beautiful gift! It has already won many admiring glances. To think that a woman wore it two hundred years ago! I wonder who she was. She cannot have been luckier than I.

Will you visit me soon? My bed is so cold without you. I miss your kisses and – you know what else. Come to me soon, before I have to find another to stop this aching! Perhaps even Annie, or Katherine – strange creatures who love their own kind – if I cannot find a good man. There! Does that not quicken your blood? Perhaps you might find me in a hot condition with them. Then you may carry me off and give me what I really desire.

With all my love and in anticipation of giving you everything you want of me,

Ophelia

I felt sick on reading the letter. But I knew that even a boor such as Mr Ambrose must have been loved. Indeed, it was a regrettable fact that some women were particularly attracted to aggressive men, presumably stemming from a primitive desire for protection above all else.

But my queasiness aside, what did this letter mean for Mrs Ambrose? It did not surprise me that Mr Ambrose had a mistress, but this evidence could prove extremely damaging for his wife's case. It gave her another motivation for murder, assuming she knew about her rival – but that nuance could easily be shrugged off by the prosecution. Ophelia's existence might help condemn Mrs Ambrose, and I realised I would have to hide this letter.

I was now doubly compromised: by my night-time capitulation to Mrs Ambrose, and by the necessity to suppress evidence. But the letter held the tantalising promise of further clues hidden in the safe: there must surely be other sensitive correspondence. It was crucial that I find the key.

CHAPTER FOURTEEN

THE following morning, I rode Celeste into town for several purposes: to check Felicity's well-being, to see Mrs Ambrose, and – the least pleasant task – to talk to Mr Wakeley.

At the Harrises, I found a charming scene in the drawing room. Phyllis, Victoria and Felicity were occupied in a kind of conference around a table, with paper strewn across it. For a moment, they did not notice me quietly enter. Mrs Harris was reading, and she looked up and nodded in the direction of the absorbed group.

"Such industry!" she whispered. "It's delightful."

Felicity finally noticed me. "Mr Rufford! Come and see what we're doing. We're planning the book!"

Phyllis and Victoria smiled at me, and I approached the table to examine some of their work. Squirrel sketches abounded, and several pieces of paper each documented a particular story idea.

"'Pantoufle becomes a painter,'" I read. "'Pantoufle finds a hoard of Roman treasure.' 'Pantoufle finds a wife.' Amazing! I didn't expect to find such a creative bustle."

"We cannot decide," said Phyllis, "whether there should be one story for the whole book, and perhaps several books, or a new story in each chapter."

"I think the latter," I said. "Not that I know anything about children's books!"

"I think so too," said Felicity. "We have so many ideas!"

"Pantoufle is greatly honoured," I said. "Is he not to be freed soon? The last time I saw him, he was full of energy."

Felicity frowned. "Oh – I don't want to think about that.

Yes, soon enough. But he is so happy with me!"

"Would it be very wrong for you to keep him?" said Victoria. "You are good friends. And good friends should never be parted."

I saw her eyes watering, and she abruptly got up and left the room, after excusing herself.

"Oh dear!" said Mrs Harris. "Is Victoria all right?"

"Perhaps it's because she's so intense about this endeavour," said Phyllis. "I often find when writing that I'm tearful – and not even when I'm writing a tragic scene. It's rather strange. I have worried my father on many occasions, and I find it hard to explain to him."

"Maybe," said Felicity, "or I wonder if she lost a friend, too? Or a pet, perhaps?"

"That may be it," said Phyllis. "I have had that bitter experience. A lost friend, that is."

"I will just go and see if she is all right," I said, and left the drawing room, putting my head around various doors. I found her in the library, staring out of a window as I had found her at Ramsburgh.

I waited for her to finish blowing her nose, and then said, "Are you all right?"

"Oh! Mr Rufford. You must stop making me jump like this."

"My apologies," I said. "I just wanted to see if there was anything I could do. Perhaps a cocoa would put the world in a better light?"

"Oh – no, I'm fine!" she said. "Thank you. No, it's just that the past sometimes has a habit of leaping out of its box, no matter how many locks and chains I put on it."

"You are not alone in that," I said. "The past recently tried to kill me. But I'm sorry – unpleasant thoughts can be hard to dislodge. Felicity must be providing a good distraction, though."

Victoria smiled. "Oh, quite," she said. "I am very grateful.

It's a pleasure to be in any way helpful – though I feel sometimes that I have imposed myself upon you all!"

"Nonsense," I said. "You are brightening up our lives. And you have done Felicity a great deal of good at such a difficult time."

"Thank you," Victoria said. "I feel a little less gloomy. We had better get back to the Adventures of Pantoufle!"

We returned to the drawing room, where Phyllis glanced at me, perhaps nervously. Was she alarmed that I had left the room so promptly to comfort Victoria?

"I'm tempted to stay and watch the birth of a new book," I said to Felicity, "but I'm going to see your mother now. Will you come with me?"

Felicity shook her head. "I went this morning, with Miss Drummond. She was so unhappy, I can't bear it. You must find out who killed my father, Mr Rufford! Please!"

"I'm sure he's doing his best, my dear," said Mrs Harris.

"Yes, of course, sorry," said Felicity. "But it's so unfair and stupid. I would like to kick that pea-brained detective. How dare he do this to Mama?"

"I know," I said. "Mr Simmons has a habit of jumping to conclusions. But we will right this wrong."

"Oh – I nearly forgot," said Mrs Harris. "I heard the Antiquarian Society is holding a special meeting tomorrow evening, to consider the matter of the castle. You might find that interesting!"

~

"I cannot tell you where it is," said Mrs Ambrose. "And it wouldn't do any good."

"You mean you will not tell me," I said, "or you cannot tell me because you don't know? You should at least have mentioned the existence of the safe. It was fortunate that your daughter knew about it."

"It makes no difference. I don't want you going through Yorick's private things. Anything he put in the safe, he put there for a reason of his own, and to think of anyone looking at it and telling the whole world about it – it's intolerable. Someone has taken away his life – the least we can do is let him keep his privacy!"

"But he is dead," I said. "Surely his privacy is subordinate to finding the truth? And I wonder – forgive me – whether you are actually thinking more of your own privacy than his?"

"Thomas! How can you speak to me in this way?" Her eyes were beginning to fill with tears.

"Because I want Felicity to have her mother back," I said. "I fear you are not being entirely straight with me. What is it you fear in that safe?"

She looked away from me. "Nothing."

"So let me have the key, if you have nothing to fear."

She looked back at me and showing a new determination, said, "I have let you into my home. I have shared confidences with you. I have" – she glanced at the constable standing in the corner of the room – "shared other things. But some things I shall not share. Do you not have secrets of your own? I can't believe you don't. Please let it rest. I trust in God to set me free, one way or another." She sighed and sat back in her chair. "I'm so tired of everything."

"So help me fight on your behalf! After all, God helps those who help themselves. Your daughter is worth the fight."

"I am thinking of Felicity, of course I am," she said. "But some things are best left alone."

I leant forward and lowered my voice so that the constable could not hear. "Are you referring to Yorick's mistress?" I said, hoping that if some truths were already out in the open, the exposure of other truths might become easier for her.

"Oh!" said Mrs Ambrose, and dissolved in tears.

The constable cleared his throat. "That's enough for today, sir," he said. "You've gone and upset the lady."

I was forced to say goodbye, and mutter my apologies, as she was taken back to her cell. I felt wretched at what I had done. But I told myself that I had to try anything to save her, however painful.

On my way out, I encountered Inspector Simmons holding a sheaf of documents.

"Mr Simmons," I said, "have you spoken to Mr Wakeley?"

"You may be sure, Mr Rufford," he said, "that we have interviewed those we deem necessary to interview. Nevertheless, the case is clear to me. I'm about to charge Mrs Ambrose. Good morning, sir."

~

Reginald Wakeley was renting a small, ancient cottage that sat in a small gap between grander modern houses on Wansbeck Street, and it looked incongruous, like a hunched peasant in a line of aristocrats.

I was surprised to find a black woman answering the door – such exotic skin colouring was a rarity in Hawksbridge.

"Good morning, ma'am!" I said. "I was hoping to find Mr Wakeley in."

She shook her head. "Mr Wakeley? No, not in," she said. "Sorry."

"Ah," I said, and scratched my head. "Well, may I wait for him for a while? I know him through his friend, Mrs Campbell. Is he likely to be back soon?"

In answer, she opened the door, and led me to the sitting room, where I took a rather hard country chair.

"He went for walk. Not for long, I think," she said. "Tea, sir?"

"Ah, yes please!" I said. "That would be very welcome."

She gave me a smile and disappeared into the kitchen.

I tried to place my hostess in the usual categories, but I found it hard. She was dressed in a colourful robe that gave her an unusual appearance for a housekeeper, and she moved with a deliberate grace.

When she came in with the tea, I thanked her, and said, "How do you find Mr Wakeley? Is he pleasant?"

A brief smile flickered across her face, and she shrugged. "He takes care of me," she said.

"Are you sure?" I said. I found it hard to believe Mr Wakeley was capable of caring about anyone but himself.

She looked at me suspiciously, and said, "Why?"

"Oh, no reason," I said. "I'm just trying to understand him. He is in business with a friend of mine – Mrs Campbell, as I mentioned – and obviously I have the interests of my friend at heart."

She gave a furtive look at the door, and said quietly, "Mrs Campbell must take care."

Before I had time to quiz her on this alarming remark, the door opened noisily opened and I heard Mr Wakeley's voice. "Catherine! My shoes. And whose horse is that?"

My hostess went to change Wakeley's footwear, and I heard a brief exchange about my presence in the sitting room.

"Ah, Mr Rufford," he said. "What an unexpected pleasure to see you. So you have met my housekeeper, Catherine! Useful, if rather sluggish. Not what you expect here, is she!"

"I confess not," I said.

"Found her in West Africa!" he said. "I had some business there. And not a little pleasure," he said, winking unpleasantly. "Now, sir, what could make you stir from the comforts of your splendid castle to visit me in my squalid little hovel?"

"I wondered if you had heard about Mr Ambrose."

He laughed. "Oh, yes. The fool apparently fell off his horse! What an unfortunate and banal end. Well, it's no more than he deserved for trying to swipe our prize from under our noses. Natural justice, I should say."

"Isn't that rather callous, Mr Wakeley? He left a wife and daughter."

"Quite right, Mr Rufford, quite right. I bow to your superior sensibilities. So is this all you came for? To berate me for my lack of Christian virtues? I rather think that if you were to catalogue all my sins, you would need to stay longer than either of us would care for."

"You had a financial interest in Mr Ambrose being out of the picture, given how much time and energy you had invested in your scheme – would you not say?"

Mr Wakeley first look astonished, and then burst into a loud and long peal of laughter. When he had finished, he said, "Of course – you think I killed him! What, did I wait in the bushes and push him off his horse? Is that it? Really, you are too humorous! No wonder you amuse Francesca so much. I was beginning to wonder what she saw in you. But your comic qualities were well hidden."

If I had hoped to read Mr Wakeley's expression for a sign of guilt, that hope had been extinguished. I began to feel that my visit had been foolish; guilty or not, Mr Wakeley was an accomplished operator and was unlikely to give himself away.

"So you don't know anything about Mr Ambrose's death?" I asked.

"No more than you," he said, "and perhaps considerably less, since Francesca tells me you are intimate with the Ambroses!" An unpleasant expression formed on his face. "How intimate, who can say!"

It was an unfortunate guess, but I did not give him the satisfaction of a reaction.

"And I was a guest of Francesca's on Friday night," he

continued, "which is when I gather this accident happened. Mrs Campbell is a warm and hospitable woman! I assure you that was too attractive a berth for me to be creeping about wickedly on a snowy winter's night."

My stomach turned at this.

"Then I am sorry to have bothered you, Mr Wakeley," I said, getting up. "Thank you for the tea," I said to Catherine, who was standing at the door. "I will see myself out."

"Good morning, Mr Rufford!" said Mr Wakeley. "What a funny fellow you are, to be sure!"

~

Mounting Celeste, I felt like a cavalry officer in ignominious retreat. Talking to Mr Wakeley had achieved precisely nothing except my own humiliation, and I preferred not to dwell on Wakeley's innuendos about the nature of his relationship with Francesca.

However, Catherine's warning about Francesca was interesting. For what reasons did she not trust her master? What might she have witnessed and experienced on the long journey from her homeland, and since? While what I had learned that morning may not have been directly helpful to Mrs Ambrose, it did at least paint a picture of Mr Wakeley as a man with a dubious past. My instincts were confirmed, but the chances of Francesca altering course were slight.

As I had before at the nadir of my morale, I arrived at Bess' door, seeking the chance to wipe out my anxieties.

"Are you sober this time?" she said.

"As sober as a judge, more's the pity," I said. "I need port."

"Oh dear," she said, leading me inside. "Now what's happened?"

She called for Lizzie to look after Celeste, and brought me a glass of port.

"I am failing a friend," I said. "Mrs Ambrose. She has been wrongly charged with murdering her husband, and I cannot find anything that could save her."

"Lord!" she said. "It's hardly your responsibility, though, is it?"

"Then whose?" I said, gratefully taking a gulp of port. "Inspector Simmons is wrong again."

"Are you sure?" said Bess.

"As sure as I can be. Simmons thinks she did it because Ambrose was cruel to her, and he even had the cheek to suggest she was after me, as a husband and a father to her daughter!"

"Can you blame her?" said Bess. "You're not the worst fit for those positions. But you are too young for her."

"Well, it's nonsense, even if she was rather warm to me."

The port was already working its disarming magic, and I had let it loosen my tongue. I badly wanted to confess my sins to someone.

"Warm?"

I briefly wrestled with the urge to spill my secret, and lost.

"She came to my room – it was the night before her husband died, and I was staying there because of the snow. We had rather too much to drink. She was shivering and she asked me to warm her up."

"I see," said Bess. "And you obliged her, of course?"

"Stupidly, I did," I said. "Then she... she moved against me."

"Interesting. Not, I take it, in the way that Brutus moved against Caesar, or Cromwell moved against Charles?"

"No," I said. "More as if Caesar had fallen upon Brutus' sword."

"Where Mrs Ambrose is Caesar, and you are Brutus, with your mighty sword?"

"Precisely," I said, and finished my port.

"Well," Bess said, and stood up. "I don't know what to make of that, Thomas, I really don't."

"I'm sorry," I said. "It seemed impossible to resist at that point."

"Well, you're a man, and men have absolutely no control over themselves, so I suppose it's entirely predictable. I don't know why you told me about this, though. Am I meant to absolve you, or congratulate you?"

"Neither," I said. "I don't know. I just needed to say it. Now I think about it, that was selfish of me."

"Yes, Thomas, it was. Finally, you talk some sense."

"Should I go?"

Bess considered this for a moment. "No, don't be silly," she said at last. "At least you've been honest. That's worth something."

"Thank you," I said. "It's been tormenting me. And now I can't even redeem myself by solving this damn case. I have got nowhere."

Bess laughed. "Goodness, but you do get yourself into some strange predicaments. What am I to do with you?"

She sat down again and put her arm around me, and I put my head on her shoulder.

"More port?" she said, and I nodded.

She administered our drinks, and we sat for a while. Presently said, "Maybe you were only being kind, in your own peculiar way."

"That's a generous interpretation," I said. "But initially, yes, before..."

"Before you were seduced," she said.

"Perhaps that word could be used," I said.

"How weak you are," she said, unbuttoning my trousers.

"Yes, deplorably so," I said.

"And how easy to coax into submission," she whispered, her hands in my trousers, causing the inevitable reaction despite the port. "Ah, behold the mighty sword of Brutus."

~

After we had amused ourselves, Bess came in with coffee and sandwiches.

"Oh, Thomas," she said after we had started on the sandwiches. "Don't you think we need to take stock? Am I to sit here forever waiting for you to come and take your pleasure? And it seems as though you may not even need that."

"Bess, it's not like that, I assure you –" I began.

"It's exactly like that. Is this how we want to carry on? I know what I said at the beginning, but..."

She trailed off, and I nodded. I had been dreading it, but I had known that this time would come. "Of course," I said. "You are right. It's not fair of me."

"Or me," she said. "The point is, it's not truly helping either of us, is it? You have to be free to marry the woman of your dreams. I'm perfectly aware I don't qualify for that – it's all right, you don't need to feel sorry for me. But – how can I put this?"

She sipped her coffee and continued, "We have had our fun, Thomas, haven't we? But perhaps we should be sensible, before our lusts become a liability to ourselves. I might find someone who can give me more time."

"I suppose so," I said, reluctantly. "Yes, you're right. It has been selfish of me."

"Don't think of it that way," she said. "Just that our little affair has run its course."

I sighed. "I shall miss you," I said.

"I know," she said. "I shall miss you too. So we will have to create some new beginnings!"

"Have you anything in mind?" I asked.

"Not really," she said, "but I do miss the shop and all the comings and goings. Perhaps I should try being a shopkeeper, and not just the shopkeeper's wife that I was. But I don't know if I have it in me. Or the necessary funds, for that matter."

A thought occurred to me. "I was at a dinner a while ago, and a guest – Mrs Harris – made an intriguing suggestion. Let me ask you this: have you ever thought how pleasant it would be to visit a coffee shop now and again?"

"Well, I might if they were not disreputable, raucous places! Even if I went with a gaggle of friends, I doubt we would last five minutes for all the disgusting innuendos and cursing from the men."

"Exactly," I said. "And there's the idea."

"Ban cursing and salacious behaviour?" she said. "I doubt that would work."

"No. Ban the men."

Bess put her coffee cup down and stared at me. "Goodness! What a marvellous thought – pardon me, but you know what I mean."

"So – open a coffee shop for women only. What do you think?"

"I think it's a wonderful idea. But Mrs Harris – would she not like to pursue it herself?"

"No – indeed, I was encouraged to do it myself! Which of course I won't, since anyway I would be banned from my own shop."

"It's a very fine thought," she said, "but I would need money, and I only have my pension, and this house, and a little put by."

"That shouldn't present a difficulty," I said. "I will invest, if you wish! It would amuse me, more than most of my other, rather dull investments."

"Really? It might be risky."

"Not so much as to put me off," I said. "Would you like to write a plan? And we can both keep an eye open for likely properties in town."

Bess smiled broadly and kissed me on the cheek. "You may have given me my new beginning!"

CHAPTER FIFTEEN

A LITTLE unsteadily, I returned to Ramsburgh with a mixture of emotions. It pained me deeply that I would no longer have recourse to the pleasant interludes in which I could indulge in whimsical exchanges with an affectionate, warm creature whose voice and flesh were balms to my troubled mind. Such intimacies would be badly missed.

Still, it also marked, I hoped, a retreat from behaviour of which I was ashamed, and which was a bar to a more fruitful relationship. I might have had plenty to forgive, but at least it was behind me – if I could get a grip on my baser instincts.

I still had the comfort of my little study next to Victoria's room. With a sore head from the port, I settled on the sofa to mull over the day's events. It was not even dusk, and yet since this morning, I had witnessed the creation of a book, pleaded with a prisoner to reveal her secrets, confronted a rogue in his den, and dissolved a relationship.

But for all this activity, I had achieved none of my objectives. I was no closer to the moment when Mrs Ambrose would be freed, her place taken by my unidentified quarry. I decided to visit again with Felicity, and not leave until the key to the safe was found. I could do no less: I had made my promise to Felicity and her mother.

I tried to concentrate my mind on what else I knew. Mr Ambrose had certainly struck the wrong note with the Antiquarian Society: presumably, on Friday he had delivered his promised triumphant rant about the land that he was about to acquire. I would need to find out what had happened, and who might have reacted badly – the special meeting of the Society might provide that information.

Who else had Ambrose clashed with? I recalled my trip to Mr Blackwood's antique shop, and the bad-tempered exchange between Blackwood and Ambrose. There was a disagreement about a past transaction, and Ambrose's annoyance about losing the cassone, but it was hardly a blood feud.

Then there was the death of the Ambroses' maid, Susan. Mrs Ambrose had been tight-lipped about the cause of her dismissal – 'impertinence' was highly subjective and could cover almost anything. Perhaps Mr Ambrose's murder was an act of revenge. And yet, some years had passed, so it seemed unlikely. And I had no evidence to confirm improper conduct on Mr Ambrose's behalf regarding Susan – simply rumour and conjecture.

However, the letter from his mistress, Ophelia, implied a complicated emotional life. This was also a dead end, as I had no present way to find Ophelia and question her. I possessed so many tantalising little pieces that added up to nothing at all.

The packet of Mr Jeremy Davison's letters still lay on the bureau where I had last left them, unable to digest all their uncomfortable secrets. I got up, and willing myself to look at them again, I found one I had not yet read.

My dear John,

How do I begin to explain my predicament? You have listened patiently to all my doubts about Dr Rufford, and as his friend you may have given him the benefit of the doubt: loyalty is a quality I admire, of course. It is also in my nature to take a liberal view of the relations between friends of different sexes. After all, I have one or two dear female friends from whom I would not wish to be estranged.

And yet Dr Rufford has taken advantage of my admittedly strained tolerance – I felt I had to appease my wife by once again allowing their association – and here is the pitiful position in which I find myself. My wife is pregnant, but as she and I both know, it cannot be due to any efforts of mine, since we have been physically estranged of late, within the consequential interval of time.

> There will soon be a cuckoo in my nest, John! I cannot bear it. If I could summon up any respect at all for Dr Rufford, then I might entertain the thought of bringing the child up as my own. As it is, I do not know how I will restrain myself from dashing its brains out as soon as it enters our cursed household and draws its first breath.

I could not bring myself to read any more. I felt dizzy, and had to sit down quickly on the sofa as the realisation sank in. Assuming this child had survived, I had a half-sibling. And the most likely identity of the child was Flora.

~

As before, I sat at the back of the room, and acknowledged Mr Fountain as he took his seat. I would collar him afterwards. I also recognised Mr Redpath and Mr Blackwood. As the Antiquarian Society assembled, I attracted some cold looks from some of them, presumably for my connection to the unfortunate Mr Ambrose. But even though, strictly speaking, I had no right to be present, Mr Fountain did not object: it appeared that my guest invitation from Mr Ambrose held good for a second time, even after his demise.

Mr Fountain stood up and cleared his throat as a sign for all to be quiet.

"Gentlemen," he began, "thank you for coming to this special and most regrettable meeting of the Society. As you will know by now, Mr Ambrose departed this world shortly after he departed the Society. I'm sure we would all like to extend our condolences to his family, even though the circumstances are quite... unusual."

There were some murmurs of dissent. Mr Fountain held up his hand, and continued, "I know that what he said at the last meeting was unfortunate and distressing. This was not the behaviour of a man in full possession of his faculties. Since he must have been impaired by melancholia or some other mental disturbance, we should try to feel compassion. He was in the most part a loyal and valued member of the Society."

He surveyed the room. "Now we must turn to the fate of the land under Hawksbridge Castle in the new owner's hands. Mr Ambrose previously stated that there were two bidders – himself and another. Mr Dunton is refusing to say who the other bidder is. Perhaps one of you is in possession of this information?"

I shifted in my seat. No one else seemed to be about to speak, so I was compelled to leave my comfortable place in the shadows.

I raised my hand and said, "Yes, I believe I am." Like a murmuration of starlings in synchronised flight, all turned to look at me.

"Mrs Francesca Campbell has spoken of acquiring the land," I said, "together with her business partner, Mr Reginald Wakeley. I don't know if the transaction has been completed."

"I see," said Mr Fountain. "And what do they propose to do with it?"

I supposed the details would become common knowledge soon enough. "I understand they intend to sell it to a railway company – probably the North British Railway Company, as they have been surveying here recently."

"I suspected as much," Mr Fountain said with a sigh. "I fear the railway will destroy more than just the castle. We are powerless against the might of such corporations."

Mr Blackwood stood up. "I suggest we raise a subscription," he said, "buy the land from its new owners, and in the process block the railway."

There was a contemptuous laugh from Mr Redpath. "I doubt we could outbid the railway. Mrs Campbell and her friend will be after every penny they can get. And besides, don't you want more business? Quicker journeys to the cities?

More frequent visits to your relatives and mistresses?" This drew a snigger. "You can't hold back the tide of progress!"

"Progress, progress, progress," snorted Mr Blackwood. "I hear people bandy this word about as though it excuses everything. I tell you, it's a new religion! But what does it mean, really? Reeking factories, child labour, destruction of our land and traditions, the manufacture of endless baubles no one needs, to enrich the already obscenely wealthy! Everyone has been so hypnotized by this devil 'progress' that they can't see what's being lost. I defy progress, sir! I defy it!"

Red-faced, he stamped his foot on the floor before taking his seat. It was evidently a topic that riled him.

Mr Redpath shook his head and raised his hands as if to say, "It's not worth arguing against such stupidity."

Mr Fountain tried to wrest back control of the meeting. "Now, gentlemen, this is not the time or place to debate the philosophy of modernisation. My question is, is there anything we can do, or must we simply give up the castle as a lost cause?"

"I think the best we can do," I said, "is put pressure on the railway company to preserve as much as they can."

Mr Blackwood laughed bitterly, and said, "They will flatten it all, Mr Rufford, mark my words! These people don't negotiate such things. It implies they will care a jot about our town and its history – when they care for nothing but the gold in their vaults."

"Nevertheless," said Mr Fountain, "it may be the only option open to us. Mr Rufford, can you speak to Mrs Campbell, and suggest to her that she places conditions on the sale?"

"Certainly," I said. "I will talk to her."

"Unexpectedly, I find myself agreeing with Mr Blackwood," said Mr Redpath. "They will accept no preconditions. They have a business to run."

"We shall see," said Mr Fountain.

~

"Mr Ambrose was positively maniacal on Friday," said Mr Fountain. We were in the tap room, where I had bought Mr Fountain and myself a drink. "I have never seen him so worked up. He said he would soon be in possession of the land, and would take great pleasure in erasing the castle from existence, and would make it a public event. Then he resigned from the Society and stormed out."

"Extraordinary," I said. "I have seen some irritability in him, but that is extreme. And all because of his humiliation in the previous meeting, I presume."

"Yes," said Mr Fountain, lifting his drink. "And I fear I have some culpability there. We were all a trifle hard on him. Perhaps he did only what he thought was best for the castle. But he went about it the wrong way. And then, like a petulant child, he wanted to smash what he loved, so no one could have it."

"And now it's likely to be smashed anyway. Tell me," I said, "what was Mr Redpath's reaction?"

"Redpath? He laughed – thought it was a great joke. Between you and me, I can't say I care for the man. He is not anyone's idea of a gentleman."

"And Mr Blackwood?" I asked.

"He was as affronted as most people in the room. More so, perhaps. You saw for yourself how protective he is about our town. A great deal of money has changed hands between Blackwood and Ambrose, but that doesn't mean they liked each other." He drank a deep draught of ale before adding, "'Blaggard' – that was the word Blackwood used for him."

"Interesting," I said. "But not sufficient animosity for murder, would you say?"

"Good Lord, no!" Mr Fountain exclaimed. "By no means. Blackwood may have strong opinions, but the balance of his mind is sound."

"And it seems to me," I said, "that Mr Redpath was more amused by Mr Ambrose's performance than regretful about the castle's fate."

"Indeed," said Mr Fountain. "If you have come here seeking a substitute for Mrs Ambrose, then you will be disappointed, Mr Rufford. I see no one in the Society who might fit that description. But I am heartily sorry for her, and from what I know of her, I cannot believe she is capable of this atrocity."

"I agree," I said, "and I intend to prove it – somehow. Another drink, Mr Fountain?"

~

The Ambroses' butler, Rayner, was not happy to see me, but Felicity was there as my ticket to search the house again. We started from a corner of the study and worked in opposite directions, removing books and checking them for secret compartments, looking under rugs, examining marble busts, and turning out all the drawers in both desks. We pulled the furniture out, removed pictures, and even looked along the top of the door and window frames. But the key to the safe eluded us.

"I have a horrible feeling," I said, "that we will need to pull the library apart, and his bedroom, and perhaps other rooms. I fear there will be a point when Rayner's tolerance will break, and he'll threaten us with the police."

"I won't let him do that!" Felicity said. "We need to think harder – where would you hide a key, where no one would bother looking?"

"I sense a paradox in trying to answer that one!" I said. "Maybe the key is doubly protected by the fact that few people even know about the safe, so they wouldn't be looking for a key."

"True," said Felicity, "which might mean that my father didn't need to be quite as clever in hiding the key."

"So we should be looking somewhere more obvious?"

"Perhaps! My father was impatient. He wouldn't want to go out of his way to fetch a key from some elaborate hiding place. Might that be of some help?"

"Interesting," I said. "So we need to think of somewhere that would be convenient for him. Perhaps so convenient, people wouldn't think of looking there."

"Yes – somewhere near the safe, maybe?"

"Let's have a look at that picture again," I said. "You can't get nearer the safe than that."

Felicity helped me get the picture hiding the safe down from the wall and onto the floor, and we both kneeled and examined the back.

It all looked perfectly normal – an oil canvas held by wooden stretchers.

"What's that?" said Felicity, pointing to a small metal loop on the inside edge of one of the stretchers.

"Ah – there's one on the other side too. It looks as though they may have been used for the hanging cord, before these eyelets on the side were fitted."

Felicity tried to pull at the loop, but it was too close to the canvas and she could not get a grip.

"Just a moment," she said, and she fetched her father's paper knife, pushing its point into the loop. To my astonishment, she then extracted a small block of wood to which the loop was attached. It had been such a tight fit I had not noticed the seams – but Felicity's young eyesight was sharper than mine.

"Voila!" she said triumphantly. As she turned it over, I saw it had been hollowed out, and a key fell on the floor.

"My God," I said. "You clever thing." I wondered if this

hiding place had been made by the same carpenter that had created Mr Kington's secret bureau compartment. In any event, this was a tremendous step forward.

"My pleasure," said Felicity, beaming. "Come on, then! Let's open the safe."

I picked up the key and hesitated. "If you don't mind, if there are any papers, I will take them home to study. I don't think you should look at them yet, just in case there are things that are disturbing about your father."

"But that's ridiculous," said Felicity. "Why shouldn't I know about my father?"

"The information may be need to be interpreted before we have a balanced view. I don't want you to be upset. There may be intimate letters that are... distressing. Your mother wouldn't like you to see anything like that. Please?"

"Oh, all right," she said. "If you must. But promise you will tell me what you find?"

"Of course," I said. "I will summarise the facts, minus any unnecessary details."

The key turned in the lock, and the safe door swung open. There were several leather pouches, which turned out to contain gold sovereigns. There was no reason to take those. Next to these was, as I had conjectured, a thick packet of papers, which I placed in my inside pocket without examining them.

There were also some bags of jewellery – rings, bracelets, brooches, and a pearl necklace. Judging by the letter to Ophelia, this little trove was probably the source of gifts for his mistress – or mistresses.

"Treasure," I said, taking the bags and emptying them on a table in the window.

"Oh! Wonderful!" said Felicity. She held a handful of them up to the light so that the gems sparkled. "Fancy them being hidden in here. Mama hardly had any jewellery. Could I take something?"

"Better not," I said. "I don't want the police accusing us of pilfering. But your mother will inherit them, and when she gets out, she can do as she wishes with them."

CHAPTER SIXTEEN

It was with some excitement, mixed with fear, that I ran up the stairs to my lofty hideout. Was my luck finally turning, or would it be yet another dead end? If Mr Ambrose's safe was not the repository of his dark secrets and the key to his demise, then I could not imagine where else I could look. This moment, this packet of papers, might determine the fate of an innocent woman.

I cleared away Mr Davison's letters from the bureau, and emptied the packet onto the desk.

The first sheet I examined was a letter from Ophelia.

> Dearest Y,
>
> I have done as you asked – I hope my hand is close enough to your sample. I think I have done it quite well. Why is it that a man's and a woman's hand are so readily distinguished? It is odd.
>
> But my dear, you are not getting yourself into trouble by this letter, are you? It is just that for a leg-pull, it does seem so serious. 'The grievous wrongs you have done me'! How very mysterious. Anyway, there it is, a simple thing for me to do, and for such a great reward that I have no cause for complaint! I will wear it when I see you next, and then you may remove it, and everything else.
>
> Your Ophelia.

There was no sign of the mysterious letter to which she alluded, but it was obvious that Mr Ambrose had concocted a dark scheme in which he had involved Ophelia. This was promising, to say the least.

An item that stood out from the other papers was a

booklet, bound together with a red thread. On the cover there was a picture of a volcano spewing lava, flanked by two semi-naked women, in a classical style, with their arms stretched out towards the volcano as if to say, 'Behold! Such power!'. Under this, the words 'THE VESUVIUS' were printed.

I turned the cover over, and a letter fell out. This was on expensively printed notepaper, bearing the address 'The Vesuvius Gentlemen's Club, Moray Place, Edinburgh'.

> Dear Mr Ambrose,
>
> I was delighted to see you at our last meeting, and glad that you particularly enjoyed spending time with Ophelia. She is a most comely girl and a joyful companion.
>
> I enclose a memento of the meeting, drawn as cleverly as ever by the talented Mr Harrison, and a schedule of our forthcoming gatherings, at which I look forward to seeing you again.
>
> Yours respectfully,
>
> Oliver Murdoch

The booklet contained a number of interesting pencil sketches. Mr Harrison's illustrations gave me a good idea of the proceedings: naked or semi-naked females happily desporting themselves, embracing couples, and a group of four unclothed individuals who appeared to be having a splendid if complicated time. The last drawing was a rather charming head and bust portrait of a young woman who might conceivably be Ophelia, if Mr Harrison had tailored his sketch collections to each client.

It was clear what kind of a society this was: one in which a man's fantasies could be turned into fleshy reality; where all senses could be employed in the grossest indulgence, and where women could be picked as easily as the apples from Eden's tree. As I flicked through the pages, I was distracted by base thoughts, and imagined myself participating in such an event, before pulling myself together. This was a valuable lead, for it offered me an opportunity to find Ophelia. And then, if I could convince her to speak to me, I would learn the nature of the letter she had been persuaded to write. It might, of course, have nothing to do with Ambrose's death – but it must surely reveal something new about the man.

There were some more letters from Ophelia, but they mainly covered the inconsequential happenings of her life, and entreaties to visit that were embroidered with offers of varying sensuality and frankness. I was glad Felicity had not seen them. I also briefly looked through more invoices from Mr Blackwood, which I thought were rather mundane items to find in the safe.

I considered whether I should surrender this information to the police: evidence that, in raw form, they might use against Mrs Ambrose, as they provided further apparent reasons for her to dispatch her errant husband. But since Mrs Ambrose had been charged, the police investigation was over, so now it was a matter of finding evidence for Mrs Ambrose's defence, or indeed, presenting enough for the case to be dropped altogether. It was entirely proper for me to keep the details hidden until I could see the entire picture.

But how to act on this information? The awkward fact was that I was obliged to attend the next meeting of The Vesuvius Gentlemen's Club, in the hopes of finding Ophelia. I could not imagine that any other mode of enquiry was going to persuade Mr Murdoch to reveal the whereabouts of Ambrose's mistress. The next meeting was to be on Saturday, the sixteenth of December, ten days from now. So I sat down and wrote a letter, saying that I was a friend of Mr Ambrose's, explaining the sad news of his death, and expressing a desire to acquaint myself with the Club of which he had spoken so enthusiastically.

What Phyllis would make of such an excursion, I dreaded to think. However, I was acting in the best interests of a friend: and I would not, of course, succumb to the temptations on offer. I just hoped that when the time came, I would be able to sufficiently dampen my natural impulses. I did not have the best record in this matter.

~

I took the letter, and had just left my study when I heard the sound of crying coming from Victoria's room. I hesitated, and then knocked. The crying stopped, and after a moment, the door opened, revealing a red-eyed Victoria holding a handkerchief.

"Oh, hello, Thomas," she said. "Oh dear – I'm not in a pretty state, I'm afraid."

"I'm sorry – is there anything I can do?" I said.

She smiled. "Have you come to fetch me a hot chocolate?"

"Certainly, if you would like one!" I said. "Or if you would like to talk about anything...?"

"Thank you," she said. "I don't need cocoa, but perhaps you could lend me your ear. If you don't mind a silly, self-indulgent woman getting all weepy. It's not attractive, is it?"

She let me inside the room and gestured to a chair. She went to the bed and picked up a small portrait of a young woman, which she had presumably been clutching before answering the door. She sat down and gazed at the picture.

"Who is she?" I asked.

"Ursula," she said. "Ursula Tennant. My greatest friend in the..." She stopped and blinked back the tears, before handing me the portrait to look at.

"She's lovely," I said. "I assume she's...?"

"Yes," she said. "She's dead. She became ill."

"She looks so full of life here," I said. "Is it a good likeness?"

"Yes," she said. "She really was as beautiful as that. And far cleverer than me, with one little weakness."

"Yes?"

"Trust," she said. "She trusted people. A great strength, and alas, a great weakness too."

"Were you friends from childhood?" I asked.

"Yes – we went through everything together. The mysteries of Pythagoras – drawing silly caricatures of the teachers – reading stories to each other when we got ill – and then the strangeness of becoming women together. The saddest part for me is remembering how interested she was in everything. Her joy at finding a Keats poem she particularly loved, or a fossil on the beach. Her triumph at mastering a Chopin nocturne, which she managed far better than me. Her love of botany – she found the construction of a flower infinitely fascinating. And then she was amazed and grateful to meet a man who seemed to love and understand her."

She stopped to wipe away tears.

"When we were young, we would imagine the dinner parties we would have when we were married to our impossibly handsome husbands. We would invite the most interesting and famous people, and show off our tribe of children. It never occurred to us that we might not still be best friends in our old age, with great-grandchildren crawling at our feet."

I contemplated asking what had happened to Ursula, but I thought she would tell me in her own time, so I just said, "I'm truly sorry."

She shook her head like a wet spaniel, trying to cast off the muddy puddle of her dark thoughts, and got up from the bed. "But this is too maudlin," she said. "Phyllis is coming to see me this morning! Shall we go and wait for her?"

As I left my letter on the hall table for posting, we heard the sound of Phyllis' pony cart on the gravel. We went out to greet her, and when I had helped her from the pony cart,

Victoria darted forward and embraced her, somewhat to Phyllis' surprise.

"Thank you!" said Victoria when she had loosened her grip. "That has helped to banish my melancholia."

Fox slipped through the open door, and bounced around us. "He needs a walk," I said.

"Shall we all walk too?" Victoria said. "I desperately need some air."

"Good idea," said Phyllis. She touched me lightly on the arm and said, "Any news of Mrs Ambrose?"

"I saw her yesterday," I said. "She was – well, she was depressed, of course."

"The poor woman," said Phyllis. "Are you any further with finding out who might have done it? I appreciate I only saw you yesterday, but –"

"As a matter of fact," I said, "I have found some information, though its value is uncertain. I have an avenue or two to explore, at any rate."

How scandalised they both would have been, had I revealed the direction of my investigation. I was unsure if I would ever be able to be candid about it to Phyllis.

"That sounds promising," she said.

We walked in silence for a moment, and the sun deigned to emerge for a moment. Victoria sighed with pleasure.

"The air is so fresh here!" she said. "The air in Leeds is full of coal smoke. I hate the way it gets in my hair, in my clothes, the curtains, everywhere. I can even taste it."

"Then why not move to some pleasant market town?" I said. "Somewhere with plenty of peace and quiet for your writing. I know just such a place, where you will be welcomed with open arms."

"Indeed," said Phyllis. "A place where you already have friends."

"Don't!" said Victoria. "You will make me cry again. You must both be thoroughly bored of my tears by now."

"Nonsense," said Phyllis. "And why shouldn't you move here? I don't want to see you go. And you seem to enjoy Hawksbridge! What's keeping you in smoky Leeds?"

"Oh – habit, the theatre, my family, one or two friends. Perhaps that's not enough to keep me there. I shall have to think!"

She stopped suddenly, and said, "But in any case, I think we should have a picnic! An outing for us to remember. The four of us – including Felicity."

Phyllis laughed. "In December?"

"Yes, in December," Victoria said. "Not if it snows, of course. But we can all wrap up warm, and get a cab to the foot of Cocklaw Hill. I have it all worked out."

"And walk up to the Devil's Teeth?" said Phyllis.

"Exactly! I have been busy in your library, Thomas. It looks fascinating! I found a picture of the place in 'An Illustrated History of Hawksbridge'. Have either of you been?"

"I have," said Phyllis. "You're right, it's just as peculiar as it sounds. It would make for a fine picnic."

"What on earth are the Devil's Teeth?" I asked.

"Standing stones," said Phyllis. "A circle – roughly – of five very oddly-shaped stones. Thousands of years old, apparently."

"About four thousand," said Victoria. "Imagine that!"

"I first went when I was twelve," said Phyllis, "and it gave me nightmares. The stones are weathered in the most strange way, with big ridges along their lengths, and they are smaller at the bottom than the top, so they do look like monstrous teeth." She shuddered.

"It would be an excellent distraction for Felicity," I said. "And perhaps she can practise her drawing."

"Certainly," said Victoria, "if she can keep her fingers warm. Oh – so you would really like to do this?" We smiled and nodded.

"Good!" she said. "We must fix a date, and I will ask dear

Mrs Felton about sandwiches. And Fox – you must come too."

~

"A picnic? In winter?" said Mrs Felton, placing our lunch on the table. "Well, you must all be hardier than you look! But you might get some sunshine if you're lucky. Yes, my dear, of course I can make you a picnic. Let me know when you have decided on a day."

She was about to leave the room when she added, "Oh – isn't it exciting about the railway? It'll be so much easier to go to Newcastle – and I might even get to see the sights of London! I've never been."

"The railway?" I said. "What do you mean, Mrs Felton?"

"It's in the paper!" she said. "Shall I get it for you?"

"Yes, please," I said. She came back with a copy of The Hawksbridge Herald, and I found the relevant story.

"Read it to us, won't you?" said Victoria, and I complied.

> NORTH EAST LINE TO HAWKSBRIDGE CONFIRMED
>
> After long speculation, North British Railway Company Ltd. has confirmed its plans for the route along the East Coast, terminating in Edinburgh. It will pass Hawksbridge over the River Gill on the west side of town, doubtless requiring a bridge of considerable length and height to cross the Gill Valley.
>
> Mr Edward Thornton, a director of the company, said: "We are delighted to announce our intentions to bring a first class railway to the North East, serving not only passengers travelling between cities, but transforming the lives of the local population along the route. We will announce further details in due course, and we will be working assiduously with landowners and town councils to achieve the best result for everyone. This is a historic day for the North East of England!"

Shares in North British Railway Company Ltd. rose by twenty-three percent after the announcement, but then dropped twelve percent after a financial statement, which warned of unexpectedly difficult geological conditions along parts of the route.

"Well, there it is," I said. "Mr Wakeley's gamble seems to be paying off. Any redirection of the railway west of the castle will add huge amounts to the cost of the bridge, no doubt, as the valley gets much wider."

"How depressing," said Phyllis. She looked crestfallen.

"But I don't suppose they will be in the mood to pay through the nose for land," said Victoria. "It sounds as though they have some headaches. And railway companies do often go bankrupt."

"What choice would they have?" said Phyllis. "They will have to pay whatever price is asked. It's a recipe for extortion."

"Call me cynical," said Victoria, "but don't you think they might resort to other methods? I mean, the directors could face ruin if the railway failed, not to mention being chased by a mob of angry shareholders with pitchforks."

"Interesting," I said. "You mean they might threaten landowners to persuade them to reduce their price?"

Victoria shrugged. "I wouldn't put it past them. I wouldn't put it past any man where money is involved."

"Good God," I said. "If you follow that train of thought... then that sheds a new light on Mr Ambrose's death – and Francesca could be in danger, as the new landowner!"

"And Mr Wakeley," Phyllis reminded me.

"To hell with Mr Wakeley," I said. "I don't care about him."

Victoria smiled. "You still have to introduce me to him," she said, "before something terrible happens to him!"

"Yes, if you insist, I'll arrange it," I said. "I have a few more things I want to say to Mr Wakeley."

~

I turned Victoria's idea over in my mind as I rode to the Pottery for a meeting with Mr McPhee. Surely it was a huge risk for a company to simply squash any potential fly in their ointment, just to reduce their land purchase costs? Then again, that might be a bold move: to do something so outrageous that no one would seriously suspect the perpetrator, but would still create sufficient fear to soften up any remaining opposition.

How could this relate to the letter that Ambrose had persuaded his mistress to write? It could be that when he had first thought he would be owner of the land, he had got wind of a company director's indiscretion, and was hoping to enlist his help in extracting an exorbitant price. If so, he had not understood who he was dealing with, and was answered with brutality.

After McPhee had impressed me with more figures that showed the company's fortunes continuing to improve, he broke out the sherry.

"Tell me," I said as I raised my glass to the good health of the company, "what do you make of the news about the railway? No doubt this will be excellent for distribution."

McPhee's face lit up. "Ah, yes, of course!" he said. "The gods are truly with us this year. Well, not in all respects, naturally – forgive me. But this will enable us to get goods across the country in double-quick time, and I hope with less wastage. It can't come quickly enough, as far as I'm concerned."

"It may lead to the loss of Hawksbridge Castle, I fear," I said.

"That would be a shame," McPhee said. "But –"

"Yes, I know – progress," I said. "There should be a God of Progress, and we should make it in Marbleware."

McPhee laughed. "An excellent thought, Mr Rufford!" he said. "Although if memory serves me, the god Janus is a near fit. But I would prefer a Goddess of Progress: comely, curvaceous, and with a healthy disdain for clothing. Much more commercial. If you can think of other elements to include with the Goddess Progressia, I will be seriously interested to hear about it."

"Perhaps a watch for the passage of time," I said, "a locomotive wheel, and a hammer to smash up the past. I will give it some thought. I don't suppose you know anyone at North British Railway?"

"As a matter of fact I do," said McPhee. "A Mr Thornton came up to inspect the factory last week, and I am travelling to Newcastle tomorrow to sign a contract. We are fortunate enough to have been chosen to provide crockery for their dining cars."

"Ah!" I said. "Was he here last Friday?"

"Let me see – yes, Friday morning was when he came to the factory."

This coincidence disturbed me. "Could I come with you to see Mr Thornton?" I asked.

"Why, of course!" said McPhee. "I would be glad of the company. Any particular reason?"

"I desperately need a change of scene," I said, "and I would like to see you at work – I might learn something!"

"Why do I get the feeling you're up to something?" he said with a smile. "But no matter – it will be a pleasure."

~

On my return, I realised I had not spoken to Flora for some time. Her influenza had unfortunately been followed by a long period of fatigue from which she had still not recovered.

Mrs Northcutt opened the door, her customary brusqueness restored now that Flora was out of danger.

"Flora!" she said. "It's Mr Rufford. Can you stand to see him?"

The answer was in the affirmative, and I went in.

"Sorry, I would have brought some flowers, but I couldn't find anything," I said, sitting down in a chair next to her bed.

"That's all right," Flora said, sitting up. "It's just nice to see you."

"Are you feeling any better?"

"Oh, maybe slightly," she said. "But it's so tedious feeling weak like this. I feel I should be over it by now."

"I gather it can often draw out like this," I said. "You must be patient, alas."

"Yes. Is there any news about Isobel? And how is Felicity bearing up?"

"Felicity is displaying the admirable resilience of youth," I said. "She is distracted by Phyllis and Victoria. And Pantoufle."

"Ah yes, little Pantoufle. How is he?"

"Thriving. Victoria is teaching Felicity to draw him, and she is doing very well."

Flora coughed. "Good for her. And Isobel?"

"She is as well as can be expected, but I can't say I'm not worried about her. She has been charged now."

"Oh, no!" said Flora.

"But I have a few snippets of information that I'm working on," I said. "I will let you know how it goes."

"Thank you," she said. "What a dreadful business. Tell me about Victoria. Meg has mentioned her, but I haven't been well enough to meet her yet."

"How to describe her?" I said. "Clever, warm-hearted, funny. Quite pretty. I like her. It's pleasant having her around the house."

"Is Phyllis not jealous?"

"They are good friends, and no, she has no reason to be. I expect she will want to return home in a few weeks."

There was a pause, and then I said, "I wonder what you were like at Felicity's age. I expect you were just as lively and interested in everything."

"I see some similarities," Flora said. "I was mad about drawing and botany, but alas, I didn't have a squirrel. We had a cat, and a couple of spaniels. I really wanted a monkey, but my parents forbade me from having one."

"In my limited experience of monkeys," I said, "that was wise. You've never really talked about your parents. What were they like?"

Flora turned her head away, and I said, "I'm sorry – I didn't mean to pry."

"No, it's all right," she said. "I just miss them. I took them for granted when I was very young, and then gradually realised that when I was with each parent individually, I felt happy, but when all three of us were together, there was an odd atmosphere. They were always short with each other, and I never saw them show mutual affection. I suppose they fell out of love with one another. I sometimes had a strange feeling that I was to blame."

"No child can be to blame for that," I said. Flora had evidently sensed a truth that lay behind her parents' animosity – that truth was not her own culpability, of course, but a rot that had set in before her conception. A rot that my father was largely responsible for.

"And then, when I was sixteen, they caught typhoid, and I was alone. Thankfully, my aunt and uncle were kind, and adopted me. And I've been here ever since."

I reached out and pressed Flora's hand. "I'm glad you were here when I arrived." I hesitated. "Do you not feel sometimes..."

"Do I not feel what?"

"As if we are connected in some way?"

"What a strange thing to say, Thomas. Well, we live in the same house. We are friends. We have both weathered some curious storms this year. Is that the kind of thing you meant?"

"Perhaps," I said. I could not bring myself to shatter her world with the knowledge that I was probably her brother, by a shocking sequence of events, although I desperately wanted to tell her and to embrace my new-found sister.

"I'll leave you now," I said. "I have worn you out quite enough already. I will come and see you soon."

She nodded and smiled, and when I had reached the doorway, she said, "Thomas?"

"Yes?"

"Did you mean that you were like a brother to me?"

"Exactly!" I said. "Would you have liked a brother?"

"Yes," she said. "If I had one, I'm sure he would be like you."

She closed her eyes, and I tip-toed away, quietly closing the door.

CHAPTER SEVENTEEN

THE discomfort and length of the coach journey to Newcastle reminded me of the need for better transport. Even the indomitable McPhee eventually ran out of cheerful remarks, and I closed my eyes to attempt to sleep and avoid the gaze of my fellow travellers. When we finally got to the boardroom of North British Railway, shaking off the dust and aching from our confinement, I briefly had a vision of helping to tear the castle down with my bare hands and gratefully welcoming the railway workers with cups of tea. But I tried to suppress such disloyalty to my friends and to the cause of preservation that was normally close to my heart.

Mr Edward Thornton was a large, broad-shouldered man in early middle age, whose serious demeanour, I thought, was perfectly compatible with the ruthlessness necessary in his business. He might easily have been a schoolyard bully a quarter of a century ago. But had he graduated to murder?

The business of signing the contract being over, I waited for a lull in the conversation and then said, "Did you get a chance to see around Hawksbridge, Mr Thornton? Perhaps you stayed for the weekend after your meeting with Mr McPhee."

"Alas, no," said Mr Thornton. "I missed the chance this time. But I have family in Rothbury, and took a coach there on Friday afternoon. Luckily, I just avoided the snowfall on the way over."

I sipped the sherry he had provided, disappointed that, if verified, this information ruled him out as a suspect. "If I may ask," I said, "assuming your line will land on the grounds of Hawksbridge Castle, what do you intend to do with the remains?"

Mr Thornton gave me a rather patronising smile and replied, "Naturally, Mr Rufford, that is confidential at present. I'm sure you will understand. We have no public position on the exact location of the line."

He paused, and twirled a pencil in his hand. I did not respond, in the hopes that the silence would prompt Mr Thornton to comment further.

"However," he continued – whether goaded by me or according to his own will, I could not tell – "were we to take the route of which you speak, then we would of course pay for some kind of memorial for your castle."

"You mean, a plaque?" I said.

"Yes, yes," he said, waving his hands, "something of that nature. We are not entirely oblivious to our obligations where we must... make changes."

My temper got the better of me. "A plaque?" I said. "You're proposing to replace a much-loved historical monument with a damned plaque?"

Mr McPhee put his hand on my arm as if to calm me, and Mr Thornton appeared amused.

"Goodness, Mr Rufford!" he said, leaning back in his chair. "What passion! It is to be commended. We must all fight for the things we love. But sometimes, one comes to a fork in the road, and one needs courage and wisdom to take the best path. The path that may not be the most comfortable at the time, but the best for the future. Everyone's future."

He straightened himself again and fixed me with unblinking eyes.

"But I must stress, Mr Rufford," he continued, "that the details of the route are by no means fixed. The new owner of the land you mention is asking a sum that is tantamount to extortion. We are considering all options, so you may wish to delay your animosity."

"My colleague is tired after our trying journey," said Mr

McPhee. "He meant no disrespect." He turned to me. "I'm sure you will eventually appreciate the benefits of the railway – especially after that bumpy ride, eh, Mr Rufford?"

I was in no mood to apologise, and I was annoyed by McPhee's capitulation. "I only ask," I said, "that if it comes to it, you consider whether at least some of the remains of the castle may be preserved. Perhaps they can be incorporated into your plans."

Mr Thornton glanced at McPhee and smiled as though I were to be pitied in my hopeless naivety.

"Well," he said, tidying some papers in a gesture that signalled the end of the meeting, "we will see what can be done. But I fear this may well be one of those cases where the old and the new collide, and only one is triumphant. It is regrettable. It was good to see you again, Mr McPhee, and delightful to meet you, Mr Rufford. I hope to enjoy similarly robust conversations with you in future!"

We spent the night in Newcastle, and it was an even less comfortable journey back to Hawksbridge knowing that I had nearly sabotaged the Pottery's business relationship with North British Railway. But Mr McPhee was good enough not to mention it.

As the coach rumbled northwards, I considered Mr Thornton. He was a brash, smug man and I instinctively distrusted him, just as I had Mr Wakeley. If he had left for Rothbury on Friday afternoon, he could not have been personally responsible for Mr Ambrose's death. There was nothing to rule out an assassin acting on his orders, but it was an elaborate, dangerous strategy for such a large company to pursue, and that made it unlikely. And they would still need to negotiate with the new owners, Francesca and Mr Wakeley, who, it seemed, were intent on making a killing from the investment.

On my return, I found a letter waiting for me: I had been accepted into the welcoming bosom of The Vesuvius

Gentlemen's Club. It seemed that my recent contribution to the cause of Hawksbridge justice had not gone unnoticed, and the lure of my supposed distinction and wealth had overcome any doubts about my sincerity as a client. Perhaps they entertained persons of note as insurance against interference from the police. Whatever the case, my strange course was set for temptations of the flesh in the pursuit of life-saving knowledge.

~

On Saturday morning, I was in my closet reading through Ambrose's letters in the hope of squeezing a few drops of insight from them, when Shipley came to inform me that Francesca had called. Female company seemed very desirable to me after the last two days, so despite my annoyance with Francesca, I hurried down the stairs.

I found her in the drawing room, in conversation with Victoria.

"My dear Thomas!" Francesca said. "Why have you kept such an interesting person as Miss Clitheroe to yourself?"

"I've been something of a recluse," Victoria said. "Mr Rufford is not to blame, Mrs Campbell."

"You must come to my house for tea," said Francesca. "No – dinner."

"Thank you. Perhaps I might meet Mr Wakeley?" said Victoria. "I heard that he's a useful man to know. I have a little money to invest."

"Oh, yes, of course! It shall be arranged," said Francesca. "We will have the most amusing party, and we shall become great friends."

"I would like that," Victoria said, accepting Francesca's extravagant embrace.

"No monkeys?" I said.

"Positively no monkeys," said Francesca. Seeing Victoria's puzzled face, she added, "I will let Thomas explain in due course." I nodded, regretting bringing it up and wondering how I would delicately describe the incident.

"I must go," said Victoria. "I have a plot idea buzzing around my head, and if I don't write it down soon, I fear it will quite buzz away. It was lovely to meet you, Mrs Campbell!"

When Victoria had left the room, Francesca sat down with a sigh at the table in the window, and I joined her. She appeared to be worn out with the effort of being cheerful, and on the verge of tears.

"What's wrong?" I said.

She smiled and laid a hand over mine. "My judgement, mostly," she said. "I should have listened to you."

"I hope you won't do anything so alarming!" I said. "What's happened?"

Francesca looked out at the hills, covered in a picturesque layer of frost. "People are starting to look at me unkindly. I went to the bookshop yesterday, and Mr Hunter was decidedly cold."

"I'm sorry to hear it," I said. "It couldn't be your imagination?"

"No," she said. "I might as well have murdered the Mayor. I wish I'd never agreed to buy that ruin. Now everyone hates me, and I only have myself to blame."

She blew her nose, and I squeezed her hand. "Not everyone," I said, and she smiled at me, before unsuccessfully trying to suppress a sob.

"At this rate, they will remove my angel from the Town Hall," she said. "And I was so proud of it."

"After all the trouble we all had over it, I'm sure they won't do that," I said. "I will stand guard day and night if necessary."

"How gallant," she said. "But perhaps it would be best if

it were gone."

"Anyway," I said, "once the railway is finished, everyone will be so grateful for it, they'll probably want to build a statue of you!"

She laughed. "A statue of you might be more to the point. You and your trusty dog – perhaps you should be on Celeste. Yes, that would be a handsome thing."

"How embarrassing that would be," I said. "Anyway – I'm sure everyone will have forgotten all this in a few months. Are you close to selling the land?"

"Reginald is being a bit obstinate. He wants a high price, and the railway company doesn't like it. So – I don't know. There seems to be something of an impasse. I wish I had never agreed to this plan – I suppose I was carried away by Reginald's annoyingly persuasive patter."

"And perhaps by his masculine charms?"

"Perhaps a little," she said.

"Can you persuade Reginald to lower the price? Then this can be settled, and you can stop worrying about it."

"As I say, he's very stubborn. I've tried – he just says there's no point in being half-hearted in business, and that the company are just testing us. That they'll pay up eventually, as they have little choice."

"He's quite ruthless, isn't he?" I said. "I wouldn't want to be on the other side of the table from him in business."

"True," she said. "That's partly what I liked about him, to begin with. The sense of his strength and determination. Now I'm beginning to wonder if he has too much of those qualities, and insufficient softer traits! He can be very self-absorbed."

"May I ask something rather delicate?" I said.

"Oh dear," she said. "Well, if you must."

"Has he... tried to seduce you?"

She shifted in her seat and smoothed her cuffs. "I might have allowed a brief flirtation after some drinks. But I am keeping my distance now. I have told him that this is strictly a business arrangement."

"Good," I said. I decided not to press her about what happened between them on the night of Mr Ambrose's murder. She was suffering enough. "Best not to get too entangled, I think."

She nodded, and pressed her hand to her head. "Oh, bother," she said. "I have worried myself into a bad head."

I knew my healing talents would be needed once more. "Shall I?" I said.

"Oh, would you? That would be so kind."

"I haven't shown you my closet," I said, getting up.

"Closet? Are you going to shove me in a cupboard?"

"My little study upstairs," I said. "Where I sit and dream, sometimes."

"How delightful," she said, standing up, still holding her hand to her head. "Lead on."

When we got to my room, I sat her in the chair at my desk. I realised that in my haste to go downstairs, I had left Mr Ambrose's documents spread on the desk. I did not want to draw attention to them so I left them as they were, and anyway, Francesca had closed her eyes.

"You are lucky," she said. "This is a fine little hideaway." I began to massage her head, and she added, "And I am so lucky to have such a healer! I can feel the pain ebbing away already."

I did seem to have a modest talent in this area. By observation of her reactions, I had learned the parts of her skull, and the pressure and direction of stroke, that had the most effect. I had even established that she appreciated a gentle tugging of her hair. No doubt all this was codified in books – I could especially imagine the old Chinese and Indian wisdom on the subject – but I enjoyed finding it out for myself, guided by Francesca's murmurs and changes in her breathing. It was almost like playing a musical instrument – or how I supposed it to be, since I was a musical dunce.

"I saw some monkeys at the Zoological Gardens in London once," she said, her eyes still closed. "They were grooming each other. It was very sweet. Just like little people, comforting one another. As you are doing."

"Ah, is that what I'm doing?" I said. "Well, it is very soothing, I must say."

"Wouldn't it be interesting if this is what friends did, as a matter of course? Sitting around stroking one another. It would prevent all sorts of quarrels."

I thought of The Vesuvius. "Hm," I said. "There are certain clubs..."

"Not like that, Thomas," she said. "I know what you mean, and it would all be perfectly innocent."

"But human nature being what it is, or rather, male nature," I said, "it would turn into more than friendliness."

"Yes, and I thank you for your restraint."

"It's my pleasure," I said, thinking that my pleasure would be far better served by abandoning restraint. But that would put me on a moral level below that of London Zoo's gentle monkeys.

We were surprised by a knock on the door. Without waiting for me to answer, Victoria came in, followed by Fox, who at once began sniffing at Francesca's legs. My hands froze on my patient's head, and Victoria looked shocked, but Francesca remained composed and smiled at her.

"Oh, hello!" she said. "Thomas is magicking away my headache. He really is far better than any doctor for it."

"Goodness! How extraordinary," Victoria said, flushing with embarrassment. "I'm sorry to interrupt. I only wanted to say that Fox is imploring me for a walk, and I am badly in need of some fresh air, so I thought I might take him, with your permission?"

"Please do," I said. "He will be grateful."

"Good. Come along, Fox," said Victoria. "Goodbye!"

She closed the door, and Francesca giggled. "Oh dear,"

she said. "We have scandalised an innocent young woman. How like me: I have put you in an awkward position with your guest."

I sighed. "I will have a word with her. Once I explain, I'm sure she'll understand."

"And want some of the treatment for herself, no doubt!" Francesca said. "Poor girl. I wonder if she's ever been touched by a man. You may resume, Thomas."

I obeyed, and said, "No doubt she's saving herself for a better man than I. She's beautiful, clever, and sweet-natured. Quite a catch for someone."

"Interesting," said Francesca, and she lapsed into silence save for a few indications of pleasure.

"Now," she said, after a few minutes, "I think you deserve a reward. You may kiss me."

I hesitated, and then bent down and gave her a peck on the cheek.

"Not like that, you silly boy," she said, and raised her head towards me. "A proper, manly kiss."

Not wishing to disappoint her, I kissed her on the lips, and lingered there, a feeling of euphoria rushing over me. Francesca breathed deeply through her nose and when I finally let her go, she sighed. "That was very nice. Top marks."

"Thank you," I said, reeling slightly.

"You've been practising, haven't you?" Francesca said. "On the lovely Victoria, perhaps?"

"Francesca!" I protested. "Most certainly not. If you think she's here as some sort of..."

"Kept woman?" Francesca said. "No, of course not. I'm just teasing you. But as you say, she is very pretty, isn't she? With such beautiful lips, made for kissing!"

"Perhaps, but I have no intention of finding out."

"Phyllis, then?" Francesca said. "I can't bear to see you wasted, Thomas. It's your duty as a warm-blooded young man to pair up and make a woman ecstatically happy."

"Then it may interest you to know, Francesca, that I have kissed Miss Drummond, and she kissed me back, with some enthusiasm."

"There!" said Francesca. "You will be married before Easter. But, oh dear – I don't know if she will let you treat my wretched old head!"

"I might be able to persuade her, so long as I forgo my reward."

"What a shame," said Francesca. "Or maybe I could just kiss both of you, to be strictly fair."

"You are back to your normal self, I think," I said.

"Goodness, so I am!" said Francesca. "My headache has quite disappeared. How good for me you are."

She turned back to the desk. "Oh, what's this? How intriguing," she said, taking up the letter I had left so carelessly on the desk. "A letter in a woman's hand. From Phyllis?"

Before I could stop her, she was scanning the letter.

"Who is 'Y'? Oh!" she said. "How very immodest! 'Kiss me where I love to be kissed!' Well, well. I wonder where that might be."

"Edinburgh, probably," I said, plucking the letter from her hand. "It's a letter to Mr Ambrose, from his mistress. It may seem prurient, but I'm trying to find some clue as to who his real killer was. I refuse to believe it was Mrs Ambrose."

"So you are back in harness, Inspector Rufford," Francesca said, standing up. "I wish you luck. I've never met Mrs Ambrose, but I agree it seems unlikely to have been her. Edinburgh, indeed," she added, tutting.

"Now, I must go," she went on, getting up from the desk. She reached out and smoothed my hair where she had ruffled it during our kiss. "There, you look innocent as a lamb again."

We went downstairs and I ordered her horse to be brought round. When she was mounted up, she saluted me, whip in hand and said, "Good bye, my dear. I feel much better now. I shall go and devise a dinner for us all: you, Phyllis, Miss

Clitheroe and of course, Reginald. He can give Miss Clitheroe some advice in return for his duck and Burgundy."

"I will be on my best behaviour," I said.

"Second-best will do," she said with a smile, and rode off.

CHAPTER EIGHTEEN

PHYLLIS, Victoria, Fox and I started to climb Cocklaw Hill with our rugs and baskets of supplies, assisted by old Howard's nephew, Roger. We left Howard in the Kington's ancient landau, which had been unearthed from a barn, dusted down, and mated to a pair of borrowed horses.

A beautiful, crisp Sunday was not to be wasted on mere religious observance. Felicity had been excited to be invited as an honorary adult, and she went racing up the hill like a greyhound after a hare, with Fox at her heels.

We could see the stones in the distance, so carefully placed on their hill-top for a purpose now lost to humanity, defiant against the immensity of time and resistant to the fury of countless storms. It sent a chill down my spine.

Victoria stopped to catch her breath and take in the scene.

"So beautiful," she panted. "And so mysterious. Strange to think that these stones will still be standing when we are all gone, and perhaps our great-great-great-grandchildren will still be coming here, and thinking exactly the same thing!"

"Yes," said Phyllis, "it's at once comforting and terrifying."

Felicity had wandered back down the hill to us. "Do you think anyone will ever find out what the stones were for?" she said.

"I hope not," said Victoria. "Aren't they more powerful for being unfathomable? We can all use our imaginations."

"Perhaps," I offered, "they are meant to convey a message to us, the inhabitants of their distant future, if only we could decode it."

"Or it's a practical joke," said Phyllis, "merely to confound people over thousands of years."

"Oh, I hope not," said Felicity. "Although, it would be a kind of communication, from them to us. So that would still be extraordinary."

We carried on, and the stones loomed ever larger and stranger. When we were finally at the summit, weaving in and out of the circle, trying to comprehend the incomprehensible, I felt an awe and respect for these odd creatures. As Phyllis had described, erosion had given them tooth-like shapes and textures; they appeared neither natural nor man-made, as though God, in a fit of absent-mindedness, had placed on Earth something meant for another of His planets. Stranded here, they silently brooded over our landscape like monstrous shipwrecked souls.

"Wouldn't it be frightening," said Felicity, "if we turned our backs on them, and when we turned around, they had moved? Oh – now I can't look away! It's too horrible."

"That would make a good little story," said Phyllis. "You should write it."

"I just might!" said Felicity. "May we eat, please? I'm starving!"

Rugs were laid out inside the circle, and we devoured the feast Mrs Felton's had provided for us – the cold had given us all an appetite. Young Roger leant against one of the stones at a discreet distance. Fox had calmed down, and Felicity fed him pieces of chicken.

"We could be in a giant fossil mouth," she remarked. "A bit like Jonah in the whale."

"Only, we're in the Devil's mouth," I said, "not in that of a friendly whale."

Felicity shivered. "Don't," she said. "I want them to be friendly."

"Sorry," I said. "What other legends are there? Surely they have inspired some strange tales?"

"There was one about pagan rituals," said Phyllis. "Before the stones appeared, worshippers of Satan – perhaps witches – would dance around, and sacrifice babies, and do other unspeakable things."

"Ugh," said Felicity.

"Until," Phyllis continued, "there was a great flash of lightning, and the devil-worshippers were turned to stone."

"Hm," said Felicity. "They don't look much like people to me."

"Another story says," said Phyllis, "that if you move any of the stones, you will die a terrible death. Perhaps that's why they're still standing."

Roger stopped leaning on his stone, turning back to look at it with an expression of alarm before sitting down a couple of feet away.

Phyllis noticed this and smiled. "I gather some people still think the circle has the power of granting fertility. But the less said about that, the better!"

"Quite," said Victoria, and Felicity made a face. "Let us drink a toast to whoever or whatever made this wonder! Anyone else?"

We all raised our glasses, and then Felicity ran off with Fox to explore the other side of the hill. Roger had wandered some way down the hill to stretch his legs, and Victoria went to find cover to answer a call of nature.

Phyllis and I were left alone in the circle, I lying propped up on one arm, and she sitting cross-legged. We stared out across the landscape in silence for a while, listening to the birds, and to Felicity singing to herself.

"This was a good idea," I said, moving closer to Phyllis. "We should do it more often."

"Yes, but in warmer weather," said Phyllis.

"And just the two of us," I said.

She looked at me searchingly. After a pause, she said, "That would be nice. You have hair in your eyes," she added, and gently pushed away the loose lock. Then she looked around her, bent down and kissed me: not for long, but for just long enough that a world of pleasant possibilities immediately flooded into my mind.

"Thank you," I said, at a loss for a more profound remark.

"Don't mention it."

"Will you come and dine with me?" I said. "Just you?"

"But what about Victoria?" Phyllis said. "Will you send her supper up on a tray?"

"Ah," I said. "No, that would be unkind. We shall have to find some other way. But I want you all to myself. Is that so unreasonable?"

She smiled, and we lapsed once more into a pleasant silence.

I thought of Victoria's words: "An outing for us to remember!" They implied the poignancy of parting and change. It was hard to reconcile the present, living moment with the shadowy recollection of the past that it would become. If I concentrated hard enough, could I preserve it more vividly? I looked at the roughness of the stones, at the tiny hairs on Phyllis' skin, at Victoria returning with her smile of pleasure at being amongst friends. I tried to imprint upon my memory the repeated melody of the birdsong, intermingled with Felicity's cheerful voice.

I did not want to believe that the scene, perfect as it was, could be snatched away. But soon, of course, "now" would become "just now", then "yesterday", and then – "was it a whole month ago?" and finally "do you remember that time?"

~

We stayed another half-hour, but the cold was becoming

uncomfortable, and the sky threatened rain, so we returned to Ramsburgh and a great fire in the drawing room, where we warmed ourselves and drank chocolate.

"Thank you for indulging my silly whim!" said Victoria. "But it was fun."

"I would have drawn the stones," said Felicity, "but it was too cold. I shall go back in the spring. Will you still be here, Miss Clitheroe? I do hope so."

"I hope so too," said Victoria. "But I don't know. My family will be missing me. At least I hope so."

"You could come back, though, couldn't you? To visit?"

"Of course I could – and I will!" Victoria said. But to me, she didn't sound altogether convinced, and she seemed to be struggling to maintain her usual cheerful demeanour.

"Mama will be back home," Felicity said. "Oh, poor Mama, how she would have enjoyed our picnic – it seems almost wicked to enjoy anything when she's all alone in that terrible cell. When do you think she can come back home, Mr Rufford?"

"She will have to be brought before the magistrates soon," I said, "and then with luck, they will grant her bail."

"What's bail?" Felicity said.

"It means they will let her go home before the trial."

"And you will find something to make them let her go?"

"I will do my best, yes," I said.

"Thomas is brilliant at this sort of thing," said Phyllis. "So don't worry."

I sincerely hoped that I would be able to live up to this expectation.

~

Phyllis took Felicity back to her temporary home, and Mrs

Felton brought tea for Victoria and me. Neither of us were much inclined to hurry on our separate ways, when the fire was warm and the company pleasant.

"It's strange," I said, "that we shall never solve the mystery of those stones. They are so... deliberate and impossible to ignore that they seem to be taunting us."

"But there are so many mysteries in life," said Victoria. "For example, you and Mrs Campbell!"

I had been mesmerised by the ever-changing flames, and I glanced up at her. She was smiling in a manner that suggested she had got over her shock since yesterday, and was now ready to tease me.

"Ah," I said. "I had been meaning to talk to you about that. It must have looked rather incriminating –"

"Terribly," she said. "But I am just a guest, so it really shouldn't concern me!"

"And yet it does, and perhaps should," I said, "because you expect me to have certain standards of behaviour. Well, you are quite right. But Mrs Campbell has no expectations of me, nor me of her, beyond a warm friendship. She has a rare frankness and a way of quickly getting to the point. And so, somehow, I have ended up being her headache-doctor."

"It must be nice to be able to banish pain like that," she said. "And to have it banished in such an agreeable way."

"Physical pleasure is not all immoral," I said. "Sometimes it seems to exist simply to guide behaviour – and in this case, the end result is a lessening of pain. How can that be bad?"

"Oh, I agree," Victoria said. "But how hard it must be not to stray over that moral line. Especially for a man. Women are better able to control themselves."

"And I thought women were supposed to be the weaker sex!" I said. "But when I look at Francesca, whether taking possession of a room or vaulting onto her horse, I can't believe that."

"Well, it all depends on the individual," said Victoria,

draining her cup. "Do you think I'm a strong woman, Thomas?"

I thought for a moment. "Yes," I said. "From what I have seen – for example, with Felicity – I think you have great resourcefulness in a crisis. And you have had to bear tragedy, and you have torn yourself from your comfortable home to come to a small town far away, all on your own, to improve yourself and make friends with perfect strangers. A weak woman would not have done that."

"Thank you. And yet sometimes I do feel quite weak and lost. My feelings, and my past, weigh heavily on me."

"But that does you credit," I said, "and besides, some vulnerability can be attractive. Who likes a perfectly confident know-it-all?"

"By that measure," Victoria said, "I should be a sore temptation to all men."

"I would not disagree with that assessment," I said.

"You are too kind," she replied. "I was going to ask you something. What was it? Oh, yes. You never told me what Mrs Campbell meant about monkeys!"

"Ah," I said. "This is quite awkward to explain. Francesca held a dinner party in which she invited a couple and their monkey. The monkey misbehaved."

"In what way?"

I fidgeted with my teacup. "It... indulged itself in a most disgusting way, and one of Francesca's female guests was in the line of fire."

"Oh my Lord!" Victoria said, laughing. "How awful. I didn't know monkeys did that."

"Yes – yes, they do. They are like humans in so many ways."

"Speak for yourself," said Victoria.

I looked away. "This is a strange conversation."

Victoria laughed at my embarrassment. "I'm sure you would never do such a thing."

“Not at the dinner table, no,” I said, and sent Victoria into a further fit of giggles.

“Me neither,” she said, and got up. “How am I going to write sublime literature now, after such gutter talk? Thank you, Thomas. I’m sorry if I embarrassed you, but it was funny.”

And she gently touched my shoulder before leaving the room.

CHAPTER NINETEEN

"BESS, this is excellent," I said as I read over her plans for the coffee shop. She had specified the equipment and number of employees required, and estimated initial costs, running costs, turnover and profits.

"Thank you," she said, smiling broadly. "I remembered a few things from setting up our shop, so many years ago."

"What about a name?" I said.

"I still can't think of one!" she said. "Maybe you can help me."

"If you refill my port," I said, "that will help my brain work."

"That's not usually the case," she said. "It normally just makes you grab things that shouldn't necessarily be grabbed."

"Alas," I said, "my days of grabbing you are over. I shall be very good. And very boring."

"It's for the best," Bess said, and poured the port.

I started to drink, and then said, "But I do miss your beautiful –"

"Lord! What did I tell you? Names, Mr Rufford, if you please – names."

"Sorry. Yes. 'The Hawksbridge Ladies' Coffee Shop'?"

"Too specific – what if I want to expand, like you said?"

"Yes, of course," I said. "How about – 'The Ladies' Coffee Haven'?"

"Hm," she said. "Maybe. Rather long. Next!"

"'The Delilah Coffee House' – because you're cutting men down to size.'"

"I think not."

"'The Belvidera'."

"What on earth is that?" she said.

"It's the name of a famous ship. It has a kind of aristocratic feel, don't you think?"

"It sounds more like a hotel. But I'll write it down. Next?"

"'Myrtle's Coffee Shop for Ladies'. 'Myrtle's' for short. It has a friendly connotation, perhaps?"

"Yes – that's quite nice. I'll put it on the list, even though everyone will wonder who Myrtle is. Well, that will do for now."

"I will try to think of some more," I said. "Have you found suitable premises yet?"

"I might have!" she said. "Mr Jackson is retiring, and his butcher's shop will be available. He says he'll think about letting it, rather than selling it."

"On the High Street – good location," I said.

"Yes, it would be ideal. I'll know what he wants a month shortly. And then there's the delicate matter of..."

"Money," I said. "Of course. Let me know what you need, and by when."

"Thank you!" Bess said. "I have a little too. I have been putting some by from my pension."

"So, the most important thing," I said. "You truly want to do this?"

"Oh, yes, of course!" Bess said. "It will be a dream! Well, I know it'll be hard work, too, but for the first time in so long, I feel in control of something. I have something I can really work at. And that's not to be sniffed at, especially for a woman."

"Indeed," I said. "We must have an opening party."

"Yes! But we've been talking only about me. What have you been up to? No more mischief, I hope?"

"No, I don't think so," I said. "But I did just take three women up a hill – does that count?"

"Gracious! Well, it all depends on what you did with them

when you got there. I take it these were Miss Drummond and Mrs Campbell, and – who else?"

"Actually," I said, "Miss Drummond and Victoria Clitheroe, my house guest. And Felicity Ambrose, but she's only fifteen."

"Worse and worse," Bess said.

"We just went for a picnic. It was at the Devil's Teeth."

"Funny time of year for a picnic," she said. "And the Devil's Teeth, of all places." Bess grimaced.

"You know it?"

"In a manner of speaking. I have never gone there, by choice."

"Too frightening?"

"Not exactly." Bess folded her arms and sighed. "It was something in my childhood. When I was naughty and spoke back to my father – yes, I was a naughty little girl before I was a naughty plump widow – he would grip me hard by both arms and say, 'Bess! You were conceived in the mouth of the Devil, and now the Devil is in your mouth.'"

"Ah – that's a bit strong," I said. "But I have heard about that local myth."

"It was years before a school friend told me what he meant by it. I was mortified."

"I'm sure," I said. "I would imagine your mother was too."

"Horribly, poor woman. To be reminded about it so often! But my father was obviously quite proud of taking my mother up to the stones and being rather wild."

"I suppose," I said, "you don't have to believe in a fertility myth to find it a very romantic and powerful thing to do."

"Perhaps. Assuming it doesn't rain, and you don't lie on an ant's nest. Speaking of uncomfortable liaisons, what news of Mrs Ambrose?"

I poured myself more port from the decanter. "Ah. Well,

in pursuit of Mr Ambrose's mistress, who almost certainly can shed light on his death, it seems I must visit a somewhat sordid gentlemen's club in Edinburgh."

"My!" said Bess, her eyes widening. "Your dedication to these investigations is breathtaking. I take it women are provided at this festival of masculinity?"

"Apparently," I said, "one of them being – I hope – the mistress in question. There may be salacious tableaux, and so forth. It all sounds quite unpleasant."

"What a martyr you are," Bess said. "Well, I will be fascinated to hear the outcome. But I advise distancing yourself from the attractions. You must be careful you are not overtaken by lust. I know what you're like, after all. Perhaps you should nip it in the bud, so to speak, in advance."

"Yes, yes, of course," I said. "I appreciate your advice."

"On your own, I mean."

"I take your meaning perfectly, thank you!" I said a little testily, mindful that discussions of this sort were becoming an unfortunate habit with me. "Can we talk about something else?"

Bess leant back and smiled at me. "The things Thomas Rufford is obliged to do in the name of justice!"

~

Mr Andrew Barrowman, Mrs Ambrose's solicitor, sent word that Mrs Ambrose had been released on bail, with her trial set for the first week in February, so I went to the Harrises to collect Felicity and take her home to her mother.

This was a great relief for me. I now had time in hand for my investigations, and Mrs Ambrose would be comfortable and available for questioning should she remember something pertinent, without the authorities breathing down our necks.

On seeing her mother, Felicity rushed to wrap her arms around her, her tears mixing with her mother's.

"Oh, Felicity!" Mrs Ambrose said when she could finally speak. "It's so good to be home with you again. How I've missed you! Have you brought Pantoufle back?"

"He's coming later," Felicity. "I was in too much of a hurry to see you."

"Do you hear that, Thomas?" Mrs Ambrose said, blowing her nose. "Her old jailbird mother still means more to her than a squirrel!"

I smiled. "Thank goodness they had the sense to bail you," I said.

"They must think me pretty harmless, then, surely?" Mrs Ambrose said.

"Quite," I said. "It may send a message to the jurors, should it ever come to that."

"Do you think it might?" she said.

"I will do everything to ensure it doesn't," I said. "I have something I'm working on to that end."

"Oh, thank you, Thomas! Mr Barrowman will be here shortly, and we can discuss everything. Yorick's funeral is on Wednesday – might you come?"

"Of course," I said, wondering whether the funeral might flush out any further mistresses.

"Good – it will be such a comfort to me."

I left mother and daughter alone, and wandered into the library to contemplate how much I should tell Mr Barrowman, and indeed Mrs Ambrose herself. The solicitor would surely find my methods unconventional, to say the least, and I would have to admit that I got into the safe against Mrs Ambrose's wishes.

After some minutes, my thoughts were interrupted by a cough. It was Mr Barrowman, accompanied by Mrs Ambrose.

"Good afternoon, Mr Rufford!" he said. I had met him once before, and found him inoffensive. He had a deferential, kind manner that put one at one's ease. "Shall we have our discussion in here?"

"Good afternoon, Mr Barrowman," I replied. "Yes, the library will help concentrate our minds."

"Make yourselves comfortable, and I shall get us some tea," said Mrs Ambrose, leaving the room.

Mr Barrowman sat down and pulled a sheaf of papers from his case. "Did you know Mr Ambrose well?" he asked.

"Only slightly," I said. "A cultured man, certainly, but with scant patience. I do wonder if his impetuosity got him into fatal trouble."

"Ah, but if we only knew what schemes he was pursuing, we might crack the case," said Mr Barrowman.

"I'm glad you think there is a case to be cracked," I said, glancing at the door and lowering my voice lest Mrs Ambrose should hear.

"But certainly," he said. "I have known Mrs Ambrose for many years, and I know she could not have done this. So we have no alternative but to find the true perpetrator."

"Do you have any thoughts?" I said.

He sighed. "Unfortunately not," he said, "other than the obvious suspect – Mr Reginald Wakeley. Mrs Ambrose has told me about the land purchase."

"Yes, I thought of him also, and I truly can't stand the man, but he has an alibi. He was with his business partner on the night of the murder – Mrs Campbell is a friend of mine, and she assured me that there was no possibility it was him."

"Ah. A pity," he said. "But I didn't think it very likely."

Mrs Ambrose came in with May who was carrying the tea tray.

"Here we are, gentlemen," she said, settling herself at the large library table. "Thank you both for helping me! I would be lost otherwise."

"It's a pleasure, Isobel," said Mr Barrowman. "I'm only sorry that my assistance is at all necessary." He took a draught of tea. "I thought I would first speak of what the police think they know, before reviewing our own understanding of the situation."

"Please do," said Mrs Ambrose.

"Firstly, your presence outside the house early in the morning and discovery of your husband. This, of course, is of little value as evidence. Your presence in front of your own home is hardly extraordinary, although the prosecution may argue that an early morning walk in the snow is unusual."

"As I told you, Andrew, I was restless – perhaps I had a strange feeling something was wrong!"

"Quite. Secondly, you might have had access to piano wire due to the recent restoration of an instrument. Again, highly circumstantial, and there is nothing to say you ever had any in your possession. Thirdly, the gossip from your servants about remarks you made concerning your husband. Tittle-tattle that any servant might hear in their household: another foolish thing for the police to give any weight to."

"Anything else?" I said.

"I think not," he said. "Separately, these pieces of information are laughably insubstantial. But together, a jury might – just – be persuaded, in the absence of any other suspect, that they add up to something. Our best defence will be to offer an alternative explanation, although even without that, we can and will argue very strongly that the evidence is nonsense."

"If the police had done their job properly," I said, "we wouldn't have to do this at all!"

"Indeed," said Mr Barrowman, "but alas, they haven't, and we do. Mrs Ambrose is fortunate, though, to have such a friend as yourself with some experience in this line."

I nodded. I did not feel that my experience necessarily warranted this kind of trust, but I did not want to diminish Mrs Ambrose's hope, so I accepted the compliment.

"Now," Mr Barrowman said, looking at his notes, "what

we know. The police think Mr Ambrose died some time between four and six o'clock on the Saturday morning. Perhaps he didn't feel comfortable wherever he was staying, or he had pressing business to attend to."

"It strikes me," I said, "that the culprit must have known something of Mr Ambrose's movements. At least that he was due to return late at night, or early in the morning, before anyone else came or went. Isobel, was he in the habit of travelling early in the morning?"

"Yes," said Mrs Ambrose. "He was a light sleeper, and tended to be up before most other people. He would often rise early to ride – not much fun for our poor groom! So it was quite in keeping."

"Interesting," said Mr Barrowman. "So knowledge of this would make it much less likely that his trap would ensnare anyone but him – assuming Mr Ambrose planned to return on the Saturday."

"How thoughtful of the murderer," said Mrs Ambrose.

"The question is," I said, "who might know these details?"

"Members of this household, naturally," said Mr Barrowman. "Is your groom reliable, Mrs Ambrose?"

"Goodness! Yes, he is a loyal man, and has no reason to kill his employer. In fact, Yorick was so pleased with the way he cared for his horse when it cut its leg that he gave him a pay rise a couple of months ago. And that's a rare thing indeed!"

"I see. And no other members of your staff have any motivation, that you know of?"

"Absolutely not."

"Despite reporting your remarks to the police?"

"I regard that as my fault, Mr Barrowman, for joking in poor taste."

"Do you think, Isobel," I said, "that Yorick might have told his friends and acquaintances about his riding habits?"

"Unlikely," said Mrs Ambrose. "I don't think it was an

eccentricity that he would have boasted about. He saw his insomnia as an ailment – a weakness. And of course sharing such information can make one vulnerable, if that was something that occurred to him."

"The culprit knew that he was away," I said, "and would be returning quite soon. So – someone who knew he was at that meeting."

"Someone present at the meeting?" said Mr Barrowman.

"Quite possibly," I said, "although Mr Fountain was adamant that none of them had the motivation. And then there's the inn staff, and anyone who saw him in town."

"Did he stay in the inn where the meeting was held?" Mr Barrowman asked.

"Unlikely!" said Mrs Ambrose. "I suspect him of having had a convenient berth in Hawksbridge. A woman."

"Oh dear," said Mr Barrowman. "I'm sorry. Do we know who she is?"

"No," said Mrs Ambrose. "I don't know, and I don't want to know. But he often disappeared for the night, and when he came back – well, a woman can tell."

I wondered whether this could be Ophelia. But it was unlikely that she would have been transplanted from Edinburgh – in her letters, she complained about not seeing Mr Ambrose for long periods. So this was likely to be another mistress.

"Well, we shall have to see if we can find out who this was," said Mr Barrowman. "She may be the last person to see your husband alive. It's unfortunate she didn't see fit to present herself to the police. Or perhaps she already has?"

"I would imagine Isobel would have been questioned about it if that were the case," I said.

"Probably," said Mr Barrowman. "Well, I shall make discreet enquiries of the police."

"If you must," said Mrs Ambrose.

"Meanwhile," I said. "I have two names that may be of

interest. One is Mr Oswald Redpath, a rather aggressive builder who clashed with Mr Ambrose at a previous meeting of the Antiquarian Society."

"I know someone who has represented him in the past," said Mr Barrowman. "A nasty piece of work. Was this clash of significance?"

"Not really," I said. "It was mostly about wounded pride when Mr Redpath exposed Mr Ambrose's plan to buy the castle land. I can't see how it could have become a fatal vendetta so quickly."

"I see. And the other name?"

"Mr Peter Blackwood, an antique dealer that Mr Ambrose frequently used. I heard him argue with Mr Ambrose in Mr Blackwood's shop. Again, it didn't seem especially serious."

"Interesting," said Mr Barrowman. "Isobel, what do you know of this man? Did you meet him?"

"I have met him, yes," said Mrs Ambrose, frowning. "I didn't care for him. But I had to be polite, as Yorick was a client of his."

"I have seen some of the invoices," I said. "Mr Ambrose spent an extraordinary amount in his shop." I gestured towards the furniture and pictures in the library. "I would imagine most of this was from Mr Blackwood. And many of the fine paintings."

"Thomas," said Mrs Ambrose, fiddling with her teacup, "I know you're trying to help, but I don't feel entirely happy with you going through Yorick's papers like this."

Mr Barrowman came to my rescue. "I'm sure, Isobel, that you know how important it is that we have all the information we can possibly glean. It's a serious situation. And Mr Rufford will no doubt be the very soul of discretion."

"Of course," I said. "The only unusual thing about those invoices, apart from the sheer quantity, was the substantial special discounts that Mr Ambrose managed to get. It was impressive."

Mrs Ambrose shrugged. "He spent a lot there, so it was in Mr Blackwood's interest to encourage him."

"Like a gambler occasionally letting their mark win, perhaps," said Mr Barrowman.

"Yes, perhaps," said Mrs Ambrose. "It was almost an addiction with him."

"So why would Mr Blackwood want to kill one of his best clients?" said Mr Barrowman.

"No reason I can think of," said Mrs Ambrose.

I shook my head. "I'm still not happy about those discounts. Were they colluding in something?"

Mrs Ambrose stood up. "Excuse me, gentlemen. I will be back shortly."

When she had left, I looked at Mr Barrowman. "Is she avoiding the topic, do you think?" I whispered.

He looked bemused by my question. "I don't see why," he said. "A discount seems neither uncommon, nor particularly significant."

"Probably not," I said. "Still, it intrigues me. And there's one more fact – or rather, rumour – that is bothering me."

"Yes?"

"A maid called Susan Lipton committed suicide shortly after leaving the Ambroses' employment several years ago. According to rumour, she killed herself after being dishonoured by Mr Ambrose. Of course, I have heard nothing to substantiate this. But isn't it remotely possible that someone close to her has taken vengeance?"

Mr Barrowman sighed. "Yes, yes, I suppose so. I recall the name now. So now we need to interview friends and relatives of this poor girl? At this rate, the whole population of the town will be suspects."

"Well, I have a line of investigation from Mr Ambrose's papers that I need to follow, and I will be out of town for a few days. Might you be able to follow up Susan Lipton?"

"Yes, of course. Can I ask the nature of your

investigation?"

"I'm trying to find one of Mr Ambrose's correspondents, who wrote about a letter that Mr Ambrose asked her to forge."

"Really? A letter to whom?"

"That is the crucial question. I fear it may be embarrassing to Mrs Ambrose, so I'd rather not elaborate further just now, but I will keep you informed if I find anything."

In truth, my mission was potentially just as embarrassing to me; I could hardly tell this decent, bespectacled, professional man that I was about to visit a notorious institution to find a woman of loose morals.

CHAPTER TWENTY

SINCE the matter of the discounted antiques was bothering me, I decided to go on a shopping trip the next morning.

Mr Blackwood was alerted by the jingle of the shop bell, and came into the showroom from his office.

"Good morning, Mr Rufford!" he said. "Good to see you again. Such a terrible tragedy about Mr Ambrose. To think he was here, fit and well, only a few days before!"

"Good morning! Yes, it's very hard for his family."

"It must be," he said. "Have you come for anything special, or shall I just let you alone?"

"I'm just in for a browse. But I might pick up something small if I see a suitable piece. To cheer up an invalid."

"Ah! Let me have a think what I've got that might do. Some good pieces of Staffordshire pottery. I've a beautiful Anthony and Cleopatra pair. Quite pricey, though."

He gestured at a couple of little statues: colourful if mournful representations of the reclining lovers. Cleopatra was holding an asp to her bosom, where it had apparently latched onto her left nipple, while Anthony looked into the distance as if in a tragic reverie. I could not help thinking that he was ignoring the opportunity to save his lover, if he just snapped out of his daydream.

"Beautiful," I said, "but I think something more modest is in order. That is, in price as well as dress."

"How about this?" he said, pointing to a statue of a woman clasping an urn that looked like a giant egg.

"Also a tragic theme," he said. "That's an urn containing Hector's ashes, with his wife Andromache unable to let go."

The woman wore a long floral robe and a sad expression.

I was touched by the way one arm curled protectively around the urn, her head tilted against it.

"I can let you have it for half a guinea. As you can see, she has a toe missing, and her nose has had a small repair."

"She is rather charming," I said. "I'll take her."

"Very good, sir," he said. "I'll wrap her up for you."

As he was doing so, I said, "I gather he was a good customer of yours. Mr Ambrose, I mean."

"Oh – yes, sir, he was. Practically furnished his home from my shop."

"I've seen his house," I said, "and I must say I was astonished by his collection."

"Well, I don't sell rubbish, that's for sure!" Mr Blackwood said.

"I would imagine that a good customer such as Mr Ambrose would get a discount from time to time."

Mr Blackwood stopped wrapping Andromache and looked up at me suspiciously.

"He might," he said. "What are you driving at, sir?"

"Oh, nothing, really. I was just wondering what kind of discount such a customer might get."

Mr Blackwood resumed his task. "Mr Ambrose was a special case. I don't think I've had any client like him. So I couldn't really say, sir. It all depends."

"Say, a fifty-per-cent discount on a very large, expensive piece?"

He frowned. "That would be a big loss for me. I wouldn't do that lightly. That is, for the right person, I would consider it, of course."

He appeared mildly flustered. His correction suggested that he was keen to avoid implying that such a discount was especially noteworthy. He may have been starting to guess that I had seen the relevant invoices.

"There you are, sir. Half a guinea."

As I paid him, I detected a distinct chill between us, but I pretended to be unaware.

"Thank you, Mr Blackwood!" I said. "I'm pleased with Mrs Hector."

He nodded, unsmiling, and I could feel his gaze as I left. I sensed I had touched a nerve.

~

I was enjoying a cup of coffee in the sitting room when I noticed some movement at the door. Victoria was standing there, leaning against the doorway observing me with a smile.

"Hello! Are you spying on me?" I asked.

"Perhaps," she said, still standing at the doorway, her head tilted. She must have known that she looked stunning – her hair had been carefully put up, and she wore a red dress that showed her figure off to full advantage. "You are amusing to watch."

"I'm not sure why," I said. "Are you going to a party? You look –"

"Yes?"

"Fetching."

"Thank you," she said, coming into the room and sitting down opposite me. "I just wanted not to look a complete frump today. It sometimes helps me write. What is that mysterious parcel?"

"Ah – the ashes of Hector. A small statue I bought to try to cheer Flora up."

"With ashes? What a strange, considerate man you are. How is the invalid?"

"Improving, I believe, but very slowly. Would you like some coffee? I can ring for another cup."

"No need," she said. "I would just like a little." She leaned forward and took my cup from its saucer, taking a dainty sip from the unused side. "I hope you don't mind," she said. "I am perfectly healthy."

I was somewhat surprised, but also flattered by her cordiality.

"Have as much as you want," I said. "There's still some left in the pot."

"Thank you," she said, refilling the cup and taking another sip.

"How is the novel?" I asked.

"Oh... I am making slow progress. I rewrote a scene so many times this morning that it gave me a headache." She pressed her temples with her fingers.

"Oh dear," I said. "Bad luck. Perhaps the coffee will help."

"Possibly," she said, still pressing her head and frowning.

"Is it bad?" I said.

"A bit." She looked up at me. "Thomas?"

"Yes?"

"I don't wish to be a burden, but..." She hesitated. "Perhaps a little of Mrs Campbell's medicine...?"

"Well – yes, if you wish," I said, unsure whether I should agree to such a request. I did not have a doctor's credentials to excuse the intimacy of this treatment, especially for a second patient.

"Oh, thank you – that would be so helpful. Shall we meet in my room in ten minutes?"

"Yes," I said. "If you don't mind –"

"What people might say? No one could grudge me a cure for my headache, I'm sure. And you are the most trustworthy man I know."

"In that case," I said, "I'll see you shortly."

~

I finished the pot of coffee, and my knock on Victoria's door was greeted with a "Come in, Thomas!" and I entered, with some trepidation.

She was ready for me, sitting in a chair, her hair now down and flowing over her shoulders.

"I thought it would be easier if I let my hair loose," she said, as if it were perfectly normal to receive male visitors in this manner.

"Yes, that will help," I said, transfixed for a moment by her beauty. "I'll begin, shall I?" I said, going to stand behind her. "Please let me know if it hurts."

"I'm sure it won't," she said, closing her eyes. "I know you'll be very gentle."

With a feeling of wickedness, I touched her hair, trying to suppress the pleasure I got from it, and began to apply pressure to her head.

"Oh!" she said, and I saw her shoulders slump. "Now I see why Mrs Campbell appreciates this. The temples, please – that's it."

I massaged her jaw muscles, and she let out a surprised "Heavens!" as her jaw loosened. "I clench my teeth without realising it. That's better."

"Good!" I said, and began to work across the top of her head. This elicited a series of sighs.

"Say when you'd like me to stop," I said.

"I will," she whispered, and I continued, dragging my fingers up the back of her head, her hair running through my fingers. "Lord," she said, bending her head forward to indicate that more of this was required.

Then, holding up handfuls of her hair, my self-control finally deserted me, and I kissed the back of her neck. She breathed more heavily, and I kissed her neck again. But then I thought of Phyllis' hurt face, and I desisted, letting go of Victoria's locks.

"I'm sorry," I said.

Victoria quickly stood up, and I braced myself for the slap I so richly deserved, but instead she threw her arms about me. She held me tightly for several seconds, and then pushed me away.

"Now we're even," she said, going to the door to open it. "And don't you dare be sorry."

I bowed and left the room, struggling to understand what had just taken place.

~

"I've brought you something."

I had got past Flora's gatekeeper, Mrs Northcutt, and was sitting by Flora's bed with my parcel. Flora put down her book.

"Most intriguing!" she said, taking the parcel and starting to unwrap it. "Thank you."

"How are you feeling?"

"Slightly better," she said. "I managed a walk in the garden yesterday."

"Good," I said, taking a seat. "Your colour is improving. You'll be glad to know that Mrs Ambrose has been bailed until February, and is now at home with Felicity."

"Oh! That is such a relief," Flora said. "Thank goodness, even if it's a small mercy." She removed the final layer of brown paper, and held up the statue. "Extraordinary," she said. "What's that egg thing she's holding? Oh! It's an urn."

"Yes, it contains Hector's ashes, and she's Andromache, Hector's wife. Sorry – it's a trifle morbid, isn't it? But I thought she was quite sweet."

"Yes, and I like her dress. What an unusual present. Wherever did you find it?"

"I have a confession to make – I bought it partly so that I

could ask some questions of Mr Blackwood, Mr Ambrose's favourite antique dealer."

"Really? You suspect him of Yorick's murder?"

"I'm not sure. The two of them had a slightly odd relationship – for all the business they did together, they were peevish with one another when I heard them in the shop. And Mr Blackwood previously gave him very large discounts."

"Is that unusual?" Flora said. "If he was such a good customer?"

"Perhaps not," I said. "But we're speaking of a large amount of money. Of course, I don't know what Blackwood's profit margins are. Perhaps they comfortably accommodated his generosity."

"Did you glean anything?"

"Not really, but he didn't much like my questions."

"Oh. So you're no closer to exonerating Isobel?" She sounded disappointed.

"I have something I'm going to chase up at the weekend," I said. "And Isobel's solicitor is going to look into the maid whose suicide you told me about."

"Good," Isobel said. "Could you put her on my chest of drawers for me?" She handed over Andromache, and I carefully placed her next to Flora's walnut mirror. I thought she made an appealing addition to the room's decor, although Mrs Northcutt would doubtless turn her nose up at it and make a caustic remark.

"There was something else I wanted to speak about, now you're feeling stronger," I said.

I did not actually want to speak to her about this at all. It painted my family in an even worse light than before, it would tarnish the memory of her mother and her childhood, and to top it all, it would substitute a terrible reprobate in place of a loving father. Her very sense of herself could be cut loose. For a moment I wondered if I should hold my tongue; but I had talked myself into thinking that she deserved to know the truth.

She turned to me in alarm. "What's happened? You're scaring me. Please tell me."

"Very well," I said. My mouth was dry and I could feel my heart pumping more quickly. "But first, if you knew something about me that changed my perspective on the world, would you tell me, or leave me in blissful ignorance?"

"What kind of question is that?" she said. "It all depends on what that something is. You need to just tell me, Thomas. I'm not such a feeble woman that you have to hide bad news from me."

I cleared my throat. "I have read some letters from your father to your uncle. They were in your uncle's bureau."

"Oh. I don't think you should have done that, Thomas. They were no business of yours."

"Well, perhaps, perhaps not," I said. "It turns out that they do involve me, in a way."

"In what sort of a way?"

"Because they concern my father. My father was a friend of your mother, as well as of the Kingtons."

Flora frowned. "And?"

"Your father wrote to your uncle to tell him of his feelings about this. He didn't like my father at all. I don't blame him."

"And yet my mother persisted in this friendship?" she said. "That would certainly explain why they were always quarrelling."

"Yes, that's true."

I let this sink in for a few moments, so that the final blow would be softer, if infinitesimally. I thought of leaving it at that for now, but knew I had to finish the unpleasant task. But how to phrase it? I decided on a direct route: to reveal the other side of this coin – a strange and delightful truth.

I took her hand, and she looked at me, puzzled. "A few days ago," I said, gently, "you said that if you had a brother, you would like him to be like me."

"Yes – so?"

Tears pricked at my eyes, and I had difficulty getting out the words. "I believe you do have a brother, Flora. And I am not an only child any more!"

Understanding and astonishment began to show on Flora's face.

"I believe we are brother and sister!" I continued, to remove all doubt.

"What? But that's ridiculous! Are you playing a trick on me?"

"The letter from your father confirms the truth of it. I'm sorry. But I'm not sorry that you are my sister."

"I don't believe it," Flora said. "What utter nonsense. Hasn't your family done enough to us, that you have to start making hurtful things up?"

"I'm afraid I'm not –"

"All this investigating business has gone to your head! Now you think you're the guardian of special knowledge, and want to cause a drama. Thomas, I thought better of you."

I expected denial, but it was painful to see, and I hated that she could think so badly of me. I shook my head, and reached into my waistcoat pocket to retrieve the fateful document.

"This is the letter. All I'm doing is interpreting the words on this paper. If I have read it wrong, I'm sorry. Perhaps there is some mistake after all. But you may be the judge."

I handed the letter to Flora, who threw it down on the bed unread.

"You are being too absurd. My mother would not do this, especially not with a man of your father's type."

She put her hands to her face and said, "Oh, I'm sorry. But you know what I mean."

"Yes, perfectly," I said.

"I won't ever believe it," she said, "so you may as well get used to it. I think I would know if you were my brother."

Mrs Northcutt came in to investigate the cause of Flora's raised voice, and saw a tear roll down Flora's cheek. "What's all this? What are you doing to her, Mr Rufford? Leave this instant, you wretch! Miss Flora, what has he done to you?"

Flora sniffed, and said, "Nothing, Meg. Please leave us."

"It doesn't look like nothing to me, Miss Flora! He's upset you something rotten – when he knows you're unwell, too. But you know best. I'll be in the sitting room." And she limped out of the room, giving me a dirty look on the way.

"Will you read it?" I asked, gesturing at the letter.

"I might," she said.

"Perhaps you would like me to be here while –"

"I don't see why. It won't change anything."

"Very well," I said. "But if you want to talk to me..."

"Yes, thank you," she said. "I'm tired now."

I pressed her shoulder lightly in the hopes of comforting her, since my words were clearly incapable of doing so, and left.

I lingered on the stair, a neutral territory between our domains, and after a minute, I heard her disconsolate sobs. Her father's letter had disgorged its bitter cargo of indisputable truth.

CHAPTER TWENTY-ONE

As good as her word, Francesca had arranged for Victoria to meet Mr Wakeley: at a lunch party that included Phyllis and myself, a few days before my journey to Edinburgh. I did not think any amount of financial wisdom was enough to justify spending an afternoon with Mr Wakeley, but Victoria was determined, and at least there would be plenty of people present to keep an eye on Mr Wakeley. Having attended Mr Ambrose's funeral in the morning, at which the lack of mourners sadly reflected the esteem in which he was held, I was ready for the relaxing effects of alcohol.

I drove Victoria in the trap, and avoided any discussion of our strange encounter the day before until we were nearly at Halfpenny House. But then I turned and said, "You must think I'm a brute."

"A brute? Of course not," she said. "I should have known that men find it hard to master themselves. Indeed, I did know that. So it was at least as much my fault as yours."

"That's very generous," I said, "but you were blameless. How is your head?"

"It's quite all right, thank you. Although... I should make a confession. I didn't really – ah, we are here already! How splendid Francesca's house is!"

I did not get to hear the rest of Victoria's confession, as we were soon gathering in the drawing room for a drink before lunch. I greeted Mr Wakeley with as much politeness as I could muster, and then was surprised to see another familiar face.

"Mr Thornton!" I said, extending my hand. "I had not expected to see you here."

"Good afternoon, Mr Rufford," he said with a smile. "I hope we can continue our energetic and frank discussion! I did so enjoy it."

"I invited Mr Thornton so that he and Reginald could work things out in a civilised environment," said Francesca. "How can men fight when there are such lovely females around?"

"I thought that was the point of war," said Victoria, mischievously. "To kill one another over beautiful women."

"Well, I forbid that today," said Francesca. "Victoria, this is my friend and business partner, Reginald Wakeley. Reginald, this is Miss Victoria Clitheroe."

"I'm glad to meet you, Mr Wakeley," said Victoria, shaking his hand. "I heard that you have an uncanny eye for a good investment, and I'm in sore need of advice. My work is not likely to support me for quite some time."

Mr Wakeley had a gleam in his eye. "I would be delighted to assist, Miss Clitheroe. I'm sure I can find a lucrative berth for your wealth. You are very wise – most people rely on established, lacklustre investments, and simply don't have the imagination to find better ways. Which is to the advantage of those who do."

Victoria smiled and said, "I look forward to picking your brains, Mr Wakeley."

I went to sit next to Phyllis on the sofa. I realised that a nagging, empty feeling that had been with me for some days had instantly disappeared: I had missed her company.

"You are looking exceedingly lovely today," I said.

"Thank you, Thomas," Phyllis said. "I'm glad you think so. You are quite acceptable, yourself. So," she added, lowering her voice, "I find myself in a room with three people who are intent on knocking down an ancient monument that I love. I hope I can remain civil."

"You'll manage," I said. "If not, I will put my hand over your mouth."

"I might bite," she said.

"I might not mind," I replied.

~

Francesca did her best to promote the flow of lunch-time conversation.

"Mr Thornton, you or your wife may perhaps have read one of Miss Drummond's novels. She writes as Iona Tavistock, and I have read three already. They are very absorbing."

"Ah!" said Mr Thornton, turning to Phyllis. "Fascinating. I am not familiar with your work, Miss Drummond, but I'm sure my wife is. What a splendid diversion for a woman writing must be."

Phyllis frowned, and I said, "Miss Drummond is something of a national treasure, and this 'diversion' is more lucrative than you might think."

"Although," Phyllis said, "perhaps not as lucrative as wielding the sledgehammer of progress."

Mr Thornton laughed. "Sledgehammer of progress. Very good. I gather you are not a great admirer of the railway?"

"It's not so much that, Mr Thornton, as not wishing to see the unnecessary destruction of historic buildings."

"Well, there's the rub, Miss Drummond. I quite agree about unnecessary destruction. But then there's necessary destruction."

"Thank goodness," said Victoria, "that railways don't like to run up and down hills. So our Devil's Teeth are safe for now."

"Devil's Teeth?" said Mr Thornton.

I admired Victoria for trying to deflect the conversation. "It's an ancient stone circle we visited recently," I said. The wine made me unguarded. "I know a woman who was conceived inside them! And her father always reminded her of this fact when she was naughty as a child."

"Oh?" said Phyllis. "Do tell us who, Thomas."

"Unfortunately I can't say," I said, "to avoid embarrassment to the person in question." I was aware of a frostiness in Phyllis' tone and demeanour.

"Astonishing," said Francesca. "Did you know I have my own ruin, in the grounds? Not as ancient as a stone circle, of course, but still picturesque."

"You intrigue me, Mrs Campbell," said Mr Thornton. "What manner of ruin?"

"It's an old water mill," Francesca said. "It last ground corn over twenty years ago, and the roof is starting to fall in now. It's quite overgrown and romantic."

"I'd love to see it," said Victoria. "Might we have an excursion after lunch? I'm going to need some fresh air and a walk anyway."

"A capital idea," said Mr Wakeley. "We can take a few bottles and glasses." I wondered whether he was thinking a romantic interlude would be on the cards, chasing Victoria through the ruins.

"That would be delightful," said Victoria.

"I wonder – why not," said Mrs Campbell. "We need to be quite careful, as some of the floorboards have gone. But it is very beautiful there, and the sun is out. I hope you all have warm coats! There's quite a good path down to it."

~

It was further down the valley than I was expecting, but it was good to walk off my two helpings of duck. The mill was impressive in size, on three floors and made with stone blocks that were in parts crumbling to sand. Much of the roof remained, but most of the window frames had been pillaged or had rotted away, giving the building a hollow-eyed look.

The path brought us to the front of the building; the river and the mill race that used to turn the wheel lay behind it.

We clambered over as much of the structure as was advisable, and then we sat on the rugs that Yates, Francesca's butler, had put down next to the mill, and enjoyed a glass of wine. Our little trip across Francesca's estate had introduced some informality, with birds and trees to be identified. Mr Wakeley and Mr Thornton had been sequestered in Francesca's little sitting room before we had departed for the mill, and they appeared to be relaxed with one another, indicating a possible breakthrough with their land purchase negotiations.

Mr Wakeley came over to Victoria and said, "Miss Clitheroe – we still haven't spoken of your investments. Might we...?"

"Oh – yes, please, Mr Wakeley," Victoria said. "Perhaps, to be private, in the mill."

"Good idea," he said, and the pair of them walked off towards the ruin.

I regarded them suspiciously. "Should I spy on them?" I said to Phyllis. "Can he be trusted? I must say, the man makes my flesh crawl."

"Give it a few minutes," Phyllis said. "I don't think she wants us to know all about her financial affairs."

Mr Thornton lit up a cheroot, and wandered over to the other side of the ruin, while Francesca took the opportunity to answer a call of nature in the woods. Phyllis and I were soon alone together, apart from Francesca's butler sitting some distance away.

"So you're not going to tell me who this mysterious child of the stones is?" Phyllis said.

"I would rather not," I said. "It was said in confidence."

Phyllis stared at me. "What female has your confidence, if I may ask?"

I looked away. "Does it matter?"

"I rather think it should matter to me, yes. Would you not be concerned if I had taken a man into my confidence?"

She had a point. "I suppose so. Very well – it's Bess Shannon. I met her in September, when I went to ask her some questions about Mr Shaw."

Frowning, Phyllis opened her mouth to speak, but at that moment there was a thudding sound, and then a scream from the direction of the ruin. I got up and ran towards where Victoria and Mr Wakeley had disappeared from view.

Victoria came running out of the ruin. "He went over! He went over, into the river! Oh, God!"

"Show me," I said, and we ran to the river bank. We could see nothing.

"Let's look from inside," I said, and we ran into the mill and to the back of the building. Through a doorway, we could see the rotten remnants of the wheel, and Mr Wakeley was draped over it. From the damage to his body, it looked as though he had hit his head on the iron parts of the wheel; the water in the mill race was turning red. His body was twisted and limp and it was clear that he was dead.

Victoria retched, and she rushed to the front of the building, where I could hear her being sick. The others were now gathering, looking on horrified at the grisly scene. Thornton had reappeared, cheroot still in his hand.

Francesca had her hand over her mouth, her eyes wide with dread. "God, no!" she howled. "It's my fault! I should not have let anyone come here. God forgive me! God forgive me!" And she sank to the ground, leaning against crumbling plaster. Phyllis squatted next to her and put her arm around her, and Francesca rested her head against Phyllis and cried.

"We need to decide what to do," I said, trying to steady my mind. "Yates, go and fetch the police!"

"Certainly, sir," he said, and ran up the path.

"Should we try to bring Mr Wakeley in?" said Mr Thornton. "It seems wrong to leave him there like that."

"No," I said, "the police will need to see the body where it is. Besides, it may be a tricky undertaking. We don't want to send him down the river by mistake."

Mr Thornton nodded. "What an awful business. I only just spoke to the fellow. Simply awful."

Phyllis led Francesca outside to where she could not see the wheel, and they sat on the grass with Victoria. When Francesca had recovered her composure a little, Phyllis took her arm and we progressed back up the path to Halfpenny House in silence.

~

We sat in the drawing room awaiting the police, while Yates brought us tea and brandy to help with the shock.

Victoria was still pale, huddling in a blanket.

"Victoria, if I may ask," I said, "what happened when you went to talk with Mr Wakeley?"

She closed her eyes and groaned, and Phyllis put her arm around her. "I walked with him up to the first floor, and went over to look at the water wheel through a window. He said we'd get a better view from the second floor. He ran up the stairs, and I was just starting to make my way up, when I saw a shadow pass across the window, and heard a thump. Fearing the worst, I ran up to the second floor, and he wasn't there. So I knew he must have fallen."

"I see," I said. "He made no sound as he fell?"

"No," she said. "I didn't hear him cry out."

"I noticed how low the window was," said Mr Thornton. "You'd have to be a fool to fall out, but if you weren't taking care, it's certainly possible."

Francesca buried her face in her hands and whispered, "Oh, God."

"It's not your fault, Francesca," I said. "Just think about the town walls! They're potentially deadly to walk around, but we're all trusted to be careful, and most people are."

She nodded and blew her nose.

"It's just a terrible accident," said Phyllis. "It's no one's fault, except perhaps Mr Wakeley's. He may have had a drop too much to drink, and thought he was invincible. I suspect he may have been showing off."

"Very likely," said Mr Thornton, "speaking as a man. Beautiful women make us do stupid things."

"Then in a way," said Victoria, "it *is* my fault. And my stupid obsession with getting the best possible return for my investments."

"No, Mr Wakeley was responsible for Mr Wakeley, and no one else," said Mr Thornton.

"I hope it's not in poor taste to ask this, Francesca," said Phyllis, "but what will happen to the castle now?"

"No, of course you may ask," said Francesca. "My agreement with Mr Wakeley specified that if he died, his portion of the land would pass to me. So I shall agree something with Mr Thornton."

"All in good time, Mrs Campbell," said Mr Thornton. "Do not concern yourself about that now."

"Thank you," said Francesca.

Yates appeared. "The police have arrived, ma'am," he said. "Shall I show them in here?"

"Yes, of course," said Francesca, straightening up and wiping the tears from her face.

Inspector Simmons entered, hat in hand, with another man whose attire and bearing were not those of a policeman. I recognised him, but could not immediately place him.

"Good afternoon, Mrs Campbell, ladies and gentlemen,"

Mr Simmons said. "I am very sorry to hear about the unfortunate death of Mr Wakeley. Most distressing, ma'am."

"Thank you, Mr Simmons," Francesca said. "It is a nightmare. Or rather, I wish it were just that."

"Quite so, ma'am. Allow me to introduce Dr Philip Weldon." Simmons gestured to his companion, who bowed gravely. "Dr Weldon is here to examine Mr Wakeley. I also have four constables to assist us."

I realised where I had seen him before: at Flora's bedside, but previously he had had a beard, which was now absent. He was an elegant man, and I instinctively glanced at Phyllis. I could tell from her gaze that his aesthetic qualities had not gone unnoticed.

"If you could all remain here, please, I will go and examine the scene with my constables and Dr Weldon, and then I will talk to each of you individually. Might one of your staff act as my guide?"

"Certainly – Yates? Can you take Inspector Simmons and his colleagues to the mill?"

"Of course, ma'am," said Yates. "This way, gentlemen, if you please."

~

As was traditional with Mr Simmons, the interviews took place in the dining room where the formality and the large table had a faintly intimidating effect on the interviewee.

"Another chance to catch up, Mr Rufford," said Mr Simmons drily. "It must be, oh, days, since I last had the pleasure of your company."

"The pleasure is all mine, Mr Simmons," I said.

I had previously observed that responding to his sarcasm with my own riled the Inspector, which is, naturally, why I did so. He glared at me, and then looked down at his notebook.

"I don't think this is the time for smart remarks, Mr Rufford," he said. "Do you? A man has died in mysterious circumstances mere feet from where you were standing. I would like you to tell me exactly what happened, if you would."

"Certainly, Inspector. We had gone for a walk to the mill after lunch, and we all explored the mill for a few minutes, and came out again. I was talking to Miss Drummond outside, and after about three or four minutes, I heard a thump, and then a scream. Victoria – Miss Clitheroe – came running out, screaming 'He fell into the river!' Or something of that nature."

"And Miss Clitheroe had gone into the mill with Mr Wakeley...?"

"Ah, yes, sorry, I omitted that part. They went into the mill to talk confidentially about financial matters. Miss Clitheroe was keen to get Mr Wakeley's investment advice."

"I see. Had they met before?"

"No – Mrs Campbell set the lunch up so they could meet."

"And whose idea was it, this meeting?"

"Several people's, I think. I told Miss Clitheroe that he was a friend of Mrs Campbell's, so she expressed an interest in meeting Wakeley. Mrs Campbell was keen to have Miss Clitheroe over to see her house, and Mr Wakeley was enthusiastic to impart his knowledge when he found out that she was interested."

"And Mr Wakeley had a reputation for financial acuity?"

"Well, apparently. Miss Clitheroe was aware of something of the sort. And of course, his deal with the land shows a certain acumen."

"Indeed. I had heard about that little controversy," said the Inspector. "Have you known Miss Clitheroe long? I gather she is staying at your house."

"Yes – no, not long. Since around the middle of November."

"And how do you regard Miss Clitheroe?"

"Let me see – kind, reliable, upright, even-tempered. The sort of person one is glad to have as a friend."

"Am I correct that she saw Hawksbridge as a kind of retreat, and came to write?"

"Yes," I said. "She contacted Miss Drummond for help with her novel."

"Thank you." Mr Simmons scribbled in his notebook for a minute. "And Mr Wakeley – what sort of man was he?"

"I confess I didn't like him, Inspector. He seemed full of himself, and perhaps untrustworthy. I don't really have any evidence for that, though – just an instinct."

"I see. And he appeared healthy to you? Not clumsy, or short-sighted?"

"No, he was quite vigorous, as far as I could see." I suddenly remembered Catherine. "Oh, Lord! His housekeeper! Someone needs to tell his housekeeper."

"I'll send a constable," Mr Simmons said. "His relationship with Mrs Campbell – was it strictly business, or also personal?"

"From what she said, I think there may have been a small flirtation, but very brief, so mainly a business association."

"I gather that the ownership of the land in question now reverts fully to Mrs Campbell. Do you have any comment about that?"

I frowned. "I see what you're driving at, Inspector, but Mrs Campbell is above suspicion. She had gone into the adjoining woods when Mr Wakeley fell."

"Very well. Let's talk about Mr Thornton. Where was he when Mr Wakeley fell?"

"I'm not exactly sure; he disappeared for a smoke and a walk, in the direction of the mill but on the opposite side to where Miss Clitheroe and Mr Wakeley went. Possibly he went into an outbuilding."

"I will ask him. How did you get on with Mr Thornton?"

"The only other time I met him, I crossed swords with him on the subject of his railway and the destruction of monuments. But today, he didn't seem to bear me a grudge."

"I gather he was still in negotiation with Mr Wakeley about a price for the land. Would you say he would benefit from Mr Wakeley being out of the picture? Perhaps Mrs Campbell would be an easier negotiating partner?"

I considered this for a moment. "It's possible. But Mrs Campbell can be quite tough. I'm not sure it would make very much difference. Not enough to kill someone over, anyway. But who knows?"

"I believe the butler, Yates, was visible to your party when Wakeley fell, so that accounts for everyone, yes?" I nodded. "In which case, I think we are done here for now, unless you can supply me with any other information."

"Not at present, Inspector, but I'll let you know if I think of anything."

~

After an hour or so, everyone had been interviewed, and I found Victoria sitting on her own in the small sitting room.

"I had to be alone for a few minutes," she said. "I'm so tired."

"I'm not surprised," I said. "I think we'd better be going soon. Shall we say goodbye to Francesca?"

"Yes, let's," said Victoria. "Though I don't even know how, in these circumstances."

In the drawing room, Dr Weldon was earnestly entreating Francesca to rest for several days.

"Oh, Thomas!" she said on seeing me. "You must get

home, the pair of you – it's almost dark!"

"Will you be all right?" I asked.

"Yes, I think so," she said. "Phyllis has very kindly offered to stay the night. And Dr Weldon has given me my marching orders. Or rather, my staying-in-bed orders."

"Has the... has Mr Wakeley been removed?" I asked.

"Yes, Mr Rufford," said Dr Weldon. "He died of a contusion to the brain – I was just telling Mrs Campbell that it would have been quick and painless."

I nodded, and turned to Phyllis. "Goodbye, Phyllis. I will come and visit you and your father soon – next week."

"As you wish," she said. I could not tell whether her cool manner was because of what I had told her, or because of Mr Wakeley's death. I found I was uncomfortable at leaving her in Dr Weldon's company.

I pressed Francesca's arm. "And I will visit you soon too. Don't hesitate to send for me."

"Thank you, Thomas. Now off with you, before you're obliged to stay here all night!"

~

The trip home was a melancholy one. We should have been recalling pleasant conversation with friends, in a faint alcoholic glow, not grappling with the death of a fellow guest.

"I think that might be the worst day of my life," said Victoria.

"Unfortunately, it only ranks about fifth worst in mine," I said.

"Oh dear!" she said. "I would ask about the other four, but I'm too exhausted."

"I don't care to remember them anyway," I said.

"I wouldn't blame Mrs Campbell if she never invited me

again."

"I'm sure she will," I said. "It's not as if you killed her business partner."

"I might as well have," she said. "If I hadn't wanted to talk to him in confidence, then we wouldn't have gone in that wretched mill, and he would still be alive."

"But you couldn't know there was a risk of him dying. Put it out of your mind."

"How do I do that?" she said.

"Oh, I don't know. Think of something pleasant. Your novel. A beautiful painting. Picnics in the spring."

"Or a stolen kiss," she said. It was uttered so quietly and it seemed such a strange remark that I was not sure I had heard correctly.

"I beg your pardon?"

"Or people I miss, I said. At home in Leeds."

CHAPTER TWENTY-TWO

IN the morning, I took Jenny and the trap into town in the vague hope of persuading Phyllis to come back to Ramsburgh for lunch, so I could try to repair the damage our relationship had lately suffered. I had the painful impression that she was slipping away from me. My first task, however, was to ensure that Catherine had been told of her master's demise.

When I reached the cottage, I heard raised voices inside. I tied Jenny to a post and knocked, and getting no reply, opened the door. Catherine, her arms folded, was addressing a heavily bearded man.

"I do not have it, and I do not know where Mr Wakeley is. You must wait."

"I have already waited a month, ma'am," said the man, in a calm but faintly menacing manner. "How long do you expect me to wait? You will both have to find other lodgings – there's plenty of folk wanting a roof over their heads, and this is quality accommodation. It's an abuse of my trust, ma'am, and I have run out of patience."

He stopped to draw breath, and noticed me. Turning, he said, "And who, sir, are you? A friend of Wakeley's? Perhaps you would like to pay his rent for him? Did you know he was a rogue about his debts?"

"No, I'm not a friend of his, and I know little about his financial affairs," I said. "But I have something important to discuss with Catherine. Might you be so kind as leave us?"

"Not until I've had my money!" he said.

I shrugged, and said to Catherine, "I take it you haven't seen the police today?"

"No," she said. "Why should I? Is it about Mr Wakeley?" The constable, or Mr Simmons, had evidently forgotten to inform her, or were leisurely in doing so.

"Then I'm afraid I have some very bad news to tell you. Mr Wakeley is dead."

"Oh!" she said, as if she had been struck, and sank into a chair.

"Good God," said the landlord.

Catherine stared ahead, unseeing, her hands gripping the chair arms. "Dead!" she whispered. After a moment she shook herself out of her trance, and asked, "How, Mr Rufford?"

"He fell from an old building, at Mrs Campbell's estate. A horrible accident. He died instantly."

"Oh," she repeated.

I turned to the landlord, whose self-righteous demeanour had been replaced with an embarrassed expression. "The rent will be paid out of the estate," I said. "You will get your money. I'm afraid it won't be today, though."

"Yes, of course," he said, putting his hat on. "Thank you, Mr Rufford. I'll be off now, ma'am. Sorry to have troubled you."

He left, and I wondered what I could say to Catherine. I sat down on a chair opposite her. "You have my sincere sympathies," I said. "Do you know what you will do now?"

She sighed, and continued to stare blankly at the opposite wall. "No. I have nowhere to go."

"No relatives nearby, I take it?"

She laughed, and looked at me. "No, Mr Rufford. They are far, far away. And they have forgotten all about me. I am alone now."

I deliberated. Mrs Felton had been grumbling about her workload, and her position as both housekeeper and cook could not continue indefinitely. "Catherine," I said, "how is your cooking?"

"My cooking, Mr Rufford? I have been cooking for Mr

Wakeley for many years. He sometimes complained about it, but only because he liked to complain. I think I am a good cook."

"Then how would you like to be my cook? On a trial basis, of course. My housekeeper, Mrs Felton, will show you the ropes and help when it gets busy."

"Oh – that would be good, Mr Rufford. Very good. But your people – will they – I am not like them..."

"Will they accept you? Of course they will, Catherine. They are not bigots – I wouldn't employ them if they were. Mrs Felton will be overjoyed to have her burden lightened, and I know everyone will like you. How could they not?"

Catherine smiled and wiped away a tear. "Then, thank you, Mr Rufford. I will be glad to try my best for you."

"Good. When would you like to start?"

She looked around at the cottage. "It makes no difference to me. I could start today. I would be glad to forget this place. And to forget Mr Wakeley."

"Splendid!" I said. "I can wait while you pack, if you like. I have a trap waiting."

It did not take her long, and I put her bags in the trap and helped her up. This was not at all what I was expecting when I had set off this morning, but I was happy to solve two problems in one stroke. I was looking forward to Mrs Felton's reaction. She would probably enjoy administering any training that Catherine might need.

We passed the Drummond's house, at the precise moment that Dr Weldon emerged from the front door. He noticed me, and looked surprised at my cargo. He tipped his hat, and I waved, wondering, with some anxiety, what business he had with the Drummonds.

"Catherine," I said after a few minutes' silence, "may I ask your surname?"

"Yes, Mr Rufford," she said. "Wakeley. I am Mrs Catherine Wakeley."

I nearly dropped the reins in surprise. "I'm so sorry – I didn't realise. Mr Wakeley was your husband?"

She nodded. "His husband. His housekeeper. His slave. His whore."

"I confess I didn't like him," I said. "It seems I had more reason than I thought."

"Your judgement is good, Mr Rufford," she said. "I wanted to leave, but I was afraid. Where would I have gone? 'I am your protector', he said. He did not let me make friends with anyone. People are suspicious of my kind. He let everyone believe I was just his housekeeper, so he could go off and – make love to women. And tell them lies to get their money."

I grimaced. "I expect your relatives were too distant to help you."

"Help me!" she scoffed. "I was sold, Mr Rufford, in exchange for a few guns. My father was a chieftain. I am" – she laughed bitterly – "a princess! Can you believe this?"

"In the last few minutes," I said, "you have already been promoted from housekeeper to wife, and from wife to cook. So yes – I can believe it." It made some sense to me, as I had already been aware of a dignity of deportment and manner in her that was not characteristic of any housekeeper I had previously met.

"Where were you before," I continued, "before you both came to Hawksbridge?"

"A big city," she said. "So much dust and noise. I did not like it. No, I was glad to be gone from Leeds. Will I have to go to his funeral?"

"Not if you don't want to. I'll tell the Rector not to expect anyone, if you like."

"Good," she said. "That man means nothing to me."

~

"Let me introduce you to Mrs Catherine Wakeley," I said to Shipley as I dismounted and helped Catherine down. "Our new cook! On a trial basis."

"Very pleased to meet you, ma'am," said Shipley. "Mind you break it to Mrs Felton gently, sir," he added with a smile. "She might need to sit down for such uncommonly good news!" He took down Catherine's bags. "What room shall I take these to, sir?"

"The room next to Mrs Felton's is free, isn't it?" I said. "Please make sure it's comfortable."

"Might need a new mattress," he said, and took the bags into the house.

"This is all yours?" said Catherine, looking up in wonder at Ramsburgh's façade.

"Yes, I inherited it unexpectedly," I said, almost apologetically. I still did not believe I deserved it.

"It is beautiful," she said.

"Thank you. I think it needed a princess," I said, and she smiled.

I took her to the kitchen, where I presented her to Mrs Felton, who was darning in a Windsor chair.

"Our new cook!" I said. "Mrs Catherine Wakeley, meet Mrs Norah Felton."

Mrs Felton stood up. "Oh, Mr Rufford – how wonderful! Welcome, Catherine!"

She was so thankful that she first embraced Catherine heartily, who looked pleased if overwhelmed, and then me.

"Thank you, my dear! I didn't mean to complain, but I'm not getting any younger. And you will keep having house guests."

"I know," I said. "I have been dilatory about it. Please forgive me. Anyway, Catherine is on a trial period for – what shall we say, a month? She has some experience, and I'm sure she'll be glad to learn our particular habits."

"I will, sir," Catherine said.

"Thank you, Mrs Felton. I'll take Catherine to her room. I thought we'd use the one next to yours."

"Goodness – let me dust it first. And find some blankets, and a better chair. It's been a bit of a dumping ground."

I took Catherine to her room, and then, while Shipley and Mrs Felton fussed over it, I showed her the reception rooms.

"You must be happy here," Catherine said. "Do you have a wife?"

I was amused at the direct question. "I do not, at present," I said. "I have been negligent on that score. I would like one, though. The house can seem too big for one man."

"There should be little ones, making lots of trouble," Catherine said.

"Yes, yes, there should. I will have to see to it. After I find a wife, of course."

She smiled. "I was never able. But it is as well."

"I'm sorry," I said, and she made a dismissive gesture.

I remembered an important detail of this arrangement. "I haven't mentioned pay – how remiss of me. Let me find out what the usual rate is, and I will let you know this evening."

"Thank you," she said.

"And if you have any problem, or you're not comfortable – you will come and tell me, won't you?"

"I will, Mr Rufford. You are very kind."

"Well, I hope you'll be happy here. In fact, I insist upon it. It will be written in my terms!"

~

Francesca was looking stronger, and was pleased to see me when I was ushered into the drawing room.

"Oh, Thomas – how kind of you to come. Phyllis has been an angel; she left this morning."

"Ah," I said, sitting down. "I saw Dr Weldon coming out of her house this morning. It would appear they are getting on well."

"Now, now! Are you jealous?"

"Well, frankly, yes. He is extremely handsome, and I have blotted my copybook with Phyllis."

"Oh, dear, Thomas! Whatever have you done?"

"I mentioned a woman. Bess Shannon. It was she who was conceived in the Devil's Teeth, and Phyllis wormed it out of me."

"And?"

"And I was seeing Bess for a time."

"I see. You naughty boy. I expect you will be able to win her round. But I fear you're right – Dr Weldon is tremendously appealing. When he was tending to me, I didn't know if I was weak from shock or from having my pulse taken by him!"

"I don't know how I shall compete," I said. "I barely have a profession any more. Oh well, that's trivial compared with... yesterday. How are you feeling?"

"I keep seeing poor Mr Wakeley on that wheel. It's too horrible." She shuddered. "But I'm feeling rather better, thank you."

"Good. This morning I went to tell Mr Wakeley's housekeeper about his death. The police hadn't been yet."

"Oh dear – how did she take it?"

"Surprisingly well, considering she is also his widow."

"What?" said Francesca. "Surely you are joking?"

I shook my head. "He kept it quiet. And he wasn't nice to her, apparently. Not nice at all."

"Lord," she said, clutching at her head. "What a fool I've been. I should be beyond flattery and deception at my age. And that nonsense about his business partner running off with his money, so I had to take most of the risk! What was I thinking?"

"Well, that's all behind you now. I have taken Mrs Wakeley on as my cook. She was about to be evicted."

"Oh, good for you, Thomas!" she said. "What an excellent idea."

"I assume Mr Simmons will treat Wakeley's death as an accident," I said. "Mind you, given his habit of jumping to the wrong conclusion, who knows?"

"True," Francesca said. "But I don't really see any way he could possibly conclude it was murder. I think I convinced him I was emerging from the woods just as Victoria screamed."

"And were you?" I teased.

"Thomas!" she said. "Yes, of course. I had just – well, you know."

"Indeed," I said. "And Mr Thornton still had his cheroot in his hand, which would be unusual if he had just committed murder."

"And there's no access to the second floor from that side of the building, as far as I know," said Francesca.

"Which just leaves Victoria," I said. "She was the last person to see Wakeley alive."

"Impossible," Francesca said. "She is such a sweet girl. I may have been wrong about Wakeley, but I know an innocent, caring girl when I see one."

"I agree," I said. "She would have no reason to do this, and she was as upset as anyone."

"Then no doubt it will be recorded as an accident, and we can try to forget this whole ghastly episode," she said. "Speaking of which, I know a good distraction."

"I don't think you're strong enough for that," I said.

She laughed. "You are incorrigible! Not *that*," she said. "Life is complicated enough already. No – I thought you might like to see my cassone."

"Ah – the Wicked Cassone! I had clean forgot about it. Yes, I would like to see this mysterious object."

"Very well," she said. "It's where you would expect it to be – in my bedroom."

~

It was a privilege to once again stand in the room that she had made magnificent, with its extravagant red and gold wallpaper and elegant furniture. Now, at the foot of the elaborate four-poster bed, there was a large chest.

"Look at the front," said Francesca.

I crouched on the floor and examined the exquisitely-painted front panel. A beautiful, naked woman was stretched out in a landscape of rocks, trees and distant hills. A clean-shaven young man in a robe was kneeling and engaged in intercourse with the woman, whose head was thrown back as she smiled with pleasure.

"Is that wicked?" I asked. "It's certainly highly erotic."

"Look more closely," said Francesca, kneeling next to me and steadying herself with her hand on my back.

I scanned the scene carefully, and then noticed, above the rocks that lay behind our ecstatic lady, that her right hand was holding that of a person reaching out from behind the rocks. I noticed that what I initially took to be foliage was actually a bearded face.

"Good heavens," I said. "Who is that holding her hand?"

"Her husband!" Francesca said. "She is Aphrodite – her husband Hephaestus is holding her hand."

"How scandalous," I said. I stared at the scene, trying to make sense of the painter's intentions. "But why...?"

"It's strange, certainly," said Francesca. "These chests were supposed to aid fertility – Mr Blackwood told me that the husband or family member would commission the painting, and the married couple would be encouraged to look at the scenes on the chests. That way, their offspring would be similarly beautiful and healthy."

"And yet this scene would seem to encourage infidelity," I said, "which is surely not to be condoned at the start of a marriage?"

"Perhaps the husband was unable to give her a child," Francesca said, "and they had an arrangement whereby another man would impregnate her."

"Astonishing. Or perhaps there's another explanation – it was a message to her that he could offer her up to whomever he wished. Or it was simply a symbol of his power, whether he wished to share her or not."

"Or this was a fantasy that he had," said Francesca. "I'm told that some men like that sort of thing."

"Well, whatever the explanation, it's extraordinary," I said.

"There's more," Francesca said. "But I'm not sure you're ready for it. You're very young, after all. I don't wish to corrupt you."

"I think I'll survive looking at a salacious picture," I said. "You should have seen what the previous owner of Ramsburgh left behind in his bureau."

"Interesting," said Francesca. "Remind me about it some time. Now – are you ready?"

"Yes!" I said. "Open, sesame."

She opened the lid, still hanging on to my back to balance herself.

On the underside of the lid, a woman – perhaps the same wicked woman – was crouching over a young man, with a pleased look on her face. The man held onto her sides, and an older, bearded man – seemingly the husband, again – was kneeling behind the couple.

"Is he – er – joining in?" I asked.

"I fear he might be," said Francesca. "He's certainly getting quite cosy with them. Isn't it deliciously wicked?"

"Good God," I said, staring at it. "It certainly is."

"Aren't the colours sublime?" said Francesca.

"They are. It's survived well. What age did you say it was?"

"Fifteenth-century, apparently."

"Astounding. It looks as though there's another picture on the bottom," I said, standing up and peering in.

"Ah yes!" she said. "That one is lovely."

On the bottom panel, a woman lay stretched out on her front, viewed from above, as if she were taking a nap inside the chest. A wispy wrap floated over her, hiding very little, and her pear-shaped figure was lovingly painted.

"She's gorgeous," I said. "I wouldn't want to put anything in the chest."

"There's a provenance," Francesca said, picking up a piece of paper from the bottom of the chest and handing it to me. I read:

'The Wicked Cassone', a marriage chest from about 1460.

The paintings on the chest are thought to depict Aphrodite and her husband Hephaestus seducing an unknown man.

It was given to the Museo Vecchio in Florence in 1810, after the owner became convinced it was bringing his family bad luck. The Moretti family had experienced a large number of deaths from feuds, accidents and disease, and so the immorality of the cassone's depictions of love was blamed.

Its nickname was thought to have been given to the cassone by a priest who visited the museum in 1815.

A popular exhibit for several decades, a change in the museum's governance meant that certain controversial objects, including the cassone, were sold off to buy sacred paintings.

Blackwood's acquired the piece at auction on a tour of Italy in 1847.

"So," I said, "you bought a cursed chest."

"Oh, Thomas, don't," said Francesca. Then she added, with a look of horror on her face, "You don't really think poor Mr Wakeley...?"

"No, of course not!" I said. "I'm sure the mortality rate in Italy was already high enough not to need a curse."

Francesca stood up and said, "I won't mention how much it cost. It would shock you far more than the paintings."

"You didn't get a discount?"

"I haggled a little," she said.

"I dare say it's worth it," I said. "Especially since this chest is guaranteed to inflame any male you wish to take to your bed."

"You mean he wouldn't be sufficiently inflamed already?" she said, with a mock-offended expression on her face.

"I am sure he would," I said. "I take it back. The merest promise of a kiss from you..."

"Stop!" she said, laughing. "Thank you. But I don't wish to test your sincerity."

CHAPTER TWENTY-THREE

I DINED with Victoria, and Catherine – I could not bring myself to call her Mrs Wakeley – brought in a pheasant broth that she had prepared with Mrs Felton's help.

"That smells glorious," Victoria said, and Catherine looked pleased.

"It does," I said. "How are you getting on?"

"Well, I haven't burned anything yet, Mr Rufford," she said. "And I am happy. That is something I am not used to."

I smiled and nodded. "Good!"

When Catherine had left, Victoria said, "She's delightful. Where did you find her?"

I sipped my wine. "She is Mr Wakeley's widow. I offered her the job when I came to tell her about Mr Wakeley, and she was about to be evicted."

"Oh, good Lord!" Victoria said, her face turning white. "I had no idea he was married."

"No one did," I said. "He kept it secret, presumably so he could court his victims with greater ease, and perhaps also so people wouldn't talk. He treated her very badly."

"That is terrible," Victoria said, her spoon still poised above her bowl.

"But things are improving for her," I said, impressed by the strength of her empathy for Catherine. "Although this may seem heartless, Mr Wakeley's death was probably the best thing that could happen to her."

"Yes, I suppose so," she said, starting to eat again. "That's a comfort."

"How are you feeling?" I asked. "I mean, after yesterday?"

"Still slightly queasy when I think about it, which is too often," Victoria said.

"Sorry, I should not have brought it up."

"That's all right," she said. "But I am trying your remedy of thinking about happier things. And this wine may help," she added, raising her glass to her lips.

"Before we change the subject," I said, "the police have not wanted to interview you again, I take it?"

"No, not since yesterday," she said. "Thank goodness. So I presume they don't imagine I pushed poor Mr Wakeley out of the window!"

"I'm sure they don't," I said. "He was just a clumsy fool."

She nodded. "Is Mrs Campbell feeling better?"

"Yes – well enough to show me a very interesting antique she recently purchased."

"Oh? How interesting can an antique be?"

"I'd say, captivating, when it's covered with fifteenth-century erotic paintings. It's the chest that Mr Ambrose was so furious about losing when we were at Blackwood's shop."

"My word!" she said. "I would not have thought she was the type for that sort of thing." She drained her wine glass.

"Francesca has hidden depths," I said. "I'm sure she will invite us again soon, and then you can watch her expression when you ask to see her cassone. Preferably in front of the great and the good of Hawksbridge."

"That might be amusing," Victoria said. "How... frank are these paintings?"

"Well, you can get some indication by the name of the thing – it has been called the 'Wicked Cassone'. It's the first time I've come across a piece of furniture with a nickname."

"Perhaps," she said, "if you were to have a drop more wine, you could be persuaded to describe the pictures. Surely it's better than embarrassing Mrs Campbell?"

"Actually, she would probably revel in it. And I would have to be fairly merry, Victoria, before I were to speak of such things to a respectable, innocent woman."

"Ah, but how do you know I'm innocent?" she said.

"A gentleman always assumes –"

"I might have had dozens of lovers, for all you know."

I realised that she might have drunk rather too much. "I suppose you might. Have you?"

"No," she said, with a hint of regret in her voice. "I have led a dull life in that respect. Not many men appeal to me, to tell the truth. They have too much confidence, or not enough, or they have scratchy whiskers" – I laughed at this – "or they have primitive ideas about women, or just stupid ideas generally. Or they're ugly, or so pretty they're conceited about it. And occasionally, of course, they're just plain evil."

"Victoria," I said, "however will you find a man when you have so little tolerance for the species?"

"Oh!" she said. "Do you find discernment a redundant quality? What do you suggest I put up with?"

"Perhaps you have a point about the tickly whiskers," I said, taking some more wine.

"Shall we move to the drawing room?" she said.

"Let's," I said.

After we had settled ourselves, I turned to Victoria and said, "As you are such an expert on men's qualities, or lack thereof, what should I improve to attract a female?"

"Let me think," she said, looking me over. "You're physically an acceptable specimen. But I do think you need to learn to sing, or play the piano, or possibly both."

"I see. I will consider singing lessons, but I draw the line at the piano. I tried when I was younger, and failed conclusively."

"You have quite a nice voice," she said. "A pleasant inflection."

"Thank you."

"And rather a good head of hair." She raised her hand and ran her fingers through my hair; I glanced at the door nervously in case someone should see this exhibition. "Soft and thick. A woman would like to feel that against her skin."

I felt I was seeing a different, intimate side of my guest: one that I had no right to see. Perhaps, I thought, I should encourage her to go to her bed and sleep off the wine. On the other hand, it was entertaining – and flattering.

"Your kisses are perfectly tolerable," she said, "so your lover will have no cause for complaint on that score."

I cringed. "I was wrong to take advantage," I said. "Mea culpa." Then vanity got the better of me, and I added, "But – only tolerable?"

"I didn't say how long they could be tolerated. Shall we say, half an hour? Perhaps a little longer?"

Victoria was looking at me intently, smiling and slightly flushed, and I suddenly felt like a cornered animal. Although my instincts were to encourage her, and more, I knew that I would be compromising my future – and hers – in giving in to my baser needs.

"I need some fresh air," I said. "I'm going to take Fox for a walk."

She looked alarmed. "Oh dear – have I offended you with my silly chatter? I'm sorry. I'm not usually like this at all."

Her forlorn look melted my heart. "I enjoy your silly chatter, Victoria, I truly do, but that's the difficulty. I'm not strong enough to withstand such pleasantness. You are very charming, and I'm very fallible." I kissed her hand and went off to find Fox.

~

The following morning, on the coach to Edinburgh, I turned over recent events in my mind. How strange that I should suspect Mr Thornton of Mr Ambrose's death, for him then to be present at Mr Wakeley's. The two unfortunates were connected by a wretched ruin. Could Mr Thornton really be arranging for the demise of those who stood in his way? He did not seem to have had the opportunity to kill Mr Wakeley, although there was a lingering doubt in my mind, as he was not seen at that precise time. But the police – flawed as they were – would surely have investigated the area around the mill to see if that might have been possible. I determined to check it myself, the next time I was at Francesca's.

And then there was poor Victoria. After the previous day's ordeal, her nerves had rallied enough to flirt with me, but I had crushed her. I had not had the time to talk with her again since last night; I would seek her out on my return and reassure her (and myself) that we were still friends.

It was flattering and frustrating that she should be warm towards me. If it were not for Phyllis, I would no doubt have thrown myself into her delightful arms. She was beautiful, clever, and available. She would be at ease at Ramsburgh – indeed, she already was. I could too easily picture waking up to her warm, yielding body and giving her everything she craved.

And yet: she was not Phyllis. Somehow I could not imagine myself and Victoria growing old together. The connection I felt with Phyllis was altogether deeper. I cursed myself for my shilly-shallying, which, together with my licentious behaviour, might have cost me my prize. I would need to find a way to best the handsome Dr Weldon and obtain forgiveness for my past sins.

I would also have to eschew distractions of the feminine kind. In any case, soon enough Victoria would be returning to Leeds, to entice me no more.

Leeds: where the Wakeleys had also recently lived. Despite the complaints I had heard about the city, it seemed a surprisingly popular location amongst my acquaintances. It must possess charms that I knew nothing of. I would have to ask Victoria about it – perhaps I could visit, and she could be my guide. But no – that would present temptation again.

This swirl of events and emotions threatened to divert me from my most important task: the dispersal of the dark cloud hanging over Mrs Ambrose. I fervently hoped that my unusual visit to Edinburgh would provide the key to this, but the closer to the capital I got, the more absurd this avenue of investigation appeared. How could a tart give me such critical knowledge? Would she even be there? Would I be thrown out as soon as I started asking questions? If Mrs Ambrose knew that her fate might be decided in the darkened rooms of an unsavoury Edinburgh club, she would be in despair.

~

I was too nervous to take Bess' advice and prick the balloon of my appetites in advance. It was a short walk from my hotel to the club, which was fortunate as the streets were slippery from freezing rain mixed with dirt.

It was a mystery how the activities of the club had not yet caused its ejection from the respectable classical environs of Moray Place, but blackmail would be a likely weapon if the clientèle were drawn from the higher echelons of Edinburgh society. I stood in front of The Vesuvius for a moment, harbouring a strong desire to cancel my appointment with fate, slip into a pub, and drink the evening away. The sandstone building towered before me, five or so storeys in height, shadowy figures moving behind its glowing grid of windows.

Finally I plucked up courage and knocked. A footman ushered me in, checked my invitation, and announced me to a man standing smiling next to him.

"Ah, Mr Rufford!" said my host. "How pleasant to meet you. Oliver Murdoch at your service. I do hope you enjoy the evening. Was your journey from Hawksbridge comfortable?"

"Tolerable, thank you, Mr Murdoch!" I said, looking around and taking in the improbably high ceilings, opulent decoration and expensive art, most of which featured nudes. "Your house is magnificent."

"Thank you, sir! I have a programme for you, which I believe is at least the equal of any of our previous gatherings."

"My congratulations," I said. "I'm heartily looking forward to it."

I took a printed programme, and Mr Murdoch pointed in the direction of a large drawing room. A dozen or so men were already lounging on sofas or standing leering at a belly dancer who was providing fleshy entertainment during the wait for dinner, to the accompaniment of a small band of musicians.

It was with acute embarrassment that I made my way to one of the sofas. I wanted to be anywhere but here, where all present were assembled solely to indulge their lustful imaginations, and perhaps more. A flunky proffered a tray of wine glasses in my direction, and I gladly took one.

"New chap, are you?" a voice behind me said. I turned around to see an extravagantly-whiskered man with red cheeks, setting me thinking immediately of Victoria's loathing of such facial decoration.

"Yes – yes, I am," I said, trying to think how I should conduct myself so as to avoid suspicion. "I've been promising myself a visit for some time, and I have high expectations. Are you a regular?"

"Me? Oh, yes. Wouldn't miss it for the world. Even helps me put up with the wife – the old girl should be grateful!"

"Ah, quite," I said, horrified.

"Just have to think of the beautiful ladies here to stiffen the old sinews and do one's marital duty, what?"

I smiled, hoping my tormentor would get bored and go away.

"You married?" he said, lighting up a cheroot.

"Not yet," I said. "But I have someone in mind."

"Good man," he said, and took a drag. "Got to repopulate the nation. Our chaps taking a bit of a pasting in Ceylon."

He turned to the belly dancer. "Lord! Look at her go. Wonder if my old girl could be trained to do that."

He roared with laughter at the thought. "Would have to feed her up a bit first. Love a bit of weight on a woman." He turned back to me. "Do you like 'em fleshy too, Mr...?"

"Rufford. Thomas Rufford. I confess I do, a little, although it's not my prime criterion for a wife."

"Ah, well, indeed," he said. "Harold Nuffield." We shook hands. "But for a mistress, I find a good covering is desirable. I've a tip for you, Rufford, since you're fresh to this."

"Yes?"

"The slave auction. My favourite part. Don't be tempted to bid too early. Just wait until the bidding is nearly closed, then swoop in with your bid. Will save you a shilling or two! And you'll startle the other chaps if you make a strong bid."

"Thank you, Mr Nuffield. I'll remember that."

To my relief, Mr Murdoch rang a bell and welcomed us all to the gathering, and we were invited to progress to the dining room. As I took my seat, I prayed that Mr Nuffield would not sit next to me; happily, he found another victim, and my immediate fellows were engaged in their own conversations.

Dinner was exhausting. Oysters and artichokes were followed by beef tenderloin, veal tongue, and a sorbet to cleanse the palate. The feast relentlessly continued with roast chicken, sole with truffle coulis, and a peppered onion soup, followed by champagne and pastries. For dessert, we were treated to jellies in interesting shapes and, with our coffee, suggestive little cakes adorned with cherries.

As we sat back and adjusted our belts, Mr Murdoch read, in a lugubrious manner, erotic poems by Ovid, Burns and

Donne.

At last he said, "Very well, gentlemen – I can see some of you getting restless. I have tortured you long enough. If you'd like to make your way back to the drawing room, we start with Beauties of the Empire!"

I wondered where Mr Murdoch had found the representatives of far-flung nations that now paraded in front of us, wearing costumes that were short on material and large on stereotype. Perhaps he had scoured the lodging houses of Leith, where ships regularly disgorged migrants looking for work.

A vulgar cheer went up when Africa, wearing an ivory necklace, dropped her brightly-coloured robe to show all of her beauty save that which was covered by a minuscule patch of cloth around her waist. Hong Kong wore dragon-decorated red pyjamas enticingly open at the front, while India sported a head-scarf and a revealing diaphanous robe.

It went on this vein, and then the last nation, Scotland, appeared in a tartan robe. She was the picture of modesty until, with a twirl, she threw off her robe to reveal her naked body entirely painted with the same tartan. She proceeded to dance a jig, accompanied by the band, and the roar of approval and lasciviousness from my fellows almost deafened me.

Next, lubricated by more wine, we were treated to more belly dancing and music, and a series of tableaux, including one involving several naked, chained white slave girls posing submissively before their black master.

Finally, Nuffield's favourite part of the evening arrived: the slave auction. Rather sickeningly, the 'slaves' had bound wrists and bowed heads, and were topless.

Our host, Mr Murdoch, was the auctioneer. "Pandora! What do I hear for this buxom beauty? Let's start at five guineas. Five guineas, and you can find out what's in Pandora's box!"

Guffaws ensued. "Ten!" someone said.

"Any advance on ten? Do I hear fifteen?"

Pandora sold at twenty guineas, and Ariadne at twenty-five.

"Now – Ophelia!"

So this was Ophelia. I recognised her from Mr Harrison's sketch. She had thick, dark brown hair; she was older than the others, but still pretty, and it was evident that she earned enough to keep hunger at bay. However, it was not sufficient to keep her from shivering.

"Don't you want to have her do your bidding? No riverside walks, mind. Let's hear five guineas for Ophelia."

"Ten!" someone said.

"Fifteen!"

"Twenty!" said the original bidder.

"Twenty-two!" said the second bidder.

The original bidder shrugged, and gave up.

"Going at twenty-two... going..."

"Thirty!" said a voice. It was Nuffield. I was horrified by the thought that not only would my mission fail, but Ophelia would have to put up with that oaf. I wondered if Mr Ambrose had always managed to 'buy' Ophelia, or whether he had had to share her with others in the club.

"Thirty-five!" I called.

He looked at me, surprised. "Thirty-eight!" he said.

"Forty-five!"

Nuffield hesitated, and then nodded to me and said, "Fairly won, old man. I'll pass."

"Going at forty-five! Going... going... gone!"

Mr Murdoch's assistant untied Ophelia, threw a blanket over her, and led her over to me.

"Hello," she said without enthusiasm, barely looking at me. "Let's find a room. I'm freezing."

"I'm Thomas Rufford," I said, walking hastily and with extreme self-consciousness as cheers and whistles followed us.

"Charmed, I'm sure," she said drily. "I'll get my clothes."

She disappeared into the basement and returned with a bag. We then climbed the ornate staircase to the fifth floor, and Ophelia led me into a room under the eaves and shut the door.

"This will do," she said.

The room was small but pleasant, with clean sheets on the bed and an outlook onto a row of similar houses on the other side of Moray Place. I wondered if their inhabitants knew just what went on here.

Discarding her blanket, she dived into the bed and curled up in a ball, still shivering.

"So cold," she said. "Quick, come and warm me up."

"Very well," I said, realising that this was a necessary step, even if it was a strange and discomforting echo of my night with Mrs Ambrose.

I kept my undergarments on, and gingerly took hold of Ophelia. After the amount of food I had consumed, lying down was slightly painful.

"That's better," Ophelia said. "I haven't seen you here before. Normally I get the same fellow, but he hasn't turned up today."

"I wanted to see what all the fuss was about."

Ophelia snorted. "And what do you think of Mr Murdoch and his circus of sensuality, as he sometimes likes to call it?"

"I'm not sure," I said. "I suppose the programme is quite... colourful."

"Colourful? That's not the enthusiasm I would expect from someone who paid forty-five guineas for a night with a woman. Well, a couple of hours – that's all they allow."

"Sorry," I said. "I'm a little distracted by the death of a friend."

"Oh dear," said Ophelia. "You do need cheering up, then."

"Perhaps," I said. "You might have known my friend."

"How's that?" she said.

"He used to come here," I said. "Yorick Ambrose."

Ophelia turned around and sat up in horror. "Yorick? Dead?"

I nodded. "I'm afraid so."

"Oh God," she said, and slumped back onto the bed, burying her face in the pillow.

"I'm very sorry," I said.

She lifted her head and said, "How did it happen?"

"Someone killed him when he was on his way back home."

She turned again, and stared at me, her breasts pressing against my arm. "Why would anyone want to do that?" she said.

"I have no idea," I said. "But I'm trying to find out."

"What do the police say?"

"They have charged his wife with it. But they've made a terrible mistake. I have to find out who really did it, or she hangs."

"Oh my Lord," she said. "Thank you for telling me." She looked at me for a moment before sniffing and adding, "Can you roll over?"

Slightly surprised at this, I complied, and she suddenly embraced me tightly, pressing her tearful face against my back. I could hear and feel her sobs and her muffled voice, saying, "Yorick, Yorick, Yorick!"

"Are you all right?" I said, feeling quite unequal to the situation.

Her arms tightened around me once more, and she said, "I wanted to pretend you were Yorick and hold him for the last time. There, I'm done. You can be Mr Rufford again now."

She sat up and dried her eyes, and I also sat up.

"So you knew Mr Ambrose well?" I said.

"Yes," she said. "He was good to me – most of the time. When he wasn't in a temper, anyway."

"He didn't mind your... work?"

She laughed. "Of course not. It meant that I wasn't his problem. Just a bit of pleasure, now and again. But I was fond of him. Maybe too fond for my own good. But if a gentleman like him has an eye for a... a woman like me, what can I do but be grateful, and perhaps a bit more than that? Besides, you won't believe it, but I come from a good, honest family. It's only hardship that has forced me into this. And sometimes I think I deserve a gentleman like him. You'll laugh, of course."

"Not at all. I can tell that you don't belong in this line of work," I said. "If you were fond of him, perhaps you could help me catch his killer."

"Me? Help catch a killer? How could I do that?"

"Simply by telling me anything you know about him," I said. "Then there's a good chance we can work out who he's been meeting, and who might have wanted to harm him."

"Oh. I see. Well, I don't know anything. Sorry."

"You might know more than you think," I said. "Perhaps something he put in a letter."

She shook her head. "He didn't tell me anything like that," she said. "Just how much he'd like to... well, you know."

"Quite," I said. "But perhaps he asked you to do something for him?"

She looked suspiciously at me. "What kind of thing?"

"I don't know. You tell me," I said.

She shrugged, and stared at the marks on the opposite wall.

"Perhaps he asked you to write a letter."

Ophelia glowered at me. She jumped out of bed and started to put her clothes on.

"How the devil did you know that? Have you come here just to trick me? I don't know what your game is, but I'm not playing."

"Ophelia," I said, "please calm down. I'm sure you want to help me catch whoever killed your friend. Just tell me about the letter, please. And don't forget, I've paid forty-five guineas!

I'm only asking for a scrap of information, and then I'll leave."

She let out a sound of exasperation and sat down on the edge of bed. "All right. Yorick asked me to write a letter, so it appeared to come from a woman. It was all a bit strange, but he told me he was playing a trick on someone, just for a bit of fun."

"Can you remember what was in it?"

"Let me think. There was this phrase: 'The wrongs you have done me'. Or 'grievous wrongs', I think it was. And asking for a lot of money to stop her telling everyone. An awful lot of money."

"So, a blackmail letter?"

She hesitated. "Yes, I suppose so."

"Anything else?"

"Not to tell her husband about this, and where to meet to get the money."

"Interesting. Quite an elaborate trick. Who was it to, and from?"

"I don't know. I think Yorick was going to fill those in himself. But it was strange, as surely that would give away his hand?"

"Perhaps he was just going to use initials," I said, "so it would be obvious to the recipient, but relatively easy to copy the initials from your hand. That way he wouldn't have to reveal any names to you."

"Ah, yes. He did also ask me to copy out capital letters on a separate sheet. Clever of you to think of that!"

"I don't suppose you have a copy of the letter, do you?" I said.

"I did practise, so I still have a copy at home. I remember thinking it was so odd, I had better keep it, just in case."

"Could you let me have it?" I said.

"Oh, but the police will be after me, won't they? For forging a letter."

"No," I said. "You were led to believe it was for a prank.

No blame whatsoever can be attached to you."

She sighed. "Very well. But I live out in Musselburgh. I could send it to you, though."

"That would be perfect. I'll give you my card – and four guineas. And here's another card for you to write your own address on." I got out of bed and fished these items and a pencil out of my jacket pocket, before sitting on the bed next to her. "And when I get the letter, I'll send you four more guineas. How does that sound?"

"That sounds very fair, Mr Rufford."

I was relieved beyond measure and smiled at her. She smiled back, and proceeded to write her address on one of the cards before playfully tucking it into my undergarments, her hand briefly lingering against me. "There," she said. "If you had to come and visit me, I dare say I wouldn't be too annoyed."

In the next room, I could hear a woman brazenly moaning, and there was the sound of a bed frame repeatedly hitting a wall.

"Pandora is a noisy one," Ophelia said. "Your hair is sticking up," she added, leaning over and carefully smoothing it down. "Are you sure you wouldn't like to...?"

Before I could answer, she had swung her leg over, and sat on my lap facing me. I felt her skin against me and her breath against my cheek, and my body ached for a yet more intimate embrace.

"I would like to, very much," I said, gently disentangling myself. "But I won't."

CHAPTER TWENTY-FOUR

IN comparison with my progress northwards, the journey back to Hawksbridge was a joy. I had exceeded my own expectations, and would soon be in possession of a letter that would surely illuminate Mr Ambrose's fate; and I had shown myself that I could resist female temptation. But it had been a close thing, a near-impossible exertion of will. I allowed myself some speculation: was Ophelia's willingness to indulge my pleasure simply the habit of her kind, or was there an inkling of affection? When held up against men like Mr Ambrose, I might seem a relatively benign example of my sex. But in any case, it did not matter – it was unlikely I would ever see her again, despite her invitation.

Waiting for me at Ramsburgh was an excited letter from Bess. I had only to deliver a letter to Mr Jackson containing financial assurances, and the tenancy of the shop would be hers. She also enclosed a list of expenses for setting up the shop and the sum she needed from me. In view of the amount I had just spent on procuring evidence, it seemed more than reasonable.

In the morning, I knocked on Flora's door, anxious to know whether our last conversation had had an adverse effect on her recovery, but was surprised to be told by Mrs Northcutt that she had gone early to resume work on the Town Hall mural.

"I told her she was being foolish," Mrs Northcutt complained, "but she wouldn't see sense. Said she had a lot of catching up to do, and it would distract her from things. Things you said to her, no doubt."

"Well, perhaps some exercise will help strengthen her

muscles after so much time spent in bed," I said, ignoring her last comment. "So long as she doesn't overdo it."

"Bound to overdo it, stood at the top of a ladder with a brush like a common decorator. It doesn't bear thinking about."

"Then, Mrs Northcutt, I suggest you don't, for the sake of your nerves. Thank you – I will call later."

I did not wait for a reply, and went to fetch Celeste from the stables. In town, I delivered my letter to Mr Jackson, who was pleased with the arrangement, and called on Bess to give her a cheque.

"I can't believe it's really going to happen!" she said, bringing me a cup of coffee. "And don't worry, coffee in the shop will be better than this, as I'll be getting the latest equipment and superior beans."

"Have you settled on a name yet?" I asked.

"I think 'Myrtle's'!" she said. "As you said, it has a reassuring feel about it."

"And what about staff?"

"I have made some enquiries, and have a list. One or two of my students are keen to help, against their parents' wishes, of course. But whenever I mention it to young women, they get quite enthusiastic about the idea! And generally the reverse when I'm talking to men."

"I'm not surprised," I said, sipping my coffee. "You're making a bold statement – in some countries, you would be persecuted for it. But perhaps one day it won't seem unusual at all."

"Well, progress can't all be about railways and clever inventions, can it? The way we see one another has to improve, one step at a time. After all, we got rid of slavery in this country. It's about time men and women looked at each other with greater charity and understanding. And respect, frankly."

"I totally agree," I said. "Speaking of railways, I haven't

seen you since Mr Wakeley's accident. I was only a few yards away when it happened."

"Oh! How awful!" Bess said. "I had heard about it. At Mrs Campbell's place, I believe?"

"Yes, it was an innocent expedition to see her old mill. Poor Victoria saw it happen."

"Ah – Victoria. How are you getting on with her?"

"We are friends," I said. "Nothing more. Although she is quite warm towards me."

"Of course she would fall for you," said Bess. "Oh dear – you won't break her heart, will you?"

"I assure you I won't. You would be proud at my forbearance in Edinburgh at the weekend."

"The club!" she said. "I had forgotten. What happened? You must tell me every disgusting detail."

I laughed. "It was quite as sordid as I had imagined. Boorish drunks leering at a lot of nearly-naked young women displaying themselves as women of the Empire, and white slaves, and suchlike. I admit it was quite interesting to see the different shapes, especially the African –"

"Thomas! I'm shocked," Bess said. "You should have looked away."

"That would not have been very authentic of me, would it?" I said.

"I suppose not," she said. "A convenient excuse. And did you find what you wanted? I mean, besides a satisfactory parade of women's bodies?"

"I think I did," I said. "The woman I was after, and some information. And I also found my willpower. You would have been impressed. An attractive female climbed onto my lap, and I resisted temptation."

"Bravo, Thomas!" said Bess. "Well done. You're growing up!"

"Perhaps," I said. "Or perhaps it's just self-interest. I need Phyllis' good opinion of me, and my stock is low at present."

~

I rode home under a grey sky and reflected that Bess would have been mortified to know that she was the main cause of Phyllis' disapproval. Or was she more hurt by my failure to confide in her about my past sins, rather than by the sins themselves? But giving up all one's secrets in the name of openness was a risky gambit. I could not imagine that I could ever reveal the extent to which I had comforted Mrs Ambrose. That incident was surely left buried in the past, for everyone's sake.

Flora was in when I tried a second time around four o'clock, and she had retired to bed.

"You must be exhausted!" I said as she smiled rather wanly up at me. "Were you really ready to go back to work?"

"I enjoyed it," she said. "I missed the sense of creating something. And the smell of the paint. But it has rather worn me out."

"Please be careful," I said. "After all, you probably haven't recovered from – well, my revelations."

"It's all right," she said. "I'll get used to it. Anyway, I'm too tired to think about all that properly. I don't have the energy for battling the past."

"But you believe we are brother and sister?" I said.

"If you say so. If the letter says so. I hear and see the words, but I can't turn them into a certainty in my mind. You need to give me time."

"Of course," I said. I was disappointed. I wanted to be able to celebrate the best part of this discovery: that neither of us was an only child any longer, and this house that had been so full of mystery and darkness had united us in the most unexpected way. But Flora had been weakened by illness, and I was asking too much of her. I changed the subject. "Are you coming to the Harrises' dinner party tonight? Victoria and Felicity will be there."

"No, I don't think so. I'm far too tired. And besides, Phyllis will probably be there."

"Oh, I'm sorry. You will be missed."

"Thank you. But you enjoy it, Thomas. I'm sure you deserve some amusement. Oh – did you find anything useful at the weekend?"

"I think I did," I said. "It's all a bit odd and somewhat scandalous – but I'm hopeful. I'll let you know about it properly soon."

"If you would."

"I'll let you rest," I said, getting up.

Flora closed her eyes. "Send my love to everyone! Including Pantoufle!"

~

It was too cold for the trap, so I had extravagantly hired a covered coach for Victoria and myself. When she appeared in the hall, I stared, for a moment unable to find any words. Her hair had been done beautifully with assistance from Catherine – who, it turned out, had many admirable skills – and she wore a turquoise dress she had recently had made in Hawksbridge. It was cunningly constructed to show off her figure, with a neckline that was on the daring side.

"Hello, Thomas!" she said, smiling with the full knowledge of the effect she would have on me, and indeed all the men at the party. "Will I do?"

I helped her into her wrap. "You will do," I said as we stepped into the drive. "You will do tremendously."

"Good," she said, and we climbed into the coach, where she took my arm. "Isn't this glorious fun? We can pretend we're a couple."

I must have looked awkward, since she said, "Don't worry. I'm quite aware I'm just warming Phyllis' seat, so to speak."

Mrs Harris welcomed us with her usual enthusiasm, and I was glad to see Felicity, who immediately came up to Victoria brandishing a sketchbook.

"Goodness!" said Victoria, putting it on a table and turning the pages. "How you have improved! I am astonished. You are now better than me. You won't have any trouble illustrating your book!"

Felicity looked pleased, and responded by giving Victoria a hug. "Thank you!" she said.

"Now careful, Felicity, you'll make Miss Clitheroe spill her drink!" said Mrs Harris, although she looked as charmed by this spontaneous display as Victoria was.

"How is your mother?" I asked.

"She's a little quiet," Felicity said, "and didn't feel in the mood for a party. But she thought I should come anyway. Even though everyone else is frightfully old."

"It just shows how mature you are," I said.

"Oh, and Mama said to tell you to come and visit," Felicity said, before running off to find a canapé.

"It must be a great comfort for Mrs Ambrose," Mrs Harris said, "for her to know that you are standing up for her. What a good friend you are to her."

I cringed at her choice of words, but said, "Thank you – I hope so."

"Now, Victoria," she said, "I want you to meet a great friend of mine, Mrs Florence Tambard."

"Miss Clitheroe, I am so delighted to meet you. I have heard all about your drawings, and I can see the effect your skill has had on Felicity. And Mr Rufford, how nice to see you again. Olivia continues to speak highly of you – I might almost warn David to be on his guard!"

"What nonsense you do talk, Florence," said Mrs Harris, digging her elbow into Mrs Tambard's arm. "Mrs Tambard is a great collector of antiques. Which must account for her tolerance of me."

"Actually, it was my husband who was the keen collector. Some of his enthusiasm has rubbed off on me. But he has already filled the house with the stuff, so I can scarcely squeeze in any more!"

"Interesting," I said. "Did your husband make use of the services of a Mr Blackwood, by any chance?"

For a split second, I thought I saw a troubled look on Mrs Tambard's face, but it was quickly replaced with a smile. "Oh, yes, indeed. Most of it came from him, in fact. We must have made Mr Blackwood a thoroughly wealthy man! He had a knack of knowing just what would pique my husband's interest."

I sensed an opportunity to find out more about Mr Blackwood. She might even shed further light on Mr Ambrose, as their paths must have crossed. "I would very much like to see your collection, Mrs Tambard – that is, if it's not too much trouble."

Mrs Tambard looked delighted to be asked, and touched my arm. "But certainly, Mr Rufford! You must come for tea, perhaps with Miss Clitheroe, if she would like to come too. It would be a great pleasure. Let us arrange something."

I nodded gratefully, and at that moment Phyllis came through the door.

"I'm so sorry to be late!" she said. She was followed by Dr Weldon, and my heart sank. "We thought it would be sensible to share a carriage, but it was rather slow to arrive."

"You're perfectly on time," said Mrs Harris, "and extremely welcome. I'm so glad you could come, Dr Weldon – I hope you don't mind bumping into some of your patients here!"

"Not at all, Mrs Harris," said Dr Weldon. "It's always reassuring to confirm that my patients are still alive."

Mrs Harris laughed heartily at that, further increasing my sense of annoyance. I could not cope with the man being indispensable, handsome and a wag to boot.

Introductions were made, and I tried to find an opportunity to talk to Phyllis, but failed to do so before were ushered into the dining room.

Dr Weldon was placed next to Phyllis, as if they were a couple. Perhaps they already were, I thought gloomily. I sat next to Victoria, which I did not object to, except to the extent that it might encourage Phyllis to see me in the wrong light. In a bid to lift my despondency, I began to consume wine at an unwise rate. I noticed that Victoria was not holding back either.

"Felicity," said Victoria, "how is Pantoufle? And your book? Are you making progress?"

"He's fine, thank you," Felicity said. "And the book is coming along, slowly. But we don't want to spoil it by showing it to anyone until it's ready."

"Yes," said Phyllis, "creativity can be a delicate flower."

"Perhaps like a potato plant," I offered. "The best bit is underground until it's ready to be dug up."

"Why, Mr Rufford," said Dr Weldon, raising his glass to me, "what a striking image. Creativity is naught but a humble potato."

Phyllis smiled at him and said, "Well, that's put me in my place. On the other hand, potatoes can be a lot more useful than some people's writing."

"Your writing is, I assure you," said Dr Weldon, "far more delicious than any vegetable."

I was not certain whether they were mocking me, but it made me very uncomfortable to see them so easy with each other.

Victoria must have sensed my pain, for she whispered in my ear, "I thought it was a fun analogy. And he's a bit pompous, isn't he?"

"Thank you," I whispered back gratefully.

"Anyway, I'd rather have you take my temperature," she continued quietly. "Or raise it."

"Shush!" I hissed, and fortunately, Mr Harris cleared his throat.

"Speaking of Pantoufle, I have a scrap of doggerel I thought I might share with you," he declared, "in honour of the soon-to-be-famous animal. Might I?" He shot an enquiring look at his wife.

"Yes, go ahead, dear," she said, patiently. "I think we've had just enough wine. And it is very short."

He retrieved a piece of paper from his breast pocket, stood up, and cleared his throat again. "An Ode to Pantoufle, A Handsome and Talented Squirrel," he said. "My apologies for sacrificing pronunciation in favour of rhyme. But if Shakespeare can rhyme 'prove' with 'love', I can take some liberties too." He held forth:

Of all my friends with a beautiful tail,
One is uppermost, no longer frail
But strong as an athlete, quick as a dart
With inspiring profile, a model for art
A hero for stories of daring and skill
In short, unique, not run-of-the-mill.
Should we sadly be parted from the great Pantoufle
We would gladly remember, but remain ever rueful.

Mr Harris bowed and sat down, to laughter and applause. Felicity was particularly pleased, and took Mr Harris' poem to read.

"Very witty, David!" Mrs Tambard said. "What a clever husband you have, Olivia."

"Oh, the joys of retirement," muttered Mrs Harris.

~

"It's such a shame Francesca couldn't come," said Mrs Harris after we had finished our dessert. "I could have served syllabub, and she would have demonstrated her knack for food sculpture."

"Food sculpture?" said Mrs Tambard. "I think I'm missing something. Do tell."

"Mrs Campbell has a strange party trick," said Mr Harris. "If the syllabub has the right consistency, she carves it into a tongue. It's most entertaining. The way it wobbles around is truly horrible."

"Oh, how silly!" said Felicity. "I must try that."

"She sounds a most unusual woman," said Mrs Tambard.

"She is," said Mr Harris. "I like her enormously. But no doubt she is affected by the death of her business partner, Mr Wakeley. I'm not surprised she's not ready for company."

"I fear she is also embarrassed by her purchase of Hawksbridge Castle," I said. "She regrets it, after seeing the strength of people's affection for the ruin."

"I'm glad to hear that," Phyllis said. "I was struggling not to think the worse of her for it. But it will be sold soon, alas, and then she can put it behind her."

"Such a terrible business, Mr Wakeley dying like that," Mrs Tambard said. "Do we know what happened?"

I was going to speak, but Victoria evidently decided it was her responsibility to tell the story.

"Yes," she said. "Mrs Campbell took us to see her old water mill. I wanted to talk to him about my investments, so he and I went inside, as I didn't want everyone to know about the state of my finances. I stopped for a moment while he went up to the second floor for a better view, and as I was starting to follow him, I saw him fall onto the wheel."

"A tragic accident," I said. "I didn't like the man, but he

certainly didn't deserve that."

"How do you know?" said Victoria.

I was taken aback. "Well, I don't know for sure – but who would deserve such a thing?"

"Perhaps he did something awful, and God was punishing him," Victoria persisted.

"I'm not sure that's how God works," said Dr Weldon. "But you may be right. Our amateur detective here –" he gestured at me – "would no doubt sniff out any foul play if there were any of the human kind. But even you, sir, would be hard pressed to arrest God!"

I had the distinct impression I was being patronised, but far worse was to come – from the usually mild Mr Harris, whose cheeks were now thoroughly flushed with wine.

"And in any case," Mr Harris said, waving his empty glass in the direction of the butler, "Mr Rufford might not be the man to indict God, when he has been entertaining himself amongst the rakes of Edinburgh at the weekend! In The Vesuvius, no less!"

Mrs Harris was open-mouthed in shock. "David, whatever can you mean by that wicked remark? Apologise at once!"

"Oh, nonsense, dear, I was merely making sport. You don't mind a bit of sport, Mr Rufford, do you?"

I looked at him and shrugged, and this chastened him somewhat.

"Oh," he said. "I'm sorry. I just heard a silly rumour from an old friend, about a new member of the... you know, a club of a particular... no matter, please talk amongst yourselves. It's a habit of mine to put my foot in it." He drank from his refilled glass and stared at the table in mortification.

"How interesting," said Phyllis. "Thomas, please tell us about your exciting trip. What kind of club is it?"

Mrs Harris said, "I'm sure Thomas has no need to explain himself, my dear."

By now all eyes were turned on me. An explanation was indeed expected.

"Thank you, Mrs Harris," I said, "but I need to set the record straight. I went to a gentlemen's club at the weekend, as Mr Harris says. It was not a genteel club. They do not just smoke and play billiards. But I had a specific reason – to find information that may clear Mrs Ambrose of her husband's murder, and find the true killer."

Dr Weldon laughed and tried, rather too ostentatiously, to turn it into a cough, while Phyllis kept her steely gaze on me.

"That almost sounds too good to be true," she said. "Why on earth would you need to attend this club to find such information? Why not simply ask people, in the usual fashion?"

"Because I could not identify the person otherwise without scaring them away," I said. "You don't just ask to speak to their... employees, unless you're a police officer. And even that would be no guarantee."

"And did you find the information you were looking for?" Phyllis said.

"Some of it, and I expect some more shortly. So I think my expedition was not in vain."

Mrs Tambard had been following the conversation intently, and looked at me with some seriousness. "Mr Rufford," she said, "I think it's admirable that you are trying to get to the truth. I never thought Mrs Ambrose was guilty. And Mr Ambrose's ghastly death must be properly – well, avenged is not too strong a word for it."

She looked around the room. "I must say," she continued, "I am glad Mr Rufford is taking his mission seriously, and I'm glad he went to Edinburgh. I'm sorry, Mr Harris, but I don't find this to be a laughing matter. Congratulations, I say, Mr Rufford! Congratulations and good luck!" And she raised her glass to me.

There was an awkward murmur of reluctant agreement,

followed by a painful silence.

Felicity broke it, by saying brightly, "So, Mr Rufford, what *does* everyone do at this club?"

~

"Well done for evading Felicity's question," said Victoria on the way back to Ramsburgh. "You can tell me, though, can't you? What did you get up to?"

"Perhaps later. I'm still smarting from the knowledge that everyone now thinks I'm a degenerate."

"I don't," Victoria said. "And neither does Mrs Tambard. I think you impressed her."

"She was kind," I said, "which is more than can be said for Dr Weldon."

"I know," she said. "Isn't he a dreadful prig?"

"He was quick to put you down," I said. "But do you really suspect Mr Wakeley of being so bad?"

"Oh, who knows," she said, yawning. "Let's not talk about him. I'm so tired." She shuffled up the bench and laid her head on my shoulder. "Do you mind?"

"No," I said. Victoria's warmth was welcome after Phyllis' frostiness. I had hoped that I might speak to Phyllis alone and restore our friendship – and now things were worse between us than ever, and apparently Dr Weldon had insinuated himself further into Phyllis' affections. My increasingly elaborate visions of a future married life with the woman I could not imagine being without, so often rehearsed by night and by day, were crumbling into dust.

CHAPTER TWENTY-FIVE

THE following day, I went to visit Mrs Ambrose, after being tipped off by Felicity the night before. Before we left the party, she had told me about a picture that her father had been given by a 'friend'. Her mother had been especially upset about it when it had arrived.

"It's been bothering me," Felicity had said. "I even had a dream about it. I don't suppose it's anything, but I want you to have every little scrap of information there is! Given my mother might – well, you know. It's a picture of a woman holding a cat."

Mrs Ambrose embraced me tightly with a hint of the hunger I had experienced before her husband died.

"It's so good to see you, Thomas," she said. "I have a fresh pot of coffee – let's sit and talk. How are you? Have you made any progress? Forgive me –"

"It's quite all right, Isobel," I said. "Yes, I think so, but I don't want to give you false hope, so I need to work on it. There's something of Yorick's I need to look at, if you don't mind."

"Yes?"

"A picture. Felicity described it me: a woman with a cat. In his bedroom, I think."

"Oh!" she said. "I can't imagine why she would mention that. It's of no interest, truly."

"Your daughter has good instincts," I said. "It might be important. If I could look in his bedroom?"

"Oh, very well," she said. "But it's not in his bedroom any more. I put it away in a cupboard. I never liked it. I shall fetch it for you."

Mrs Ambrose soon returned with the picture, which was as Felicity had described, albeit smaller than I had expected, being an oval about ten inches at its largest dimension. The artist had captured the flesh tones beautifully, perhaps with flattering exaggeration, and the composition was charming. The sitter, in her early twenties, wore a mischievous smile and held a tabby cat that echoed her gaze out of the frame. Without context, it was hard to see why Mrs Ambrose would object to it.

I turned it over in my hands, and then saw the reason. In small, feminine writing on one of the stretchers had been inked the words: 'For dearest Yorick, from his F.T.' There was evidence of a torn label that might once have identified the painter and subject.

Mrs Ambrose looked down at her knotted hands. "Now you see why I never liked it. It's as though she's laughing at me."

"I'm very sorry," I said. "It must have been very painful to have to see this hanging in his room."

"I never knew of the inscription until a few days ago," she said, "when I removed it. But I hated it anyway, because I knew he didn't buy it, and he was evasive when I asked him – even rather proud of the secret. It was bound to be from some woman."

"And you have no idea who F.T. might be?"

She shook her head. "No, and I don't want to know."

"Judging by the ageing of the paint, and the clothes, I don't think it's a portrait of the giver," I said. "She will be long gone by now. But she is rather pretty." I started. "Oh! Of course!"

"Are you all right, Thomas?" said Mrs Ambrose, concerned by the look of surprise on my face.

Something had needled me last night, something I could not put my finger on. Now it made perfect sense, if I had correctly surmised the identity of 'F.T.'

~

"Mr Rufford! What a splendid surprise. And so soon! Well, make yourself comfortable, and I will order some tea. Or coffee?"

"Coffee would be excellent, thank you!"

Mrs Florence Tambard's house was a fanciful, neo-Gothic pile with ornate, latticed windows and a tower finished with a small turret that gave it the appearance of a rectory that had fused with its church. The drawing room was reminiscent of Mr Ambrose's, in the density of objects and paintings that it hosted. Mr Tambard and Mr Ambrose had shared a passion for old things – had they also shared a woman?

I looked around me. "Your house is exquisite, Mrs Tambard. This room reminds me of another."

"Thank you, Mr Rufford. What room might that be?"

I watched Mrs Tambard's expression as I said, "The drawing room at Mr Ambrose's house."

I was not disappointed; I could see from her face that she knew I was making the connection for a purpose.

"Oh – yes, perhaps," she said, composing herself. "Well, as you know, my husband and Mr Ambrose were both keen collectors. Perhaps they competed a little. You know how men are!"

"Yes, indeed. Did they compete in another way, Mrs Tambard?"

"Another way?" Her usually deep voice rose in feigned innocence.

"I'm sorry to ask," I said. "I wouldn't if I didn't need to. I need all the information I can get –"

"For Mrs Ambrose, of course, of course," she murmured.

"Thank you," she said to the butler delivering our coffee. She took a sip and sighed before answering.

"My husband and Mr Ambrose were friends, as well as

rivals. They used to love discussing their finds, and they played golf together. Sometimes Mr Ambrose would call when my husband was out, and we would talk. I know he could be an irascible man, but he was interesting, and I confess my husband was beginning to be less so."

"And so you became lovers?"

"Only after my husband had died," Mrs Tambard said. "I was surprised to find that Yorick quite disregarded the disparity in our ages, though I like to think I have preserved myself reasonably well." She frowned. "I was acutely aware of the wrong I was doing to Mrs Ambrose. But it was too much of a pleasure to give up. It was wicked, I know."

"I don't judge you at all," I said. "Especially when you were so kind as to come to my defence last night."

"Oh! Well, I may look like a fusty old widow, Mr Rufford, but I'm not a prude. And I could tell immediately that you are a man of honour."

I did not argue with this assessment, although I doubted its accuracy.

"Were you still seeing each other when Mr Ambrose died?" I asked.

"Yes," Mrs Tambard said. "Yes, we were. I am so sorry. I should have come forward, but... it would have been so humiliating, and so painful for Mrs Ambrose."

"Did Mr Ambrose visit you on the night before his death, after the Society meeting?"

"Yes," Mrs Tambard said, blowing her nose. "My darling Yorick was here. As usual, he was restless in the small hours, and left early. If he hadn't come to me, then perhaps he would still be alive."

"Not necessarily," I said. "His killer was evidently quite determined. I'm sure he would have struck another time."

"I suppose so. It's a strange sort of comfort, but thank you."

"Is there anything he said that was unusual – that might

shed some light on his death? Anyone he was seeing, or doing business with?"

Mrs Tambard gazed into the fire and considered this. "I can't think of anything. But he did keep talking about marriage lately. That seemed odd, all things considered."

"Oh?"

"Yes, he said: 'If I were free, would you marry me?' And I said, 'Perhaps, but you are not free.' He said it two or three times over the last few months."

"That is strange. Perhaps he was just looking for reassurance that you loved him enough to marry him, if things were different."

"That's possible," she said. "He could be unsure of himself like that, for all his bravado."

She looked pensive. "Mrs Ambrose wasn't ill, was she?" she said.

"No, she seems very well to me," I said, "apart from the recent jolt to her nerves. Why?"

"Oh, nothing, just trying to think of a reason for what Yorick said. He seemed... Oh, I don't know. He was just in a strange mood, that's all."

"He was very caught up in the matter of the castle land," I said. "Might that have accounted for his strange mood? A kind of mania?"

"It might. I don't know. Oh, it's all so vexing. Would you like a tour of the house? I know you are here for your investigations, but now I've got you –"

"I'd be honoured to see around your house," I said, finishing my coffee. I entertained the hope that some useful tidbit might slip out in an unguarded moment.

CHAPTER TWENTY-SIX

MRS Tambard had an admirable collection, including a Henry Raeburn of superior quality: a full-length portrait of a characterful, middle-aged lady whose demeanour, clothes and expression suggested that she had achieved everything she wanted in life, including being painted by the foremost portraitist of her time.

Although there was no single, definite clue amongst these treasures, the aggregate effect was significant. It strongly impressed upon me the desirability of marriage to a woman in possession of such riches. With what intensity Mr Ambrose must have envied Mr Tambard his chattels, both material and human! How he must have dreamt about marrying Mrs Tambard, so that he could at one stroke add the Tambard treasure-house to his own collection and sate all of his desires. All it required was the absence of his current wife. And yet, his wife lived, and he was dead.

A letter awaited me: from Ophelia! I fairly grabbed it from Shipley's hand and took it to the top of the house to read. I scanned the covering letter.

> Dear Mr Rufford,
>
> You see, I am as good as my word!
>
> Here is the letter – the content is the same as the one I gave to Yorick.
>
> I hope it is of some use. I am not sorry to have the thing out of the house. It gives me the shivers.
>
> I was glad to meet you, although I feel you have not got everything you paid for! If you care to visit me in Musselburgh, we can see about putting that right.

Yours,

Ophelia

With trembling hands – so much had I invested in the acquisition of this piece of paper – I unfolded and read the letter that Mr Ambrose had asked Ophelia to copy out.

> I write after all these years to obtain redress for the grievous wrongs you have done me. You have balanced your pleasure and my place in Heaven against mere trinkets. The corruption of my soul, far from being a faded memory, has only increased over the years, to the point that now I must have acknowledgement, apology and compensation if I am to live in sanity. Otherwise I have no alternative but to expose to everyone what you have done, and what you are: and this will surely mean the end of your comfortable existence in Hawksbridge.
>
> I have the means to prove it, but I will return all of this information to you in exchange for the sum of a thousand guineas. I am sure this is possible for you, knowing as I do the nature and success of your business.
>
> I will meet you with this information at the ruined chapel off Dewberry Lane on Sunday the 3rd of December at 6 o'clock. If you fail to arrive, or if you mention any of this to my husband or anyone else, I will immediately submit letters to the newspapers detailing your crimes.
>
> Once this painful exchange has been made, you may live in peace, and my soul may also find balm knowing that you have paid a price for your barbarism.

I re-read the letter, horrified. The stakes implied by this letter were enormous, and certainly enough for murder to be the outcome. Blackmail had a habit of being accompanied by death. But why Mr Ambrose's?

My first deduction was trivial enough: the mention of a husband confirmed that the letter was masquerading as being from a married woman. A woman who had been the victim of some kind of harm – real or imagined – at the hands of the recipient. How much of it reflected reality, I had no way of knowing.

But let us suppose, I thought, that the hurt mentioned in the letter was genuine. The forgery indicated that Mr Ambrose did not want this woman to know about the scheme, but he himself knew of the harm that had befallen the woman. This implied, perhaps, some degree of intimacy; so the woman might be Mrs Ambrose, or a mistress, such as Mrs Tambard.

The letter put the supposed author in not inconsiderable danger, and the amount of money demanded was suspiciously high. It was very possible that the recipient would not want to pay, and would instead have the opportunity – at a remote location with no one else about – to dispatch his victim, assuming she had been persuaded to present herself at the appointed time on some pretext or other.

I had to conclude that in all probability, this was an attempt to have the woman killed. It carried a certain amount of risk – what if she did not turn up? Then, I supposed, another rendezvous could be arranged, if Mr Ambrose was watching and aware of the situation. What if she professed no knowledge of the letter? That might appear as some strange deception, and be disregarded by the potential murderer. Indeed, the fact that she did not have the promised material might provoke him all the more.

It quickly dawned on me that Mrs Ambrose was the likely target, as her untimely death would allow Mr Ambrose to get his hands on Mrs Tambard and her treasures. In which case, if I could find out who had perpetrated offences against Mrs Ambrose some years ago, I would know the identity of the recipient and would-be murderer.

Perhaps not 'would-be', I realised. Was it possible that this person had rumbled Mr Ambrose's plot, and decided that he was too dangerous an antagonist to remain at large?

My mouth was dry from this grim train of thought. I went

downstairs to find a drink to steady my nerves, and in the drawing room, I found Victoria and Catherine deep in conversation on the sofa by the fire.

Catherine started to get up. "Sorry – I shouldn't be here."

"Nonsense! Do sit down," I said. "You both look so comfortable and decorative, and I sorely need company. Port, ladies?"

"Yes, please," said Victoria, and Catherine looked doubtful.

"It is nearly Christmas!" I said. "And I think we all deserve it."

"Thank you, sir," Catherine said, and I went to the sideboard to pour the drinks.

"Catherine has been telling me about Mr Wakeley," said Victoria. "It seems he is something of a villain."

"I hope this isn't too painful for you, Catherine," I said, bringing the glasses to the table in front of the sofa. "You don't have to talk about it if you don't want to."

"I want to," said Catherine. "It feels good." She sipped her port and added, "And this tastes good."

"Excellent!" I said, taking a seat and raising my glass. "Here's to making peace with the troubles in our lives!"

My companions raised theirs, and Victoria said, "Apparently Mr Wakeley has been making a habit of attaching himself to single women of means and making promises he had no right to make, and no intention of keeping. And then when he had captured their affections, he extracted large sums for non-existent investments, or to save his allegedly failing business."

"In that case you had a close call, perhaps, Victoria," I said.

"He was not romantically interesting to me," she said, "and I hope I would have seen through any financial bluster."

"But was he on the verge of going straight?" I said. "After all, the castle land investment was, as far as I know, sound –

and quite astute. I gather from Francesca that he worked hard on calculating the optimal spot for the railway on the north bank of the river."

"Yes," said Catherine, "he studied for long hours – and even read books about rocks!"

"Perhaps he tired of his previous methods," said Victoria, "and saw a more lucrative opportunity. But his old habits were still in evidence in befriending Francesca."

"She resisted his romantic charms, fortunately," I said. "But he still persuaded her to put down a lot of money, to the detriment of her standing in Hawksbridge."

"I am so sorry," Catherine said. "He terrified me. I wanted to help Mrs Campbell, and the others, but... I was weak. And I am not the sort of person people listen to." Tears rolled down her cheeks.

Victoria linked her arm with Catherine's and squeezed her hand. "You have nothing to reproach yourself about," she said. "He was entirely to blame – he knew how to wield power over women."

I nodded. "Victoria is right," I said. "You must try to stop blaming yourself." I tried to move the conversation to calmer waters. "How strange that you were both in Leeds at the same time!"

"Not quite," Victoria said. "I was in Florence with my parents over the summer."

"Was Florence everything you hoped it would be?" I said.

"Well, it was beautiful, of course, and a cultural feast. But it was also very noisy, and I was not happy. I was a sore trial for my parents."

"I'm sorry to hear that," I said. "Were you home-sick?"

"In a way," she said. "I was receiving distressing letters from a friend – but enough of melancholy thoughts. May I have some more port?"

"I must go and start on dinner," Catherine said, and got up.

"I look forward to it!" I said, taking Victoria's glass and mine to refill.

When I sat down again, she smiled at me. "I want it to be like this forever," she said, sighing and resting her head on the back of the sofa. "But Mrs Rufford might have something to say about that."

"Whoever she may be, if she's in my future at all," I said.

"Hush now! Don't be a defeatist," Victoria said. "But you will need to improve your game. I went to see Phyllis this morning to show her some passages in my novel." She took a sip of port.

"Oh?"

"Dr Weldon was just leaving. Perhaps he was seeing her father – I don't know. But she did ask me what I thought of him. Dr Weldon, I mean."

"Ah. That's not a good sign. What did you say?"

"I said I thought him quite good looking, but a trifle smug, and with a cruel sense of humour that she might grow to hate. I said he appeared to lack warmth, and that she could do better, and find a man with a generous heart who understands her! I think it was clear who I meant by that."

"Well done," I said. "I don't suppose she liked that very much."

"No, but she thanked me for my opinion. So you see – you must make a move, Thomas! Sweep her off her feet. Show her what a lovely, desirable fellow you are. Kiss her!"

"I already have."

"Well, kiss her some more. And take her to the theatre! Write her some love letters! Oh, I'm sure you can write enchanting letters."

"Yes, you're right," I said. "I have been so fixed on this case that I have neglected other things. But speaking of which, may I take advantage of your brains?"

"My dear Thomas," she said, draining her second glass of port, "you may take advantage of me in any way you wish."

"Alas, I shall only be requiring your brains," I said, and explained the relevant details of the Ambrose case, including the blackmail letter.

"So you see," I concluded, "if we can find the intended recipient of the letter, in all probability we have our murderer."

"Extraordinary," Victoria said. "I can see that it might be a sufficient motive for Mr Ambrose's murder. Not proof, of course."

"Once we know who it is, we may be able to find proof," I said.

"Or trick the truth out of him."

"Perhaps," I said.

"But surely if Mrs Ambrose was the intended victim, and some great wrong has been done to her, she should be able to just tell you who it is?"

"I will speak to her again – but she can be very obstinate. She was not happy about me going into Ambrose's safe. There's obviously a chapter of her life that she desperately wants to keep buried. But I will try again."

"A shameful, dirty secret," Victoria said. "How fascinating. That reminds me – there's a secret you still haven't shared with me, Thomas."

"Oh? What secret was that?"

"That antique of Francesca's – the 'Wicked Cassone' – you never told me what was so wicked about it."

"That's true, I didn't."

"Well?"

"I will need another glass of port," I said, and she waved her empty glass at me.

Having poured us another glass each, against my better judgement, I gathered my thoughts.

"It depicts," I said, "Aphrodite in the throes of passion with a lover. But her husband is concealed behind a rock holding her hand."

Victoria nearly spat out her port. "Oh my!" she said.

"That's horrible. Why on earth would anyone want that on their wedding chest?"

I shrugged. "That's just on the front. On the inside of the lid, there's a painting of the same three people making love together."

Victoria's eyes widened. "How astonishing," she said.

"And on the bottom of the piece, there's a naked woman stretched out on her front. That one is relatively tasteful. Although it does make me think that she's been locked in the chest."

"Goodness," Victoria said. "I should like to see it. It's too fascinating."

"Yes, in a horrible way."

"And Mr Ambrose was so upset in losing it to Francesca," Victoria said. "I wonder why. I mean it's obviously an extraordinary piece, but Mrs Ambrose would hardly approve of such a thing in the house, surely?"

"I don't think her opinion counted for very much in that household," I said.

"No. But – Thomas, I have had a terrible idea." She sipped her port, lost in thought, and after a moment continued. "Do you think Mr Ambrose had an affinity with the chest, somehow? Is that why he wanted it?"

"You mean he wanted to emulate the scenes in the paintings?"

"Worse than that," she said. "That he had already done something of the sort, and wanted the chest as a sort of homage to it. So he could show the piece off, knowing that it had a significance that no one would guess at."

"Good Lord," I said. "It's an interesting theory. So if this is true, he may have sanctioned the immoral union of his wife with another. Perhaps even forced her into it."

She nodded. "That would explain a great deal, wouldn't it?"

"Yes," I said. "Mrs Ambrose's intransigence, and the

'grievous wrongs' in the letter. Mr Ambrose was quite aware of how it might have affected his wife, but nevertheless was simply using it to get her killed. He really was an evil brute if this is the case."

"It's ingenious, in a twisted way," Victoria said. "Now, if we could guess the name of the person involved, you can go to Mrs Ambrose and see what her reaction is! What else did you find in Mr Ambrose's study?"

"Invoices for his antique purchases," I said. "With some hefty discounts for being a good customer."

Victoria stared at me. "Just how good a customer?" she said.

"Oh my God," I said. "You're not suggesting...?"

"Why not?" she said. "We know the man has no scruples whatsoever. If he can plot to have his wife killed, he can also sell her in exchange for his precious *objets d'art*. It all makes perfect sense."

"It was the only way he could have afforded all the pieces in that house," I said. "Mr Blackwood – I should have seen it before."

"It does you credit," Victoria said, "that you could not even imagine it."

We sat in silence for a minute, ruminating on our unpleasant insights.

"But something bothers me about this whole theory," I eventually said. "How on earth could Mr Ambrose know that his plan would work? I mean, Mr Blackwood may have been immoral enough to accept the offer of his wife, but to have the ability to kill a woman?"

"Presumably, they knew one another quite well," said Victoria. "Well enough for Mr Ambrose to even make the offer in the first place. So if he knew he would agree with his scheme, then what else did he know about him?"

"I saw a lot of military memorabilia in Blackwood's shop," I said. "It made me uncomfortable. It suggests a spell in the army, which means he knows how to kill."

Victoria pulled a face.

"Otherwise," I continued, "was there a specific incident that assured Ambrose that Blackwood could kill? Has he killed before?"

"You could go to the police office and ask for records of unsolved murders," Victoria suggested.

"Or suspicious deaths," I said. "Lord Almighty – the maid!"

"The maid?"

"A maid called Susan," I said. "She was employed by the Ambroses some years ago, and later left under a cloud, and shortly afterwards killed herself. Except not everyone thinks it was suicide."

"Oh no!" Victoria said. "The poor woman."

"Yes, it's ghastly. So why did Mr Ambrose's plan rebound on him so spectacularly? Presumably Blackwood rumbled it as soon as he got the letter, since the scheduled meeting didn't even take place."

"And then," Victoria mused, "having discovered it was Ambrose who was trying to use him to kill his wife – which could lead to Blackwood himself being hanged his anger led him to murder Ambrose. That would mean one fewer person who knew about the arrangement with this wife."

"True. And it's just possible," I said, "that Blackwood felt some pity for Mrs Ambrose – maybe even some guilt? – and in killing Ambrose, knew it might save Mrs Ambrose's life. A kind of penance for doing her wrong."

"A chink of hope for the man's soul, then. And yet, not so much hope if he killed that maid for something that happened in the house... what on earth happened at the Ambroses?"

"I need to find out," I said, getting up. "Right now. Can you tell Catherine I'll be back late? Whatever she's making, I'll eat cold."

CHAPTER TWENTY-SEVEN

THE cold, late afternoon air was what I needed to shake off the effects of the port, and my mind was racing from the bleak deductions that Victoria and I had made. Celeste seemed to sense my urgency, and I arrived at Houndswood before the sun had sunk much lower.

"Why, Thomas!" exclaimed Mrs Ambrose when I strode into the house, giving the butler no time to announce me. "You are most welcome, but is something wrong? You look agitated."

"I'm sorry to visit so late," I said, getting my breath back. "But the truth is revealing itself. There are things I must know – that I must ask you. May we speak in private?"

"You are starting to alarm me, Thomas," she said. "But of course. Let's go into the library. You look as though you need a strong coffee – Rayner, some coffee, please."

When I had closed the door, I sat down and encouraged Mrs Ambrose to do the same.

"I have made much progress," I said. "I'm sure there will be no need for you to stand trial. But my task isn't complete, and unfortunately I will first have to tell you some unpleasant things, before I ask you some more questions."

"Oh dear," Mrs Ambrose said. "That is, I am very pleased about your success, but surely I have told you everything you need?"

"Perhaps not," I said. "Let me first show you a letter that your husband had made for him." I unfolded the letter, and placed it in front of her.

"I'm afraid I don't have my spectacles –"

"Then I will read it for you. It's in a woman's hand." I

read the letter aloud, and Mrs Ambrose looked deeply pained.

"But – why? What is the purpose of this?"

"Unfortunately, the purpose is your death. Yorick intended to goad somebody else into killing you, Isobel, but his plan only led to his own death. I'm sorry to have to tell you this."

I could see Mrs Ambrose trying valiantly to control herself, and starting to form a response, but it was no use. She began to sob uncontrollably, and I squeezed her arm sympathetically.

"I'm sorry," I said again. "It's very hard to comprehend, but I believe it to be the truth."

Rayner came in with the coffee.

"Are you well, ma'am? Should Mr Rufford perhaps return on another occasion?"

"No, it's quite all right, Rayner," Mrs Ambrose said. "I will be myself soon."

The butler hesitated, throwing me a hostile glance, and left.

"Why would Yorick want to kill me, Thomas? I mean, I may not have been much of a wife to him, but I think he at least appreciated my domestic virtues. And I am the mother of his child! How could he even think of doing such a thing?"

"I believe he had thoughts of marrying his mistress, who had inherited a fine collection of furniture and paintings from her husband," I said, hating myself for hurting her with this revelation.

"Oh!" She laughed slightly hysterically. "Of course. For more of his precious antiques. Well, I should have seen it coming. And who is this mysterious widow?"

"A Mrs Florence Tambard."

"I see. 'F.T.', I suppose?" she said.

"I think so."

I took a swig of coffee. "I need to ask you a difficult question," I said. "What are the 'grievous wrongs' that Yorick refers to? Clearly Yorick, the recipient, and you all knew about this. Otherwise it would make no sense as a blackmail letter."

Mrs Ambrose covered her eyes with her hands. "I cannot tell you," she said. "I will not."

"You can," I said, "and you must – to save your own life. Let me make a suggestion as to the identity of the recipient – and the perpetrator. Please look at me, Isobel."

Reluctantly, she dropped her hands and gazed at me.

"It was Mr Blackwood, wasn't it?"

Her bottom lip trembled and tears rolled down her cheeks. She nodded.

I continued: "This is difficult for me to say, but I think I know the nature of the wrongs that Mr Blackwood did you." Mrs Ambrose looked away and fiddled with her handkerchief. "I believe Yorick allowed you to be subjected to certain attentions from Mr Blackwood in exchange for a discount on his purchases. Is that right?"

Again she nodded and blinked back the tears.

"Oh – you deserve to know everything, Thomas. It will be a relief to tell someone after all this time. I'm sorry I kept it from you. I'm so ashamed."

"I understand," I said. "It was a terrible thing to happen to you. But if I may ask – why did you submit to it? Could you not have refused?"

"It makes no sense if you don't know everything," she said. "Maybe it still won't make sense. But you must know that my marriage to Yorick was never an equal match. Before he took to spending all his money on old fripperies, he was something of a philanthropist. One of his favourite charities was the Hawksbridge Magdalene Asylum, and in the course of his visits, he became friendly with a woman who had had a baby out of wedlock. The baby died, and he took it upon himself to extract her from the Asylum, and thereby keep her grateful and beholden to him for the rest of her life."

"I'm so sorry," I said. "I had no idea."

"My place in Hell was assured before I ever met Mr Blackwood. Yorick told me that it made no difference if I gave myself to another man – I was already a miserable sinner. And he made it plain that I would feel the back of his hand if I refused. So I gave into it. Wives should do what their husbands say – especially this wife, who barely deserved to be rescued and improved. Yorick made sure that young, feckless Isobel from the Asylum was transformed into elegant Isobel Ambrose, a woman he could bear to be seen with when the occasion demanded. Another piece for his house. And a helpful commodity."

She fidgeted with her coffee cup.

"Yorick would hand me a piece of paper on which were written the words 'Special Discount', the date and time, and the amount of money it would save him, to encourage my diligence. I would dutifully go up to the attic room to receive Mr Blackwood at the appointed hour, having ensured that there were clean sheets on the bed and fresh flowers on the chest of drawers. And a jug of water, and towels. Small, civilised things to make the whole sordid business more bearable."

I shuddered as I recalled the cyclamen in my room – the same room! And I too had made use of the towels so solicitously provided.

"At first," she continued, "I was disgusted by what I had to endure. But over time, my terror of it dulled, and as Yorick lost interest in me, I even started to welcome it. Someone was at least paying me attention. And although Mr Blackwood was not always gentle, neither was he entirely oblivious to my own needs. I expect it increased his pleasure to see that I was not merely a cold vessel. I even think he might have had some affection for me, although the circumstances were hardly conducive to him expressing it."

She paused to wipe away her tears.

"Strange as though it will seem to you, Thomas, I came to

look forward to these encounters. Hell could not burn any hotter for each additional sin, and so I believed – as Yorick told me – that it made no moral difference. I enjoyed it, God help me: I came to crave the pleasure and the depravity. I encouraged Yorick's expenditure, so he would have to rely more heavily on discounts. I became dependent on the pleasure, and the transgressive nature of it. It was a terrible secret that I could think about in the drawing rooms of Hawksbridge, where everyone was so proper."

"But – if I may ask," I said, "were you not afraid of getting with child?"

She shook her head. "It was a strict condition of Yorick's that I should not get pregnant by Mr Blackwood. So he resorted to – certain means."

Mrs Ambrose looked down at the library table, flushing pink. "I won't elaborate on that, if you don't mind, Thomas."

"No, no, that's quite all right," I said, truly not wishing to hear the details.

"Now do you see why I didn't want you to find out? And especially not Felicity. Can it be hidden from her? How could I face her if she knew what a monster I am?"

"You are not a monster," I said. "You have simply been used badly. I will make sure that the police are presented with only the necessary facts. And certainly no one else needs to know that it was not always a wholly coercive transaction."

"Thank you," said Mrs Ambrose. "I just wanted to be completely honest with you, at last. You have done so much for me, and I have foolishly resisted your help. I feel better for telling you everything."

She reached out her hand and placed it on mine, smiling as she wiped away her tears.

"There is one more thing I need to ask you, Isobel," I said. "It's about your former maid, Susan Lipton. Is there anything you can tell me about her? There is some doubt about the manner of her death. Was it connected with this house? Can you tell me why she really left your employ?"

"Oh – I forgot about poor Susan," said Mrs Ambrose. "I haven't told you everything yet after all, have I? I'm sorry. I didn't want to think about her again. But I *will* be a better person, now."

"Thank you," I said.

"Susan was forbidden from going up there during the time of the 'appointments'. But one day, she did. I think she wanted to protect me. She flung open the door in the middle of – well, it – and tried to pull Mr Blackwood off me. She was screaming to him to stop raping me, and how she was going to tell everyone about what an evil bugger he was – excuse my language!"

"That's quite all right," I said. "And how did he react to this?"

"He was furious. He flung her across the room, and told her that if she told a living soul, she would be a corpse floating down the river the next day. To my shame, I didn't do anything."

"And then she was sacked?" I said.

"Yes, Mr Blackwood must have told Yorick to sack her. And not long after, she killed herself."

"Or she was said to have killed herself. Is it not more likely that Mr Blackwood either suspected her of telling someone what she had seen, or he had killed her just to be on the safe side?"

"Oh, God," she said. "Perhaps. Especially if he had it in him to kill Yorick. It's possible. Oh Lord..." She buried her face in her hands again. "I might have stopped that, somehow."

"I don't think so," I said. "Is there someone in the household I could talk to who might have known Susan?"

"Yes – yes, May knew her quite well."

At that moment Rayner came in to announce that dinner was ready.

"Would you join me for dinner, Thomas?" Mrs Ambrose said, drying her eyes again. "You're very welcome."

"No, thank you. I'm not hungry. I'd better be going. I'm sorry I had to ask these painful questions."

She nodded.

"I think we have our man now," I continued. "But we need something else, so that no doubt remains. I have an idea about it. I'll come back tomorrow to speak to May, if you don't mind? I might bring my friend Victoria."

~

After returning and eating my cold chicken, I went to bed but lay awake for some hours turning all the facts over in my mind and weighing up the dangers and benefits of attempting to trap Mr Blackwood. My plan involved invoking May's sympathy for her friend, and perhaps even for Mrs Ambrose, and that would be achieved more easily with gentle persuasion by one of her own sex.

At about two o'clock in the morning, I thought I heard someone talking, and then a scream. It had appeared to come from upstairs. Throwing on my dressing gown, I ran up to Victoria's room. She was sobbing. I knocked, and hearing no reply, I opened the door to find her sitting upright in bed, perspiring and with a look of anguish on her face.

"Victoria!" I said, sitting on the bed. "What happened? Are you all right? Should I fetch a doctor?"

"No," she said quietly after a moment. "It was just the night terrors. It happens sometimes. Ever since..."

"Mr Wakeley?"

She nodded. "There's a jug of water and a cloth on the chest over there," she said. "Could you please get me a damp cloth? I need to cool down."

"Certainly," I said, and fetched the cloth, and dabbed it over her face and neck.

"Ah! That's better," she said, unbuttoning the neck of her nightdress so I could apply the soothing cloth to her chest. "Oh, lovely," she whispered. "Almost worth the terrors."

I hung the cloth on the bed frame, and held her hand. "Are you feeling better?" I said, after a while.

"Much," she said, smiling. "Did Mrs Ambrose confide in you?"

"Yes," I said, "almost too much! It confirmed all our suspicions. There's no doubt in my mind – and I think hers – that Mr Blackwood is the culprit, but it's not quite enough to take to the police. As you said, we need to trick him into giving us more."

"Do you have a scheme in mind?"

"Yes," I said, "and I would like your help, if you don't mind getting involved –"

"Of course!" she said. "Anything. We must catch this dog. And I might as well make myself useful, as I have only caused trouble so far."

"You are no trouble," I said. "I'm very glad you appeared on the scene, seemingly out of nowhere!"

"So what can I do to earn my keep?"

"I'd like you to talk to May, Mrs Ambrose's maid, and persuade her to tell us what she knows about Susan, and to help set up a meeting with Mr Blackwood. I want May to write to Mr Blackwood saying that she knows what happened to Susan, and to meet her to discuss the terms of her silence."

"Goodness!" said Victoria. "Isn't that rather dangerous? And do you think Blackwood would fall for it, after the last blackmail letter?"

"We would need to enlist help to ensure May's safety," I said. "I haven't properly thought that through yet. And I think Blackwood is going to be curious enough to turn up. He can still deny everything, so the plan might fail, but there's a chance he could threaten May – if he's the thug we think he is – and we will make sure this is witnessed."

"I hope May will agree to this," said Victoria. "It's very risky for her. If Mr Blackwood doesn't show himself, or simply denies everything, then we would have painted a target on her back."

"In that case, we go to the police with what we have. At the very least, Mr Blackwood would know that if May met an untimely death, it would be scrutinized very carefully, so it wouldn't be worth the risk. And at best, the police would agree with us and put him on trial, not Mrs Ambrose."

"We can certainly try to persuade her," Victoria said. "If not, we must think again. Oh – I said 'we'! It seems I have been thoroughly drawn into one of your investigations. How exciting!"

"You are an excellent assistant," I said.

"Thank you," Victoria said. "I have been meaning to ask you something."

"Yes?"

"You have been so kind, letting me stay. You're probably wondering when I'm going to leave you in peace."

"Not at all!" I said. "I've got rather used to you being here."

"Might I perhaps stay for Christmas?"

"But of course! I assumed you were," I said, squeezing her hand. "And in any case, you are not released from detective duties yet."

"Oh, thank you! That's so kind. My parents are wintering in Madeira. Isn't that decadent?"

"I'm envious," I said. "But wouldn't you prefer the warmth of Madeira to cold, damp Northumberland?"

"Perhaps, but not with my parents. We had rather too much of each other in the summer. I'd rather be here with you. It's strange how happy I am when I'm with you."

She looked up at me, and it pained me to see the affection

written on her face, which I was not at liberty to return.

"I'm sorry," she said. "It's not fair of me. But indulge me for just a short while longer, and then I will always have the memory of the friends I made here."

"Of course," I said. "If it weren't for Phyllis..."

"Shh," she said, wiping away a tear. "I know."

~

"What did you want to ask me, then?" said May, suspiciously.

We had come over around ten o'clock the following morning, and we decided to interview her in the drawing room in front of the fire where she would be warm and therefore more at her ease.

"This is Miss Victoria Clitheroe, May," I said. "She's helping me find out who killed Mr Ambrose."

May nodded, and Victoria said, "It's very nice to meet you, May. It's such a pretty name!"

"Thank you, miss."

"We wanted to ask you about Susan," I said. "I think she was your friend."

May frowned. "Yes. What about her?"

"Had you known her long?" I asked.

"I knew her for about three years," she said, "as we were in service together at the Watson house. The master couldn't afford us both, so she came here, and then when Mr Watson died, I came here too. But by that time, Susan had died."

"I'm sorry to have to ask," I said, "but do you believe her death was by her own hand?"

"That's what everyone said, sir, and the police, so it must be true, mustn't it?"

"But a friend," said Victoria, "would have an intuition that might contradict what everybody else said. You would know whether Susan really wanted to end it all."

May fidgeted and shifted in her seat. "Perhaps. But Susan said it was dangerous to tell the truth. Look what happened to her. I don't want that to happen to me."

"So you believe she was murdered?" I asked.

After a moment, May said, "Yes. I know who by, too."

"Ah – so Susan told you that she was afraid of someone in particular?" Victoria said.

"Yes."

"It was Mr Blackwood, wasn't it?" I said.

May looked up at me, and nodded. "She said he threatened to kill her because of what she had seen in this house. She was terrified."

"May," Victoria said, "would you like to help catch this awful man and ensure no one ever has to fear him again?"

May snorted. "Well, of course, miss, but it's not that easy."

"We think he murdered Mr Ambrose as well," I said, "and we have a certain amount of evidence that points to him. But we need more, and we need your help."

"Why me?" May asked. "I'm a nobody."

"The fact that Susan confided in you," I said. "And it's partly your testimony that has led to Mrs Ambrose being wrongly arrested and charged. Perhaps you would like to help right that wrong?"

"I'm sorry, sir, really. But knowing what she got up to upstairs – Susan said she looked like she was enjoying it! – and then the dreadful things she said..."

"I know," I said. "But those things don't make her a murderer. She is as much a victim of Blackwood as Susan was – especially if they hang her, and Blackwood remains free."

"Please help us," Victoria said. She knelt beside May and took her hands. "You can help save a life, and give justice to your friend Susan – and make Hawksbridge a safer place! You have so much power to do good, May! What a tremendous thing to be able to say to your children, that you helped good triumph over evil."

May looked wide-eyed at Victoria, and then to my surprise she dissolved into tears. Victoria put her arm around her shoulders, and when her sobs had died down, May said, "I miss Susan so much!"

"I know," Victoria whispered. "Of course you do."

"Sorry, miss, sir," she said after drying her eyes. "I'll listen to what you have to say, and then I'll decide. I would like to help. But I have to think of my own skin too."

"Of course," I said. "Thank you. I had a letter this morning from Mrs Ambrose's solicitor – I asked him to find out what he could about Susan. He said that she was engaged to a constable. Constable Taylor – is that right?"

She nodded. "He didn't think it was suicide either, since they were making plans together. But he couldn't go against what his boss said."

"I think there's a chance we could enlist Mr Taylor," I said. "I will talk to him this evening, and then I will return with a plan."

CHAPTER TWENTY-EIGHT

I WAS anxious to see Constable Taylor, but I would have to wait until evening when I hoped he would be back from the police office. I could hardly speak to him with Inspector Simmons breathing down my neck. I decided to occupy myself by writing to Phyllis, as Victoria had suggested.

At my fourth attempt, I wrote the following letter.

Ramsburgh, 20th December

My dear Phyllis,

It is too long since we sat in a mystical circle of stones and kissed! Strange events have conspired to keep us apart since, to my great regret.

I would like to explain what I was unable to in our last meetings.

It is true that I was seeing Bess Shannon, but no longer. Or rather, very infrequently and only to talk business. I put to her Mrs Harris' excellent suggestion of opening a ladies' coffee shop and she has taken it up with enthusiasm. I am investing a small amount. I hope you can forgive my weakness in lonely and difficult moments earlier this year: I know it was unworthy of me.

My visit to that insalubrious Edinburgh club must seem to be a continuation of my moral laxity, but I assure you there was no pleasure in it. As I mentioned, I was following a trail of information to find the evidence necessary to save Mrs Ambrose and avoid a gross error of justice that could leave a killer at large in Hawksbridge: however grandiose this statement appears now that I write it down! I believe I am close to success, but it is by no means guaranteed.

I have been guilty, though, of neglecting you in the pursuit of this affair. It is no wonder that you cast your gaze on another. But I believe with all my heart that you and I belong to one another; have you not felt it? I think you have, or you would not have kissed me. All that I do seems without meaning without the hope of your affection and respect.

Will you and your father perhaps honour me with your presence for Christmas dinner? I hope you are able.

Yours with devotion and tenderness,

Thomas

~

Fortunately, Constable Taylor was not on an evening shift, and answered our knock on the door to his little cottage.

"Mr Rufford, isn't it?" he said. "What can I do for you, sir?"

"Good evening, Mr Taylor! I'm sorry to interrupt your evening, but I would like to discuss an important matter with you. This is my friend, Miss Victoria Clitheroe."

"Pleased to meet you, miss. Won't you come in?"

The door led directly onto the sitting room, which was gloomily lit and rather rustic in decor. He gestured to a couple of battered armchairs. "A drink of some kind?"

"No, thank you, Mr Taylor, we'll try to keep this as brief as we can. To begin with: do you believe Mrs Ambrose is guilty of her husband's murder?"

Mr Taylor pursed his lips. "To be honest with you, Mr Rufford, I can't see it. My opinion is that there was nowhere enough evidence to charge her. But Mr Simmons must know what he's doing."

"And do you think he knew what he was doing with the sad case of Susan Lipton's death?"

He looked at me quizzically, and I added, "I'm sorry to

have to bring it up. You have my deepest sympathies."

"Aye, well," said Mr Taylor, "it's been a few years now. It's true I wasn't happy with the result of the investigation, but there wasn't much in the way of evidence."

"Still, from what I hear, she had no reason to kill herself."

"No, that's true enough. We were going to be married. She never said anything to me about being unhappy. Quite the opposite, Mr Rufford. And she would be here, next to me on this sofa, if she hadn't..." He was unable to continue.

"It must hurt terribly," said Victoria. "We talked to her friend May Ettrick, and she thinks Mr Blackwood was responsible. Do you think so too?"

"I thought that the most likely explanation, yes," said Mr Taylor. "Susan was petrified of the man, and she told me all about what went on in that house." He shivered. "It wasn't natural. But like I say, we had no hard evidence."

"What if I told you," I said, "that with your help, Mr Blackwood could be brought to justice, for Susan's murder as well as Mr Ambrose's?"

"I should say you were mad, begging your pardon, Mr Rufford," Mr Taylor said. "How do you intend to work this miracle?"

I explained what we knew, and how we intended to lure Mr Blackwood. When I had finished, he stared at me for a few moments, his sceptical expression gradually dissolving.

"Well, Mr Rufford. That's put a different complexion on things. Your scheme might work. You do know you could get me sacked, if I had anything to do with this?"

I nodded. "Yes," I said. "But I was gambling on you wanting to right a grievous wrong, close to your heart."

"You're not wrong there. Well, let's think about it. How do you intend to protect May if he turns violent, either at this meeting, or later if he fails to incriminate himself?"

"Would it not be possible," Victoria said, "to leave documents with a solicitor, so that she can say that he will be immediately exposed if anything happens to her?"

"Yes," he said. "That would help. But we would need to be near her. Hiding in a cupboard? No, he could easily find us in there. Tell you what – I sometimes have family stay in The Duke's Head, and I noticed that one time, their room had a door to an adjoining room. The door was locked, and probably never used – but if we could get both rooms, wouldn't that work? If I remember right, the door is just like all the others – just the usual ledge and brace. Hardly anything to them."

"So we could all listen in to the conversation," Victoria said. "What a clever idea!"

"And I know Mr Minto, the landlord, quite well," he continued. "I'm sure I could persuade him to keep both rooms free for us."

"And to keep it a secret, I hope," I said.

"Yes, I'm sure he would," he said. "Now, we'll need a few people. I won't be able to hold him on my own, and with respect, Mr Rufford, you don't seem cut out for a fight. What about one of your people?"

"I can enlist my butler, Shipley," I said. "He has proved very reliable in past adventures. So the three of us should manage. And Victoria – can you come along so you can look after May? It's going to be a very difficult task for her."

"Of course," she said. "You may rely on me."

"Are you sure you want to do this?" I said to Mr Taylor.

"You've convinced me, sir. Anything to avenge my Susan. I don't care what Simmons says. I'll be able to get work somewhere."

"Thank you," I said. "If we're successful, I don't think Mr Simmons will be able to touch you."

"So, what next?" said Victoria.

"I'll set a date, and write a letter to Blackwood for May to copy out," I said. "Then we'll arrange the rooms in The Duke's Head, and set it in motion. Let's try to get this done by Christmas."

As we left, Mr Taylor shook hands with us both heartily. "Thank you, Mr Rufford, Miss Clitheroe. Good luck to us all. I can't wait to see that bastard hang – excuse my language, miss!"

~

I wasted no time that night composing a letter for May to send, with help from Victoria. We set the date for the meeting at The Duke's Head for the twenty-third. But whether it was due to our scheming, or still the memory of Wakeley's death, poor Victoria had her night terrors again, and I repeated my care of her with the help of a cool cloth. She agreed to send for a doctor the next day, and she insisted on Dr Weldon, in view of the state of Dr Drummond's joints.

In the morning I wrote a letter to be made public by Mrs Ambrose's solicitor in the event of May's untimely demise. I rode into town with a handful of errands, and started by visiting Houndswood with instructions for May to send her letter later that day. I next delivered my letter to the solicitor, and dropped a note in at Mr Taylor's cottage keeping him informed so he could arrange for the rooms to be made available.

Dr Weldon's rented house, a squat villa perhaps two decades old, appeared mean for an ambitious doctor, but I imagined that he would move to grander premises before long. The only memorable aspect of the house was the presence of several glazed boxes of butterflies hung in the hall, and also in the dining room that was being used as an office. I was happy not to see Dr Weldon, to whom I had developed a visceral aversion – the greater for picturing him sticking pins in defenceless insects – and instead left my message with his sister.

I was left with just the letter I had written to Phyllis. If I could see her, then so much the better. I knocked on the Drummonds' door slightly nervously, rehearsing some conciliatory words.

The maid answered the door. "Yes, sir?"

"Good morning," I said. "Could you tell me if Miss Drummond is in?"

"No, sir, she is not."

"Ah. Do you know when she will be back."

"I'm afraid I couldn't say, sir."

"Do you know where she is?"

"I couldn't say, sir."

I had my suspicions. "With Dr Weldon, perhaps?"

"Like I said, sir. I couldn't say."

"Well, would you please give her this letter when she returns?"

"Yes, of course, sir. Was there anything else?"

For a moment, I contemplated speaking to Dr Drummond and asking him how things stood, but then thought better of it. "No – no, thank you."

The door slamming in my face felt like a rebuke from Phyllis. Disappointed, I returned to Ramsburgh. As I rode, my mind was full of confected scenes involving the two of them, from walking arm in arm on the ramparts to kissing in a carriage, and worse. Who was this arrogant man who had arrived in Hawksbridge to steal my happiness? Would I one day have to subject myself to treatment from a doctor whose wife was my beloved Phyllis? This was a grim prospect indeed.

~

In my study, melancholia had draped its heavy blanket of gloom upon me as I stared out of the window at the colourless skies. I should have been in a state of excited anticipation of what lay ahead: the culmination of my Ambrose investigation. But my mood only permitted me to predict a negative outcome for that adventure. Mr Blackwood might not turn up, leaving us – and especially May – in a dangerous limbo. Or he might turn up, but say nothing of interest, and deny everything. Perhaps we were meddling with things we improperly understood, with consequences we could not at this moment conceive. All because of my own arrogance, far surpassing that of Dr Weldon's: in the event of failure, my humiliation in front of him, Phyllis and the whole town would be devastating.

I threw myself on the sofa and wallowed in my dark thoughts for some time, and then I heard the faint sound of voices outside. Getting up and looking out of the window, I sensed movement on the lawn below. Victoria was walking with someone I could not quite see. But then they turned, and I saw it was Dr Weldon, as if my bleak ruminations had been strong enough to conjure him up from thin air. They looked friendly and animated and I could see Victoria laughing at something he said.

A fresh wave of loneliness and alienation washed over me. It was a blow that even Victoria, who had apparently shared my view of Dr Weldon, had now capitulated to his charms. I was out of step with everyone.

I went downstairs to seek out the comfort of a friend who I knew would not disagree with me, nor judge me. Fox was curled up by the fire, having been taken for a walk by Catherine. I fell into a reverie by the fire, wondering what it must feel like to be a dog, with no responsibilities except to exhibit a moderate amount of loyalty and fetch the occasional stick.

As I was about to nod off, Victoria came in.

I started. "Oh! Victoria. What was Dr Weldon's verdict?"

"Hello, Thomas! He said it would be simply a matter of

time and rest, and to not put myself in a position of stress."

"Ah," I said. "So that would rule out our appointment with Blackwood."

"Nonsense! I didn't say I would take his advice, did I?"

"Well," I said, "I don't want you to make yourself even more unwell –"

"I'm absolutely fine. As Dr Weldon says, it's mainly a matter of time. And he gave me a thorough examination."

I stared at her. "How thorough?"

"Very." She laughed. "Oh, your face! Actually, I asked him to. I had an aunt who died from the most innocuous looking mole. I told him this, and he asked if I wanted him to examine me. So I said yes. He has elegant hands."

I screwed up my face. "Was that entirely necessary?"

"Entirely? Probably not. But I thought it might be interesting."

"Interesting?" I exclaimed. "Victoria, I don't think I understand you at all."

"Of course not!" she said, sitting down opposite me. "A woman should be an enigma to men. Our mystique is the greater portion of our charm. But to be less flippant – I thought it would help me to understand him better. Know thine enemy, and all that."

"Well, you seemed to have an understanding earlier, in the garden. You appeared to be having a grand old time."

"Appearances can be deceptive, Thomas. Anyway, I thought I was being rather clever. He thinks I have lowered my guard, when in fact he has lowered his, and so I might find out some information that could be useful to you."

"Thank you, but about what?"

"About him and Phyllis, silly! Didn't someone say 'knowledge is power'?"

"That's very kind of you," I said, "but please don't do any more of this sort of thing. I will make more efforts with Phyllis, and if she chooses Weldon, then so be it. I wrote to her, by the way."

"Oh, good! Did you propose marriage?"

"I wasn't quite that forward," I said. "I'm not sure we're at that –"

"Poppycock!" Victoria said. "Just propose marriage, before Dr Weldon does. It's what you want, isn't it?"

"Yes – yes, it is," I said. "Thank you. I will consider it." To change the subject, I added, "Dr Weldon seems to be keen on collecting butterflies. He has quite a collection of them in cases at his home."

"Has he?" she said. "More information for our campaign! But it makes sense. I can just see him pedantically writing all the Latin names on labels, with his tongue sticking out!"

I laughed. "How attractive. But as to it being pertinent information, even you would be hard pushed to find a way to use his butterflies against him."

"I accept your challenge, Thomas," she said. "You underestimate my cunning."

CHAPTER TWENTY-NINE

I HAD a day to kill before the culmination of our plan, and to divert myself I thought I would visit Francesca and find out the state of the castle land sale.

As I was wiping the breadcrumbs from my mouth after breakfast, I heard footsteps on the stairs and the door open and close. From the drawing room window, I saw Victoria, looking stunning in a green cloak and feathered hat, climbing into the pony trap with old Howard at the reins.

Shipley brought me a letter from Phyllis, briefly and a touch formally accepting my invitation for Christmas dinner and thanking me for my explanations. It was disappointing that the warmth in my letter was barely returned, but if she had decided to come to Ramsburgh, rather than – Heaven forbid – spend Christmas with Dr Weldon, my rehabilitation had surely started.

Before going out, I looked in on Flora.

"Hello, Thomas!" she said, answering the door herself. I was glad to see her dressed and looking more like her old self.

"Good morning, Flora!" I said. "Have you got your energy back? Your cheeks are positively rosy!"

"Yes, I am much better," she said, leading me into the sitting room. "Nearly a normal human again. Mr Falkirk and I have almost completed the Town Hall murals! I won't be sad when they are done. My limbs ache after a day's painting. But I'm pleased with our angels."

"I can't wait to see the finished work," I said. "I bet Francesca will be curious, too. Seeing yourself half-naked in an expansive posture, in a public place, must be quite something."

"Not to mention being bestowed with magnificent

wings," said Flora. "I think they suit her."

"I fear she would like to fly away from Hawksbridge altogether," I said, "after selling off the town's heritage to the highest bidder."

"Is it done?"

"I intend to find out this afternoon," I said.

"And what news of Mrs Ambrose?" Flora said.

"I came to ask you to wish me luck. Victoria, Shipley and I – and Mrs Ambrose's maid – are going to play our trump card tomorrow in the hopes of getting a confession. Our target is Mr Blackwood."

"Ah! I remember you were suspicious about him previously. Well, I do wish you the best of luck, but you won't take any risks, will you, Thomas?"

"As few as possible," I said.

"After all," she said, "I only have one brother."

I threw my arms about her, being unable to articulate my happiness at hearing such simple but significant words.

~

"Oh! It's you, Thomas. I thought it must be Dr Weldon. Yates, please get us some coffee!"

"I'm sorry – are you unwell?"

"Oh, it's nothing, really," said Francesca. "I did something to my leg when I mounted my horse rather too enthusiastically. I forgot that I'm not a young thing any more. It's probably only a sprain, but I thought I would have it looked at."

"By the most handsome and eligible doctor in town."

"But of course, Thomas," she said. "Aesthetics are important. However – he is not the most punctual man."

"Curious," I said. "From what I've seen of him, he's

highly efficient. But I imagine he's becoming popular, especially amongst the ladies. Anyway," I added, "he would probably only look at your leg, prod it, and then tell you to get plenty of rest. That seems to be the main function of doctors. And then they have the cheek to charge good money for such wisdom!"

"What a splendid cynic you are, Thomas," said Francesca. "You are a man after my own heart. But the very act of confidently dispensing prods and platitudes can still be effective in itself."

"Simple reassurance? You could be right. We are anxious creatures, always seeking solace. On that subject, wish me luck for tomorrow. I will be trying to rid Hawksbridge of a menace."

"Oh?" said Francesca, sipping her coffee. "Who or what is this menace?"

"The man who helped to furnish your house, in fact. Mr Blackwood, who we suspect of murdering Mr Ambrose and an innocent young woman."

Francesca looked shocked. "Really? Mr Blackwood? He didn't look like a murderer to me. Well, maybe on reflection there was something slightly rough about him. But where am I going to buy my antiques if you are successful?"

"You have enough already, Francesca. I will be doing you a favour."

"You're right," she said. "Heavens – yes, best of luck, Thomas. I hope the police are involved this time."

"Unfortunately the police tend to disregard my opinion. Perhaps after this they will be less dismissive, assuming it goes well."

"I'm sure it will," said Francesca.

"I also came to invite you for Christmas dinner at Ramsburgh!" I said. "Please say you'll come."

"Oh! That's so kind. Are you sure your other guests will want me there?"

"Of course they will! Nothing has changed as far as your and my friends are concerned. You will be missed if you don't come."

"In that case, I would be delighted to accept."

I drained my cup. "That is excellent coffee," I said. "If I may be so bold, Francesca: how is the land sale going?"

She grimaced. "Mr Thornton and I have agreed terms verbally, and I am poised to sign. But I can't get out of my head the idea that I'm signing a death warrant. I wanted to talk to you first, just to make sure I'm not missing anything. I'm aware I have the eyes of the town on me."

"So – you have a chance to fix the terms of the transaction in your favour," I said. "I don't mean necessarily in monetary terms. What if we were to oblige them to preserve the castle?"

"Do you think that's possible?" said Francesca. "Surely they will need to flatten everything for the new line and station."

"Perhaps, but surely it's worth a look, isn't it? Did Mr Wakeley have any plans of the land?"

"He did!" Francesca said. "I'll get them." She winced slightly as she stood up, and I poured myself another coffee while I waited for her to return.

After a few minutes she came back with a large case, and said, "Let's spread them on the dining room table."

We looked through the sketches and charts that had been made by the surveyor that Mr Wakeley had employed for this purpose. One plan showed in detail the pieces of the castle that remained, and there was a helpful map at a smaller scale that showed the relationship between the castle and the river.

I unfolded and smoothed out the two documents on the mahogany table.

"The main hall is about fifty feet by a hundred," I said. "Isn't this plenty of room for a double railway track to go straight through, if archways were made in the end walls? Look

– where the railway comes in over the river, you only need a slight deviation for it to go through the great hall instead of having to demolish it. And once it clears the hall, some of these smaller ruins could be incorporated into the platform and station."

"Goodness," Francesca said, examining the documents. "I see what you mean. In which case, most of the castle could be saved! This is too good to be true, surely?"

"We'd have to consult an engineer to confirm this would be possible. A lot of walls would need to be strengthened. But it looks promising. And the company could promote it as a spectacle. What other railway goes straight through the great hall of a castle?"

"I do hope you're right," said Francesca. "I might just be able to shed my reputation as a scheming, wanton vandal. Thomas, whatever would I do without you?"

~

In the middle of the afternoon, I heard a crunch of wheel on gravel, and Victoria opened the door. I met her in the hall.

"Hello!" I said. "Have you had an exciting day? You look exhausted."

"I'm fine," she said. "Well, rather tired, yes." When she turned towards me, I saw the hall lantern catch a glint on her cheek. Had she been crying? I thought it better not to pry.

"Shipley has found a Christmas tree for us," I said. "It's in the sitting room. I don't suppose you want to help decorate it?"

"Oh – yes, of course," she said. "That might be fun. Let me have a rest first. Have you got any decorations?"

"Just ribbon and candles, alas. And I'm not too sure about the candles – not with Fox in the house."

"I could cut out some of my drawings," she said. "And couldn't Catherine and Mrs Fenton make some little cakes for it?"

"I'll ask them," I said. "Not that I want to make extra work for them with Christmas Day coming up."

"True," she said, and made her way upstairs.

Victoria returned after an hour with scraps made from her animal drawings, and we attached them to the tree with thread after winding red ribbon through the branches. She seemed to regain something of her lost sparkle, especially after a glass of sherry.

"Well, it won't win any prizes," she said, "but I do feel a little more festive now."

"I'm sorry if you've had a bad day," I said.

"Thank you," she said, looking at me and then into the fire. I had the impression that she was looking through the flames into a darker realm. "But it's nearly over, and you have cheered me up. Tomorrow will be far too busy for brooding."

CHAPTER THIRTY

THE day on which my reputation and Mrs Ambrose's life both rested had come – the twenty-third of December. We prepared May as much as we could, and then made sure to arrive a good two hours in advance of the appointed time, since it was possible that Blackwood would arrive early in order to ensure that May was alone. Having settled May in her room, with reassurances that we were but a few feet away, we sat silently in the adjoining room with our pencils and notebooks at the ready.

Eleven o'clock passed, and then another agonising thirty minutes. I began to rehearse the embarrassing, not to say dangerous consequences of the failure of this mission, and I found my palms had become clammy with sweat.

Finally, at about half past eleven, we heard footsteps on the stair and then on the landing outside. There was a knock on May's door, and we heard her say, "Come in!" with just a hint of nervousness in her voice. We looked at each other, and held our breaths. The rat had walked up to our trap. But would he take the bait and doom himself?

"May Ettrick?" he said.

"Yes, Mr Blackwood," May said. "Thank you for coming."

"How could I resist?" he said. "Your letter was so charming."

I imagined he would be looking around the room, and sure enough, he rattled the connecting door which we had locked from our side. We froze, holding our breath, praying that the lock was secure. Then we heard him draw up a chair, and we quietly exhaled.

"Now then, Miss Ettrick. You're very bold to take me on, aren't you? A mousy little thing like you, up against a big bad man like me?" He laughed. "Let's hear your story, then. This should be highly amusing."

"Well, as you know, sir, I have a copy of the letter that Mr Ambrose must have sent to you. It angered you enough to kill him."

"And how the devil did you get hold of this letter?" demanded Mr Blackwood.

May gave her prepared answer without hesitation. "I found it in his desk, when I was dusting."

Mr Blackwood snorted. "A nosy little bitch, aren't you? So why didn't you give it to the police, if you thought it was so important?"

"I thought it might be useful to me," May said, "even before I really worked out the meaning of it. I thought I might use the matter of your meetings with Mrs Ambrose to get an increase in my pay. Here she was, admitting it on paper. And then I realised that it was far more valuable than that."

"What do you know about me and Isobel?" said Mr Blackwood, tetchily. "You weren't even employed at the house at the time."

"I know what Susan told me," May said. "That you both often went to an attic room and you... seduced her."

"And you believed this nonsense? Then more fool you."

"Oh, I believed it all right. She was my best friend, and never lied to me. And now this letter says she was right. And the fact that she died after telling me she was scared."

"And you think I killed her? Let's just say I did. Aren't you afraid I'll do the same to you?"

"No, because if I disappeared, my solicitor would send sealed letters to the police and the newspapers, with a copy of Mr Ambrose's letter and an account of everything I know."

There was a pause. "Well, well," said Mr Blackwood. "You're smarter than I thought. Very good! But that threat only works if I believe you. I think you're bluffing. Besides, there's no proof I killed anyone. It's all so much hot air."

"Perhaps you're not capable of killing anyone," said May. "Perhaps Susan did kill herself after all. In fact, now I've met you, you look to me the type who's all bluster. But that doesn't matter so much as how it looks to other people, does it? If it looks as though you might have been driven to it, you could still hang."

"You think you know my type, eh?" said Mr Blackwood with menace in his voice. "I assure you, Miss Ettrick, that you have no idea about me. It's quite easy to overpower a young woman and string her from a rafter with some old reins."

I glanced at Taylor, who looked back at me with wide eyes and nodded.

Mr Blackwood continued. "Military training never leaves you," he said. "Dispatching the enemy becomes second nature. Have you decided to become my enemy, Miss Ettrick?"

"On the contrary," said May, whose courage in the face of this terrifying man deeply impressed me. "I have already saved you from the gallows by hiding Mr Ambrose's letter from the police. And I told the police that Mrs Ambrose had said she wanted to kill him, which further distracted the Inspector. So I think I have earned your gratitude, and more besides."

"What a greedy hussy you are, Miss Ettrick. Again, I ask you to present the evidence that I killed either Yorick or Susan. Your letter could at most harm Isobel's reputation, and make me the butt of jokes in the inn. I think I can live with that. But since you are so curious, why don't I tell you my sinful tale? I think you'll find it interesting, and perhaps you'll learn to be more careful in future.

"I was friends with Yorick for a few years. But he was like you – greedy. He wanted treasures on the cheap, and so he made an outrageous suggestion to me. How would I like to spend time with his wife, in exchange for a discount on his next purchase? Well, Isobel was a fine woman. She still is. I don't know how Yorick persuaded her, but I agreed to his proposal. She resisted my charms at first, and then seemed to grow accustomed to me. By the time Susan burst into the room, Isobel had been in the habit of making quite a noise – but not out of distress, you understand! Yorick had lost interest in her, so I was simply doing his job for him.

"But pleasuring Isobel cost me a lot of money. I grew to resent Yorick, and we fell out. As for Susan, I suspected that she would not be able to keep a secret, so she had to go. It was unfortunate – she was a pretty young thing.

"And then, a few years later, I get a letter purporting to be from Isobel, signed with her initials. But Yorick made a bad mistake. You see, Isobel had written to me early on, begging me not to accept her husband's offer of her. I retained the letter, so I compared it with the new letter. I realised it was a fake, and deduced that Yorick was the sender. I realised too that he was trying to get me to kill her, knowing full well that I had it in me."

He cleared his throat. "Now call me sentimental, but I have a soft spot for Isobel. I spent many pleasurable moments with her. It occurred to me that I had to dispatch Yorick, to prevent him from any more attempts on Isobel's life. I had a mind to then marry her myself, whereupon I could resume our delightful congress, with the additional benefit of reclaiming all the antiques I had sold to him at such a loss. And young Felicity might be an amusing distraction, so to speak."

We grimaced at this disgusting thought.

"I frequently have pianos repaired in my shop, so I have a plentiful supply of wire. Yorick had confessed about his mistress in town, and I saw him go off in the direction of Mrs Tambard after giving an intemperate diatribe at the Antiquarian Society meeting. I knew about his inability to sleep for long, and guessed that he would be returning in the early morning. It was easy to set up the wire without being seen. A suitably dramatic death for a man with a disposition for drama. He was highly strung, you might say."

He guffawed loudly at his own joke.

"But the police thought it must have been Isobel. Well, it was unfortunate in one sense, as she's a fine woman. But if I had to choose between her and me for the drop – it would certainly be her."

After a moment, May said, "Thank you for being so frank with me, although I must say I pity your black soul. Now, sir, will you buy this letter, or not?"

"Well, I'm a generous man," Mr Blackwood said. "Damned, yes, perhaps, but generous. So I propose a sum of five guineas for this scrap. What do you say?"

"I say twenty, sir, and then you shall hear no more from me."

"Greedy, damned greedy. No more than ten."

"Let us compromise at fifteen, then, sir."

He sighed. "Oh, very well. Fifteen. Let's see the letter."

After a few moments, he said, "Very well." There was the chink of coins, and muttering. "There. Fifteen. Happy?"

"Yes, sir," said May. "Thank you."

There was the noise of a chair scraping, and footsteps as he went to the door. We stood up carefully, poised to jump into the landing, but the footsteps stopped. Was he about to tie up a loose end, violently?

But Blackwood had only paused for a final remark. "Oh, and now that you're a wealthy woman," he said, "come and visit my shop. Perhaps I can arrange a special discount for you!" He laughed, and opened the door.

Taylor and Shipley darted into the corridor and grabbed Blackwood just as he was closing May's door, before he had any time to react.

"What's this?" he cried as Taylor wrestled Blackwood's arms behind him and slapped on handcuffs. "Landlord! I'm being assaulted! Get off me! Get off me, I say!"

He struggled violently, and I tried to help restrain him, but he kicked me in the face and I went reeling across the landing.

"Mr Rufford! I should have guessed. What a pathetic specimen you are, making everyone's business your own. Don't you have anything better to do? So that's why you were asking about discounts. You will pay for this, you pustulent son of a whore. You don't know what I'm capable of!"

I picked myself off the floor, holding my bruised jaw. "But we do, Mr Blackwood. We know exactly what you're capable of, because you gave us a detailed account of it. There are five witnesses to your confession. You will hang, and not before time."

Blackwood struggled and shouted, "I will not, and I will come for you! I will come for all of you! You're all dead!"

The landlord, Mr Minto, had appeared with a length of rope. "You've got him! Well done. Would this be of any use?"

"For tying, or hanging?" said Taylor. "I'd be happy to save everyone the time and trouble. What sort of a coward kills a defenceless woman?" said Taylor, and he spat in Blackwood's face. "Let's get him inside."

In the room, Victoria was comforting May, who was breathing quickly. Victoria led her out of the room, and we got Blackwood into the chair May had vacated. Taylor tied him securely to it. "Can someone please fetch Inspector Simmons?" he said.

~

When Inspector Simmons arrived with three more constables, he had a curt conversation with the defiant Mr Blackwood before coming into the adjoining room where we waited, exhausted by the morning's events. Mr Minto had kindly provided us with sandwiches and drinks. I could hear the still-cursing Mr Blackwood being taken out of the room and downstairs, presumably to be incarcerated at the police office.

Mr Simmons surveyed us with furrowed brows, and sighed.

"It's quite the conspiracy, isn't it?" he said. "Constable Taylor has given me a summary. It beggars belief. What's the ruddy point of having a police force if the town simply takes matters into its own hands? I cannot tolerate this."

He ran his hands through his depleted, greying hair.

"I take it you are the ringleader, Mr Rufford, as always?"

"I'm afraid so, Inspector."

"Then I will interview you first. Please come with me and Constable Taylor downstairs to the dining room."

For once, we both had a notebook to open. The simultaneous gesture evidently unsettled him: it was his exclusive opening gambit, designed to punctuate the start of the interview and perhaps intimidate. He scowled and said, "Blackwood's admissions? Let me see."

He glanced over some of the pages and grunted, but dispensed with the initial sarcastic remarks to which I had become accustomed.

"Take me through it, then, Mr Rufford."

"Certainly. It's rather complicated. It starts with the purchase of some antiques by Mr Ambrose."

I did my best to describe what I knew whilst compromising Mrs Ambrose to the smallest extent possible. But I could not hide the indecency of the conduct between Mr Blackwood and Mrs Ambrose, and he reacted with a variety of expletives.

After I had spoken for about ten minutes, he said, "So you deduced that this letter was an attempt to have Mrs Ambrose killed? Where did you say you got the letter?"

"From one of Mr Ambrose's mistresses. I found her via correspondence in Mr Ambrose's safe."

"So Mr Ambrose didn't send the letter?"

"He did – this was just a practise copy."

"Ah, yes, of course," Mr Simmons said. "This confounded case is giving me a headache. And you contend that Mr Blackwood is capable of killing Mr Ambrose because he killed Susan Lipton. Which was concluded to be suicide, was it not?"

"But Mr Blackwood just confessed to it, citing a detail that was not reported in the press."

"Ah, yes, sir," Constable Taylor said. "The use of reigns to make a noose. The godless scumbag."

"Thank you, Constable," Mr Simmons said. "I see. And so you took it upon yourself, Mr Rufford, to conspire with Constable Taylor here" – Taylor looked awkwardly at the ceiling – "and several other of your acquaintances to set a trap for Mr Blackwood, offering poor Miss Ettrick as bait."

He shook his head and tutted.

"This was an extraordinarily foolish, dangerous, misguided thing to do." He stood up and walked over to where I was sitting, looming over me, and then looked at the constable. "I shall have to decide what to do about you, Constable Taylor. This was an unforgivable act of insubordination."

"Yes, sir," said the unfortunate constable. "Sorry, sir."

"And yet," I said, "Constable Taylor has helped prevent a terrible miscarriage of justice. I'm sure the newspapers will call him a hero."

"The police doesn't operate with tawdry newspaper stories in mind," Mr Simmons said. "Our aim is justice, not heroism!"

"I'm sorry to say this, Mr Simmons, but your approach has achieved neither. Had you been more amenable to alternative viewpoints, you would have been the first person I would have talked to. But you can be a tad – inflexible."

"How dare you question my methods, Mr Rufford!" Mr

Simmons fumed, pacing up and down the dining room. "I could have you on a charge of withholding evidence."

"I don't think so," I said, "because your investigation had been completed. I was merely collecting evidence for the defence."

He stared at me, and then sighed and gestured to the door. "That will be all for now. I have the rest of your fellow reprobates to interview. Come to the office first thing tomorrow, Mr Rufford, and I'll take a proper statement then."

~

When I returned upstairs, May had composed herself after her ordeal.

"You were extraordinary, May!" I said. "Without your presence of mind, all of this could have been for nothing. You have saved a life today."

"I'm glad," May said, "after getting Mrs Ambrose into trouble. And I won't get Susan back but at least that brute will come to the same end as her."

"Quite. And thank you both," I said to Victoria and Shipley. "I shouldn't really have asked you to take the risk."

"Happy to, sir," Shipley, swigging some beer that Mr Minto had provided. "We did all right, didn't we?"

Victoria smiled sweetly at me. "It's not what I was expecting when I came for a quiet writing retreat," she said, "but I wouldn't have missed it. My only fear is that life will seem a bit dull now."

"Dull can sometimes be welcome," I said.

Mr Taylor came to fetch May to talk to the Inspector, but she was spared a lengthy interview out of consideration for her nerves, and when Victoria and Shipley had been questioned briefly, we set off for Ramsburgh, by way of Houndswood to drop May off.

Victoria and I went with May into the drawing room, where both Mrs Ambrose and Felicity were sitting reading.

"Thomas! Victoria! What news?" cried Mrs Ambrose, jumping up.

"Isobel, May has been incredibly brave. I'll let her tell you."

"Oh, ma'am! Mr Blackwood is in jail." She could say no more, and ran to Mrs Ambrose, and they both cried and embraced.

Felicity ran to me and threw her arms about me. "Oh, thank you, thank you, Mr Rufford! You did it! I knew you would!"

"Your help was indispensable, Felicity," I said.

Victoria could not refrain from weeping too. "I have no one to hug!" she said, sniffing, whereupon Felicity obliged.

When everyone's emotion had subsided a little, I said, "May was extraordinary, and said just the right things to Mr Blackwood to goad him into a confession. It must have been terrifying."

Mrs Ambrose untangled herself from May and said, "Am I safe now, Thomas?"

"You are safe," I said. "Five people witnessed Blackwood admit his guilt. I expect you will hear from Inspector Simmons soon."

"I would imagine he's feeling quite sheepish," said Victoria.

"As well he might," said Mrs Ambrose.

"I'll go and make tea, ma'am," said May. "I'd like to just get back to normal now."

CHAPTER THIRTY-ONE

THE following morning, I went with Victoria and Shipley to give our statements. The interview room in the police office was by now very familiar to me, and for all its austerity, it had lost its ability to daunt me. Inspector Simmons was in his usual place, drumming his fingers, but this time he had not brought in a constable as a witness.

"Here's the thing, Mr Rufford. If your little investigation was the work of vigilantes, and Mr Taylor's involvement was unauthorised by the police, we would have a problem. Mr Taylor would have to be disciplined – perhaps let go – and public confidence in the police would be compromised. Do you not agree?"

"Well, yes, perhaps. But –"

He lifted his hand to silence me.

"But supposing instead you had brought me your information as soon as you found it, and Mr Taylor had been operating under my command. Then we would have quite a different state of affairs. Mr Taylor would be commended – promoted, perhaps – and the enforcement of law would be seen to be working smoothly in Hawksbridge, as it normally does. There is no erosion of trust, and you and your friends could take a share of the credit for helping the police with their enquiries. Now doesn't that sound like a story with a happy ending?"

"Yes," I said, "but something of a fairy tale, Inspector!"

He smiled. "Nevertheless, fairy tales sometimes come true. All it takes is a little belief. Would you like to believe in this fairy tale, Mr Rufford? Because I will, if you will."

I stared at him, astonished. "Really? You would take all

the credit for this?"

"Is it credit you want, Mr Rufford?" said the Inspector, leaning back in his chair, seemingly confident that I would agree to his proposal. "Because I don't think it is. I think you are concerned with justice and harmony. The triumph of good over evil. I admire you for it, even if I can't overlook the fact that you have set yourself against the police."

He leaned forward again to make his point.

"No, Mr Rufford, I believe you are for the greater good. And the greater good here is to put aside the prosaic matter of credit, and tell a story that will keep everyone safe and happy – you, me, Constable Taylor, and every man, woman and child in the town. What do you say?"

I found it hard to fault this line of reasoning. "If you put it like that, Inspector," I said, "you do have a compelling argument. If you don't mind telling a white lie, I dare say I can too."

"And you can persuade your friends?"

"I think so."

"Good! Good," said the Inspector. "I knew you would see it, because for all your transgressions against this institution, I believe you are essentially a man of honour and intelligence. I'm not a great one for effusion, Mr Rufford, and you may not hear me say this again: but I have to say your pursuit of Blackwood is a decent achievement."

"Thank you, Inspector!" I said. "That means a great deal to me."

"I'm not condoning it, mind. I don't want to be in this position again. Please behave like a normal citizen in future."

"I'll try, Inspector. Has Mr Blackwood been charged?"

"He has – with both murders."

"And Mrs Ambrose?"

He exhaled noisily. "I will be calling on her this afternoon to let her know personally that the charges have been dropped."

"You will make her an extremely happy woman, Inspector. Shall I write my statement now?"

~

Flora had agreed to attend Christmas dinner so long as she could bring her bag of crochet for any awkward moments before or after the meal. This would allow her to avoid unnecessary eye contact with Phyllis. I regretted that my own flesh and blood was still so estranged from the object of my affections, but at least she would be present.

"Miss Ambrose," Francesca said when we had sat down to the splendid venison dinner that Catherine and Mrs Felton had prepared, "I gather you and Miss Drummond are writing a book together! Am I right?"

Not wishing Mrs Ambrose and Felicity to spend Christmas day alone, I had invited them, and they had gladly accepted.

"Yes, Mrs Campbell," said Felicity, "it's going very well. It's called 'Pantoufle the Artist', about my squirrel. Miss Clitheroe has taught me how to draw animals – in addition to what Miss Davison has already taught me of nature drawing, of course."

"Goodness!" said Francesca. "So much talent has gone into this book. I look forward to reading it. Have you a publisher?"

Felicity looked at Phyllis for an answer.

"I have written to my publisher," she said. "They don't usually publish children's books, but they may be able to recommend us to another."

"I do hope Felicity isn't distracting you too much from your own work," Mrs Ambrose said. "The world is waiting for your next novel!"

"It's a very pleasant distraction," said Phyllis, "but don't worry – I am making progress on my own book."

"I'm very glad to hear it," Mrs Ambrose said, "as I have started reading your novels all over again. The trouble with such fine books is that it spoils one for other authors! I find too much fault with other novelists now."

"That's very kind," said Phyllis. "But I'm always nervous about each new effort. One day, a reviewer will say I have lost my touch."

"That day will never come," I said, "unless the reviewer has a grudge against you."

Victoria sipped her wine. "I would be happy with any kind of review!" she said. "Or even a publisher."

"Is Hawksbridge inspiring you, Miss Clitheroe?" said Flora.

Victoria considered this. "Yes," she said. "Just not always in the most helpful way." She glanced at me and smiled. "But I am getting there, slowly, with Phyllis' help."

There was a lull in the conversation and the musical sound of cutlery on plates.

"My daughter tells me that the police have seen sense about you, Mrs Ambrose," said Dr Drummond. "You have my whole-hearted congratulations – and of course my commiserations on the sad death of your husband."

"Thank you, Dr Drummond," Mrs Ambrose said. "I am very lucky with my friends, otherwise I don't know what would have happened."

"And do I understand correctly that Thomas was instrumental in Mr Wakeley's downfall?" Dr Drummond said.

"The official line," I said, "is that I – and my accomplices, including Miss Clitheroe – simply helped the police with their enquiries. It means, among other things, that Constable Taylor can keep his job."

"I see," said Dr Drummond. "Well, with such unpleasant events happening all too regularly in Hawksbridge, I'm glad my duties with the police have been taken on by young Dr Weldon. What do we think of him? Do we like him?"

"I might if he turned up when I was expecting him!" said Francesca.

"Medical skills apart," Victoria said, "he has a quite magnificent –" At this point she stopped to sneeze. "Oh – excuse me," she said, finding a handkerchief.

"He has a quite magnificent what?" said Phyllis, curiosity written on her face.

"Butterfly collection," Victoria said. "Including one that looks exactly like a leaf. Don't you think camouflage in nature is just extraordinary?"

I wondered if she were making this up, or if she really had visited Dr Weldon's house.

"As extraordinary as it is in humans," I said. "A killer masquerading as a respectable antique dealer; or a cruel trickster with the appearance of a slightly pompous but harmless businessman."

"It's terrifying, isn't it?" said Victoria. "Who knows what any of us might be, underneath?"

"Oh, but not you, Miss Clitheroe," said Felicity. "I know you are exactly the kind and clever person you appear to be!"

"Well, thank you, Felicity!" Victoria said. "You are very generous."

I saw Dr Drummond's eyes widen and wondered if he was going to say something. But then he slammed the table with his fist and clutched at his throat, and it was immediately clear that he was in trouble.

"Dr Drummond!" I said, standing up. "He's choking!"

It was a dreadful sight, as he tried to catch his breath. Any hope that he would clear the obstruction himself started to fade in a few seconds, and Phyllis screamed, "Father! What shall we do?"

Flora darted to her bag and pulled out a crochet hook. "Excuse me," she said, pushing Felicity out of the way. "Hold him, please! And get me light!"

Phyllis and I held Dr Drummond's flailing arms, while Francesca and Mrs Ambrose held up candles near his head. As Dr Drummond started to turn blue, Flora pushed a crochet hook down his throat, and after several attempts managed to hook the offending piece of meat out, to our immense relief.

Dr Drummond fought for breath for some time, still clutching his bruised throat, and no one spoke. Finally, he said, hoarsely, "Thank you!"

Phyllis stood with her hand over her mouth for a moment, and then embraced her father. "You gave me such a shock! Please chew your food properly in future, Father." He smiled and nodded.

Phyllis looked around to where Flora was wiping her crochet hook with a napkin. She ran over to her, and flung her arms around her, bursting into tears. "Thank you, Flora," she said. "Thank you for saving my father. And I'm so sorry about everything. I was such a fool, using your name in my story. Please forgive me!"

To my gratified surprise, Flora returned her embrace, and her own tears were soon flowing. "Of course I will," she said. "I'm sorry I've been so silly about it."

"Oh, thank you, thank you!" Phyllis said. "Let's always be the best of friends, as we once were."

The rest of us stared, astonished and moved. The other females were also afflicted with tearfulness, and when Catherine and Mrs Felton came in to clear the dishes they stopped by the doorway, alarmed.

"What's going on?" asked Mrs Felton. "What on earth's happened?"

"It's all right, Mrs Felton," I said. "Dr Drummond's life has just been saved, and two old friends have been reconciled."

"Gracious!" she said. "What a Christmas."

"I think we should move into the drawing room now," I

said. "We can have our desserts in there."

"Very good, dear," said Mrs Felton.

"Thank you, both of you!" I said. "The venison was splendid."

~

Dr Drummond's throat was soon soothed with the application of port and jelly. Phyllis and Flora sat together on the sofa, renewing their friendship with talk of art and literature – mainly that of their own devising – and Mrs Ambrose and Francesca were, as far as I could make out, comparing notes on the behaviour of horses. Felicity sat on a rug by the fire, fussing over Fox, while Victoria had lapsed into a happy silence, drinking her wine and enjoying the scene.

"Catherine – Mrs Felton – why don't you come and sit down for a while?" I said, as they were about to leave the room after setting down trays.

"Well, I'd certainly be glad to take the weight off my feet, dear," said Mrs Felton, and Catherine smiled sweetly.

"Let me get you something. Port?" They nodded.

I poured out the drinks and pulled a couple of chairs nearer the fire for them.

"Lovely," said Mrs Felton, sipping her port. "Catherine is such a boon, Mr Rufford. A quick learner, too!"

Catherine smiled. "Thank you," she said. "I am enjoying it here. I am nearly starting to forget... all the bad things!"

"Oh, that awful Mr Wakeley," Mrs Felton said. "Has she told you all about him? Dreadful! And to think Catherine tried to tell that poor girl, and no one would listen. Just because of her colour!"

"Oh?" I said. "I haven't heard that story."

"Yes, I think that was the worst thing he did," Catherine

said, "even worse than taking me away from my family. The poor girl was so in love with him, and she gave him a lot of money. I tried to warn her. I looked in my husband's papers, and found out where she lived. When he had gone out drinking, I went out – which he would have beaten me for, if he had found out – and knocked on her door. They thought I was mad, or a gypsy, or some kind of wicked woman. They wouldn't let me in. If only they had, perhaps she would not have died."

I looked at Victoria, and she avoided my gaze, fidgeting with her glass.

"When Reginald finally got all her money, he bought some expensive wine and poured it out for us both. I remember it well. 'Let us drink to our generous benefactress!' he said. 'To the lovely, stupid, formerly wealthy Miss Tennant!'"

I started on hearing the name and spilled some port on my waistcoat. Dabbing it with my napkin, I said, "How odd. That name seems familiar to me. Can you remember her Christian name?"

"A pretty name," she said. "Ursula."

Again I looked at Victoria, who was pretending not to have heard.

"I'm feeling rather tired," Victoria said. "This has been delightful, but I need to retire. Please say my goodbyes to the others. I don't want to disturb them." And she walked quickly out of the room.

I did not wish to be rude to Mrs Felton and Catherine, so I talked to them for a few minutes more, and then excused myself. I ran up the stairs two at a time and knocked on Victoria's door. There was a silence, and I knocked again. "Oh, come in, then," she said.

She was sitting on her bed, the portrait of Ursula in her hands, tears rolling down her cheeks.

I drew up a chair by her bed. "Do you have anything to

say?" I said.

She sniffed. "What would you like me to say? That I'm a horrible human being? Oh, I'll happily say that, since it's true. I'm wicked. I'm as wicked as Mr Wakeley, or Mr Ambrose, or Mr Blackwood. In that, I'm a fine advertisement for equality of the sexes, am I not?"

"Are you telling me you killed Mr Wakeley?"

There was a pause. "Yes." She turned over and pulled the pillow over her head. I pulled it off her and she looked up at me, miserably. "And now you will hate me, forever."

"I don't hate you, Victoria," I said. "I just want to understand. Did you plan everything? Did you even want to write a novel?"

"I did want to write. And I didn't plan everything." She sat up and dried her eyes.

"Let me start from the beginning. After I had been in Florence for a few days, I got a letter from Ursula saying she had met a wonderful man, and they were secretly engaged. Mr Wakeley told her to keep it a secret from her family until his business affairs were in order. I got several more letters where she was ecstatic in his praise of him, and she said how blissfully happy she was."

She picked up the picture again. "And then I got a terrible letter from her, saying that she had given all her money to him to help his business survive, and then he had disappeared. She was distraught. In the next letter, she appeared to have given up on life. He had taken her virtue, she said, as well as her money. There was no point in anything. That was the last letter I got. I wrote back several times imploring her not to despair, and to think of everything she had, not what she had lost. But I got no reply."

She stroked the bumps of the paint with her finger. "And when I got back from Italy, she had simply faded away. She died of misery. And I hadn't been there when she had needed me most."

"I am so sorry," I said. "But you could not have known this would happen."

"Perhaps not," Victoria said. "But I failed her nevertheless. And I made myself – and her – a promise that justice would be done."

"Was Mr Wakeley not apprehended?"

"No – Ursula left me a letter saying if anything happened to her, not to embarrass her parents by going to the police. That it was her fault for being so stupid. So it was left to me to redress the balance."

"How did you find out where Wakeley had gone?"

"In Ursula's things, I found a letter to Wakeley that she hadn't sent, with the address of his lodgings on it. I talked to his landlady, and she said that he and his housekeeper had gone to Hawksbridge. She didn't have their exact address."

"So you decided to enter Hawksbridge society through Phyllis? Quite an ingenious idea."

"I had read her books, and knew from a newspaper article that she lived here. I got her address from her publisher by pretending to be an old school-friend visiting Hawksbridge."

"My God," I said. "Everything has been a sham!"

"Oh, Thomas, don't say that!" said Victoria. "I've become so fond of you all. You and Phyllis really are my friends. And charming Felicity! You have been so good to me, while I..." She began to sob again, and I held her hand.

When she was calmer, I said, "It didn't take long for you to locate Mr Wakeley. I imagine your tale of hearing about his reputation in The Black Bull was fictional?"

"Yes, I'm afraid it was. It was fortunate for me that you knew of him through Francesca. I think he didn't get all that he wanted from her."

"And yet for a change, it seems his business plan was sound, and legal," I said. "Had you planned to kill him when we went for lunch at Francesca's?"

"No, no – I didn't even think I was going to kill him.

Simply expose him, and ruin his reputation and his finances. I didn't really know how. But then the mill presented an opportunity that I knew would never come again."

"So you did go up to the upper floor with him?"

"Yes. He crouched on the edge of the big window, overlooking the wheel, and while he was talking in that arrogant way of his and looking at the river, I simply went up to him and gave him a push. He was too surprised to even cry out."

"I see," I said, trying to take this casual confession in.

"I'm sorry," she said. "I wish I hadn't done it. But at that moment, I had a vision of Ursula dying in her bed, having been utterly destroyed by the man in front me. And it seemed perfectly fair that he should pay. Can you understand that?"

"Yes," I said. "I think I can." I squeezed her hand, and there was silence for a while.

"So, what happens now?" Victoria said. "Am I your next victim, Thomas? The next triumph in your quest for justice?"

"I don't know," I said. "I truly don't know what to do with you."

"You could let me go."

"I could," I said. "But that would make me complicit."

"Yes, of course," she whispered. "You do know I love you most horribly, don't you?"

"Yes, I know," I said softly. "I am not ungrateful."

"You ought to go back to your guests," she said. "I'm so sorry to be such a disappointment."

I smiled at her. "And yet you are still a fascinating and beautiful creature. I will send your regrets to the party. And I will think what to do. I won't make any hasty decisions."

"Thank you!" she said. "Good night, Thomas. I'm so sorry about everything."

CHAPTER THIRTY-TWO

I WOKE up with a sore head to find that it was already ten o'clock. With a jolt I remembered Victoria's confession. I hurriedly dressed and washed, and ran up to Victoria's room. To my horror, there was no sign of her or her belongings, but the candles had been burned to stumps. On the bed lay four letters. One was addressed, 'To Thomas', a second 'To Phyllis', a third 'To whom it may concern regarding Dr Weldon', and the fourth 'To whom it may concern regarding Mr Wakeley'.

I opened my letter with shaking fingers, and read:

> My dear, sweet Thomas,
>
> I am sorry to have to leave without saying a proper good bye. Just know that in my mind I have wrapped my arms around you and kissed you, and cried salty tears all over your neck. I know that you would have not denied me the comfort of your arms and a last kiss.
>
> I am so grateful for all that you have done for me. I have truly cherished the warmth and love of my new friends, and you cannot know how much it breaks my heart to leave you all. I do not know if I will ever see you again, but I suspect not. It is hard to bear.
>
> Please deliver my letter to Phyllis. The other two letters need an explanation.
>
> My 'Mr Wakeley' letter is a full confession. You may do with it as you see fit. I hope this will lighten the burden for you: you have only to present it to the police, and you will not have to carry a secret and therefore be contaminated by my guilt.
>
> The final letter, regarding Dr Weldon, is my strange gift to you in your pursuit of Phyllis. I know that you and Phyllis are destined to be together, and will make each other so happy. I

am truly glad for that, even though I may wish it for myself! And so Dr Weldon cannot be allowed to spoil your happiness. Please do not condemn me for this, Thomas, but I have to do penance for my misdeeds, and I will never have the only lover I have ever craved. Therefore my own innocence is meaningless to me.

I have seduced Dr Weldon, and provide proof in my letter, by way of knowledge of his bedroom that could only derive from intimacy, by the location of a certain mole, and by a description of this occasion that he may find it hard to deny. You asked me how his butterflies could be used to his disadvantage, Thomas, and this is how: the day before our adventure in the inn, I went to his house to thank him for his advice earlier. His sister was visiting a relative, so he was alone in the house apart from his housekeeper, who was in bed recovering from the influenza. I said I was interested in butterflies and had heard about his hobby. He offered to give me a tour of his collection, and I maintained my interest as much as I could, despite his quite dull descriptions of the habitats and life-cycles of these insects.

He had some boxes of the things in his bedroom, and when I was in the room, I feigned palpitations from the coffee he had given me. He helped me onto the bed, and I loosened my clothes for him to examine me. As he bent down, I kissed and embraced him, and said that perhaps some help with my blood circulation would cure my palpitations. This was probably the opposite of the appropriate medical wisdom, but nevertheless the poor man could not contain himself any longer, and began to kiss me. The rest you may imagine for yourself, Thomas, but rest assured I would rather it had been you.

He was a little ashamed afterwards, and our parting was awkward. It was an unkind thing to do, perhaps, but it is your insurance in case he becomes a nuisance. Phyllis would never consent to marry him in these circumstances. I am glad if I have been some use after all the trouble I have caused. Claim your beautiful, clever, prize, Thomas, and have many, many children!

And so I must now bid farewell, my love. I am headed for Southampton and then Madeira, where I will contemplate what is left for me. Perhaps I shall become a nun, or start a school in Africa. I have much atonement to do.

Know that I will always love you, and think about you, wherever I am.

Yours forever,

Victoria

I had not got to the end of the letter before my eyes misted over, and when I had finished reading, I collapsed on the bed, howling with grief like a child.

~

When I had recovered myself, I rode into town to see Phyllis. The cold air revived me and I realised that Victoria's disappearance was for the best. Perhaps she would find happiness in time, and look back at the more innocent of her Hawksbridge days – not least her winter picnic – with fondness. But how I would miss her company, more than I had imagined. I fervently wished, though, that she had not compromised herself with Dr Weldon. I had no wish to win Phyllis on such terms, and Victoria had paid far too high a price for such a well-meaning but ultimately futile gesture.

Christmas evening had ended as congenially as was possible in the circumstances – I had tried to push Victoria's revelations to the back of my mind, and we sang carols. Mrs Ambrose had revealed that she and Felicity would be moving to a suburb of Newcastle, which had pleasant associations of her childhood, but extracted a promise from me to visit when the new railway had been built, if not before.

When I arrived at the Drummonds, Phyllis and her father were reading in the drawing room in front of a blazing fire.

"Ah, Thomas! You didn't have enough of us last night?" said Dr Drummond with a smile. "I'm sorry about my performance. Most embarrassing."

"That's quite all right," I said. "I'm just glad Flora was there to save the day."

"It seems I was the cause of a touching reconciliation," Dr Drummond said. "I never did understand why you fell out with Flora, Phyllis."

"Well, that's all in the past now," said Phyllis. "Thomas – was there a reason for calling on us? Not that you need one."

"I'm afraid there is a reason. May I speak to you alone? Sorry."

"That's all right," said Dr Drummond, heaving himself out of his chair. "It's time I went for a wee stroll. I'm seizing up again."

When Dr Drummond had gone, I said, "Victoria has gone away – this morning. She was gone by the time I woke up."

"Gone away? You mean for a trip?"

"No, permanently."

"What?" I could tell that this was a heavy blow: the two had grown close. "Why would she do that without saying good bye?"

"There is something we didn't know about her. Please prepare yourself for a shock."

"Thomas, you're alarming me," Phyllis said. "What on earth could it be?"

"She came to Hawksbridge for a purpose: to settle a score for the death of her friend. She came for Mr Wakeley. It wasn't an accident."

"Oh! No, this can't be right," Phyllis said. "She's my friend! You must have got hold of the wrong end of the stick. You can't be right all the time!"

"I'm sorry. I imagine this letter will explain." I handed Phyllis her letter, which she took as though I were handing her an unexploded shell.

She read the letter with her hand over her mouth, and stared blankly into the room before giving way to her emotions. I put my arm around her, but I felt inadequate. If only Catherine had not spoken of Miss Tennant, we would have remained in blissful ignorance, and everything might have stayed as it was. A few words had ruined two friendships and led to exile.

"And there was another letter," I said, producing Victoria's confession. "She invited us to give it to the police, to absolve us from keeping her secret. What do you think we should do?"

Phyllis took the letter, turning it over in her hand unopened. She thought for a moment, and then said, "Is it me, or is the fire becoming a little weak?"

"Yes, you're right," I said. "It does need something."

Phyllis got up and walked to the fireplace. She threw the confession on the fire, and we watched for a moment to make sure it had been consumed completely.

"Father and I are thinking of travelling to Europe for a couple of months," she said. "I need fresh sights and sounds. I'm getting stale here."

"But I thought he hated travelling?"

"It's really his last chance," she said. "And I think it will do him good, too. And now this..." She gestured at Victoria's letter. "I do need it."

"I shall miss you," I said. "Rather badly, in fact."

"I'm sorry," she said. "But you understand?"

"Yes," I said. "It makes sense. Phyllis..."

"Yes?" she said.

"I want everything to be out in the open between us. Everything else seems to be, except..."

"Oh goodness," Phyllis said. "What next?"

I hesitated. Did I really want to do this? But it was too late to stop now.

"It's about Mrs Ambrose. On the night before Mr Ambrose died, Mrs Ambrose did something rather strange. I think she wanted to recreate what had happened between her and Mr Blackwood years before."

"Why in God's name would she want to do that?" Phyllis said.

"I don't know," I said. "Because it had somehow become associated with getting attention – the closest thing to affection she could find. It was a kind of sickness with her."

"And?"

"And she came into my bed."

"Oh, for heaven's sake, Thomas. Why did you let her do that?"

"She was cold," I said. "I know that sounds ridiculous now."

"Yes, it does. Is that it?"

"No. She... seduced me."

Phyllis sighed, and shook her head. "I'm tired, Thomas. Tired of Hawksbridge. Tired of drama. I'm even sick of myself. I need time somewhere different, to see things in a new way."

"Yes, of course. Will you write to me? To tell me your address, at any rate?"

She shrugged. "I expect so. Good bye, Thomas," she said, and led me to the front door.

EPILOGUE

WITH the snowdrops and daffodils of February came hope that Phyllis might return soon – in a better humour with me after a change of scene, God willing. The hint of spring also saw a new presence on Hawksbridge High Street, marked by a sign that read: 'Myrtle's Coffee Shop for Ladies'.

It was Mixed Company Afternoon, which meant that I could legitimately join Flora and Francesca there for coffee and cake. They were already there when I arrived, talking to Catherine, whom we had allowed to work for Bess for two days a week.

"This looks marvellous," I said, looking about me. "I like the blue walls and lithographs. And the stalls – nice and private."

"For interesting liaisons," said Francesca.

"Well, they will obviously only get interesting on mixed company days," I said.

"My dear boy," said Francesca, "how naive can you be?"

Flora smiled. "Now, now. You can't speak to my brother like that."

"Your – what?" said Francesca, staring at Flora, and then at me. "You two never told me –"

"What can I get you, sir?" said Catherine. "Coffee and sponge cake? I made the cake myself."

"In that case, Catherine," I said, "yes, please. Is Bess about?"

"She's in the back, sir. Shall I get her?"

"No, I'll come and look. I want to see what she's done there. Excuse me, ladies!"

I left them to discuss the finer points – and the less salubrious points – of our shared family history, and went through to the kitchen and office. It was all neatly fitted out with cupboards and gleaming utensils, and the staff were cheerfully bustling around.

Bess was coming through the back door holding a bunch of herbs, and when she caught sight of me she smiled broadly. "Thomas! How lovely to see you. Do you approve?"

"More than that – you have worked wonders!" I said. "And it all seems to be running like clockwork." I gestured at the filled booths. "This place is popular. I'm sure it must have been harder than it looks to set all this up."

"Yes, it was a struggle at times," she said, putting the herbs on a table. "But it's all been worth it. The Hawksbridge Herald wrote a flattering report. It got quite crowded after that. And I have you to thank for it all!"

"Well, and Mrs Harris, of course. Has she been yet?"

"Yes! She loved it. But Thomas, how have you been? The newspapers said you were just helping the police to find Mr Blackwood's murderer. It's funny – it sounded when you spoke to me as though you were working quite on your own."

"I fear I am apt to exaggerate," I said. "The police are to be commended this time."

"Hm," she said. "There's more to this than meets the eye, isn't there?"

"It's possible," I said. "But don't tell anyone."

"I thought so. Well, I must be getting on. I'm so glad you like it!"

"It's perfect," I said, and embraced her.

~

The Town Hall was crowded for an event that had been

advertised on posters around the town as 'The Grand Unveiling of the Hawksbridge Station Plans: A Presentation by the North British Railway Company. All Welcome!'

We were surrounded by the finally completed murals, in memorial to the lost of Hawksbridge's tragic factory fire. They were getting admiring looks, as well they might. The chief angel that had been modelled after Francesca now led a company of angels in flowing robes energetically pulling souls from the burning factory, and the mural continued across the ceiling with a bearded God observing the proceedings with compassion from a cloud. Flora and Mr Falkirk had done well.

On one side of the hall, a curtain had been hung to conceal whatever wonders lay behind. I hoped that they reflected at least some of the ideas Francesca and I had been putting forward to Mr Thornton and his employees over the last two months, with help from the Hawksbridge Castle Preservation Committee. I glanced at Francesca, and squeezed her hand for support. She looked nervous: her standing in the town depended on the reaction of the crowd.

Mr Thornton stood up, and the murmuring subsided.

"Ladies and gentlemen," he said, "thank you for coming this afternoon to see what we've been working on. Now, I know that there have been disagreements about the balance of things: progress versus the status quo. But I think you'll be pleased with what we've come up with. It serves both the needs of the modern world, and the obligation that we have to respect our precious heritage. All credit to Mrs Francesca Campbell for firmly holding us to this worthy principle. I would like to give special thanks to the Hawksbridge Mechanics' Institute who have created an ingenious miniature... well, let me not spoil it. Let me just say that their skills have brought movement to our model, to let you appreciate more fully how it will be two short years or so from now. Without further ado, I give you: Hawksbridge Castle Station!"

He pulled back the curtain and for a few moments, the crowd remained silent as they took in the model. I looked around me and saw confused faces: were they looking at the new station, or a restoration of the castle? It was not obvious at first glance, but realisation began to dawn, accompanied by awed whispers.

The station was growing out of the ruins – the station was the castle, and the castle was the station. The new parts discreetly took their cue from elements of the castle, such as towers and castellations, and – in the model, at least – the colour of the new stone was a decent match for the old sandstone. The contours of the joins had been accentuated where necessary so it was still possible to tell the new from the old. Some of the smaller remnants of the castle remained untouched. Next to the station, the great hall was represented in a better condition than current reality, with iron struts and additional masonry. A soaring arch had been cut into each end.

Looking past the station and great hall, there was a model of the proposed bridge, with impressive stone arches, albeit truncated to fit the space available, and a young man in a white overall was fiddling with something on the far end of the bridge: an object that had been making hissing noises for some minutes.

A lever was pulled, and a cheer went up a model steam locomotive was advancing noisily over the bridge, pulling brightly coloured carriages in red and yellow livery. Briefly, the locomotive disappeared into the great hall, with smoke emerging from the top, and then it appeared again and puffed into the station, whereupon another young engineer pressed a lever to stop it.

The applause was immediate and loud, and Mr Thornton looked suitably gratified. To my surprise, I saw Mr McPhee and Mr Fountain turn to Francesca and direct their smiles and applause at her. She smiled back, inclining her head in acknowledgement.

I was immensely relieved. The people had been won over, the castle would largely be preserved, and Hawksbridge was on the brink of entering the age of the railway. My one regret was that Phyllis was not here to share this moment.

~

"Good morning, Mr Rufford!" said Mr Hunter, as I entered the bookshop. "May I congratulate you on your triumph with Mr Blackwood?"

"You may, Mr Hunter," I said. "Thank you. But I cannot claim all credit for it."

"Perhaps you'll write a memoir? It would sell by the cart-load."

"That's good to know," I said, "but I don't believe I'm a natural story-teller. And I'm sure the papers have already written all that's to be said on the matter."

"I'm not so sure," said Mr Hunter. "And the public are always hungry for the personal side of a story like this."

"Alas, the public will have to wait," I said. "I'd like to put it all behind me. Perhaps one day."

"May I humbly suggest you write a few notes," Mr Hunter said, "so you don't forget too many of the details? You may be glad of it later."

"Good idea," I said. "I'll do that."

My aim was to find a present for Phyllis to give her when she returned. A novel? But it might be tactless to give her something by one of her arch-rivals. Poetry, perhaps? I did not know what she liked, and in any case, I was not an ardent admirer of the form.

I moved along the aisles, and was confronted by a title I recognised all too well: 'The Predilections of Reverend Malamor'. Idly, I pulled it out to see if there was an inscription, following Phyllis' habit. For a moment a fantasy came into my mind that it might read, 'To my dear Yorick, from his adoring F.T.' But when I turned the cover, the fly-leaf was quite blank.

I became aware of a customer's footsteps approaching, and hastily put the book back.

"Have you found something interesting?" said a familiar voice.

"Oh, Phyllis! You're back!" I said, turning and tipping my hat. I wanted to throw my arms around her, but I felt I could not be demonstrative in the shop. "No, it's nothing much."

She pulled the volume out. "I see. Were you looking for an inscription, by any chance?"

"I confess I was. But there's no romantic story here. It's a pristine copy."

Phyllis smiled at me and pointed out its dozen or so brothers on the shelf. "It's a brand new edition, and it's entirely down to you."

"How so?"

"All the newspaper reports from the summer mentioned Malamor, of course, and there was so much interest, the publisher had to order a run of ten thousand."

"Good Lord!" I said. "The author will be able to retire."

"The author," she said, "does not wish to retire – or so I've heard. But the author is grateful. Even though he knows it's a terrible book."

"Simply awful," I said. "Would he want to turn back time, and never write it?"

"Perhaps. What would you do, Thomas, if you could turn back time?"

"That's easy," I said. "I would be a better, bolder man. Come." I led the way to the door, and in a moment, our eyes were adjusting to the crisp afternoon sunshine after the gloom of Mr Hunter's shop.

"Miss Drummond," I said, "I'm new to Hawksbridge, and I want to explore the town walls – I've heard they're remarkable. I know this may sound a little forward, but is there any chance you would be my guide?"

"Well, Mr Rufford," she said, stroking her chin with her gloved hand. "It goes against my better judgement to be seen alone with a strange man." She looked me over with a critical eye. "But today I will make an exception. I will be your guide. I think you will find Lover's Bastion of particular interest."

"I will?"

"You may depend upon it," she said, offering me her arm. "Shall we?"

~ THE END ~

DRAMATIS PERSONAE

Ramsburgh

Mr Thomas Rufford: owner of Ramsburgh

Miss Flora Davison: niece of the previous owners, the Kingtons

Mrs Margaret Northcutt: Flora's housekeeper

Mr Matthew Shipley: Thomas' butler

Mrs Norah Felton: Thomas' housekeeper

Old Howard: the groom and dogsbody

Jenny: a pony

Celeste: Thomas' horse

Fox: Thomas' dog

Hawksbridge

Phyllis Drummond: a novelist

Dr Anthony Drummond: a doctor and Phyllis' father

Mrs Francesca Campbell: friend of Thomas

Victoria Clitheroe: friend of Phyllis

Mr David Harris: a former banker

Mrs Olivia Harris: Mr Harris' wife

Inspector Ralph Simmons: a detective

Constable Taylor: a policeman

Constable Gawley: a policeman

Mrs Bess Shannon: a widow

Lizzie: Mrs Shannon's maid

Mr Johnny Falkirk: a local artist

Mr Frederick McPhee: a director at the Pottery

Mr Peter Blackwood: an antique dealer

Mr Reginald Wakeley: a businessman and friend of Mrs Campbell

Catherine: Mr Wakeley's housekeeper

Mr Leonardo Fountain: a member of the Hawksbridge Antiquarian Society

Mr Oswald Redpath: a builder and member of the Hawksbridge Antiquarian Society

Mr James Dunton: owner of the land containing Hawksbridge Castle

Mrs Florence Tambard: a wealthy widow

Dr Philip Weldon: a doctor with a new practice in Hawksbridge

Houndswood

Mr Yorick Ambrose: a member of the Hawksbridge Antiquarian Society, and a collector of antiques

Mrs Isobel Ambrose: Mr Ambrose's wife

Miss Felicity Ambrose: the Ambroses' daughter

Pantoufle: Felicity's squirrel

Miss May Ettrick: the Ambroses' maid

Miss Susan Lipton: the Ambroses' former maid

Mr John Rayner: the Ambroses' butler

Elsewhere

Miss Ophelia Doyle: a young woman of scant virtue

Mr Edward Thornton: a director of the North British Railway Company Limited

ABOUT THE AUTHOR

Julian Smart was born in Nottingham, England, and studied Computer Science at the University of St Andrews. He has a doctorate from the University of Dundee. Julian has worked for the University of Edinburgh, the Artificial Intelligence Applications Institute, the Scottish Crop Research Institute, and Red Hat UK.

Julian started the wxWidgets open-source GUI toolkit project which is used by many organisations and individuals worldwide, and by Julian for his own projects, including the e-book editing software Jutoh. Jutoh was used for creating all books by Julian and Harriet Smart.

Julian collaborated with Harriet Smart to write *Emma Vernon's Northminster Ghost Stories*, a spin-off from Harriet's Northminster Mysteries which he has edited since 2010.

Julian is currently working on *The Thomas Rufford Mysteries*, a series set in nineteenth-century Hawksbridge, a fictional town in the north east of England.

Printed in Great Britain
by Amazon

16491012R00203